NO SAFE HOUSE

JAN GARNETT

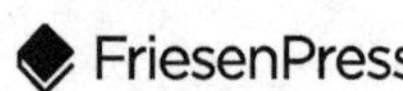

One Printers Way
Altona, MB R0G 0B0
Canada

www.friesenpress.com

First Edition — 2024

ISBN
978-1-03-830516-9 (Hardcover)
978-1-03-830515-2 (Paperback)
978-1-03-830517-6 (eBook)

1. FICTION, THRILLERS, CRIME

Distributed to the trade by The Ingram Book Company

For my parents, Daphne and John Rumball, with gratitude for a childhood full of stories.

~ ONE ~

Late March

The snow lining the scar of pavement through the mountains is deep and stubborn, but traffic is light, and the spring sun warms Kot's face. For five hours she has nothing to do but drive, worry, and watch for omens. Probably almost five hours too long.

In spite of all the good reasons to just go straight to the ferry terminal, by the time she is approaching Vancouver Kot knows that she's going to risk trying to see Ben first. Seize the day and all that. She takes the exit towards the dockyards like a high dive, and is rewarded to find Ben's car alone in the Northcott Shipping parking lot. Still, in case there is anyone else still inside the building this late on a Friday afternoon, she swings sharply at the bottom of the entry ramp and then up into the shadows of the leafing trees bordering the street. Her side mirror provides a clear view of Ben's Land Rover down in the CEO slot near the door.

It has been a demanding day. She's tired and still unsure of the wisdom of surprising her ex and future lover (Kot chooses optimism.) But she has a choice of ferries back to Victoria this evening, and time to wait. Anticipate. Anyway, now she's here, she might as well follow through.

Kot's heart does its usual backflip when Ben Northcott exits the building, his eyes on the ground. She grabs the envelope on her seat but an SUV races down the ramp beside her before she can get out. The two men inside are focused on Ben and in her mirror she watches the driver trap him between the building, his vehicle, and theirs.

Disappointed that she may not get Ben to herself, Kot is also amused to witness a couple of his friends playing one of their famous practical jokes. Their backs are towards her, so she gets out quietly and leaves the door open. Perhaps the performance won't take long.

The thing is, Ben isn't laughing. And one of the men sounds aggressive, his voice abrasive and memorable. The only word that Kot hears clearly is "pissed." She assumes that the gun in his hand is a toy until a dull shot echoes off the building and Ben folds to the ground. A stream of blood carves a jagged path from his thigh across the pebbled asphalt. The shooter goes to lean over Ben and continues his growling monologue.

Kot stops breathing and hits the 911 speed dial on her cell. She disconnects as soon as the dispatcher answers, assuming that her GPS coordinates will be enough to bring police. Frozen, she forces her eyes back to the inexplicable scene below.

A cheery tune rings out from her phone and both of the strangers whirl around. She'd forgotten that the dispatcher would try to call back, and to mute the thing. She leaps into her car and pushes the lock button, then yells into her phone, "Police. Ambulance. Northcott Shipping." She tries to flatten herself sideways over the console, her arms protecting her head.

The SUV's doors slam shut It races up the ramp and stops level with her car. A bullet shatters her window and enters the passenger door, sending shards of glass into her arms, neck, and scalp. Another shot goes through the seat back above her, and a third sprays more glass fragments around the interior. The wail of a siren begins, not far away, and Kot hears the shooter yell: "Go! Go!"

When the sound of the vehicle is gone Kot stumbles down to Ben. His eyes open long enough to register surprise and pain, but nothing else for her to hang onto. Her fingers fumble in panic as she attempts to tie a tourniquet around his thigh with the sleeves of her thin cardigan.

She tries for calm. "I'm here, Ben. You're going to be okay. I've called for help. I was just dropping off the tax receipt to you on my way home from a work trip. Hang on, my love."

Even to herself, she sounds crazy.

The police arrive first, and a firm grip hauls Kot upright. She sees her blood on his uniform as the cop talks on his radio and another one gets to work on Ben. Two more emergency vehicles arrive, and Kot is led to a squad car. By the time the screaming ambulance takes Ben away, she has blurted out what she'd witnessed and answered their questions about the men and their vehicle. Then, apart from an officer outside the car, she is left alone behind tinted windows and loses track of time. Police tape is set up and evidence markers placed. Eventually, a cop in street clothes gets into the car and introduces herself. She hands Kot a drooping sun hat and instructs her to pile her long hair under it. Kot isn't allowed to access her car or anything in it.

She is whisked straight into an elevator of a hotel near the airport. Even under warm blankets she shivers on the bed, exhausted. When a doctor arrives to check her over and tend to her cuts, the plainclothes officer closes the bathroom door behind her and turns on the fan. Kot can hear her talking quietly on her phone. Even later, when an older woman slips in to cut and dye Kot's hair, nothing seems real.

It is only when she is strapped into a police helicopter halfway across the inky Strait of Georgia that Kot fully understands that she has lost the plot of her life.

~ TWO ~

Saanich, BC

Derrick considers himself a nocturnal creature. The need to be outside before the pubs open is making him nervous. Nevertheless, he gets all of his equipment down the reeking stairs of his apartment building safely until a strap gets caught on his truck's wing mirror as he's loading up and his tripod tumbles to the broken asphalt. His eloquent curses provide counterpoint to the song of a city-smart robin in the brambles blanketing the fence.

At the drive-thru, he balances a box of Timbits on the pile of trash on the bench seat and squints at his map app. By the time Derrick reaches the country roads north of Victoria the coffee is doing its work.

For too long, nothing fits. Finally, the right kind of fence appears on his left. The driveway gate has a security keypad. He stops for a minute. Everything is exactly as described. Brilliant.

He goes back to park in a trail pull-off, and sticks his last two joints and a couple of uppers into the pockets of his utility vest. Strolling back to the gate in the warm spring sun, binoculars around his neck, camera bag over one shoulder and tripod balanced on the other, it has become a surprisingly fine day to be Derrick B. Tunstall, recently of Hoxton, East London, United Kingdom.

Derrick turns his back when a car is coming, and pretends to focus his binoculars on a random spot in the greater nothingness of his surroundings.

Most people ignore birders, so the only serious risk in his chosen persona is an actual expert stopping to chat. His late dad's tired old joke also holds true for Derrick: he wouldn't know a red-breasted booby from a tit.

It doesn't really bother him that he knows nothing about the chain of command above his supervisor, "CallMeWayne." The pay is good, and the work is mostly intermittent, leaving ample time to indulge his choice of recreational activities. Derrick is of the firm view that the enjoyment of various chemicals on his own time—and, generally less rewarding, during working hours—is his business alone. And so far, so good. Wayne has never said anything, even paying him in substances at times, and Derrick has no doubt that he can control the increasing cravings.

His instructions are to hide somewhere that allows a clear view of the gate keypad, with the goal of obtaining the access code when someone—statistically likely to be a right-handed someone—punches it in. Stupid wankers; the vegetation across the road from the gate is almost impenetrable. He eventually finds access to a big stump, wide enough for both his tripod and his bum. He breaks enough branches to line up a telescopic sight line but still hide his presence, and Derrick has himself a lookout for as long as this job will require.

By rationing the intervals between mood enhancers, there's always something to look forward to. Occasional cars go by at the gentle pace required of the twisty road, but none stop. Suspicious spouses create most of Derrick's assignments. Judging by the posh area, this job may also be about nailing a rich bitch for bad behaviour. Just consequences, and all.

As usual, he takes a few artsy shots on his personal mobile, and adds a brief description of the job to his voice memos. Finally, bored out of his mind, Derrick packs it in for the day, just before five.

The second day brings persistent drizzle. By mid-afternoon, his goodies are gone and he's coming down hard, nearly in tears from the need to drag his freezing ass and the rest of him somewhere warm. There is always the choice of going home and phoning Wayne later to say that he'd watched all day for nothing again. Unfortunately, based on something his boss had dropped about the nature of this particular client, Derrick has a feeling that might be one of the stupider things a guy could do.

Besides, he chooses to believe that the fictional tales he serves up for his mum will one day manifest into reality. A brighter future, higher in the ranks, so to speak. A deserved progression into a permanently stoned and serene middle age.

The rain finally stops, and Derrick decides to sort out the uncomfortable bind in his wet jockeys. His pants are still down when he hears a vehicle approaching from the direction of town. Of course, this is the one that is significantly slowing down.

An old Accord pulls into the driveway across the road, and the driver gets out. He looks more like an aged George Costanza from *Seinfeld* than the object of illicit passion, so maybe it's the husband. Derrick hobbles sideways, whips the protective cover off his camera and blows on his hands. He focuses, gets the video rolling, and grabs his binos.

Sure enough, the guy is right-handed. He must also be far-sighted, since he extends his arm and leans back from the keypad. Derrick has a clear view, and gives a nod to the old Tunstall luck as he confidently records the code.

The gate relocks with a clang, and he can hear the car carry on down the driveway. Derrick prepares to head back to the city and collect his pay, now able to focus his mind on how much better he'll feel in… oh, about an hour.

~ THREE ~

Kot and Medley follow one of the property's little trails in air made sharp and clean by rain. The distant hum of highway traffic to the east confirms her suspicions about where they are; even exhausted, she'd managed to follow some of the turns from the back seat on the midnight drive.

Vehicles on the road are invisible behind a high wooden fence at a good distance from the house. Occasionally, a commuter floatplane buzzes overhead, and sometimes there is a distant siren or a dog barking. Mostly, it's just the comforting hum of bees and the songs of competing birds. A growing choir of frogs at night. This is only the third time that Kot has heard the unique sounds of another human entering her space as the driveway gate creaks and rattles open and a car door closes. Through the trees, she can see the driver wait inside while the gate locks again before he continues to the house. Medley races off to perform his indiscriminate greeting rituals. Less enthusiastically, Kot follows.

When the man has left again, she paces the house and mumbles to herself, then turns to the dog.

"Screw it. I'm calling Mich."

Medley knows that name and his head swings hopefully to the door. But Mich's voice comes out of the thing in Kot's hand, and he sees his human smile for the first time in many days.

"Michaluk PR. Suzanne Michaluk speaking." The remnant Irish lilt.

"Mich, it's me."

"Christ, Kot! Are you okay? Did you get my thousand messages? I've been trying to reach you since Thursday. What's going on?"

Besides Kot's brother, Mich is the only person to still use her childhood nickname, and there is unexpected comfort in hearing it right now. Kot began introducing herself by her birth name of Kathleen when she left home for university. Ben claimed to love her name, and anyway, he'd shown no interest in her past.

"I'm so sorry you've been worried, but to be honest, I'm nervous about using this phone. I think it's what they call a burner. But then, I'm nervous about pretty much everything right now. Are you alone, Mich? Sorry—how are you?"

"Fine. Crazy… never mind. Yeah, this timing's good. Tell me what's going on."

"Well, believe it or not, we're in a safe house."

Mich sounds impatient. "Yeah, right. Just tell me where you are, okay?"

"Trust me, being in a safe house isn't something that I will ever joke about again. And I'm desperate to know how Ben is, if he's out of the hospital."

Mich is wary now. "Okay. I'll start with, who is 'we'?"

"Medley and me. Apparently, only a select few know where I am, and that doesn't include me—although I think I have a fairly good idea. Mich, I did something awesomely stupid. You won't need to tell me that."

"What are you talking about? Sweetie, I'm not about to lecture you. Ben is a privileged, philandering prick and I would love to bust him to hell and back for the way he ended it with you. Okay, maybe not back. But I promise, no preaching. What happened to him? And why are you in a safe house? I'm still hoping you're not serious about that."

"Sorry, but it's true. Apparently, this is just temporary, and Medley's happy here because he can run free on a couple of fenced acres. But it's lonely, and the only drama is in my head. It's not at all like in books. The house is probably from the 1950s. There are only a few pieces of furniture, and they may have started life in a seventies motel. No visible neighbours. I know I've been complaining about needing a break from my job, but I'd be back at it in a heartbeat if I could. I'm the only one who knows a lot of what needs to happen at work this week. I don't know if anyone there has any idea what's happened to me. I was allowed to send my assistant one email the first night, and I had to lie and say that I was sick and *blah blah*. Anyway, a Witness Protection guy named Doug comes to visit. I think of him as Warden Doug. He came for the third time today and brought the food and stuff I needed, but zero information. In fact, Ol' Doug's not much for conversation of any kind, but he's all I have."

Mich listens with her mouth hanging open. It's completely unlike Kot to babble like this. She recognizes post-trauma when she hears it, and also the need to be patient. She can picture her friend's furrowed brow and the anxiety in her beautiful blue-green eyes.

"Wow, that all sounds really hard. But you still haven't explained what's happened. I've just locked the office door, so please tell me."

"Well, I'm pretty sure I'm not even that far from home, and I had no idea there was a safe house in this area. It's just not something you think about, right? There are signs that this place was well loved for years. But things are pretty overgrown now. The only benefit is that I hardly see anyone, so I've already stopped wearing a bra. I wonder what comes next."

"Hey, entire reality shows are based on less."

Kot can hear Mich's fingers tapping, and it's her turn to imagine the impatient shake of Mich's dark bob and the worry in her deep blue eyes—gifts among many from her Irish mother. The problem is, now that she finally has a loving listener, Kot is surprisingly unable to tell the story. She hears her own torrent of words as if it's someone else speaking.

"Maybe the high fence and gate are for more than just deer. The extra security here might be because it's specifically designed to be used when the risk is highest. Anyway, I assume they'll soon figure out there's no further threat to Ben or to me, and I can go home. Right? I mean, my plants will need watering, and I'm really missing my stuff. Plus, I'm so anxious to know how he is."

"Kot Cafferty. Dear God. Please. Tell me what happened. Now."

Kot wonders if she should have looked for a safe way to send Mich a written narrative, but there isn't one. This is risky enough. She steadies herself and tells Mich about leaving Medley with her next-door neighbour, and driving to a big ranch near Kamloops to discuss a conservation partnership with the owners. "Their grasslands are as good as at the time of the buffalo.

And apparently there's a brother who's also interested in protecting some of his huge spread in Alberta."

Mich keeps pushing Kot onward until she blurts out her decision to stop at Ben's office on the way home.

"I had a thank you letter and a tax document for the Northcott Foundation, and figured I might as well deliver it in person."

"So you used a flimsy professional rationale as a way to stalk him?"

"Yeah, pretty much."

Mich is quiet. "Okay. Well, I get it that you wanted to try and re-establish a little personal power. And I promised no lectures, so please carry on. What happened?"

"You're right. I really didn't enjoy feeling like a victim. Ironic as hell, given these results. I'd visualized a cheerful handover, then either getting a dinner invitation from Ben or just simulating a carefree exit. I was prepared, either way. And hey—I should tell you this."

Mich sighs. "What?"

"Remember the first time Ben and I broke up, and I was such a wreck? Then you arranged for a large bag of sour cream glazed to be delivered to my office, and I realized that life was still worth living? Well, this was sort of the same. While I was sitting there in Ben's parking lot, I was super unsure but—honestly—also sleepy, and I had an epiphany. I definitely still wanted to be with Ben, and of course that probably wasn't altogether healthy. But I also knew that if he didn't appear—or if he did and rejected me again—I would cry and feel very sorry for myself. But I wouldn't have a breakdown or anything. I would grab some shreds of dignity, and carry on."

"Hey, many believe that time and donuts heal all."

"Finally, a religion I can believe in."

"So did the wretched man come out?"

"Yes, after I'd spent quite a while lounging in the sun with Leonard Cohen."

"Story of your life."

"I know. But not once has that man let me down."

Mich has done a lot of listening to Kot in the weeks since Ben announced that he wanted to finally end the affair, and she knows that it is far from over for Kot. And to be fair, for a long time, Ben had given Kot every reason to believe that he'd do whatever it took for them to be together. The change in him was abrupt enough to be questioned.

Kot's voice is stronger. "I mostly wanted to closely observe Ben when he saw me. You know, watch his eyes. He's such a social pro, but I was prepared to catch any signs, and also to not fight them if they weren't what I wanted to see."

Mich listens to her friend then describe what had happened in the parking lot.

"Holy shit, Kot."

"Yeah. I'm pretty sure I was screaming by the time I got back in my car. But at first, Ben kept his cool with them. He actually put on his sunglasses. It's one of his self-guarding things, like when I said we needed to talk about something. Maybe he even did it in bed, and I just couldn't see him in the dark."

Mich values Kot's attempts at black humour, but right now can't respond in kind.

"This is so crazy. You should *not* be alone right now. What the hell are they thinking?"

Kot blows her nose. The worst of the telling is over. "Thanks. It's harder to talk about it than I'd imagined, but this has helped." She hears Mich sniffling. "Oh Mich, why don't we talk about the Canucks now? Except I don't think you know what the Canucks are."

"A boy band, right?"

"You nailed it."

"Do you think it was some gang thing?"

"That's a good possibility. Anyway, I would know both of their faces, and that one guy's voice, for sure. I was able to tell the cops the first three numbers of their licence plate, but of course the car might have been stolen. And yes, they had a solid look at both me and my car. Definitely a problem."

"Damn right." Mich notices that she's shivering at her desk. "What about Ben? Many times have I wished him ill, I admit, but that's horrible… Oh man, I didn't mean—"

"It's okay, Mich. He's recovering." Kot doesn't feel like divulging how she knows that, so carries on. "You know, I still can't piece together what it was all about. It's not like Ben carries a lot of money around. And people who witness stuff like that aren't necessarily shoved into safe houses, are they?"

"I don't know. It's not my area, thankfully. But I have to ask: did the cops have guns on you as well? At first, they wouldn't have known what had happened."

"Yes, but just briefly. I probably presented as the opposite of a threat, and I told them what had happened. It all seemed like one of those horrible dreams, you know? When you should really just get up and pee?"

"How did you explain why you were there, waiting for Ben?"

"Three different cops asked me that, probably trying to see how consistent I'd be. I gave them the truth, at least the professionally ethical version of it. I felt ridiculously guilty, like I had something to hide. Well, obviously, I did, but not on the criminal side of things. And you know, even Jack Latrie wouldn't see anything seriously wrong in me going the extra mile to thank one of our top donors. Basically, as long as Ben's happy, Jack's happy."

"I wonder how much Jack has been told about what happened." Mich knows that Kot's relationship with her boss includes friendship.

"I was asked to provide his contact info. So I assume they've told him something about the attack and sworn him to secrecy, or else they just fudged something. At this point, it feels like I'm supposed to be the last to know anything. Ben's attackers could have killed him, but they didn't. So, who knows?"

"Lots more questions than answers, for sure. And I know how much you love that, my little control freak."

"I was a hot mess, Mich. I felt like a little kid. Fortunately, the cop who took me away was calm and lovely. She just took charge." Kot pauses. "You know, I go around in circles. If it was a robbery, they must have been watching from the road, waiting for Ben to come out. His wallet was on the ground but I don't know if anything was missing. Or maybe they had a bone to pick with Northcott Shipping. My cop said the dockside area is getting worse, and based on my expertise from movies and TV, those guys could also have been mafia goons."

"Sorry, but that scenario makes me grateful you're under official protection right now."

"I know. But it still sucks, and I'm crazy for information. I don't even know where my poor car is. I'm sure the police went through my stuff and they would at least have found the letter and tax receipt to back up my story. I wonder where those are now. Anyway… God, Mich, it was such a comfort to pick up Medley, and even a few of my own things to have while I'm here."

"It must have been. I'm so glad Meds is there. Such a solid little dude."

"He sure is, which is good, since my only human contact has been Doug in the past week. I feel safe here, but it's lonely and super boring. That said, if you and some good wine were to show up, it could easily turn into a getaway."

"Hmmm. Wouldn't I be elbowing out the handsome Doug?"

"Ah, yes. Our stolen hours of passion. Perhaps if this drags on, I might get desperate enough. He's just my type. Married, I sense unhappily, a smelly smoker, and I've caught seductive hints of a troublesome teen or two."

"Wow. Sounds perfect."

"I tried to visualize us once, but, suffice to say, I felt unwell."

"Oh, Kot, you'll have quite a story to tell. But then, I suppose it may never be smart to tell it. And please let me say this, with the greatest of love: you absolutely need to stop yearning for a guy who can't connect the dots between his cock and his marriage licence. Right?"

"I know. I'll try. I've never been good at knowing when to hold or fold, or—okay—even which game to play. But this is definitely a new low in outcomes. Anyway, it's been an amazing relief to talk to you. If I get away with this call, I'll do it again soon."

Later, Mich has more questions, and tries to call Kot back. A recorded voice says that the number is not in service. Through both of their early marriages, beyond the tragedy of Kot's ectopic pregnancy and her eventual sad acceptance of infertility, the divorces, jobs, the deaths of Kot's parents, and, six years ago, Kot's renewed interest in life through her new career, through all of the messy confidences and confessions that form the warp and weft of a close friendship over many years, she and Kot have had each other's backs and held each other's hearts. Too bad, on so many levels, that selfish Ben Northcott has messed up Kot's life again.

And now this.

Mich wonders if she made the right decision not to tell Kot about the recent CBC documentary around breaches in Canada's Witness Protection Program. She decides that, on the whole, she'd been right not to mention it.

For her part, Kot regrets that she didn't consider in advance whether to tell Mich that she'd also called Ben on her second day in the safe house, while he was still in hospital. Too embarrassed, probably. Oh well, with luck, she'll be able to talk to her about it soon, in person.

~ FOUR ~

Atticus Island

These waters are rich enough, but during birthing season the river otter still needs to up his game. He scuttles from the shallows and shakes, sending sparks of saltwater through the early rays of the sun. When he reaches the tideline of bark and seaweed, he stops and sniffs the air, evaluating the unfamiliar thing ahead.

The fish in his mouth must be delivered to his mate and pups in the bank den above the beach, and the otter won't retreat without good reason. However, even soaked in seawater, this creature has a dangerous scent. Instinct drives him back to the safety of the ocean and the protecting boulders at the end of the cove. This longer route will take more time and energy, but getting food to the pups is all that matters.

The new day triggers hunger in the bellies of two bald eagles, but they will wait before gliding down from their snag to investigate the strange flotsam. The male raises his head and his incongruously squeaky call echoes over the bay. His mate is immobile, her gaze fixed on the beach.

Temporarily abandoned by the Salish Sea, the small body may be reclaimed in the next tidal assault. But that is hours away, and eagles know patience. They are aware of the future prey in the otter den, but until the pups are old enough to venture out the eagles steal what fish they can from the adults.

Soon, they will have their own chicks to feed, and anything potentially dead and edible is worthy of observation.

Clams shoot tiny fountains from beneath the sand, and a flock of sandpipers peep and forage in the shallows stretching to a small islet. Apart from the body on the beach, it's business as usual.

The collar of a blue life jacket cushions the girl's head. Her dark eyelashes rest on a high-boned cheek with abrasions from the coarse shingle. A dark helmet of hair extends over the neck of her soaked sweatshirt, and sopping grey jeans cover her bent legs. The strap of a daypack lies across one arm and the other is extended, fingers curled into the gravel.

Predatory crows and ravens move into the green margins of the bay, secure in their belonging. So far, only the otter has spotted the slight rise and fall of the life jacket, and the tiny puffs of mist as warm breath meets morning chill.

She has woken many times to a sightline of beach sand, but everything else feels wrong. Camas recalls being on the boat, but has no idea why she is lying here, frozen to the bone. In the past, she was always watched over by a parent, and while she can't remember anything else, her resident grief knows that she is alone in the world now.

A crow is standing on the shingle, regarding her with shrewd and eager eyes. It retreats when Camas struggles to her knees. Her pounding head brings a wave of nausea, and vomit stings her throat before splashing her pants and coating the pebbles. Memories of last night begin to surface. She collapses onto her side again and curls into a ball, eyes closed. Hazel eyes, like her father's. Her damp hair is as glossy as the crow's wing.

From the time that Camas could walk and talk, her Coast Salish mother taught her the basics of wilderness survival and traditional ethnobotany—skills learned from her own grandmother. Now eleven, Camas knows a considerable amount about food foraging, first aid, and basic survival within her home territory. But right now, she is only sure that, for some reason, she has hypothermia and maybe a concussion, and that finding a way to get warm is the most critical priority.

Eventually, she is able to stand up and wait for the world to stop spinning, then stumble along the beach toward the boulders at the end. Not knowing why she is so afraid makes the fear worse. She must be visible from the water, and perhaps also from places in the forest above the beach, and certainly by someone on the bluff. She can only hope that no one is around this early in the day. Camas can't even remember what is inside her heavy daypack. She needs hot water and a safe place to lie down. A chance for her body to recover, and her memory to return.

She hears the sound of a waterfall, somewhere to her left. Her soaked sneakers slosh heavily as she crosses a wide stream carving small channels to the sea. An opening forms in her mental fog: fresh water, filtered through forest cover. Good.

Camas suspects that the life vest saved her life, but it is a cumbersome thing on land. Her frozen fingers can't undo the stiff buckles, but the attempt triggers a clear memory of last night and her heart beats faster with the urgency to get out of sight. Is this the bay where they anchored? Brett could probably spot her easily with his powerful binoculars, and being found by him would be worse than dying of hypothermia. There were times in recent weeks when Camas longed to die. But right now, the realization that she has somehow escaped that hellish life makes her want to survive in a different one.

At the end of the beach, she sinks down behind the first boulder she reaches, and peeks out at the bay. There isn't a boat in sight. The cliff face is warming and she lies back against it, exhausted. The spring sun has no impact on the deep chill inside her.

The thicket of salal bordering the beach is impenetrable, but she saw a lighthouse on the bluff above, and there must be some way to get up there. In her misery, Camas almost misses the old staircase. A rusty padlock secures the gate at the bottom, but the fence is falling down on one side. She slips through it and begins to climb the rotting steps.

After she finds warmth and food, Camas intends to disappear. If she is discovered, she would probably be handed over to some authority and most likely returned to her stepfather. Who would believe her story against the varieties of convincing crap that Brett invents? And if anyone does look for her, won't they eventually assume that she must have drowned? It's no comfort that, besides Brett, Camas can think of no one who would even notice that she was missing. And Camas suspects that her stepfather would be just fine if he were certain that she was dead.

At the top, she collapses on the ground behind the trunk of a big arbutus tree, shuddering and sick. A car door bangs not far away, followed by a second one soon after. A motor starts up and the car noises slowly fade, brakes squeaking as it presumably descends a hill. Camas stays hidden, listening.

Everything is quiet, and after a few minutes she manages to sit up. A bungalow is close by, with the lighthouse on a rise just beyond it. So this must be the lightkeeper's residence, and that car would have been parked near it. There are no other vehicles. Thin smoke curls gracefully from the chimney, like in a storybook. The place feels familiar. Mama had once taken her on a tour of a lighthouse and they'd gone up to the giant light at the top, but Camas has never been inside any of the residences.

With no other way to tell if someone is still in the house, she scuttles to a window beside the front door. No lights are on, but the door is unlocked. She creeps inside, feeling like a raven-haired Goldilocks, but far more afraid. There are lingering smells of bacon and toast, and some dirty dishes on the counter. For now, is seems that she is alone. Most people probably wouldn't turn away a freezing child, but she neither wants nor needs help from others.

She struggles out of her wet shoes and socks and heads for the wood stove. Finally free of the life jacket and sodden clothes, she wraps herself in the blanket that was on the living room couch. Her headache has dulled, but she is overwhelmingly sleepy. Camas huddles by the fire and follows Mama's protocol, counting to five hundred in a whisper and rocking to and fro. Then, still frozen to the bone, she forces herself down the hall. Only one bedroom is furnished. Based on a large pair of tattered leather slippers and the box of denture cleaner on the bedside table, an old man sleeps there.

The bathtub is small and won't take long to fill. She gradually adds warmer water and lies back to rinse the salt from her hair, fighting her panic at being discovered. Still, she waits until her extremities are stinging and she can move her toes before she gets out and dries off. She heads for the man's closet and chest of drawers and quickly dresses, taking only items that she imagines won't soon be missed. She has to roll up the sleeves and pant legs, but it could be worse. She makes a pile of additional clothes on the floor. Everything smells and feels foreign. The activity has brought a return of the headache, but at least her fingers work a bit. Camas will steal only what she can carry, and she now recalls doing the same thing when she took items from the boat last night, the things that are in her daypack: snack bars, water, nuts, her only photo of her parents, Mama's ring and favourite scarf, and Grizz, Camas's beloved stuffed bear.

She tidies the bathroom and assesses it for signs of her use, then swallows two pills from the bottle of arthritis painkillers by the sink, taking some more for later. She's a little warmer, but pain and exhaustion are slowing her down. She dumps her wet shoes and clothes into a green garbage bag, and stuffs a couple of wool blankets from the linen cupboard into another.

The old man has a far better stock of food in the pantry than Brett had on the boat, and Camas adds some packaged food as well as a few pieces of cutlery, a plastic bowl and plate, scissors and a can opener to the bags. She finds a warm camo jacket in a jumble on a coat rack and puts on the toque and dirty mittens that are in its pocket. Tennis shoes from another pile are too big, but at least they're dry. Forcing herself to take another last look around, Camas can see nothing different from when she came in.

There is a tourist map pinned to the wall beside the door. As she thought, this is Atticus Island, and someone has circled the location of the light station beside the beach where she woke up. A ferry horn blares, departing from the terminal nearby. There is a national park stretching from the light station obliquely to the north, bordered by a road. Camas may not be far enough from people, but she is apparently right next to an ideal bit of wilderness in which to hide.

The next beach is the one where she and Mama had spent time last summer, the one where Brett had also anchored yesterday. So Camas must have been swept around the point while she was unconscious. She tries not to imagine that, but is glad that it happened.

Brett is usually sullen with a hangover in the mornings, and chooses to pull anchor alone. But what if her stepfather did things differently today, and is already searching for her? He might have opened her cabin door and discovered that the lumps under the blankets were just clothes.

Sudden, useless tears arrive. She craves another bath, hotter and much longer this time. But she has to go.

Camas hauls everything outside and quietly closes the door. An idea arrives: a faint possibility, but a short-term alternative to the exposure of the forest. She slowly drags the bags up the grassy path to the lighthouse. Its thick door is locked, so she abandons the bags and follows the tower's circular wall in a forlorn search for another entry.

She ducks low on the far side to avoid being seen from the boat passing by, and through spindly vegetation spots the outline of a wooden panel at the bottom of the tower's stucco wall. The swiveling wood slats holding the panel in place are stiff with disuse, but she is finally able to pull it outwards and crawl inside to the deep gloom behind a circular staircase. Higher up, dust motes do a lazy, never-ending waltz in sunlight streaming through a window. It's colder in here than outside, and damp, but it is shelter.

Camas retrieves the bags and pulls the hatch door into place again from the inside. The lacy cobwebs across the bottom of the stairs suggests that no one has used them for some time. Even the spider is gone. Camas climbs up one level and finds a room with a long narrow window facing the house. Up another level, a stairwell window lets in light from the ocean side. Apart from two metal beds with bare mattresses behind the partition, the room is empty. She brings only the stolen blankets upstairs, slips off the big shoes, and covers herself on one of the old beds, waiting for the pounding in her head to ease.

The sun is much lower when Camas is awakened by the sound of an approaching car and the crunch of tires on gravel. From the edge of the window, she watches a woman help an old man out of the passenger seat. He waves her away and pegs into the house on two canes. His helper waits until he is inside, gives a vague wave, and leaves.

Thankful for the timing, Camas sends a prayer to Mama that she can just hide where she is until she feels stronger. She lies down on the musty mattress and covers herself again. Maybe shipwrecked people have lain here and felt the same strange mixture of gratitude and grief. Her future is no more certain than the unluckiest of them, but Camas goes to sleep.

FIVE

Kot barely caught the shadow that sliced the moonlight across her bed, but the raucous noise that woke her was familiar. A pair of barred owls is nesting on the property, and one had called to its mate from the roof above her bedroom. Still… she sits up and listens hard.

Budding lilac branches nod conversationally in the dark, tapping lightly on the window. Kot loves the scent of lilac, but she counts on being home again by the time this one blooms. A dream is still drifting in her mind, like blowing snow. She'd been dying, with a peaceful awareness that it had happened many times before. In fact, in the dream, the process had felt as simple and natural as a sigh. Kot can imagine expert analyses: obvious evidence of frayed nerves, rapid displacement syndrome (okay, she made that one up), or even post-traumatic stress disorder. Things are bad enough right now without mental self-sabotage. And aren't owls mythical precursors of death?

Almost as strange, Medley is standing in his dog bed, tense and on guard. He is sometimes alarmed by owl calls on bedtime walks, but Kot has rarely seen him this vigilant at any time of the day. He has a menacing growl for his size, and races to the entry hall to let loose. Each volley of barks launches him into the air and is followed by a precarious landing on the slippery wood floor.

Medley has provided many false alarms in his young life, but he occasionally gets it right. In addition, Kot wasn't reassured to be told that he might be her most effective security system while she's living in the safe house.

She slips out of the warm bed and reaches for her fleecy robe. Sometime in late adolescence, she had secretly abandoned nightwear, such decisions finally beyond the control of her straightlaced mother. The current temperature of this house is a reminder that there's also a downside. She tucks her hair inside the robe's collar, a habit from childhood that has acquired a more recent association, connected to a far more glamorous robe and a luxury hotel room: Ben, whispering how sexy it was when he released the belt and her abundant curls came tumbling out "with everything else."

Now Kot's hair is not only shorter, but auburn. No more long blonde mane. And tragically, no more Ben.

Kot drops the little flashlight from the bedside stand into a deep pocket. She can't find her slippers, or the phone. She's already becoming too complacent, too careless. The ugly clock on the hall table shows that the wee hours have progressed to almost 4:30, meaning that she'd managed to get three consecutive hours of sleep—a new record since coming here.

She leaves the lights off and stays away from windows. The rattling fridge motor shuts off and the sudden quiet makes even the air feel emptier. Medley is calmer now that Kot is apparently taking charge, and just follows her around. Everything seems peaceful. Normal. And Kot has lain awake enough in this house to know what constitutes normal. In less than a week the place has become a trusted landscape—at least for what essentially amounts to solitary confinement.

After disabling the door alarm, Kot slips her bare feet into rubber boots. She feels more vulnerable out on the rear porch, but does a long visual scan before closing her eyes to give her other senses full rein. Then she goes back through the house to the front steps. The moonlight is bright and unbroken in the meadow across the driveway. Not even deer can get into this property. Kot closes her eyes again. Her heightened sensitivities pick up echoes of energy, but nothing more than the movements of small mammals under bushes, the stirring of early birds, a final flurry of bats, and the first swirl of a rising breeze.

Reassured, but her heart still pounding, she goes back inside to the same joyful welcome from Medley as if she'd been gone for days.

In the event of something unusual happening, there is one more thing that Kot was told to do: report it. She turns on a light and finds the little flip phone on the kitchen counter. She'd forgotten to charge it after that long chat with Mich. Another bad sign that her attention is wandering. Wondering if being woken by an owl and Medley's unusual behaviour qualifies as an "incident," she waits, undecided. But the instructions had been clear, and repeated, so Kot presses the only programmed button on the phone. It's answered right away.

"Report desk. Marty. What's up, Kathleen?" He sounds really young. And he knows her name. Kot wonders what kind of need-to-know system exists around that.

She paces the kitchen, dealing with adrenaline. "Hey Marty. I think things are okay, but I know I'm supposed to report anything unusual. My dog was going nuts a few minutes ago, and that's really not like him at night. He's usually pretty comatose. Anyway, I've had a good look around, and I guess there's not really anything to report except that there's nothing to report. Everything seems copacetic."

Shit. Kot wonders if this guy's generation even knows that word.

"Copewhaaaat? Where you are, I'd guess your biggest worry might be a big ol' cougar, but hey, you did the right thing to call."

Again, if this Marty knows where she is, how many others do?

Marty continues, "I'll type it up and Doug'll probably give you a call. The caller ID. will just show RCMP, so go ahead and answer it. Meanwhile, try and relax. Just let me know if you two have any more uprisings."

"I will. Is there anything else I should do?"

"Nah. Probably good if you just make a cup of tea and go back to bed."

Stereotyping. Her gender, anxious voice, or the situation? Probably all of the above.

"Um… I might have a little single malt, thanks. Sorry you have to write a report about nothing." *Canadian to the core, Kot. Apologize to someone for making him do his job, eh?*

"No worries. Get some sleep now."

He sounds gentle. Maybe he's just a nice person. *And you are a stressed-out jerk.*

After Kot disconnects, she's struck by how welcome even that bit of human contact was. Anyway, she was right to make the call, and now Medley clearly needs to pee. Putting him out alone in the dark usually results in him lifting a leg on the closest post, so Kot plugs in the phone and shrugs a long, hooded jacket over her bulky robe. It doesn't quite meet the top of the gumboots. She feels like the Michelin man, but apart from Doug's short visits (she can hear Mich calling them "quickies" already), she has no witness in this isolated form of protection.

On their return, she'll make the suggested cup of tea. Medley stands beside her on the porch, tuned in to her watchfulness. A barred owl calls from further away, sounding like: *"Who cooks for you, who cooks for YOU-awwllll?"*

Kot answers it silently. *No one. No one cooks for me.*

A few solar lamps along the downhill path still work, casting dim spheres of light, and nearby clumps of creamy narcissus generate a luminescence of their own. The half-moon peeks through the tall firs along the back of the garage. Medley is snuffling through the detritus of dead leaves over by the perimeter fence, presumably honouring the purpose of this unprecedented outing. Pungent, almost metallic smells rise from the ground and disperse in the slight breeze that is rattling the arbutus leaves above. One dry husk sails down to land with a gentle rasp on the pavement below her.

Maybe it's the emotional release of calling Mich, followed by the stress of tonight's events, but Kot is angry. It seems inconceivable that no one will provide her with core information—anything that might allow her to regain any sense of control over her life. In this context, Doug's stonewalling phrase "foreseeable future" has no meaning. It's maddening.

Also, that call to Ben had probably been a bad idea. On her second day in the safe house, Kot had disobeyed the advice of the police, and caved to her all-consuming need to know he was alive. His phone rang several times before Ben answered, and his voice was so hoarse and weak that it was unrecognizable above the background noise of a hospital paging system.

"Ben? It's Kathleen. I just needed to know how you are. I won't keep you."

A pause. "Ah, hi. It said unidentified number and I almost didn't answer. But I'm glad to hear from you. Apologies for my voice. I think they call it post-intubation croaking syndrome."

He told her that he was in a private room after emergency surgery to remove the bullet from his leg. Ben told her that, until the police had confirmed it, he'd wondered if he'd dreamed that Kot was with him after the attack. Kot had to repeat her flimsy reason for being there. Ben was quiet, and then told her that he'd been shot because he'd refused to give the men his wallet and car fob.

"There was another attack near our building, not long ago. Apparently, there's been a rising number of robberies in the area. All gang-related. I probably should have just handed over my wallet to begin with." That matched what the police had told Kot. "I've been worried about you, Kathleen. Where are you?"

Kot instinctively told him the truth, but since Ben was clearly medicated, she wished him a fast recovery, said she'd be in touch again sometime, and ended the call. She felt uncomfortable not knowing if his wife was there with him. Her affair with Ben aside, Kot's opinion remains that Lauren doesn't deserve him.

That call had hollowed her out, and she'd howled into a pillow for a long time. Calling Mich yesterday evening had taken some courage, but at least it had resulted in more comfort and support.

At the bottom of the path is what Kot calls the Sentinel Fir. A massive thing, it seems to guard an unused little gate, overgrown with tangled vegetation, and the only opening in the high fence apart from the driveway gate. Kot has no idea who owns the land on the other side, but if this incarceration drags on, she might force the gate open and follow the little deer path through the forest on the other side, just to see where it goes.

A grey shadow zips across the path in front of her foot. Kot's visceral fear of rats increases her urgency to empty her own bladder, and using the old toilet in the garage is a more appealing option than encountering other ratty relatives out here. Medley whines and snuffles outside while Kot sits on the cold seat and listlessly decides to have toast with her tea. And maybe some of the honey that Doug brought yesterday.

After she stands to flush a massive explosion splits the air. Kot is thrown off her feet and lands heavily on the concrete floor. Deafened, she can't tell whether the disaster is happening inside of her or outside. She squints upwards to a world that is surely ending. Flames are devouring the opposite garage wall and licking at the roof. Through the opening, a tower of fire rises from the house to the sky and the trees are giant tiki torches, dripping flame.

The cedar shakes on the house and garage roofs are dry as kindling and will soon be consumed. The quiet of moments ago is now a Renaissance artist's rendition of the infernos of hell.

Instinct and adrenalin take over, and Kot uses her good arm to reach up to the worktable and pull herself up. Her body has too many points of pain to even acknowledge, and in the searing heat, it feels like her bones are starting to melt. She keeps her eyes closed and gropes her way toward the door. The smoke is becoming suffocating. She finally makes the doorknob turn, then trips on the raised sill and has to grab onto the door frame for balance as she goes through. In that moment, the propane tank beside the house explodes, and the blast thunders in Kot's ears as the air is sucked from her lungs. She cowers down behind the garage, her screams inaudible in the roar.

The only possible escape is through the gate beside the huge fir and into the forest behind. She crawls like a drunken beetle along the fence line, her hands and face clawed by blackberry and salal branches. She hadn't had time to refasten her robe, and her breasts and stomach scrape on the rough ground. At least it's still cool from the rain.

The top of the giant fir catches fire with a roar. In the terrifying light, Kot can see the gate just ahead. Using her coat sleeve to press the hot latch, she pushes hard against the weight of vegetation and forces the gate open enough to squeeze through the opening to the little track beyond.

The forest canopy provides protection from the thundering heat, but now it's more difficult to see. Her burned fingers find the little penlight still at the bottom of her robe pocket, and she points its beam at the ground, slowly putting distance between herself and the inferno.

Then the horror hits. Medley. *Oh my God.* Kot stops and tries to call him, but her voice is too feeble. She can't go back to that hell. And she knows the odds. The gate is still slightly open, so her desperate hope is that Medley will follow her if he has survived. He was probably somewhere behind the garage, near her. He is such a good little tracker. Could be a truffle dog.

Tears channel through the grime on Kot's face, making it even harder to see where she's going. She limps forward, her prayer for Medley a whispered loop in time with each step. She can hear several sirens, but can think of no reason to trust the police or anyone else right now. The overriding instinct is to flee.

She leaves the deer trail and heads east toward the pre-dawn light, breaking her way until she eventually finds another track leading downhill. Glimpses of reflected lights on a body of water and the occasional sound of traffic mean that Elk Lake must be at the bottom of the slope, bordered on its east by the Pat Bay Highway. Her guess about the general location of the safe house was correct. A sob catches as some tiny measure of control returns.

She trips over vines and roots, falling more than once in the dark, but eventually Kot crawls through shrubs to a big maple trunk and turns off the light. Beyond the highway and the grid of houses climbing the hill beyond it, the new day is arriving in a wash of pastels. Behind her, the sky is still lit by a very different glow. The multiple sirens have been stilled, but the smell of smoke is strong. Shivering, she tries to catch her breath.

So far, she must be the only one who knows that she has survived, and for now, she needs to keep it that way. Kot recognizes shock symptoms in addition to her injuries. She'll need to come up with a solid strategy before moving again.

~ SIX ~

Soon after becoming the President and CEO of NatureSave Canada, or NSC, whether in his office, on the road, or even on holiday, Jack Latrie had quickly figured out that his number one priority is a call from their biggest donor representative. It requires him to interrupt anything, up to and maybe including a heart attack, and take it.

Ben Northcott, his main contact with the Northcott Foundation, is a keen adventurer. Over the course of multi-day NSC field trips and expensive whiskies, Jack has forged something that might be called a friendship with him, at least by Northcott standards. Jack knows that Ben's personal trust in him is a critical factor in keeping the copious Northcott Foundation money flowing in NSC's direction. It also provides him with some pretty sweet job security.

He closes his office door, and grabs his desk phone before even sitting down. "Ben! How's things on the wet coast?"

"Ah, good to hear your voice, Jack. Not bad, not bad. You're right—it's a bit damp today. But of course, we're also drowning in blossoms, even if they're wet. Sorry about my voice. I've been battling a cold. But it's almost gone. How are things at home?"

Fresh out of the hospital and still hoarse from intubation, Ben is working hard to sound a lot more energetic than he feels. Still, he is relieved already. If Jack had somehow learned about the attack, he would have been immediately solicitous. Instead, they are just lobbing the usual conversational ball, and it's in Jack's court.

"Hey, it warms my heart you still call Toronto home. And I'm glad to hear you're beating the bug, buddy. Hey, try saying that three times fast. It's crazy busy… but a shitload of great projects, so that's the good kind of crazy." Jack adopts a confidentially humorous tone. "Of course, a couple of the regions are giving us grey hairs, but what else is new? Nothing we can't handle." They share a collegial chuckle about the perils of running large organizations across a huge and complicated country.

Ben rises above his pain to achieve just the right casual tone, his usual mixture of bonhomie and noblesse oblige. "Hah. Challenges, no doubt. But you've put together such a crackerjack team, Jack. Kudos to you, as always. Speaking of which, I've left a couple of messages on Kathleen Cafferty's voice mail and heard nothing back. I'm hoping she isn't ill. Is she on holiday?"

Jack can feel the moisture surfacing on his forehead. There has been no time to prepare for this question. Kathleen's assistant in Victoria called a couple of days ago to say that she had received a unusually terse email from Kathleen, saying that she would be taking some sick days. Nothing too serious, but doctor's orders were for complete rest, and she would be in touch with a date when her staff could expect her back. Until then, they should handle everything as best they could. Jack had sent a text to Kathleen, wishing her a fast return to health, and had heard nothing back. So he gave it no further thought, beyond hoping, for everyone's sake, that his Western Division VP would soon be back in the saddle.

But then he'd received the call at home last night, one that he was still trying to get his head around. Kathleen is not sick, but rather the sole witness to a crime, and for her own safety the RCMP had her housed somewhere secret and presumably safe. And no, Mr. Latrie, there would be no further information provided. Jack's confidentiality was demanded and given, and the blunt sergeant had hung up, leaving Jack stunned and staring at his phone.

He has allocated time later today to craft appropriate internal and external messaging about Kathleen's absence, meant to suffice for as long as the situation lasts; he intends to reference "a family matter." It's now obvious that he should have taken care of it already. However, this scenario is unique, and could have organizational repercussions. The ins and outs of keeping the truth from both the National and Regional Board Chairs isn't covered in any not-for-profit leadership manual. Also, not to be too dramatic, but Jack himself could be incapacitated by any number of fluke accidents or medical events. So shouldn't someone else know the real scoop on Kathleen?

He particularly resents having to withhold information from Ben Northcott. Jack knows himself to be a bad liar, and also that Ben has an advanced ability to sniff out deceit. Probably part of his business talent. Or maybe his genetic legacy.

The temptation to be honest is strong. Jack thinks Ben would be fascinated by the tiny but titillating information that the sergeant had provided in that call. It would also be a relief to share the burden of knowledge and enjoy some fruitless phone speculation together. But it had been made clear that, to date, Jack is Kathleen's one and only point of exposure, and that her life could be threatened by more people knowing the truth. And Jack genuinely cares about her wellbeing. He has no choice but to risk this all-important donor relationship and fudge the truth. In the long term, Jack has to count on Ben understanding the serious reasons for that.

Jack's troublesome blood pressure has risen. He's delayed responding to Ben's question for a few seconds, and now hopes that his voice won't betray him. Whatever he tells Ben must also match all other communications about Kathleen. He settles on the KISS principle: Keep it Simple, Stupid. He'll also put his university acting talent to use. They don't pay him the not-so-big bucks for nothing.

"Sorry, Ben. I was just told that Ted is on the other line. But he's okay with me calling him back when we're done."

Normally, Ben would courteously suggest that Jack interrupt their call and take the one from the National Board Chair. Today, he is silent, so Jack continues.

"Anyway, yeah… Kathleen. I only got word late yesterday." That much is the truth, but there it ends. "Apparently, she was off work with the flu, but then had to ask for a leave of absence to deal with some family matter. She didn't offer any details, but she didn't sound too upset. She thinks she'll be back at work in a couple of weeks, so of course I agreed. Can we help you with something, Ben? I'll be heading west soon, and could have a day or two in Vancouver."

"That's kind of you to offer, Jack. But no, it's nothing urgent. Just a quick question about a project. Sorry to hear Kathleen is having a tough time. Please just let me know if you're in touch with her at all, and do give her my best wishes. And it would be so good to see you! Maybe you'll have time to grab dinner with me at the club?"

Jack's shoulders relax in relief, although he's confused about why Ben wants to know if he hears from Kathleen.

"Sounds good. But do let me know if there's anything we can help you with, okay, buddy? By the way, we're starting to line up that Galapagos trip for major donors that I told you about. It'll likely be this fall, and it would be great on many levels to have you along, if you can make it."

"Tempting, tempting. Send me the dates, and I'll get Isobel to take a look at my schedule. I don't think it's Lauren's thing, but maybe one of the kids. They're hard to predict these days. Thanks for thinking of me, Jack. Let's talk again soon."

Ben wants to blurt that he needs to know every detail that Jack learns about Kathleen's whereabouts and wellbeing. He's probably already shown an inappropriate level of interest, but had only called Jack after he'd struck out with every other method of trying to locate her.

After they sign off, Jack dries his forehead. That call went a whole lot better than it might have, and maybe he will be able to tell Ben the whole story by the time they meet up in Vancouver. He might need to change a few timing details to protect himself, but surely Ben wouldn't be paying close attention.

Ben unlocks a lower desk drawer and removes a small phone from under papers at the back, one that not even his personal assistant knows about. Leaning on a cane, he limps gingerly across the wool carpet. As usual, Isobel, the assistant, chose aesthetics over comfort when selecting new furniture for his office, and the couch is too short to accommodate his length. Of course, it may also have been a deliberate move on her part to limit his recreational activities when she wasn't around. He'd ended the foolish affair with Isobel long ago, but she still shows signs of jealousy. If dismissed, she is also capable of telling stories to his wife. So on they go.

He lifts his wounded leg onto the couch, already angry and impatient with the pain. His brain is too fuzzy, and he needs to collapse at home again. He only came into the office on a Sunday to make that call, away from any possibility of being overheard, and off his usual cell phone records. He steeples his fingers and taps them together, trying to think things through. He has no intention of resuming their affair, but is increasingly desperate to know what has become of Kathleen. He wishes that he hadn't been so out of it when she'd called him in hospital. He'd tried phoning her back, but the number didn't seem to receive calls. If she only has a Witness Protection burner phone, that won't change. The voicemail on her personal mobile has been full for days.

Jack Latrie would be unlikely to lie to him, for obvious reasons. That means that Jack knows even less than he does, and also that, unless Jack calls him soon with more information, phoning him today was more than just risky; it was a waste of time.

Ben bites his lip and looks up a contact alias on the phone. Someone answers on the second ring. It's appropriate to sound a little vulnerable for this short call, so he doesn't have to work as hard. After, he closes his eyes and rests before struggling up with one of the words frowned upon in his family, and dropping the phone into a pants pocket—another necessary risk until he obtains more information. He calls a cab to the front, unwilling to even look at the rear parking lot yet.

There is still a shipping empire to be managed, and more than a few frayed tempers to control. But it will all have to wait.

— SEVEN —

The pain when Kot wakes brings memories of trying to shift positions during her fitful sleep. Her bashed hip and shoulder ache, she can feel a number of cuts, burns, and bruises, and her throat is raw from smoke, or screaming, or both. Frantic barking down by the lake makes her heart race, until she sees an Irish setter bouncing backwards along the trail as its owner teases it with a ball chucker. By the light, it must be late afternoon.

She flinches when something moves beside her. Medley places a sooty paw on her sleeve, his eyes solemn brown pools in his filthy face. Kot gasps and pulls him against her, moaning love and tears into his curly coat, a mess of embedded debris. Medley has survived, and sometime in the night his nose led him to her. He is clearly exhausted, not even squirming at being held so close.

However, if her beloved amateur sidekick located her, trained dogs could certainly do the same. After she figures out a viable escape plan, Kot will need to stay flexible. Not overthink things for a change. Just trust her instincts, one step at a time. Every item in that to-do list feels completely beyond her right now. She is distracted by thirst, and Medley also pants heavily beside her.

She picks some of the larger vegetation from his coat and tries to think. The trail that circuits Elk Lake is still too busy. In this bathrobe and boots ensemble, and possibly a face as sooty as Medley's, she would certainly be noticed and remembered. They are well screened up here and probably blend in well with the surroundings as long as they don't move.

There must be at least local media coverage of the explosion by now. Kot can't guess what information the police would release, or if they might engage the public in a missing person's search. A diligent journalist would quickly uncover a mystery regarding the property's ownership.

On the other hand, wouldn't the Witness Protection Program try to prevent all-points bulletins, or the distribution of a photo that might endanger her further? She wonders how obvious it is that she'd used that little gate. The giant fir may have dropped branches onto it as it burned, and the ruins of the house would be unsafe at first, making early forensic efforts difficult. She should have some hours yet.

Kot comes to grips with a few basics. The safe house had been bombed. The propane tank hadn't exploded until after the house and garage were already on fire, and with no other stored fuel around, nothing else makes sense. Worse, there's no avoiding the fact that she must have been the intended target.

Maybe Medley was barking because he'd heard someone outside. Placing the bomb. But how did they get inside the high fence, especially packing an explosive device? Did someone sneak in when Doug opened or closed the gate? No, he's too careful. It was nothing short of a fluke that Medley needed to go out last night, and that they were sheltered from the worst of it by the garage. Perhaps the owl had also been disturbed by the intruder. If so, Kot clearly owes her life to it and Medley. She plants more kisses on her dog's dirty head.

Whoever tried to kill her must now have a keen interest in knowing the outcome. A forensics team will soon determine that there are no human or canine remains in the wreckage. There must have been a cop or WPP leak that gave away her location, so there could well be another one after the forensics results are delivered. Nothing good can come of anyone knowing her whereabouts anytime soon.

Someone searching for her will probably focus on the Greater Victoria area, but with no apparent resources, Kot has no idea how to get anywhere else. She closes her eyes and, piece by piece, builds an immediate plan.

Someone wants her to disappear, and she will do exactly that, but on her own terms: get to temporary safety, recover, and regroup.

By dusk, the lake trail is quiet and Kot slowly picks a way down the slope, with Medley right on her heels. When she's sure that they're alone, she crosses the trail to the water. It often has high coliform levels from the over-abundant Canada geese: fine for dogs, but it would be stupid for her to risk drinking it. An inflow stream further north should still be fresh and flowing in early April, and she will have to wait to reach that. She cleans her sore hands and splashes her face with refreshing water. Nothing more can be done about her appearance, but darkness will help.

She ducks down and holds Medley's snout closed until well after a night jogger's headlamp has bobbed past. There is a dog leash in another anorak pocket: a totem from a past life. Medley wags his tail slightly as Kot attaches it, apparently pleased that she can't get away again now.

Without swimming all the way across the lake, the shortest route to Kot's destination is around its north end. Her injuries are no worse while walking, but her bare heels are already blistered by the boots. When the trail eventually starts to bend, she hears the burbling stream ahead. She slakes her thirst, then leads Medley into the lake shallows and reenters the trail further along. She knows the simple tactic would only delay a tracker by a minute, but it feels like a start on being proactive again.

By the time they reach the highway it's been dark for a few hours and the moon has yet to rise. Besides a few deer, they have only encountered a couple of lovers hiding in the bushes. Kot is beyond hungry, her comforting notion of tea and toast before returning to bed last night a distant fantasy. She has no backup if something goes wrong with her tenuous plan and she doesn't find food and shelter tonight. Still, there's no point in worrying about worst-case scenarios—only in limping forward.

When distant stoplights create a break, Kot and Medley clamber over the highway barriers. Kot removes her boots when she reaches the sidewalk and tucks them under her arm. Being barefoot on pebbled pavement is at least a different kind of pain. When cars approach she pulls Medley out of sight behind a hedge. If there is nowhere to hide, she bends over with an outstretched arm to pick up imaginary poop: just another robed dog owner in the night, doing her civic duty. Medley trudges along, spent enough to ignore every smell.

A big view opens up when they crest the ridge to begin the steeper drop on the other side. The lights of northern Washington State twinkle far across the strait, and to the left, the sky glows orange and white from Greater Vancouver. Familiar, impossible places.

A gust of wind sends another blizzard of useless pink blossoms against her face. *April is indeed the cruelest month.* With a quarter of the distance still to go, Kot sits down on the grassy verge, unable to continue, and Medley stands over her protectively. Kot must acknowledge that he, alone, deserves the effort, and struggles up again.

The breakthrough of remembering that she has access to Anne and Gerry's waterfront place offered a perfect short-term goal. Kot has been checking their house periodically and watering plants while they winter in Baja, in exchange for the use of Anne's kayak and equipment. Medley's head comes up when they finally near the familiar house.

Kot finds the hidden key and locks the door behind them. It seems like months, but it was less than ten days ago when she was last here, and no one else would have been inside since. She gets them both water and tips the contents of one of the resident beagle's cans of food into a bowl. Medley devours it while Kot wolfs down tuna from a tin with stale crackers. They taste terrible, and terrific. For dessert, she pours herself two fingers of scotch from a new bottle that she had left on the counter for her friends' homecoming.

At last, she strips and stands in the hot shower of her dreams. Cleaning Medley will have to wait. She finds Tylenol and is asleep almost before the familiar duvet on Gerry and Anne's guest bed has settled over her.

The morning light brings a clearer head. At the very least, the Witness Protection Program can't be trusted. Someone on the inside must have revealed her location to… someone else.

It would be lovely to just hide out here and relax with Anne and Gerry when they get home. Have drinks and hamburgers on the deck. Take a brisk paddle together out to the flashing buoy, or a leisurely stroll along the beach. But such fantasies are crazy. Some office colleagues know that she goes there, and they might eventually be questioned. She might also endanger Anne and

Gerry by involving them. Kot also isn't certain that they would understand and respect her need to avoid the police.

So, she must move again, very soon. She also needs to regain as much strength as possible in a short time. She finds a heating pad and stronger pain meds, and her anger begins to build again. She has spent her life trying to please everybody, for God's sake. She can't remember ever having a serious enemy, and now, apparently, someone actually wants her dead.

She waters the houseplants and swats at winter cobwebs, and the silent hours of weeping pass. By late afternoon, she has figured out her next move, made a list, and begun to collect what is needed. In between, she rests. When night comes, she keeps the curtains closed and carries a lonely candle.

After sunset on the second day, Kot locks the back door and hides the key again, trying to suppress her fear. This departure feels like an ending, ominously permanent. They slip through the gloom of overhanging evergreens and down to the loaded kayak above the beach. Her robe and anorak are laundered and in a box in the garage. Now she is wearing mostly her own kayaking gear, retrieved from that same garage, and Anne's fleece-lined jacket with Medley's leash in a pocket. She hopes that the jacket's warmth will compensate for its bulk during this night paddle.

A dry bag full of other items of Anne's clothing and equipment is stowed in the rear hatch. Her friend wouldn't begrudge Kot any of it. However, the contents of the Ziploc bag in the inner pocket of the jacket do inspire guilt: three hundred dollars, in twenties, that Kot found inside an envelope in a desk drawer. She's left a note confessing to borrowing it, with effusive thanks and promises of repayment. But it troubles her. She also asked Anne and Gerry to trust in the crucial need for secrecy until they hear from her. Kot could think of nothing else to safely say.

She scans the empty beach in both directions, turns for a last look at the house and then back to the dark grey ocean. Her hip is still painful, but the shoulder is slightly improved and her paddling gloves protect her hands a little. She plans to take whatever painkillers are necessary to get through this first journey. It will get colder tonight, but Kot's luck with the weather continues; the winds are calm, and stars are slowly being revealed in a mostly clear sky. A little light remains, so she leaves the headlamp that is fitted over her toque turned off. There is also a new battery in the same little penlight in an upper pocket.

She drags the laden kayak to the shallows of a rising tide, and Medley jumps in happily to a blanket folded in the front of the large cockpit. He loves kayak trips, but this one is sure to be more demanding than anything that either of them have done before. And even with water-resistant gear, Kot knows what it will likely cost in comfort to have no spray skirt over her, in order to accommodate Medley.

She settles stiffly into the cockpit and pushes off hard with her paddle. Supplies in the front hatch shift and settle, but her smooth strokes send them shooting across the flat water like a spear. Even her sore body knows exactly what to do, and the glassy surface offers little resistance. The unexpected relief of being self-sufficient and on the move again begins to blanket her fear.

Kot angles northeast, heading away from both Vancouver Island and the US border. A prehistoric croak shatters the silence, making Medley cower. A great blue heron has risen from a cluster of rocks in the water and circles them with ponderous grace before heading for shore. Kot interprets its message as *Godspeed*. Or was it a warning? In any case, she is glad that she waited for darkness. They are invisible to any hunter not at close range.

Murky across the water, the outlines of undulating islands seem to have been smudged by the thumb of a weary god.

~ EIGHT ~

He made sure that there were no raptor-friendly trees nearby before first flying onto his Atticus Island estate. And every time since, after crossing the Strait of Georgia, Hunter Nott has gone out of his way to pilot his helicopter in a big loop around the north end of the island, in order to approach the ocean bluff of his property directly from the water. Besides not wanting to disturb wildlife, Hunter wants to ruffle the feathers of other island residents as little as possible. He also suspects that the usual complainants about his infrequent flights would be among the first to expect an emergency medevac in his chopper.

Back when he was a child holding a fishing rod in his father's boat, Hunter had been impressed by the cliff-top flagpole now in view and by stories about the Glenhurst "mansion" in the meadows behind it. Back then, Hunter could never have imagined doing this: flying his own chopper to land on the Glenhurst estate, which is also now his.

It's still the same sturdy old flagpole, but snapping cheerfully from it more than thirty years later is a new Canadian flag. And today, he's coming home.

Home: still a wondrous concept, and also the likely trigger for his current self-examination. With a deep bow to his new, no-holds-barred therapist, Hunter is making an attempt to evaluate his fundamental character. His very core. His rise to international star status has been free of such exercises to date. The current therapy homework is to try to "consciously identify" his emotions, and this current one is dead easy: pure elation.

He has experienced and even lived in many beautiful places, but this spot claims him like no other. Atticus Island is the thread connecting the golden summers of his youth to his present—by tabloid estimations—glamorous life, and so far the paparrazi haven't discovered his cherished bolthole. Hunter knows that every day that continues will be one of the happiest of his life. His therapist has suggested online sessions while he is here, as frequently as he would like to pay for. Instead, Hunter is counting on physical labour, real friends, and the peace of the place to reduce his stress and ease him forward. As his mother used to say, he just needs to "Go Atticus."

All of Hunter's romantic partners have been stereotypically younger, and every one of them has sported the enhancement surgeries deemed necessary in their world. Hunter had thoroughly enjoyed the early romance stage with each, and their clear appreciation of being his much-photographed escort. Nevertheless, it had always been he who severed ties. In fact, his unwillingness to commit has devastated at three (okay… maybe five) women by now. A couple of them didn't fully deserve it, and Hunter experiences bouts of feeling like a jerk.

But this last one—holy shit, what had he been thinking? Apparently, he has been *projecting fantasies, avoiding clear realities.* Expensive therapeutic hypotheses about Hunter's relationship with his mother abound. Every one, in Hunter's view, complete garbage. He admits to being a slow learner, but he just keeps returning to the same inescapable point: in order to sustain an exclusive relationship, isn't it vital to want to be not just physically, but emotionally and intellectually intimate with the other person? To consider them your best friend? In fact, no lover has ever felt remotely like a close friend since his high school sweetheart and confidante. Hunter had been crushed when she told him that she had "grown out of him," possibly setting the stage for him to be the first to leave a relationship ever since. Still, Hunter has never known a woman since who made him even want that level of intimacy. And in his opinion, all that has sweet diddly-squat to do with his marvellously healthy relationship with his mother.

The lovely Ashley, his latest abandoned lover and most urgent issue, is wreaking revenge through tabloid warfare. Hunter stopped answering

Ashley's calls days ago, and the advice now is to publish a rebuttal interview in another magazine. In the words of his agent: "Remember, buddy, there's no bad publicity. Top of public mind predicts future pay scale." However, Hunter would prefer to take the higher road, sure that the salivating tabloid media will soon move on if left unfed. Others can give him character references in the face of whatever today's libel turns out to be. He has always been monogamous, he tries not to lie, and hell, he doesn't even like marijuana much. And, it hadn't taken long for Ashley's very real instability to reveal itself, in technicolour. But then, her body had been quite a distraction. Same old, same old.

Wisely pessimistic during their relationship, Hunter was careful to ensure that Ashley knew nothing of Glenhurst. He can only hope that, during his off-radar time there, the press will get bored and move on, probably at roughly the same rapid pace as Ashley's own attention span. He'd sent her a "cease and desist" request before he left L.A. last night, and she'd replied: *"Pas de chance, darling, sans solid incentive. Ten mill. & public grovel, perhaps? Do stay in touch."*

Glenhurst remains the largest private holding on the island, and Hunter intends to place legal restrictions on the title to ensure that it doesn't get subdivided after he's gone. Roughly 105 years ago, the first owner, an immigrant Irishman, had fenced and cross-fenced his lands for racehorse breeding, even before the house was built, and, over the years, had planted hedgerows and allowed vegetation to screen its perimeters. Now the estate can only be viewed from the air. Or, as Hunter's caretaker recently put it, by "any asshole's drone."

There have been a number of owners since the Irishman, the most recent an accomplished chef who, with his lover, enjoyed one euphoric season of designing and operating an elite destination restaurant before fleeing, penniless, back to the city. Glenhurst hit the market once more, with the added attractions of updated electrical, plumbing, and heating systems and a commercial kitchen.

So when Hunter started looking for a permanent home, he was astounded to find his boyhood dream property was available. More than his improbable movie plots, he loves the unpredictable twists of real life. His financial advisor was equally delighted by the price, at least relative to other international choices and to Hunter's history of extravagance. Many expensive updates had already been done, still leaving scope for Hunter to imprint his own preferences.

Within a week of his taking ownership six months ago, a helipad was installed and his interior designer flown in. The original basement carpet bowling court is now a no-expense-spared gym, and the antique metal-gated elevator has been replaced with a slick and silent version that the caretaker requires, but which Hunter personally rarely uses.

He has sold three properties in other countries and closely monitored renovation progress from two different film locations, and Glenhurst is finally ready for him to call it home. It's also time for the landscaping to begin, and he intends to supervise that in person. Now he just needs to finalize those designs and get a commitment from his island gardener friend, Tessa Colgan.

The beach below the estate is wide with a zero tide as Hunter descends gently to wait through the cool-down cycle. He's grateful to be through the turbulence over the strait and arrive before the approaching squall. The treetops are already dancing in all directions. He plans to quickly unload before the rain hits, but suddenly breaks into the lopsided grin beloved by millions. That smile, the boyish flop of chestnut brown hair, and his big brown eyes were his as a baby, but soon became famous in the action series that first made Hunter Nott a household name. And a very rich man.

The reasons for his smile and change of plans are coming toward him from the house—just the right people to get his Hollywood detox underway: Madonna, his sweet golden retriever, crazy to see him and straining on her leash, and the smiling man holding her back.

With the rotors still slowing, Hunter rushes in a crouch to hug his ecstatic dog, and then the powerfully built man in the wheelchair. Malik Koto, a.k.a. Roller, is Hunter's former stunt man, and now his security guard, property manager, and friend. That new flag would be Roller's doing.

Camas crouches under the forest canopy and holds her breath. The helicopter coming in low over the ocean is headed straight at her. She wouldn't expect Brett to go to such lengths to search for her, but this chopper is smaller and on a different flight path from the commercial ones.

When it veers to the north, she finally exhales. It seems to be landing somewhere on the far side of the park. There must be rich Atticus residents who fly in and out, and her brain knows that it's unlikely the helicopter has anything to do with her. But during the few days since she escaped, her lethargy has been balanced by high anxiety, and she's plagued by headaches, brain fog, and loneliness. Almost every time she leaves the lighthouse, she forgets to take something with her—the stolen daypack she uses for foraging, a jacket, or the water jug—and has to return to her room. Hunger is a near-constant companion, and the need to find food and water is just as relentless as her concussion.

Camas uses a hidden deer track whenever she leaves the tower. It traverses a narrow plateau on the bluff, taking her down to the beach on the far side of the boulders. She times excursions for just after dawn and at dusk, and tries to be watchful every minute. Driven by an empty stomach, this midday foraging foray is unusual. Her collection bag of edible plants isn't filling quickly enough, but at least she hasn't seen anyone yet.

The old man in the light station residence doesn't seem to venture outside much on his own. A few different people have picked him up to drive him wherever it is he goes, and the same driver as Camas saw on the first day came yesterday morning. After she was sure they wouldn't come back for something, Camas raced back down to the house to steal some food and another blanket. She also took a pen and two puzzle books from his pile on the coffee table, and discovered the staircase that led to a musty basement and the glass bottles of canned fruit stored down there. Getting salty edibles from the ocean isn't hard, but she is desperately missing sweetness, and the peaches in syrup taste almost like candy. She promises herself more soon, but is still trying to limit what she takes so the old man won't notice. It will soon be necessary to muster enough energy and courage to investigate what lies behind other unlocked doors between the light station and the ferry terminal.

A sign says that the official camping season won't begin until late May, but one couple has already tented for a night above the beach. Camas snagged their water container while they were out paddling. The influx of legal campers in a few weeks will mean more things to steal, but also far higher risks of being seen. She'll figure that out later.

Camas has gradually explored the forest, and the best routes to move around without being seen. She's discovered stone outcrops that offer shelter, and one in particular, soft with fallen needles, offers a perfect vantage point for spying on the beach and campground. There are also secret hollows, deep with moss, where she can hide or rest in good weather. The lack of large predators, poisonous snakes, or even skunks on these islands is almost unique.

Most of the park visitors stick to the main trail, and talk so much that she has ample warning. She's always on the lookout for the quiet, solo ones, and any dog is always unpredictable. A joyful border collie sniffed her out, its white-tipped wagging tail like a flag for her location, but it obeyed a whistle from its owner further up the trail, leaving Camas feeling both relieved and bereft. She'd crept up to her higher perch, and a minute later a carefree-looking woman in a ball cap paddled a kayak around the point and past the beach. There was a cute blonde dog sitting in front of her. She would have happily become either one of them.

Camas was named after the beautiful indigo-coloured bloom of a native plant, a former food staple that was farmed by the Coast Salish people. Mama taught her what plants can make her sick or even kill her if she is careless, and Camas has discovered some safe things in the park, even this early in the year: an abundance of heavy maple blossoms, a few patches of nodding onion, and early sprouts of miner's lettuce in open areas near the stream. However, even with occasional gifts from the sea, these are nowhere near enough to suppress her gnawing hunger. She has fresh water for now, at least, steals what she can, and while her source of drinking water will shrink, better foraging will come with every week that she can survive.

Even without remembering the details of how she got it, she knows that a concussion can last a long time. She figures that Brett would do at least a cursory search, no doubt hoping he doesn't find her, but also wanting assurance that she won't suddenly reappear. He will probably try to pretend, publicly, that Camas is still alive, just for the money. While Camas is a minor, Mama's will named Brett as her guardian, and, with two others, a joint trustee of a fund in her name. After Mama died, Camas thinks that Brett found a way to access the monthly payments meant for her, and he would want to continue doing that for as long as possible.

She remains motionless for some time, listening. If the chopper takes off again she will try to get a better look. Finding food is less important than staying free. But it doesn't reappear, and by the time the wind and rain arrive she has enough in her bag to scurry up the bluff trail to her tower room.

~ NINE ~

Robert Baschel likes to introduce himself as "the number one slave of Chase Bay Café." Hardly original, and not even accurate; he chose this island life and doesn't complain.

Better still, his current assistant is both hardworking and highly adept at teasing the male dinosaurs within their customer base, while at the same time curtailing their behaviour. Rachel's skills are well above the pay grade that Rob can afford, and he is grateful, for however long the situation lasts. His former employees have shown a consistent tendency to leave for better-paying jobs, or get pregnant, or addicted to something or other. No matter the age or gender, it's always one damned crisis or another. That said, Rob will not blame Rachel when she also leaves. As long as it isn't too soon.

He lugs a bulging bag of recycling down the café's back steps, arcs it into the bin and turns to stretch and scan the wrinkled bay. As usual, he and Rachel started the day's work in the early hours, to have the glass display cases full by opening time. Now Rachel is serving up a selection of breakfast dishes and the range of espresso beverages apparently required these days, even by those who claim to be hard-up.

Like others who rise early, Rob sometimes feels the slight superiority of witnessing the quiet hours, the arrival of daylight. On these April mornings, the first folks through the door are less generically grumpy than in the dark rains of winter. Rob understands; he feels the same. No matter the season, as cars begin to line up for the first ferry at the terminal across the road, baking fragrances send seductive fingers to lure the sleepy passengers.

It will soon be time to finish the hearty soups and savoury lunch dishes, but Rob lingers an extra minute outside. The morning chill is confirmation that winter isn't long gone. Mists swirling around the lighthouse on Chase Point make the view more mysterious than the summer version, and a rainbow reminder of the morning squall is fading before the new blue sky blowing in from the west. The air is so heavy with ozone and wet evergreen that a deep breath almost hurts his lungs.

The crew of the *Salish Chinook* is skillfully holding the boat stationary. It hovers in the powerful tide and currents off the lighthouse like a clunky marine hummingbird, waiting for the larger ferry bound for Vancouver to vacate the Atticus dock. The *Chinook* is late, and with onboard food service minimal, Rob expects some hungry customers through his door soon. In fact, hyperbolic reviews of his café sometimes suggest that readers should visit Atticus Island solely to sample his Chase Bay Café pastries.

In Rob's estimation, any reason for tourists to visit is a good one. Some locals—far too many—like to arrive early and order a hot drink, then nurse the precious liquid to cold dregs through the morning. Lonely from divorce, retirement, death, or simple ennui, their strategy meets two primary needs: caffeine and company. Rob often has to ask the usual suspects to grumble off and free up tables for paying customers. After Labour Day, vacation homeowners return to their cities, and the island population shrinks by almost half, and for at least seven months of the year, local patronage isn't enough. He can't imagine what would happen if there were a catastrophe that might really halt everything in its tracks—something like an earthquake, or a pandemic.

Like most in the Gulf Islands chain, Atticus hosts an eclectic mix: ecological idealists, the wealthy or famous, writers, stoners, geniuses, conspiracy theorists, artists, cranks —and by no means are those categories mutually exclusive—and as many middle-of-the-roaders as anywhere else. Many admit that their move to such an inconvenient place was an attempt to escape, if only from pervasive noise. As one of them, Rob has no regrets. There is a strong historical rationale for the resident mistrust of visitors and newcomers, and for their hostility to change. But rampant island tribalism is something else. So another reason Rob welcomes off-islanders is the diversity of opinions they bring.

He opens the side gate to check the café entry. As he bends to pick up a piece of scrap paper slapping around the wheelchair ramp in the wind, his striped chef's apron restricts his midriff and brings to mind his tiresome new mantra: *Not every batter must be sampled.* He also has less hair for the wind to blow these days, but is past being depressed about it. He feels good. Healthy. Prime of life. Sexy, in fact, now and then, on a good day.

Rob pretends that he is a first-time customer, crossing the café's porch and approaching the heavy oak door under the budding wisteria. As usual, he's reassured by the blast of wood-fired warmth and fragrance that greets him inside. He was justified to do battle with his ex-wife (or is Marie still his wife, since she has yet to ask for a divorce?) about the commercial value of ambiance. During renovations, Marie had wanted to get rid of the fireplace and replace the leaky old windows. But Rob held his ground, and right from the beginning their customers raved about the cozy fire in the cooler months, and the beauty of the light as it bent and split through the half-mullioned panes facing the bay. People tend to linger, order more, and return, to the point that Rob now has little need to advertise.

So take that, Marie.

Still, had one of those lost battles marked a turning point for Marie? Maybe it was less complicated. Maybe she had just stopped loving him. Stranger things have happened.

He adds a couple of logs to the low flames and waves at two women at a table across the room. Tessa Colgan was in her fifties when she launched her own gardening business a year after her husband died. She's also now preparing to open the island's first garden centre. Her companion, Toni Campo, is younger and a more recent Atticus import who is already the island's top realtor.

Rob hears her ask Tessa, "Are you going to Stitch 'n' Bitch tonight?"

The bi-weekly ladies' quilting bee at the Legion is a cherished island anachronism, a venue known for ribald humour that also produces all of the category's blue ribbons at the Fall Fair. The occasional man shows up at a bee, hoping to enjoy the gender odds. Apart from requests for quilting supplies to be passed, they are always met with sombre silence. Each disappointed fellow soon loses interest in the art of quilting, leaving the women free to resume their usual discourse.

Tessa had just taken her last bite of apple Danish when Toni asked her question.

"*Mmmhp*… sorry. No, I can't. My daughter is going straight to her course from work and I'm picking up the grandkids from school. I said I'd slap on the feedbags and get them to bed at my place. I know, it's definitely a case of the overloaded overloading the overloaded, but I wouldn't have it any other way. Still, I have to admit that I'm feeling totally swamped in general these evenings. I'm nowhere near being ready to open the nursery, never mind looking after my clients. This lunch represents my entire social calendar, so be honoured."

Toni's phone vibrates and she glances at the caller ID. She apologizes to Tessa and plugs her other ear to block out the café chatter as she answers.

"Hello, Toni Campo. Sorry, I can't hear you. What?" She pauses for a few seconds. "My apologies. I'll have to call you back when I get somewhere with a better signal." She ends the call with an impish grin. "Not my favourite client, and definitely unworthy of wrecking this delicious lunch. So I pretended that the service stinks in here."

Rob has appeared at her shoulder with coffee refills, and Toni purrs up at him, "I mean the cellular, not yours, Mr. Baschel."

She isn't exactly flirtatious, but Rob is drawn by the smoldering sensuality that is part of her energy. Witty, lovely, and inexplicably unattached, he finds Toni a delight. She is undoubtedly unattainable, but a guy can dream, and he ensures that her favourite menu items are always available. He lingers to fill mugs, scrape crumbs, and inhale Toni's delicate perfume.

Toni makes small talk until he is out of earshot again. "What's his story, anyway? I don't really know Rob beyond the three group dinners you've invited me to, and in here."

"Oh, well, you know, I think he's through the worst, but he's definitely had some challenges. His wife suddenly left him, almost a year ago now. Rob took the truck to Sidney to get supplies, and Marie drove their car onto the next ferry while he was gone. Apparently, she left everything behind except some clothes and things. As Rob put it: 'including, or perhaps particularly, me.' Anyway, I'm very fond of my friend Rob."

"Aw. Poor guy. Where were they before Atticus? Did the wife go back there?"

"I don't know, and I'm not sure Rob does either. He's still forwarding mail to her sister's address in Nanaimo, but the women don't even get along so it's not likely she's still living there. Rob and Marie used to live in the Vancouver area. Rob was actually a pretty high-level cop in his former life. Gangs, drug smuggling and stuff, I think. He doesn't talk about it much, but he once told me that it all got to him, and booze was how he coped. He got sober before they moved here, and he never touches it now. Anyway, their boys were grown up, so they both quit their jobs and converted this old place. Then Marie suddenly left and went incommunicado. Rob still isn't sure what went wrong, specifically. She'd seemed really into the whole venture, but living here isn't for everyone. I think they're still married."

"Okay, that really sucks..." Toni glances down the room, at Rob and Rachel in the kitchen. "Do you think he can keep this place going? Even with an assistant, it must be hard to soldier on alone with something that was a shared dream."

"I actually asked Rob that a few months ago, and he said he hasn't come up with anything else he'd prefer to do. But yeah, it can't be easy. Just between you and me, I think he also wonders if Marie might suddenly reappear out of the blue."

Noticing the new occupants of the nearby table, Tessa stops talking. She trusts Toni's discretion, but not theirs, and knowledge of people's private lives can become valuable currency in a small community. Maybe some other time she will share with Toni that Rob had confided that his wife had taken "the coward's way out," leaving a letter on the kitchen counter: *So sorry, Rob. I've tried, but I can't do it. Take care of yourself.* And how he still occasionally studies that note, hoping that its message might become clear: "*Do it.*" Do what? Help run the café? Live on Atticus? Love him anymore? And was it "*Take care of YOURSELF?*" A fond parting, or a rebuke? Since he had done all of the cooking and most of the housework, the latter interpretation didn't seem fair.

Whatever, Tessa believes that building the café to be such a success has provided Rob with the twin salvations of mental focus and physical demands.

Rob glances at them from the plating counter and wonders what is so serious over there. Tessa seems fixated on her mug, so he grabs the coffee pot.

"You two doing okay? Refills? Can I tempt you with today's fresh crème brulé?"

Toni accepts a little more coffee. "Super tempting, but I have to get to a showing. I won't say where it is, but the front porch is only the first death trap. So if you hear a siren, you'll know I'm down another couple of clients. Hey, do either of you know when Hunter is planning to arrive?"

Rob answers, "Today, I think. He called yesterday to confirm that he and Roller will be here for the next potluck. He's pretty excited about being on-island all summer, so I hope that works out for him."

Only these three on Atticus can claim true friendships with Hunter Nott and the inscrutable Roller. Of course, Rob has heard others on the island ignore Hunter's family history on Atticus, preferring to frame his purchase of Glenhurst as confirmation of their own brilliance in living here. A few claim that Hunter has swung by their place on occasion for a coffee or beer. Or a joint. Others imply that they might find time to hang out with him, should he really insist on it. Rob tries to look suitably impressed, while he and Hunter's other real friends keep their occasional group potlucks a secret. They take turns hosting—and this summer Hunter's fancy kitchen can join the list of venues.

Tessa doesn't mention that she has also talked to Hunter, mostly because she feels conflicted about being on the verge of letting him down. She just can't see a feasible way to commit to the contract he's offered. Instead, she lowers her voice with a sly smile.

"Hey Rob, I heard something interesting about you and Hunter the other day, and I feel obligated to inform you."

"Oh, let me guess. I'm his next co-star."

"Nope. Even better. You're a couple. Word has it that you were seen noodling together at some point, and you, my friend, are the one and only reason that Hunter chose to dwell on this rock. Your secret's out."

Rob replies, "Well, that makes a change from stories about him and Roller, anyway. And if it were true, I could probably stop worrying about finances. So I should probably give it some thought. Too bad we're both so shamelessly heterosexual, though." Rob would like to make that abundantly clear to Toni, hopeless as it may be.

Toni grins, and changes the subject. "Oh my God—I almost forgot! Have you guys heard about the robbery at the gas station this morning?"

Rob straddles a spare chair to listen, thoroughly enjoying watching Toni. She sees their heads shake, and continues. "I was there afterwards, and heard about it straight from the victim's mouth. Apparently, the robber sat in his car out at the pump wearing a Halloween mask. Unsurprisingly, no one noticed. Dave told me that, as soon as he was alone in the store, the guy just sashayed in and told him to hand over all the money in the till. His hand was in his pocket and it was bulging, so Dave just did as he was told. And with most people using cards now, there wasn't much cash anyway. Apparently, the bandit almost took out a lamp standard during his getaway, and the cops could have pulled him over for the state of his muffler alone."

Tessa looks genuinely horrified. "Oh my God! That's awful. There are so many weirdos visiting here now."

Toni shakes her head. "Ah, but you haven't heard the best part yet. Dave called the cops, and our shiny new sergeant got there a few minutes later. What with Dave's yelling, the store was full of people by then, so there was no point in fingerprinting the door handle. Anyway, that won't be needed."

She takes a deliberate pause and a sip of coffee, and Rob accepts the bait. "And why is that?"

"Well, the cop asked Dave if he could remember anything specific about the robber, and again, I quote: 'For sure, I could. He tried to disguise his voice, but he couldn't keep it up and it kind of squeaked. It was Wayne, for sure. Wayne Curdle. He was driving his old Corolla and that was the same mask that he wore at the Halloween dance at the Hall last year. Plus, he was wearing that ugly sweater Edna knitted him for Christmas. No one else would wear that thing.'"

Rob notices that two local stoners at the neighbouring table have been trying to both overhear Toni's story or peer down her cleavage. He gets up and blocks their view as the women settle the bill and return to work.

~ TEN ~

Kot's first night of paddling is tough, and humbling. The pain of her injured shoulder is manageable, but her stamina is still nowhere near normal. In this frigid sea, there is a rule of one to one to ten to one. If you hit the water, you have one minute to get control of your breathing. In an average of ten minutes, your limbs become useless, and after one hour, give or take, severe hypothermia takes over and eventually kills you. But even in warmer water, it's too far to swim to shore.

She is increasingly concerned about her ability to reach D'Arcy Island, her first goal, but they are over halfway there now. When she feels at her limit, and conditions allow, she slumps forward as if asleep, or dead, as the kayak bobs in the dark like a bathtub toy and Medley fidgets anxiously. Kot can't relax for long, with the ever-present fear of being capsized by the endless wake of a distant freighter or a deep-keeled fishing boat. She constantly scans the water, looking for ship lights through the mist, and her ears and nerves strain to detect even the faint thrum of a motor.

About a kilometre from D'Arcy Island the visibility gets even worse, but each dip of her paddle is triggering aquatic fireworks. It's as if the northern lights fell into the water, merging with fairy dust on their way. The kayak is creating a glittering contrail of turquoise, blue, and green bioluminescence, and Medley seems transfixed by whatever the phenomenon looks like to him. Unfortunately, their passage has probably become visible from above.

It's after midnight when they bump onto the beach. Medley leaps into the shallows, but Kot slumps in exhaustion until waves start to smash the kayak sideways. She drags herself out and staggers to pull the boat a bit higher. She remembers from former visits to this beach that the ruins of a former leper colony are nearby. Most of the leprosy victims had made the grueling journey from China to Victoria in search of a better life, and perhaps had even found one before becoming ill and being cruelly exiled here to die while lights and life taunted from across the water. The only advantage over Kot that the lepers had in their tragic little community was each other's company and care.

Her headlamp illuminates the crumbled walls of a leper's hut, now full of blown sand and hardy beach plants. This will make a better bed than the hard rock shelves above the beach. Kot hides the kayak and takes out water and food for herself and Medley. Wrapped in the warmth of a first aid blanket, she dares to close her eyes. It feels safe enough in this random, unguessable place, under a canopy of indifferent galaxies, and she doesn't mind if the island's ghosts pay a visit. They would probably be sympathetic. Medley puts time into his own evaluation before he curls up close.

Kot wakes with the rising sun and rolls over with a groan. Then she starts thinking. Forensic investigators would no doubt have determined that there were no bodies in the charred house by now, and the cops would have discovered the little gate that she had forced open, and maybe the branches that she broke in her passage along the trail. However, she's committed no crime, and her notion of dogs tracking her was perhaps a product of panic.

Still, who will have access to the forensic reports, whether legally or not? Someone within the police systems got hold of classified information and tried to kill her once. Would they care enough to continue that effort? With few resources, this escape plan remains as good as anything else she can think of. She needs to anticipate the likely short-term challenges, and then avoid as many of them as possible. Travelling at night offers essential invisibility, in spite of its difficulties, but nothing puts a dent in her desolation.

She uses an overhanging branch to haul her aching body out of the sand hollow. So early in spring, it's likely that she and Medley will have the day to themselves in this island park, but she will still need to avoid being seen from both the water and the air.

The night mists have lingered, and branches from graceful arbutus trunks reach up like arms through a sea of vapour. She and Medley follow a perimeter trail around the island. The water reflects fragments of the pink sunrise, mixed with cobwebs of mist. Awareness spreads through Kot that she is in an earthly paradise on a warming sunny morning, and no doubt safe enough for now. Her aches are easing slightly as she walks, and she wants to also tamp her fear, get a better grip.

Back at their sleeping spot, Kot spreads out her gear to dry and lights the little stove for tea. Later on, her nap is broken by the unmistakable sound of whales breathing. A resident orca pod is feeding just fifty metres off the beach, a new baby among them. When the show ends and the whales move off to the north, Kot heats a can of soup and prepares to follow them. There is only enough fresh water for one more day of camping, and there are no streams on these small islands. She rubs numbing gel on her injured muscles, and pulls up the blanket to watch the light fade behind the hills of Vancouver Island. Medley lifts his snout to sniff the air, and they wait.

In another hour, low tide brings quiet water and the moon is high in a cold and starry sky, pulling unimaginable quantities of water back and forth across the planet, and driving billions of female reproductive cycles. Kot is reminded that her own period will start soon. She'd put those supplies on the next shopping list for Doug, but that is irrelevant and current alternatives are not appealing.

She hauls the kayak back over the exposed barnacles, her beach shoes still wet from last night. Twinkling lights have appeared across the water, and she can hear the wail of a siren. Someone else's emergency. They trace the path of the whales around D'Arcy's northern tip. Her next goal is a dim mound of unlit land well to the northeast, dark and mysterious against the dusky sky. When she is on the edge of Haro Strait and tucked safely into a sheltered notch of Sidney Island, a thick cloud blanket lumbers across the moon. The wind is picking up, and Kot tries to assess the situation. She downs another painkiller and decides to go hard in an attempt to beat the coming ugly waters. The direction of the wind is opposite the fast-rising tide: a recipe for rough water.

As visibility lessens and the wave height increases it becomes obvious that her decision could prove fatal. She shakes the stinging spray from her eyes and must rely on the compass sunk in the kayak's deck to keep any kind of bearing. This far out, she has no choice but to push on.

Behind them, city lights reflect amber against the dark billows of clouds scudding her way. She'd packed a flare within easy reach, but even if it led to a rescue, the various negative outcomes are obvious. Nevertheless, she ponders scenarios that might make it necessary to launch it.

The cold wind is pushing them from behind, and in spite of the conditions Kot knows that she's covered a lot of water in the first two hours. The waves push her bow around, and she has to correct her course with every stroke. Medley is a quaking lump, but their destination is definitely closer now.

Even above the noise of the wind, Kot hears and can begin to feel the deep vibration of a large motor, off to the right, and getting stronger. The superstructure of an immense tanker emerges from the mists to the south, outlined in lights, and headed straight at them. Kot has been trying to get beyond the shipping lane, but she must have underestimated, and her heart is racing. The giant ship is already just a few kilometers away and threatens them with instant death by collision, or a slower one, swamped by its wake. Kot estimates that she has less than ten minutes before one of those outcomes is a reality. Her paddle hits the gunnels with each frenzied stroke. When Medley stands up she screams at him, in the absences of anyone else.

She takes a terrified glance to her right. The ship's lights look different. Miraculously, it has started to turn. Under normal circumstances Kot would have known its most likely course: turning relatively sharply south to Victoria, into the Strait of Juan de Fuca and west to the open Pacific. She gasps out gratitude. But the wake will arrive in time, and she still can't take a break.

Kot's panic subsides as the squall passes, leaving her angry again and needing someone specific to blame. Utterly spent, she finally rests when the water calms. Half an hour later, they crunch onto her target beach at the south end of Elegy Island. Kot has never been so glad to step onto land in her life. Medley races above the sand to mark new territory, and Kot again conceals the kayak and pulls out food for them both. With something in her stomach, exhaustion sends her to sleep immediately. But this time, Medley continues his vigil until a cloudless dawn gilds the ocean gold.

In the morning, Kot's mouth tastes like the aftermath of fast food and too much coffee: unfair, given the bare simplicity of her recent diet. Another short walk loosens her body slightly as she considers her options. The urgent need for supplies will require interactions with other people, but she decides to settle on a plan later on, after more sleep. There are still many hours until tonight's journey.

But it isn't yet noon when Medley wakes her with his growling. Kot scrambles up to grab his collar and put a hand around his muzzle. A small Bayliner full of people is approaching the beach below her kayak. The boat is being pitched high and sideways by heavy wake, to a soundtrack of shrieks. As soon as the rollers from the first passing ferry die down, the next round arrives. However, at some point, they will probably manage to land. Kot puts Medley on his leash and rapidly collects her gear. Then the sounds begin to fade, and she sees the boat heading around the point for a more sensible landing on the sheltered beach there. That will still bring them within close proximity, but she now has a few minutes of opportunity. As soon as they round the point, she creeps down to the kayak, and quickly loads and launches. So much for sleep, and for the luxury of time to decide what to do next.

A thin layer of overcast reflects on the water like swaths of silver silk, and a soft breeze from the southwest is a welcome contrast to the night before. Soon, there are only dark shadows of scattered cumulus moving across an ocean that is now the dazzling blue of the sky above. Kot takes a big breath of relief. The advantage of daylight is obvious: she can see and assess the water, weather, and her surroundings. Now to figure out where to aim.

The further she paddles the less familiar Kot is with the landscape. She knows the names of a few of the islands: Mayne, Prevost, Pender, Atticus, Galiano, but has no idea which one is which. Beyond the forested hills to the east is the wide Strait of Georgia, and a little further north, Greater Vancouver. Trying to cross the strait would be beyond foolhardy, so despite the magnetic pull of Ben Northcott, returning to that city is probably not wise. So one of the larger islands ahead must be her next destination, one likely to have a store. However, a loss of anonymity must not be the cost of obtaining even critical drinking water.

Potential hazards will increase with each person who comes to know her face, her voice, her dog, and her mode of travel. But there is no choice. The money Kot borrowed from Anne and Gerry won't cover much. If she has to pay for shelter, it will be gone within a day. Still, it would be difficult and time-consuming to find somewhere safe enough to sleep wild and to hide a kayak on any of these more populated islands.

Maybe it is the particular arrangement of its shadowed layers of hills and dips, but some instinct leads Kot to choose a medium-sized island, roughly in the centre of the seascape around her. She stops for a minute to open a hatch and pull out a ballcap, then tuck her dirty hair under it. She pulls the brim low and digs out some sunglasses to reduce the glare and allow her to read the water better. They will also help to hide her face. She tries to cover all of Medley except his head, knowing he will keep extricating himself. A dog in a kayak is always an attention-getter, and they will soon be visible from the island. Kot gathers herself and sets her course. She will need to pull off a fake persona by the end of this day, and that still needs some work.

The remaining passage is a blessing of warmth and smooth water. Kot takes off her jacket, and gives up her futile efforts to keep the blanket on Medley. She paddles gently along the island's western shore, careful to linger for looks at sea stars and anemones on the rocks, more like a local resident enjoying a leisurely paddle than a desperate woman fleeing attempted murder. Strangely, it isn't difficult. When someone on shore calls out a greeting, Medley wiggles and whines, and Kot acts like any annoyed pet owner trying to keep the kayak level.

This island seems like a friendly place, but she definitely isn't looking for friendly.

They cross a bay with a ferry dock and a lighthouse on the far bluff, then a curved beach backed by a big block of forest that might be parkland. Another, larger beach comes next, and some distance further on is a bluff with a flag whipping merrily on a pole and meadows in the background. Kot can now see the northern tip of the island, and her muscles have almost reached their limit for the day. She is trying to decide whether to rest and then continue around to the other side of the island when a small festival of sailboat masts begins to be visible behind the next point of land. A marina. It probably won't be crowded in early April, and as long as it's open, might be as good a destination as any.

Kot summons her nerve. She now has a simple story ready. The less to remember, the less to screw up. She can embellish it as necessary, or completely abandon it if—or probably, when she flees again. What she needs now is some faith in both the future and in what her colleagues describe as her "awesome ability to wing it."

They beach on rough shingle next to the marina's dinghy dock. Medley ignores her order and leaps out to pee on a post. He's unlikely to go far, so Kot stows her paddle and gets out. She looks around as she pulls up the kayak, pretending a casual interest entirely at odds with her pounding heart. The melodies of purple martins fill the air as they circle nesting boxes installed on the docks. A pretty path lined with huge tubs of petunias leads to the white frame marina office and store. At the bottom of the path is a hand-painted sign. Kot has been looking for signs, and as usual, her angels have a sense of humour.

Gubbins Bay Marina, Atticus Island

Remember the Magic

Kot touches her forefinger to the last word, for luck, and heads up the path.

With Medley tied to a verandah post, Kot lowers her cap brim and saunters into the marina store. After the outside glare, it takes a minute to identify the forest of objects hanging from the ceiling; all sizes of hand-carved and painted signs swing in the breeze that follows her through the door. Some are worn and barely legible, others bright and new. A few stand out as whimsically romantic or artistic. Along with slogans and messages, every one of them bears the name of a boat, and the dates go back many years.

Otherwise, the place resembles a 1950s café, complete with vinyl bar stools. There are shelves of groceries, and refrigerated deli items and baked goods. The service counter supports a massive, pale green milkshake machine and an antique cash register. In the back, a modern laptop and monitor sit on an old oak desk. Display tables and racks hold nautical and nature books, charts, postcards, local information, and the obligatory offerings of hats, mugs, sweatshirts, and souvenirs. A tee-shirt on a mannequin displays the slogan: "Republic of Atticus Island."

There are only a few people inside. Two wrought-iron tables and chairs are the same pale green as the milkshake maker. One of them is occupied by a family of four, the kids sucking through straws in tall, old-fashioned glasses, their skinny legs turned sideways. It could pass as a bucolic scene from a Norman Rockwell painting, except for one angry voice and the fact that the children are clearly on the point of fleeing with their milkshakes.

Kot steps back to allow two men to exit, each giving an apologetic glance back to the pleasant-looking man behind the counter. The wide-legged source of everyone's discomfort has her hands on her hips and her temper directed at that same man. His nametag, pinned to a popsicle-lime golf shirt, states that he is both Steve Elliot and the marina manager. Steve is tall and lanky, with greying sandy hair and weather-narrowed eyes.

The woman leans closer to him, yelling. "You can't charge moorage fees when there's no Wi-Fi signal worth a shit. What kind of backwoods dump is this? We want a full refund. Do you understand?!"

Another customer approaches from the side, apparently intending an intervention, but a nearly imperceptible shake of Steve's head holds her back.

"I'm sorry you're not happy with the Wi-Fi. You're in D16, right? The Sabre Cruiser 52? I was just going to drop down for a chat, but we can certainly have it here if you prefer. We haven't received your payment for last night's moorage, and now you technically owe for tonight as well. I'd understood you were heading out yesterday."

"You'll have to take that up with my husband. As far as I'm concerned, we owe you nothing. I haven't been able to watch a movie since we've been here, and that sure wasn't clear in your advertising."

"Well… as you say, this really is a backwoods place, and nowhere do we promise good Wi-Fi. But that's why most people come to the islands, to get away from the pressures of urban life. And sadly, that also means doing without some technical conveniences."

"Huh. Where we come from, no marina worth two bits would—"

Pleasant-looking Steve raises his own voice a notch, and cuts her off.

"Maybe you missed the big sign on the main wharf asking our clients not to stream movies. It makes it impossible for our other customers to get what connection there is at the docks. You know, people who might really need it. Like, for work. Or handling a crisis back home. So, no, I'm afraid there will be no refund. I'm thinking that you need to pay me for last night and be on your way. In fact, I'll throw in today's moorage just to get you moving." He doesn't seem flustered, and more weary than irritated.

The old-fashioned word "flounced" comes to mind as the woman storms by Kot in a bright red fury, elbows flying. Her blood pressure almost leaves a vapour trail as her Nikes pound across the verandah and down the path to the docks. The only remaining customer puts his purchase on the counter and mumbles a sympathetic comment to Steve, who smiles slightly but just rings in the item and says something about the weather. Kot notices that he simultaneously keeps track of her and everything else in the place.

She turns her back and looks through the books for sale until the door swings shut and she is alone with Steve. When she turns around, his hands are resting flat on the counter and he is quietly considering her.

"Can I help you with anything?"

Kot has decided to take a direct approach. She sustains good eye contact as she walks over to the counter. *Showtime.*

"Hi. My name is Kot Malone. That's my dog outside. We arrived in a kayak that I've left on the beach."

Steve glances outside at Medley, still huddled at the full length of his leash in the wake of the angry woman, then back to Kot with a nod and a friendly smile.

"Hello, Kot. What can I do for you?"

"I'm not really sure, but I thought this might be a good place to start. You're the marina manager?"

Steve nods. "My wife and I own the place, but I make her wear the tag that says *owner.*"

Kot gives him a wan smile. "I've paddled here from Victoria over the past couple of days." She looks down. "To be honest, I'm running away from an abusive relationship." *A relationship with a bomb and whoever planted it.* And before that, with a married man, that Mich would describe as just another kind of abuser. "All that I have now is in the kayak, and it isn't much. And my dog, of course. He's a really easy little guy. He doesn't even shed."

The new babbling has a grip on her again. She wonders if Steve can also see that she's shaking. She takes a deep breath. "Anyway, I need to find some work, and somewhere to stay. Would you be able to suggest anything on the island? I have tons of experience."

That is true. And Kot knows that she would probably have handled that rude woman exactly as Steve did. Fight rudeness with grace.

Steve's expressions flow between concern and what might be disgust at her predicament. He sits down on a stool and looks out of the window, jiggling one leg. Then he gets up, closes the door, and gestures to a table as an invitation for Kot to sit. This seemingly nice man didn't actually lock the exit door, but Kot takes the chair closest to it, just in case.

He asks, "Do you know how to operate an old-fashioned cash register?"

The possible implications of the question are obvious. Some aspects of her current career have required a pleasantly neutral poker face, and Kot searches for it now.

"Many years ago, I had a grocery checkout job and had to make change. And I used to work in a bookstore, but that system used software." She looks over at the ancient machine. "If you mean this one… well, it looks like a bit of a brute, but I could probably master it after a tutorial."

Steve laughs. That is the perfect word for the machine. When he and Nora bought the marina, back in the days of their innocence, the vintage equipment included had mistakenly been part of the attraction. The cash register hasn't completely let them down, but it has always been cranky, and the need to repeatedly take apart the even more cantankerous soda machine has also wasted a lot of his time. He calls the milkshake machine "The Diva," and from here on, the cash register will be "The Brute."

"Okay, good. Yes, I really need some help here until my wife gets back from an emergency family trip. We don't know yet when that will be. Her mom's in hospital in Saskatoon. Broken hip."

"Oh, I'm sorry to hear that." Although Kot isn't sorry to hear about the wife. She needs money and refuge, but not with strings attached.

"Yeah. Thanks. There's just too much other work. Besides the dock maintenance and the customer demands down there, there always seems to be a toilet plugged or a broken laundromat machine, or some damned thing. And at this time of year, frankly, I could just cut grass twenty-four seven. If I also have to man this place, things seriously start to fall apart."

Steve looks away, toward the docks. He knows he should be more cautious, and hasn't missed the fact that Kot is trembling. Addiction?

"To be honest, I'm so tired that the lovely lady who just left almost got to me. I had to cling to an image of her being the one to finally go through the punky board near the bottom of the ramp. But besides my temper, we're losing goodwill when people find the store locked. Not to mention losing income."

Steve has surprised himself with so much speech, and also by his own frankness, but the person sitting opposite him seems to inspire it. She is well spoken, old enough to have the experience she claims, and has expressed a willingness to work. Even if there is more to her story, it would have taken a lot of guts to do what she says she has. It's small wonder that she's shaking a bit, maybe from simple hunger and exhaustion. Nora would describe Kot as "fundamentally refined," but right now she looks like she did the rough trip that she says she did. Did she sleep outside in the cold, alone?

Steve's protective instincts are overriding the practical cautions that he imagines Nora might have put forward. Besides, he was the one to install that sign at the bottom of the path, and he still tries to live by its message.

"You'd need to learn quite a bit really fast. Nora got everything well organized into binders last summer for a high school kid we hired, so that should help." Steve's pretty sure that Kot couldn't possibly turn out worse than that kid had, but he needs to be blunt and honest with her. Better to not hire her than to lose her—or have to fire her—a day or two in.

"Besides moorage rates and the marina policies, people ask us for a lot of random information about destinations, weather forecasts… you name it, really. And you can't fake it. Better to say you don't know, than to be held responsible for someone taking a stupid risk out there. So obviously, the faster you can get up to speed, the better. And there's also some basics like keeping this place clean and tidy and sweeping the verandah and stuff. Plus reminding people to pick up after their dogs if you see them abandon a poop. Nothing can piss people off like stepping in a ripe pile of dog shit, especially if they end up getting some of it onto their boat. Oh, and while I think of it, a lot of people want to know what 'Gubbins' means, but just say that you've never thought about it or something."

Kot looks at him quizzically. "Okay, sure. But confidentially, what *does* it mean?"

"Mess. Disorder. That kind of thing. Not exactly ideal for a marina bay, right?"

Kot laughs. "Not great, no." She tries to hide her desperation and sound confident. "I'm not worried about the steep learning curve, Steve. I'm also pretty good with people, and multitasking isn't a problem."

Steve takes a big breath and blows out his cheeks with a smile. "Okay, let's give it a try. I'll give you some training first thing tomorrow. I might need your help outside sometimes, too. Nora always gets stuck doing a real mixture of stuff. But then, I guess we both do. Anyway, like I said, it's very short term, but it might let you see how you like Atticus and maybe look for other work. There's not much profit in this biz at this time of year, and I can only offer you a dollar over minimum. We'll figure out the hours, and probably play it by ear."

The pay is a pittance, considering her usual six-figure salary, but Kot knows a big, fat gift horse when she meets one. She nods slowly, pretending to think it over. Then she stands and holds out her hand.

"Thanks, Steve. I'm grateful." Finding a camp ground will be next on her agenda.

They shake, and Steve seems to be on the edge of saying something more. Kot waits, not sure that she wants to hear it.

"Our house is next door here, but see the cabins on the other side of the lawn, near the picnic gazebo? We rent them out. But the closest one isn't booked for a while yet, and you could use it if you want. Maybe just a week at a time, 'til Nora's back. There's a woodstove and about half a cord stacked outside. I'll get you some clean bedding and towels if you don't mind airing the place out and setting yourself up. You'll have to keep your dog there while you're working." Steve looks out at Medley. "Seems like he's been well behaved outside here, too. But anyway, let's see how it goes. He just can't be noisy or bother folks. Okay?"

When she has stored her kayak and settled into the cabin, Kot returns to the store to spend some of Gerry and Anne's money on a few staples and to borrow a book about the area. When the people on the docks are busy with their happy hour and dinner, she takes Medley for an exploratory stroll of the grounds, then locks the cabin door and draws the curtains, leaving not the slightest crack of an opening. She sleeps until four, the universal hour to wake and worry.

Before the store opens the next day Steve teaches Kot the basics, and she handles several customers and moorage slip bookings on the phone under his supervision. Later in the morning, Steve leaves her to it, not even trying to hide his relief.

In quiet times during her first days of work, Kot immerses herself in marine geography and learning more about BC's coastal facilities. Steve is available on the radio if there is something she can't handle, but so far, so good. Even the Brute and the Diva seem to be in a good mood, and so far, only one customer has made a serious effort to dig into Kot's history and what brought her to Atticus.

A woman named Aurora, who apparently lived "down the road in a rotting trailer with a great view," seemed to assume it was her right to have the details. During Aurora's third visit for chips, chocolate, and cigarettes, Kot had exhausted every evasion tactic in her repertoire. Just as Steve came in, Aurora's triumphant voice rang out: "Of course! You're in the Witness Protection Program! That's why you're so secretive!" Then she leaned close to Kot to confide, "Don't worry, I won't tell a soul." After a glance at Kot's face, Steve cut in with a joke, and Kot managed to join in with a weak smile before slipping outside, leaving Steve to ring in the purchases. She hid in a washroom stall until she could calm herself.

She knows that Steve must also be curious, but is too kind to pry. He asks no questions and his vibe is consistently calm, courteous, and tired. He opens the store, discusses the weather, and then disappears to work elsewhere on the grounds, returning to give Kot a lunch break. She finishes her workdays in time to take Medley and his chucker ball down an old logging trail behind the marina while the daylight lasts. It all feels surreal.

On the third evening, Kot sits on the cabin's little deck with the VHF radio by her side. The few boats booked in have already docked, and she can't see any more coming into Gubbins Bay. Steve has headed out in his truck to visit friends. Since she was taken to the safe house, Kot has badly missed her smartphone and other devices, and can no longer resist the temptation to use the marina laptop. She lets herself into the darkened store through the rear door. When she types into the browser: "house explosion, Saanich, BC, 2017," several media stories pop up. Kot scans the top three, checking for any contradictions between them, then deletes the search topic in the computer's history and hurries back to her cabin under little brown bats scooping mosquitos in the dusk.

The news stories all quoted police reports that the demolished house had an absentee owner, was unoccupied at the time of the explosion, and that a faulty heating system was the cause. It, the outbuildings, and all contents were apparently burned to the ground, and nothing could be salvaged by the time that firetrucks arrived. After the initial reports, the story appears to have died the death of yesterday's news.

Back in her cabin, Kot goes through the motions of a normal evening, but her mind is racing around, everywhere but there.

The days go by, each very similar to the one before. Kot's injuries heal, and for the first time in her life, her birthday passes unacknowledged. She has only left the marina for two nervous trips to a store on Nora's bicycle. More hair dye will soon be needed, but for now, she has the essentials—except for the one thing she needs most: some answers to the crazy-making questions, to stop her mind running on its loop of unknowns. At night, Medley scrunches the lightweight bedside rug into some personally ideal configuration of humps, and seems to have no trouble staying asleep. For sleep-deprived Kot, it's not so simple. She is slowly mastering the illusion that she is in her childhood single bed. She closes her eyes and tries to focus on the soporific sounds of nature, and the softly clanking rigging.

A vintage alarm clock by the bed jumps around self-importantly to shrilly announce the start of each day. The songbirds are going strong by 6 a.m., interrupted now and then by the uniquely squeaky croak of Herman, the marina's resident bachelor heron. Something must have damaged his vocal apparatus. Now and then, the drone of a boat motor fades away from the marina, and Medley's snores do a close imitation. It certainly isn't quiet, but Kot finds this new routine increasingly comforting.

When she gets up on the eighth morning at the marina, her soreness is almost gone. The defined tasks of each workday help, but loneliness and fear lurk beneath her skin like a disease.

~ ELEVEN ~

Vancouver

The cheap window frames of RCMP Inspector Annette Solinski's office are no match for the city's endless drizzle. She imagines mould spores penetrating her skin, her organs fermenting. But it's better than turning around to face the inbox on her monitor and the piles of paper on the desk. She scratches her head. She'd meant to wash her grey-streaked hair this morning, but as usual, the texts just kept on coming.

Four stories down, the traffic oozes in spurts, like lava. Pink-tinged clouds scatter prettily around the mountain peaks across Burrard Inlet. Solinski feels scattered, too, but never prettily. Too little sleep, crap food and coffee on the fly, and endemic stress take care of that. The bulge around her middle is relatively new, and she's feeling old.

Still, the imminent arrival of Sergeant Wade Dance could possibly lift her spirits mightily. If his report meets her hopes, it would also lead to an overdue boost in team morale. That matters to Solinski, not to mention her own pleasure in being the one to carry the good cheer upstairs to Superintendent Batra.

After over one hundred billion dollars of illegal drug trafficking last year alone, media headlines are screaming alarm. Death statistics from fentanyl overdoses were bad enough before producers decided to increase their profits by mixing carfentanil with the fentanyl, heroin, cocaine, meth, or whatever, thereby committing anonymous homicide on an unprecedented scale. After all, it takes only a tiny amount of carfentanil to tranquillize an elephant, so they didn't need to add much. Domestic supply activities are growing, but the majority of the deadly shipments still come from China and Mexico. Victims represent all ages, social strata, and nooks of the province, dying in suburban homes, cars, high rise condos, flop houses, palatial hotel rooms, at teen parties, under trees, on farms, or in the street. The citizenry are appropriately scared, and demanding more effective police measures.

Previously, Hells Angels and other gang members were openly hired to operate within all three Vancouver dockyards and in the private trucking companies that service them. A series of newspaper articles on the subject finally resulted in new police leadership, and a period of better dock hiring practices. Still junior in the ranks, Solinski remembers actually feeling hopeful back then. Then came 9/11, and the sudden re-deployment of police personnel from drug and smuggling enforcement to terrorism units. Almost overnight, the international gangs regained the upper hand, and now have members working within the shipping companies themselves. Sixteen years after the newspaper exposé, the ongoing carnage is much worse. It's the same situation in the ports of Prince Rupert, Montreal, and Halifax. Just one of Canada's dirty little secrets.

Meanwhile, too much competition for government funding means a stunning shortage of resources. As soon as Solinski's squad or their partners on both sides of the border successfully infiltrate one cell, three others are born, while the undercover man or woman who achieved the infiltration must be taken out of circulation, sometimes forever. Assuming, of course, that he or she has survived the experience.

Dance blows through the door late, with the excuse of wanting to finish a report for her. Solinski catches a micro-expression of a smile. He settles into the little armchair and tries to fit his long legs between it and the desk. Solinski feels a familiar flash of affection for her colleague. At least it makes a change from the other flashes. Black and gay, Dance has doggedly clawed his way up through the mire of prejudices still subverting the force's self-conscious attempts at political correctness. She hopes he makes it to the top. Her games-free relationship with Wade Dance is unique to her, as is his rare combination of intelligence, courage, and common sense—a most uncommon thing, these days.

Unlike the chronic wreckage of Solinski's own personal life, Dance and his husband are in what he calls "a forever kind of love." That doesn't stop him from being regularly hit on by one and all, simply because he is so goddamn cute.

Dance's caffeine consumption is the stuff of legend, and it's showing. Solinski raises her eyebrows at him. "Extra wired this morning, sunshine? What's up?"

"Well, I'm not sure if you know about our new guy on the docks…?"

Solinski shakes her head firmly. She likes to hear the full story, front to back. She also makes a point of never learning the real names of undercover personnel.

Dance taps both feet while he speaks, and the dimple in his right cheek makes an appearance. "He's an Ottawa output, circa 2001. We call him Bogart. Nice, solid background, and for the past three years, he's operated one of those enormous cranes that lifts the containers off the freighters. He's apparently kept his head down, so to speak, and his eyes open. He's made lots of friends, and by now, no one pays much attention to him. Single. Official home address is a condo in Ladner."

Solinski is doodling already. Delivering a report to her is always a lose-lose exercise. If he skips the details, she demands them. When he includes them, she looks bored or gets testy. It's also impossible to anticipate what she already knows. The only option is to keep going.

"So, he got debriefed last night. One of the Northcott freighters is called the *Novicta.* It's unloading containers in Port Vancouver right now for two or three days, and the long and short of it is that Bogart's noticed a pattern in the way certain containers from that ship and another one are handled. It's nothing obvious, unless you were looking for it, but he's now convinced that we should be ready to check the Novicta out the next time it's in port."

"Okay, when's that?"

"It's booked in again at the Centerm Terminal fairly soon, on April 20, but given the backlog and wait times, it could be anytime from then into early May. Bogart will be on a mid-ship crane, and he'll try to record anything he can. But he'll obviously have to carry on with his own work, so he thinks we should have a hidden surveillance camera installed with a good view of the stern crane. He thinks that regular operator is a key piece of the action.

He also suspects that someone senior in the container-processing Terminal is bent. It's all in that report I just emailed you. It's probably already getting buried in your inbox."

Solinski checks that it's arrived, and they start to work on a plan. She knows that she can count on her second-in-command to play devil's advocate all the way, and that the results will be better for it by the time she seeks tentative approval from upstairs.

After an hour, Dance gets up to leave. "Looks like we might have momentum at last, boss. Fingers crossed, anyway." It always amuses him to show her all of his crossed fingers.

"We'll see. It's sure overdue. You've stopped vibrating. Better go get yourself a refill."

When Dance is gone, Solinski returns to the window. The sun is coming out.

~ TWELVE ~

After her emotional dam had collapsed, a few nights ago, Camas sobbed for hours and then she slept and woke up hungrier than ever. The concussion is a little better, but still limits her stamina and she needs frequent naps. Making sure that no one sees her has become second nature.

The habits of the park's animals and visiting humans are becoming familiar. Her stolen food is kept in a stolen bin, her foraged plants are wrapped in damp, stolen paper towel on the cold cement floor of her room, and she collects water in a stolen camping jug. As the weather warms, the lighthouse is becoming less clammy.

Dusk and dawn remain the safest times to visit the waterfall and fill up her jug. Camas has only bathed in the pool below it once, too scared by being so exposed to do it again. At least she doesn't notice her own smell much anymore. The waterfall will probably dry up in a matter of weeks, and the pond will become stagnant. Then drinking water will be more of a challenge, and more stealing may be required. She can't risk a fire or cooking smells, so steals only raw or ready-to-eat food. She craves the comfort of a cooked meal, and to be warmed to the core in hot water.

Last night, Camas crept along the road in the opposite direction to the park to explore what was nearby. A café looked promising, but she had to be very careful and both doors were locked, with lights on upstairs and a truck parked out back. She hopes to develop enough courage soon to investigate the rear doors of neighbouring houses, past the ferry terminal.

She is resting in her lookout now, trying to prolong the pleasure of what she is eating. A few minutes ago, she'd watched the latest illegal campers take off in a double kayak, and she soon found something wonderful among their belongings. They couldn't seem to keep their hands off each other when they returned, and tumbled into their tent, laughing. Camas figures they won't immediately miss their package of butter tarts. She reluctantly closes the plastic container to save the last two, but suddenly freezes and then scoots her bum back under the rock outcropping.

Coming around the point is a boat exactly like Brett's. Other boats have made her stomach flip, but this one looks identical. As it passes, she squints at its stern. She can't make out the name, but there are more words with bigger lettering than on Brett's boat. Another false alarm, but her brain starts rocketing with memories.

Camas was four when her father died, shockingly quickly, from some galloping illness with a complicated name. Mama had told her that they both had no siblings, and that all of her grandparents passed away before she was born. And there was never any evidence to the contrary. Her mother often told her that they only needed each other.

Her father's life insurance money had provided the trust fund for Camas. Mama also got grants for her research work, and Camas remembers life slowly becoming happier again. Even when Mama started seeing Brett, things were okay for a time. He made Mama laugh, but even back then, Camas had the feeling that Brett was just pretending to be nice. Still, Mama appreciated not having to do all the work, and even Camas liked Brett's Sunday pancakes with syrup and sausages. And she was excited to wear a pretty dress and be Mama's only attendant at their courthouse wedding.

Her mother found a bigger rental house for the three of them in the mill town south of Nanaimo where Brett worked. Instead of putting Camas into a new school, Mama started homeschooling her, and for a short time all was well. Then Brett was fired, and Mama had to take an evening job at the White Spot. Brett began to drink more, just before he started to drink way too much. No one laughed much anymore, and a curtain of misery descended that not even Mama seemed to know how to lift. One day, Camas saw her mother find her wallet on the kitchen counter, emptied of cash. After that, Mama began to secretly slip her tips inside the hidden zipper of Grizz, the bear on Camas's bed, whispering, "Just for you and me, okay?"

The first big fight woke up Camas. Brett was drunk and pissed off about something, and they were both yelling. Camas peeked through the hinges of her bedroom door and gasped to see Mama backed against the wall, Brett leaning over her with a raised fist. The animal growl of his voice and Mama's whimpering were scarier than the shouting.

The next fight, he started hurting Mama. Each time, Camas would stay in her room with her fingers plugging her ears and praying that Brett would just move out and let them be happy again. Instead, Mama got tired and depressed. When her bruises were obvious, she didn't go to work at the White Spot. Camas heard her tell Brett that unless he could control himself, she would lose her job. Still, her mother was there to look after her, and to stroke her hair until she slept.

Mama was driving home from a late shift on a crystal January night when black ice on the highway sent a spinning semi into her little sedan, and Camas's world ended.

She heard the cop at the door tell Brett that Mama probably died instantly. He wasn't there, so how would he know? Brett didn't let him in. He closed the door, and when he saw the shock on her face, his pale eyes were empty.

"Your mom is dead." Then he went into the kitchen and started throwing Mama's best dishes at the wall, screaming obscenities.

Brett immediately dropped all pretense of caring about Camas. He knew she could hear him tell someone on the phone: "The last thing I need is her bitch of a kid in tow."

He told Camas that he'd tried and failed to find any relatives on either side, and she believed that he had. That was what Mama had said too. So maybe they really were all dead. Or anyway, not looking to take on an orphan.

Brett acted like Camas might disappear if he continued to ignore her. He was home very little and was usually drunk when he was. Camas had never had to look after herself, but soon started using her mother's secret stash of tips inside Grizz to buy food. Brett ate out, and it didn't seem to occur to him that a child needed to be fed. Maybe he was just waiting for her to starve to death.

She hadn't made any friends since they'd moved to the new area, and there were no close neighbours. There had been no obituary for Mama, and everyone was a stranger, preoccupied with their own lives. Apart from fielding concern from one of the cashiers at the grocery store, Camas spent each day alone. She liked to ride her bike to hang out at the beach, even if it was a steep pedal back up. If she saw Brett's truck in the driveway when she got home, she would keep riding. But that wasn't usually a problem. When Brett almost stopped coming home at all, Camas would lock the doors and lose herself in books, TV, and silent games on the old laptop in Mama's office. She didn't wear ear phones because she depended on hearing Brett's noisy truck so she could get to her room before he came inside.

But then the Internet was cut off. Camas was scared that the electricity might be next. Mama would have figured everything out, but Camas had no idea what to do. She became obsessed with the idea of going back in time and finding a way to die in the car with Mama.

Then things changed again. Wherever Brett had been sleeping, he stopped going there, and now spent his days on the couch, drinking, sleeping, and monopolizing the TV. He must have found figured out how to pay the cable bill. Once, Camas left her room for the bathroom, and caught him watching her with a creepy, considering look.

On the first warm day in March, she decided to run away. Then she heard Mama's voice in her head: *Wait my, darling. Not yet.* Camas cried with frustration and anger with her mother for dying, but gradually realized that she still needed to work out a few things. She bought some packaged snacks and put them into her small daypack with a bottle of water, then zipped the remainder of Mama's money into the inside pouch. When Brett went out later, she found the wedding ring that her father had given Mama, a gold raven's head carved into silver. Brett had no interest in the plastic bag from the morgue when he discovered that there was nothing of much value inside. Camas tucked the ring into a pocket, and also found the photo of herself as a toddler with her parents in her mother's chest of drawers, and Mama's favourite scarf. Back in her room, she stowed these things safely into her pack as well. She would add Grizz at the last minute. Now, she was ready to go when the right time came.

But no matter how hard Camas tried, she couldn't figure out where to go, and the late winter rains were long and heavy.

One night, Camas woke to find Brett lying beside her, obviously drunk, and starting to grope at her in his sleep. She fled to the garden shed with the couch blanket. He locked the door when he left the next morning, but she climbed through her bedroom window.

As the wet days passed, she began to wonder if she'd dreamed that episode. And then one evening Brett stumbled through the door without any truck noise first, and grabbed her, unzipping his pants. Camas drifted to the ceiling and tried to die.

After that, she spent her days in the library, or endlessly walking the aisles of stores; anywhere dry and warm, anywhere Brett definitely would not be. The nice grocery cashier told the other staff to let her be, and sometimes she bought the girl a hot chocolate from a machine with her own money. Camas would never know that the kind woman also called Social Services to report the odd child who said her name was Raven, and who always seemed to be alone. Or that there was no known result.

Brett had lost his driver's licence, so Camas had no more warnings of his arrival. She was too ashamed to tell anyone about what Brett was doing, and anyway, who was there to tell?

It was the end of March before the wet weather ended and sunshine reached inside the house. At the same time, it seemed that Brett was drinking less, and had again forgotten that Camas existed. He started driving again, and would come back late or not at all. At first Camas hoped that the police would catch him, before she realized that would mean that he'd be staying home more again.

A year ago, Mama had just married Brett when the three of them went on his spring crabbing trip. Camas enjoyed having her own tiny cabin and the novelty of life out on the water, and her mother seemed proud of how quickly Camas learned how to help. But this year it took the smell of diesel fuel from Brett's clothes before she remembered his crab boat. She was desperate for him to head out this year, but on his own. She started to think about how to get far away before he returned.

He hadn't spoken to her for a long time, so her heart sank when Brett curtly announced that she would not only be going with him the next day, but she would be working hard. Then he made sure she stayed in sight. He packed a lot of alcohol onboard, but Camas saw no food, so took some things from the stores under her bed. Mama's tip money was mostly gone after her last trip to the store.

They left the wharf in Cowichan Bay in early April, and in no time Brett was cursing the owners of crab traps that had been set in what he considered his territory. He yelled orders at Camas, and after she'd followed them, she would slip away and don an imaginary invisibility cloak until he yelled at her again. After Brett dropped a load of traps on the edge of Georgia Strait, he returned to a sheltered bay on the west side of Atticus Island. The ripples of the calm ocean reflected the colours of the sunset.

Camas recognized the nearby beach. It was where she and Mama had spent time last year. Mama was peaceful and happy during those hours on their own, laughing as she overturned endless rocks and they scrambled to collect the little crabs beneath into a pail. After a ceremony to set the crabs free, they leaned back against a warm log and ate their picnic. Camas remembers saying to Mama that she wished that they could make a shelter and live there together. Mama had just nodded and smiled sadly. Later, Camas fell asleep with her head in her mother's lap. That was as close to Heaven as she can now remember.

This year, Brett abandoned his usual after-anchoring routine of tidying the boat, in favour of cracking beers. He eventually heated some baked beans that he'd stowed somewhere, silently dumped a small amount onto a piece of white bread and pushed the plate at Camas. She'd eaten nothing since her bowl of breakfast cereal and the beans tasted good. It wasn't nearly enough, but she couldn't ask for more. Brett polished off the rest and told Camas to clean up. As she did the dishes, she heard him opening cupboards behind her back and then close the cabin door behind him.

Camas watched him hunch over to light a cigarette at the stern. The sky behind him was splashed with stars. She planned to use the head and then go straight to her bunk, securing the sturdy hook on the door. But she was still too hungry to sleep, and remembered the bag of cookies that she'd hidden at the back of a cupboard. They were gone. She looked outside again. Brett was now perched on a stanchion under a lantern in the stern. He held a beer can and a girly mag, and Camas saw a familiar-looking package on his lap.

The weeks of neglect and abuse were overcome by the rage of a child, and Camas was across the deck before Brett saw her coming. She grabbed at the bag.

"Give me those, you asshole! I bought them!"

Brett's foot sent Camas flying sideways across the deck. He bent over her, looking like a demented pirate with the cookie bag between his teeth. The air reeked of hatred. Camas suddenly knew that there were a number of ways that Brett could get rid of her out there. She kept quiet as he dragged her into the cabin. When it was over, she limped outside and heaved undigested beans over the railing.

The other boats anchored in the bay were dark, the crews already in bed for an early start. Ferry wake rolled the boat, and the cabin door slammed shut. Camas huddled under a smelly tarp in a corner of the deck, but Brett didn't emerge again. Sleep came in short, shivering stretches until she woke with a jolt. The moon was setting and she was choking on sobs that must have started in her sleep.

When the warmth arrived, it was a surprise, and immediately flooded every cell of her body. *Go now. I will be with you.* It was time. Any other life, or none at all, would be better than one more hour in this one. An escape plan took shape, bringing with it a glimmering of unfamiliar hope. Camas crept back to peer through a corner of the window. Several empty beer cans were on the table and two more on the floor. The battery lamp above the sink was still on, but no light escaped the closed doors of the head or Brett's cabin. It was quiet. She crept silently to her bunk.

Camas is a good swimmer, and was prepared to brave the freezing water long enough to reach land. She thought Mama wanted her to head for the nearest beach, where they'd been so happy. She put Grizz into her daypack at last, and slung it over her shoulder. As she headed outside, she grabbed the half-empty cookie bag from the floor and stuffed it on top of Grizz. The cookies would get wet, but… *Fuck you, Brett.*

She buckled her life vest as she headed for the rear of the boat. The breeze had stilled, but the tide or currents had the boat straining at its anchor line, and the rigging was noisy. A year ago, Brett would never have been too drunk or careless to leave it unsecured.

Camas started to back down the ladder fixed to the stern, then realized that she hadn't removed her sneakers, and that the pack was still just slung over her shoulder. She decided to leave her shoes on. They weren't heavy, but she needed to get the pack onto her back so that her arms were free to swim. Camas leaned forward against the ladder, loosened the pack's straps and buckled it over her lifejacket. Before she could continue down the ladder, enormous swells hit the hull. The boat's untethered tackle began to swing heavily against her and away again. Camas hung on as long as she could, but at the peak of the fifth wave she was hurled sideways.

She doesn't remember her head striking the corner of the boat as she fell, or the small splash as she hit the water, like a slap from the tail of a baby seal.

The swinging boat stern pushed her away, and the life vest supported her lolling head. The current carried her out past the sleeping boats, around the forested point, and into the next bay. Just as the sky began to lighten, the fast-flooding tide took over and swept floating logs, a pop can, and Camas to shore.

~ THIRTEEN ~

Tessa pulls her truck into the Gubbins Bay Marina parking lot and begins unloading bags of soil and fertilizer into her wheelbarrow. Her gloomy mood is a reflection of having finally faced reality. Saying yes to Hunter Nott will require her to seriously let down a number of loyal clients, many of them friends who not only pay her well but, in some cases, even helped to hold her together after James died. That is not an option. She is also far from confident that her landscape design skills are sufficient for the scope of the Glenhurst work. That doesn't stop her from feeling crummy about losing the opportunity. Also, there is also no one else on Atticus with the necessary qualifications, so Hunter will need to import someone. He won't be happy.

But the decision is made. She needs to call him as soon as possible, apologize for the delay, and break the bad news.

Steve and Nora were her very first customers when she started her business, and last year, Gubbins Bay Marina was awarded the title of "Prettiest Marina in North America" by a top yachting magazine. When interviewed, Steve and Nora still give Tessa much of the credit. In the summer boating season, voluptuous planters edge the marina's main pathway, and baskets heavy with blooms hang from white lamp standards and at the corners of the store's porch. Combined with the marina's location at the pastoral end of a warm bay, the contest judges described the place as "Over and above. And completely, uniquely, irresistible." In no time, Tessa had to start turning away new business.

Steve is swinging a hammer down at the docks. He tucks it into his tool belt and waves when he sees Tessa. She leaves the wagons and heads down to him.

"Hi! I finally made it! I've ordered your plants, so today's a prep day. What do you think about pink, purple, and blue petunias this year? You replacing the railings?"

Steve's eyes veer wildly sideways at the list of colours, but he lets Tessa give him a quick hug, one of very few people allowed that liberty, and dodges the petunia question.

"Yeah, I sometimes think the otters take a crow bar to them at night. But more likely it's just the weight of our customer base leaning on them."

"I was sorry to hear about Nora's mom. Is she getting better?"

"Yeah, Nora's trying to sort out some home care, then she'll probably stay with her until there's a routine in place before she comes home."

"Aw. She'll be pretty tired when she gets back. How on earth have you been managing without her? Have you closed the store?"

"It's been too much for an old fart like me, for sure. With the rains we got last fall, a lot of basic stuff didn't get done—so yeah, I did have to keep the store closed too much during the first week after Nora left." He nods up the slope at it. "I can't monitor it from down here."

Steve looks away and scratches his chin. He seems unaccountably embarrassed.

"But then the weirdest thing happened. This woman appeared out of the blue. Literally. In a kayak, with her dog. She asked me if I knew somewhere she could look for work. We chatted, and well, she just seemed to fit the bill for the short term here. Kind of like a gift from the sea, you know? And so far, it's working out. Says her name is Kot Malone. Her and the dog are staying in the top cottage 'til Nora's back. I take care of the washrooms and there's not much ice cream scooping yet. Kot's picked things up real fast, and the little guy's quiet. We can't really afford to pay her, but at the same time, we can't afford not to. Folks get out of the habit of coming here real fast if the store's closed."

He winks at Tessa. “But just between us, soon’s I hear when Nora’s flying home, I’m going to have to let Kot go the day before. No need to trigger Nora’s pesky questions about how such a good-lookin’ lady washed up here when she happened to be gone. I can’t account for it myself.”

Tessa laughs. Nora can be possessive of her lanky man, for sure, although she doubts that Steve has given Nora much cause to worry.

“Wow, funny how things work out, hey? It does sound kind of strange, but I’m glad it’s taken the pressure off. Where did this Kot come from? Any chance she’s on the lam?”

“Oh, for sure. But from a man, she says. I googled her, of course, but nothing came up. So I’m thinking either that’s not her real name, or maybe she’s the only one left besides me who isn’t on social media. Whatever—so far, it’s working out. And I can’t help how she looks, can I? After work, she just walks the dog and hides out in the cabin, so there’s not much disruption for me.”

“Well, if Nora hears about her fill-in, I imagine it’ll be even more incentive for her to get home soon. What a gossip soup this rock is. Anyway, I’ll do all the prep work for planting today, and when I’m really filthy and smelly, I’ll go up there and introduce myself.”

Steve chuckles. “I’d be interested in your take. I’ll probably make it up there in a couple more hours, too.”

Tessa yanks her work gloves on again. “Nice day, huh?”

“Yup—we have a stretch of good weather coming up. I can feel another crazy season on its way, but my banker would say that’s a good thing. See you in a bit.”

Kot has been watching them from the store window. She likes the look of the woman with Steve, her purposeful stride and authentic smile that takes over her entire face. She must be the gardener. She is older than Kot, but from a distance, she seems youthful. It’s clear that Steve is comfortable with her, and Kot already trusts his judgement. She can’t make out the conversation, but his gravelly laugh drifts through the open window. It always sounds like Steve’s vocal cords are made out of fine sandpaper.

Kot would normally be involved with her own garden by this time of year, enjoying the healthy creativity. Over time, a person might make a life here, but that won’t be happening for her—not while things with Ben still feel unresolved and the security of her real work and old friends await—not to mention that garden. She simply accepts and is grateful for the opportunity to carve out a temporary role in this world apart, pretending to others that it might be permanent.

Later, she hears Steve and the gardener meet out on the verandah. The woman's voice sounds gentle as the door opens. Her light brown hair has faded mauve highlights and she approaches Kot directly, holding out a grubby hand.

"Hi, you must be Kot. I'm Tessa Colgan. I do the gardening, and I hear you're Steve's new hero."

Kot laughs. "In that case, he must have a pretty low bar."

"That's not what I hear. And FYI, Steve and Nora are Atticus treasures. So how are you finding our quirky island? Have you had a chance to explore much yet?"

After a week here, Kot has become adept at dealing with questions. "Not much yet. Just some walks around here with my dog." She is trying to avoid using his name when people are around. "But we haven't been here long, and I'm still boning up on all this." She waves her hand around the store.

Kot senses that Tessa might try to push social opportunities on her, and changes the subject. "I've looked at the marina's website and online photos, and it sure looks stunning here in the summer. I used to work in the gardening world, and it's definitely hard labour. Especially in the fall. Planting and making things pretty in the spring feels creative, and even weeding can be meditative. But cleaning up dead stuff in a cold autumn rain—not so much."

"No kidding. And thanks for the compliments. Did you take any courses?"

"Yes, I was pretty serious about it, and I also studied landscape design. I was super privileged to be offered an apprenticeship with Mason Eppsley, and that was fantastic. I learned so much from him, until life got in the way and I had to pivot. But I'm grateful for that experience."

In fact, Kot had quit after almost dying from an ectopic pregnancy, but her stomach drops at the knowledge that she has just made her first serious mistake. Because she'd taken a liking to this friendly woman, she'd let down her guard and blurted out Mason's name, probably just to impress. Tessa might even know him, or others that do.

The phone is ringing, but Steve hesitates before going to the office to answer it. Tessa has just pulled more information from Kot in twenty seconds than he has in the past week.

Tessa exclaims, "You worked with Mason Eppsley?! He's like a *rock* star to me. I'm jealous." She shakes her head. "He wouldn't have worked with you unless you were top notch."

Kot shrugs, determined to avoid further blunders. "It was quite a few years ago, but I still love gardening."

Tessa glances at Steve on the phone in the office, then seems to make up her mind about something. "Hey, I know you're working here until Nora gets back, but would you be interested in giving me some help after that? Or maybe you plan to keep on moving? It's just that I'm at a point when I really need experienced help—earlier than I'd imagined—and I don't know of anyone with your level of knowledge on Atticus. Besides the heavy spring work, I'm also opening the island's first garden centre. Or at least that's the plan, if I manage to live that long."

She looks away, tactfully giving Kot a break from scrutiny.

"Whoa, that's a huge amount for one person to handle, for sure. Um… I haven't really thought ahead too much."

Although the words flow out, the truth is that Kot thinks of little else. One step at a time, though—and she will certainly need money, no matter what the future holds. It strikes her that perhaps she should question getting back-to-back job offers within a couple of weeks, but a number of customers have commented on the severe lack of reliable labour here and on Steve's luck in finding her. She really doesn't want to have to advertise for her next job. And there's that gift horse thing again. And her angels. And that sign about magic.

"It would be nice to stay on Atticus for a while, and I'd love to do garden work again. If you're serious, sure, we could talk about me helping you when I'm not needed here anymore."

Tessa's smile lights the room. She has avoided hiring anyone, not wanting the hassles of supervision and payroll. However, just as Steve said, there is something about this woman that inspires confidence. Kot also seems to have proved herself on several levels at the marina, at least in the short term. She's curious about Kot's backstory, but as her father used to say, "When you come to a fork in the road, take it." Or maybe that was Yogi Berra.

Steve joins them, also looking pleased. "That was Nora. She's planning to get home Sunday night." He fiddles with the nozzle of the Diva. There is nothing wrong with it, and Kot knows that the poor guy is working up to say the obvious.

"So Kot, I'm sorry, but that means we won't be able to keep you on here past this weekend." The bad news delivered, he faces her. "But you're welcome to use the cabin 'til Sunday morning. And I'd be happy to make a couple of calls or give you a recommendation for another job. The grocery store is always looking for part-time help."

Perhaps naively, Kot hadn't expected to lose the safe anonymity of the marina cabin so soon, and she feels a little sick. Things are certainly changing fast.

Then Tessa jumps in. "No worries. Kot's just agreed to help me out when she's finished here. At this point, I don't know how else I'm going to get the garden centre open." She isn't comfortable talking about the Glenhurst stuff with either of them yet, and leaves it at that.

When Steve looks startled, Tessa adds, "Don't worry, my friend. I had no intention of stealing Kot before Nora gets back, and Kot was clear with me that she wouldn't leave here before then either." She checks the time. "Okay, I have to get to another job. I'll be back here with a truckload of plants, probably in a week or so. It'll be looking gorgeous soon."

Tessa pulls a card from her jacket pocket and hands it to Kot. "Could you give me a call this evening to talk about the details? I hope to be home by seven."

Tessa plans to mull over the new idea she's just had while she's driving.

After Medley's evening walk, Kot lets herself back into the store to use the phone. The conversation doesn't begin well when Tessa suggests an hourly wage that is well below what Kot will need to pay for a place to stay. Maybe she should again consider camping, or find a basement room where a dog is allowed. Anyway, what real choice does she have, besides hitchhiking to the shopping area to look for a higher-exposure job, or paddling onwards to even more uncertainty? Still, she can't prevent the flatness in her voice as she agrees to Tessa's offer.

Almost shyly, Tessa says, "You know, after we talked earlier, your arrangement with Steve got me thinking. I might also have a place for you to live. My husband and I bought the land across the road from our place some years ago. It has commercial zoning, although to be honest we just wanted to protect our own privacy. The building used to be the old general store and after the owners left the place got run down, so we got a bargain. An engineer said it's basically sound, so I've had renos done. The nursery store will be on the main level, and it made sense to turn the upstairs into a rental suite. I haven't had time to look for a tenant, and I'm thinking you could live there on a trial basis while we see how things work out."

Not sure how to interpret Kot's stunned silence, Tess continues. "You access it by an outside staircase with a little porch at the top. Once you're up there, it's completely private, and there's a bit of sea view over my place and also to the national park and the lighthouse. The location doesn't match the marina cabins, but it's pretty cozy, and it has most of the basics and some furniture, too. It would also help me with security to have someone living on site, and maybe with insurance too. A plumber is supposed to install the fixtures in the customer washroom and a laundry room next to the shop tomorrow. If he shows up. Sometimes he doesn't. Anyway, your job would include the garden centre laundry, and of course you can do your own there, too. It's all pretty rustic, but some might say that's part of its charm. If you're interested you can have a look tomorrow."

Kot hears Tessa take a sip of something, and she exhales. "Oh my God. Thank you. That sounds completely perfect."

However, she now has no moral choice. What she must now say could be deal-breaking. "I'm sorry, but I have to be open about my circumstances. Steve may have told you that I arrived by kayak. I was in danger, and I had to get away. I don't know how long it will be until I can go back, but when it's safe, I will definitely want to go home. Don't worry, I'm not running from the law. I just really don't want to be found. I know that all sounds strange, but I can only ask you to trust me. My name really is Kot—or at least that's my nickname. But the thing is, I don't even have any identification, including a driver's licence. That's got to be a hassle for you, and I'm so sorry."

Tessa replies, "Okay, thanks very much for telling me. Steve did mention that. Look, let's just take this one step at a time, and be honest about whether it's working for both of us. I'll pay you cash, at least until the nursery's open, and I can probably work out driving you to the jobs. Oh, and there's something I should mention before I forget. Our wonderful old golden retriever died soon after my husband passed, and you can imagine… Anyway, I really miss her, and Steve mentioned that your little guy is really good, so he's welcome to come along in the truck. You'll need to ask each client if he's allowed out, though, and keep a close eye on him, pick up poops, and so on."

Kot's eyes have welled up, and her voice is unsteady when she thanks Tessa again.

Tessa pauses, as if checking in with herself one more time, then suggests a time to do that tomorrow. Kot agrees, and thinks they're finished for now, but Tessa quietly continues. "Okay, there's something that I've kept from you, too. A wealthy friend has offered me a big design and landscaping contract. I'd love to accept it, and at this point, my business needs every cent I can make. I mean, besides buying the nursery stock, I didn't realize how many up-front costs there would be. Still, I haven't been able to see a way of doing that contract without letting down a lot of long-term clients. So. I have to confess that one of the reasons I offered you the job was because of your design experience. We obviously need to talk some more, but then, if you're game, we could meet with the client soon. I know he's pawing at the ground to get going, but we would all need to assess the situation and agree on costs. The potential good news is that *if* he gives me the contract, I could pay you considerably more for that design work than for the gardening. And we could work out the rent aspects if you want to stay in the suite. What do you think?"

When the call is over, Tessa steps onto her oceanfront deck and reflects on the risk she is taking with Kot. She had noticed something that Steve probably didn't. Kot's dark auburn hair has light blonde roots that match the hair on her arms. A minority of natural blondes choose the work and expense of maintaining another hair colour, but poor Kot has underestimated how memorable her face is. Still, Tessa accepts the feeling of straight-line inevitability around it all, and is old enough not to question that—as long as there is no danger to her, or to the community.

Kot pulls her cap brim down and risks taking Medley for a walk through the darkening marina grounds to the bobbing boats. The mast rigging jangles in the breeze off the ocean. Herman the heron croaks his strange call as he flies to his night roost, and a beautiful sunset is fading to dusky purple. How strangely things can evolve. She wonders how many English words have been invented in order to describe lying to someone: to fib, dissimulate, prevaricate, equivocate, obfuscate, withhold, tergiversate… Kot feels like she has already become an expert at withholding the truth from good people who deserve honesty.

Nevertheless, less than a week ago she was living in terror, and now she is almost looking forward to next week.

~ FOURTEEN ~

When Ben examines a shaving cut in his bathroom mirror it leads to a full assessment of his appearance for the first time since he was shot. He finds it reassuring: Caribbean-warm skin, just fine lines beside deep brown eyes, a great mouth, and a full head of dark hair with touches of silver. In his late forties, his family's youthful genes are serving him well. When he is ready for a new conquest, what's in the mirror should still do the trick. He already knows of a few willing and necessarily discreet ladies.

He and his wife ceased to be lovers years ago. So, while the command of detail around infidelity can be exhausting, he isn't prepared to settle for the empty marriage without compensations. After he's alleviated the current level of business stress and his wound has recovered, he fully expects that his sex drive will as well. For now, as well as the total libido crusher of pain, his mind is still too focused on Kathleen.

Ben took so many physical risks that his parents feared he wouldn't survive adolescence, and they didn't know about a lot of them. When he did get caught, he just refined his methods in order to retain a sufficiently interesting life. He is addicted to trying to trick everyone close to him. As an adult, he moved naturally into extreme sports, exclusive, high-stakes poker, and multiple secret affairs, both before and since marrying the elegant socialite, Lauren Hoffman. Some of Ben's risky business decisions have also led to clashes with Northcott Shipping's board of directors, and those are only the ones that are on the books. However, only recently has he experienced any serious consequences of living on the edge.

He sits down in his dressing room to put on his pants, and his imagination returns to Kathleen. A glimpse of his unmade bed through the doorway brings a memory of opening a hotel room door to find her naked and waiting. Now, he'll have to lose a reassuring hard-on before going downstairs. He might have known that, even indirectly, Kathleen would be responsible for the first one since the attack. But besides the uniquely enduring passion that she'd triggered, there had been something unique about being with her. Even with an eight-year age difference, they shared important preferences. Food, music, the outdoors, and sex, for sure, ideally all together. But, far more rare, Kathleen made him laugh. He never tired of watching her tell an entertaining story. A man could drown in those eyes, and Ben had, many times.

Kathleen had also represented an escape valve from the increasing morass of his life. At one point, Ben actually decided to leave Lauren, and had made the stupid mistake of telling Kathleen. However, before long, too much changed at work, and ending the affair became one of few things that Ben could still control.

In contrast to Kathleen, social status is Lauren's highest value. Her reaction to any public humiliation would be to score a financial settlement sufficient to carry on in luxury with the children and her servants. She would also make it her mission to turn the kids against him. Besides the emotional toll, Ben's reduced circumstances would unacceptably impact his own freedom and comfort. That alone was enough to make him rethink leaving.

There was another factor in Ben's break-up with Kathleen, one that reduced his guilt. If their affair were discovered, she would bear the heaviest consequences. He would be required to quietly relinquish his direct connection with NatureSave, but otherwise would simply be following in the established footsteps of his father and grandfather's philandering lifestyles. However, Kathleen, at a minimum, would probably lose the job she loved.

The final piece in Ben's decision was the threat of Kathleen's extraordinary intuition, her ability to read his emotions, if not his mind. She never openly criticized or judged, but did call him out on inconsistencies. Or just went very quiet. Also, like most women, she clearly wanted more emotional intimacy than he did.

He only wished that she'd made it easier for him by being the one to end it. He'd broken the news in a secluded nook of her favourite restaurant, and to her credit, Kathleen hadn't fallen apart. At first, her eyes had widened as she checked out his, and then she didn't look at him again. She'd stiffly agreed to resume the relationship they'd had before: he as the representative of a major charitable donor, and she as a senior staffer in the recipient organization. Not just beautiful, but smart and proud, Kathleen had maintained her dignity until they parted. Ben assumed that she would move on, and eventually forgive him.

So why the hell had she unexpectedly turned up outside his office like that? Whatever the reason, she'd put herself squarely in the crosshairs of a very bad situation.

Ben tightens his Hermes tie and does his usual final presentation check in the full-length mirror. The spot of blood on his chin is barely noticeable, and the nuisance erection has followed the sober direction of his thoughts.

In an obligatory show for the maid pouring his coffee, Ben pecks his wife's cheek. Lauren is in a new silk robe, nursing a latté at the breakfast table. He leans his cane against the wall and waits until the maid is gone.

"Morning. What do you have going on today?"

Lauren doesn't look up. "A dressmaker fitting, and then probably lunch with the ALS fundraiser group. They're a boring bunch, but if I want Cherie to come through with an invitation to her Oprah party, I'm stuck helping with her little cause."

Conveniently, Lauren has shown zero interest in Ben's recovery progress, or, as is typical, anything else about him. Breakfast doesn't appeal, so he refills the ridiculously dainty coffee cup and massages his aching leg.

Lauren yawns. "I'd better get ready. The bridge traffic might be bad." She leaves her dishes on the table. In a minute, the annoying ring tune of her phone echoes down the stairs, followed by her affected laughter. It always reminds Ben of a manic sitcom soundtrack.

He didn't sleep much last night, and the prospect of spending another day dodging the shit recently being spat up by his own bad choices is daunting. It's hard to think straight anywhere these days, but especially in the office. So there is high appeal, in spite of the pain, in renewing his usual travel schedule. To just fly away, to almost anywhere.

First, he needs to know what has happened to Kathleen. When Ben asked him, in just the right way, an infatuated gay RCMP friend confided that the safe house where she had been living had exploded, but that no remains were found in the wreckage. Calls to her cell phone continue to go nowhere, and Ben won't make any more now. He is sure that Jack Latrie will contact him if Kathleen returns to work. Meanwhile, no one seems to know where she is.

He leans on the cane and moves the dishes to the sideboard for the maid. Maid. Halloween. The memory of a costume comes to mind. His post-op brain has forgotten someone who might well know something about Kathleen, a woman who attended a charity costume ball dressed as a French maid last Hallowe'en. She had made undisguised efforts to ignore him throughout the event, but so what?

Ben recently declined a charity event invitation from the office of that same woman. As he remembers, that gala is scheduled for tonight, and he needs to reverse his previous refusal and attend. That call, and possibly others, will be best done in his locked and insulated office, during Isobel's typical early lunch. He should be able to get out again before she returns. Suddenly, the day has new purpose beyond the urgent and unpleasant business of Northcott Shipping.

Lauren leaves for her fitting, and Ben's Porsche is soon purring down the leafy avenue of gated enclaves, heading for the dockyards.

~ FIFTEEN ~

Kot reprimands Mich for shrieking.

"I'm so sorry, but it's such a huge relief to hear from you, and there's no one else here. And I have to say, I'm hating living with this theme of fear. I saw the news about a house in Saanich blowing up. Way too weird, and so little information has been released. And I've heard nothing from you. It's been terrifying."

"I understand. But it's been unavoidable."

Kot's tone is grim, and Mich feels a chill. When Kot stays silent, Mich continues, "I couldn't come up with a way to search for information that might not put you at more risk. I actually used what is probably the last pay phone left in Vancouver to call the RCMP. I pushed a bit, but that was a lost cause. They just kept asking for my personal details, and why I was so interested."

The fact that Mich might have come close to linking herself to the situation makes Kot very uneasy. "Hmmm. I'm glad they wouldn't give out information, but it's possible that they have an internal leak there somewhere. I really don't know."

"So—are you saying that the house that exploded was the one where you were living?!"

"Yes, and it was just a fluke that we weren't killed. It had to be a bomb. Medley gets all the credit. He needed to pee, and we were a little distance from the house when it happened. In fact, I'd just used the bathroom down in the garage and for a split second I had the impression that flushing the toilet had caused the explosion."

"Okay, that's so sickening. Where are you now?"

Kot supplies the bare bones of her escape, and what has happened since.

"Right now, my name is Kot Malone and my hair colour is straight out of a box originally chosen by someone associated with the cops. 'Echoes of Auburn.' It doesn't suit me, but I couldn't care less, and I need to do it again soon. It's only been two weeks since I saw Ben get shot, but it feels like months. I'm wondering if you've heard anything about how he is."

"Yes. In fact, I've seen him in person."

"What?! That's crazy! Where? How is he? It's been hell not knowing."

"He seems to be recovering well, and I'm pretty sure that he's looking for you. He came to the Breast Cancer Gala. I'm on the steering committee again this year, and I have to say that focusing on it hasn't been easy, you being AWOL and all. Ben had already RSVP'd that he couldn't attend, but then he called my assistant on the day of the gala to see if there was a ticket left. Apparently, he asked to speak to me, but I wasn't in the office. Anyway, he chatted Jenn up and apparently told her he thought it would be good for him to start getting out again "after the accident," support a good cause, blah blah. Someone had just returned two tickets. Ben only wanted one, but apparently bought them both so we weren't left with an orphan. We were both swamped and Jenn forgot to tell me, so I was pretty shocked to see him there."

Kot is already halfway down the emotional drainpipe that is Ben Northcott. "Wow. So he went alone? How did he look?"

Mich snorts. "Butt-ugly. What do you think? And that intimate manner he turns on… like this particular conversation with you and only you is making his life complete? Masterful, the shithead. He did look tired, and he's probably still well medicated for pain. He told me the same story about his leg that I heard him tell other people: that he'd been T-boned in a car accident, and was getting better with physio. He's using a cane, but said he'll soon be able to dump it. I just told him I was sorry about his injury, then someone interrupted, and I left him to her gushing. Also, I needed some time to think."

Kot is quiet, processing the excellent news. Mich saw Ben, just a couple of evenings ago, and he is obviously going to be fine. Then she remembers something Mich had said earlier.

"How do you know he's looking for me?"

"Well, of course I was doing the crazy chicken, trying to monitor the silent auction and working the room. But it seemed too much of a coincidence that every time I looked up, Ben wasn't far away. It seemed like he was keeping track of me while he was talking to other people. I got the clear impression that he was looking for a chance to corner me for a longer chat."

"Okay. You're usually right about that stuff."

"Why, thank you. In this case, I was, because as soon as things started to wind down, he nailed me. I was coming out of a washroom down the hall. He made it look like he was just heading to the men's, but I'm pretty sure he'd been lurking outside and waiting for me. He faked surprise, and asked if I had a minute to talk. I told him that delaying his trip to the washroom was his risk, and by that point in the evening, my absence for a few minutes wouldn't matter. Mostly, I was hoping that he knew something about you, and I wasn't going to miss that. So we walked to the far end of the balcony and sat on a quiet bench."

Kot's stomach is churning. "Mich, are you sure he wasn't just coming on to you? He told me once that he thought you were hot."

"Good to know, but only for future assassination ops. And absolutely not. What I think now is that he'd figured out that I might know where you are. It may have been a mistake, but then I decided to test things a bit and I told him in confidence that I knew what you'd witnessed. I got the big brown puppy eyes, but his mouth twitched. I'd say he was startled, and possibly even angry. Which is when I figured out that it may not have been the smartest thing on my part to say that. But then he made himself look more relaxed, and confided that you'd called him while he was still in hospital. Kot, you didn't tell me that, and it would have been a lot better if you had. It really caught me off guard."

"Yeah, that was dumb, and I apologize. I was embarrassed, but I did plan to tell you soon after. When you and I talked, I thought I might be out of the safe house soon. I called Ben a day or two after I got put there. Wrong call, in more ways than one, but hopefully no harm was done, except to my fragile emotions."

"Agreed, on the wrong call part. But it's not surprising that your judgement was wonky at that point. Anyway, he said you'd told him that you were in a safe house somewhere near Victoria, but that he was sedated and out of it when you called, and he hasn't been able to reach you over the weeks since. He also said that he was worried about you and didn't understand why you haven't called him again. He really made a point of telling me that his attackers had robbed him."

"Hmmm. So he really said that he tried to reach me?"

"Yeah, but listen. I didn't buy the whole package. There was something a little too rehearsed and smarmy, even for Cool Hand Ben. Oh yeah—apparently, he called Jack in Toronto to find out how to reach you, and Jack told him you were taking a leave of absence for a family matter."

"Wow. Okay, Jack would have found it weird that Ben even asked about me. Jack would never want to risk lying to Ben, so that's maybe what the cops told him. But no, that doesn't make sense. Nothing does, Mich. My head is sore from trying to figure things out."

"Yeah, I can't either. But I was able to honestly lock the bastard's eyes and tell him that I had also talked to you when you were in the safe house, but hadn't heard from you since, and have no idea where to find you. Also, that I was scared shitless. I'm pretty sure he believed that I was telling the truth, which I was. My instinct was to not bring up the explosion, since he didn't. I just steered him into talking about the gala. And, I must admit, about our satisfaction level with the current cars that we're driving."

"I don't know if it would be good for Ben to know about the explosion. There's nothing he can do, so you probably were wise not to bring it up. It's nice that he's anxious to find me though. He wasn't exactly engaging on that phone call."

"Maybe he feels bad because he was so sedated when you called, or something has changed since then. Maybe he has regrets. Who knows? I will reluctantly admit that he certainly seemed very concerned about you. Hey, I've been wondering. Did you get the impression that he already knew those two guys in the parking lot, or do you think they really were strangers?"

"Well, they certainly weren't friends. The vibes were hostile. Why? What are you thinking?"

"Oh, nothing really, just curious. But I'd say it's certain that Ben showed up at the gala because he wanted to talk to me, and he left right after. He asked me to be in touch with him if I heard from you. As if. But I said the same thing to him, and I actually meant it, in spite of wanting to poke his eyes out."

"Oh, Mich. Usually, one person or the other has to end an affair. And I think for a while there, Ben really did intend to be with me. He's just fundamentally not very brave under that 007 facade."

"Fundamentally male, you mean?"

Kot snorts. "You know, I've been thinking how ironic it is that I was worried about losing my job if people found out about Ben and me. But the affair has ended with no one knowing, and here I am anyway, earning slightly over minimum wage and working in dirt."

"While he continues to reap the benefits of running the Northcott empire. I'll shut up, but you have to promise me not to communicate with Ben at all until we learn what all this is about. Or with anyone else. Agreed?"

"Promise. I made that call to Ben back when I thought I'd be home again soon, but at this point, I just want to hide from everyone on earth, except you."

Kot is suddenly and surprisingly tired of the subject of Ben.

Michy asks, "And what have you told the natives on lovely Atticus Island, wherever that is?"

"Oh, I'm just another damsel in distress, on the run from an abusive relationship back on what people here call 'the Big Island.'"

"That's Vancouver Island? Very funny. Your story is accurate, and you're smart to go back to using your nickname. As I remember, no one from the past twenty years knows you as Kot."

"Correct, and it's safer than a whole new name that I might not respond to. Hey, tell me how the gala went."

"Oh, rewarding and exhausting, as usual. There's still a lot of followup, but it looks like we raised a record amount. Fancy Pants Northcott was top bidder on a big item, despite his sins. So—did you have a non-birthday, or did the multi-talented Medley produce a cake?"

"I worked at the marina, and he slept. After that, I threw things, and he chased them. Good times. The day went by, and we went to bed. So maybe I'm still thirty-seven."

"You've certainly earned a year back. So, my Kottie, we must celebrate that somehow, if nothing else. I have no frigging idea where exactly you are, or where I'll stay, but I intend to find out and get myself there. Ideally, armed with a big, fat cake. Would you be up for that?"

"That's my wildest dream, besides going home. And I don't even need a cake. But let me think about it." Kot is silent for a minute. "I'll try to be in touch again tomorrow at this time, assuming you'll be alone there again. There's a second bedroom in my suite, but I'll need to check it out with Tessa tomorrow if it's okay for me to have a guest. I keep this cell phone with me most of the time— it's the garden centre one—so use it if you need to. Oh. I almost forgot. You'll get a kick out of this. Tomorrow morning, we're going to an estate where Tessa wants me to do a big design contract, and it happens to belong to a celebrity heartthrob of yours."

"Yikes. Impressive. I thought nothing ever happened on those islands. Who is it?"

"Hunter Nott."

"Holy shimmering shit! He lives there?!"

Kot smiles fondly. Mich's Irish remnants make any curse sound more interesting. "Part time, but whenever he can, I gather. I'm sure he has other places, and he's mostly away filming and stuff. But he's planning to be here all summer. Tessa says it's a huge property with some kind of old mansion. She just happened to meet ol' Kot Malone at the right time—someone with more garden design experience than she has. She's actually pretty good friends with Hunter, and they hang out with a select few on the island. He uses his helicopter to come and go. Who knew?"

"No kidding. 'Hangs out' with Hunter as in *hoochy-koochy*, or just friends?"

"Friends."

"Okay, I'm bringing stilettos and that barely-there gown with me, okay? The man will be mine in no time. I have to say, that island of yours sounds surprisingly interesting. But then, I can't imagine you in a dull life. I will need to hear every teensy detail of your time with my future husband tomorrow, okay? I'm looking at a period of relative calm on the work front, so please let me know ASAP about visiting you, and I'll start plotting. You do have Wi-Fi there, right?"

"Oh yes, you'll be able to work to your heart's content. Gardeners have to put in long hours at this time of year, and the nursery is supposed to open within days, so I'm afraid you'd be alone a lot. And if you do come, throw in some Atticus-worthy items on top of your femme fatale outfit. I mostly wear what you'd call *nonsembles*. Clean jeans are considered wedding attire here. But Mich, if this works out, you can't tell a soul where you're going, including Jenn. I have no idea how, but make sure you aren't under any kind of surveillance. I know you pay for security monitoring, but get your guy to also make sure that your personal cell phone isn't bugged or anything. I know I sound paranoid, but please just disappear in such a way that no one could ever trace you. That's absolutely critical. But, knowing you, if you plan it well, they don't have a chance. Okay?"

"Yeah, I'll do that, although I would think your real home would be more likely to be watched."

Kot has also wondered about that. And about how overgrown her garden is getting, what is happening to her mail and banking, and who is covering her work.

There is no one in the world that she trusts to be smart and careful more than her savvy best friend. It is also possible that whoever had located her in a rural safe house might also be a step ahead of even Suzanne Michaluk.

~ SIXTEEN ~

The next morning, Tessa's aging truck suspension bounces its passengers along the winding road toward Glenhurst. Medley is sitting on the bench seat between the two women along with the conversational elephant of Kot's real history. Kot knows that Tessa must be curious and has probably compared notes with Steve, but so far there has been no inquisition. Driving along the edge of the national park, they are alternately blinded by a low morning sun and the sudden dusk of overhanging firs. They are already comfortable together, and with shared silence.

Kot moved into the suite on Sunday, then stocked up on groceries in the quiet time just before the store closed. She appreciates having a good view of the road and intersection in one direction, and the ocean and park in the other. It obviously won't be as quiet and private once the nursery opens three days a week, but she hopes that wearing a hat, sunglasses, and renewing her hair colouring will help. Her kayak is now above Tessa's beach, offering a fast exit, if necessary. Meanwhile, she wants to prove her usefulness until she is free to go home.

After a few minutes Tessa says, "So, Kot, please speak up this morning if you think something won't work." She grins. "Super tactfully, of course, and maybe try to suggest something you think would be better. Hunter claims he's open-minded, because, and I quote: 'Actors have to take direction all the time.' But who knows whether his ideas are sublime or ridiculous."

"Okay. I also prefer clarity up front than an unhappy client at the end, famous or not. I do promise not to scream 'Are you crazy?' Or at least, not too much. If it's okay with you, I'll provide polite feedback, and ask for time to think. It would be good to just get a feel for his overall vision. You know, what level of eye clutter he's after, how he plans to use each space, maybe his favourite colour palette. Stuff like that."

"Perfect. I only know Hunter socially. He has a good sense of humour, but I can't predict what he's like to work with. Or for. Are you nervous about dealing with him?"

"No, not at all, thanks."

"Good. He's really just a regular guy who got blessed with looks and talent and was smart enough to use them. He's certainly worked hard, but he also got some lucky breaks."

Kot chuckles. "Yeah, our culture seems to consider pretending to be someone else the highest possible accomplishment. Whatever—every famous person I've ever known needs to eat, sleep, and use the toilet, and they'll leave their toys behind when they die, like the rest of us. And they're every bit as much a child inside as everyone else, if not more so. Still, obviously Hunter's a good guy, or he wouldn't be a friend of yours."

As soon as she stops talking, Kot wants to snatch it all back. She's been so careful, and it's no doubt her comfort with Tessa that caused her to again drop her guard and disclose that she is familiar with celebrities. Tessa gives her a speculative look, but still doesn't pry. Thousands would, so Kot quickly moves on.

"To be honest, I'm excited by the sheer scope of this project. I can't wait to see the whole place."

"And I am immensely relieved not to be trying to tackle it on my own. I think I told you that, just before I met you, I'd decided that I had to say no to Hunter. Oh, I meant to mention that Glenhurst's caretaker for the past few months is going to be joining us today. He used to be Hunter's stunt body double, and they became good friends. Roller's kind of mysterious, and I don't know him nearly as well as I know Hunter. But Rob Baschel likes him, and Rob has good judgement."

"Interesting name."

"His real name is Malik Moreno, and I honestly don't know why he's always called Roller. Ha! I just… sorry, bad taste, but Roller himself would be the first to laugh. And he probably has. He's in a wheelchair." Tessa is relieved to see Kot smile. "He's had the nickname for a long time, and the accident only happened last year, so the name isn't related. Hunter wasn't in that film, and apparently Roller was lucky not to be killed—some car chase gone wrong—but both his legs are paralyzed. Hunter's a loyal guy, and when he needed someone to look after Glenhurst, he offered Roller the job. According to Hunter, it's working out great. He's converted part of the basement into a gym. Said it was for himself, but a lot of the equipment is suitable for paraplegic rehab. Kind of sweet, but the local gossip is wrong. They're not a couple. Roller probably won't ever recover the use of his legs, but, oh my God, check out the rest of him. As far as I know, he is also unattached. They're quite the manly pair of eligibles."

"Well, that's always a bonus, but it can sometimes complicate things too, right? But they both sound pretty interesting. Tessa, will you please be blunt if I'm getting things wrong about what Hunter wants? You know him, and I don't."

"I will." Tessa pauses. "Have to admit—if we get this contract, it will make a lot of difference for me financially—for us both, obviously—and there would be ongoing Glenhurst maintenance work when it's done. But if it doesn't pan out… well, it isn't the end of the world. I have plenty of clients, and hopefully, the garden centre will make a profit."

Tessa had been impressed by Kot's efficiency and knowledge while they were working together yesterday. She had literally dug right in, and together, they did more than twice the work in half Tessa's usual time. Once the nursery gets rolling, there will be a need for more staff and for another conversation with Kot, but one step at a time.

For her part, Kot plans to confide in Tessa at some point, just not quite yet. She is starting to feel more secure, and if she can find a way to stop the endless mind loops about Ben, the old yearning that still lays waste her heart, it would be another huge step forward.

Tessa breaks the silence again. "Oh hey, I just remembered. You said you had an interest in lighthouses, so I called old Harvey at the light station last night to ask if we could visit the tower. I needed to check in with him anyway. He's been the caretaker there since the place was decommissioned, but he's more just a tenant now. He's in his eighties and having regular cancer treatment, but I've heard his prognosis is okay."

"That's really kind of you, Tessa. It would be great to have a prowl around if you have time and he doesn't mind."

"Harv said we're welcome as long as he doesn't have to provide a tour. I don't think he can even get up to the tower anymore. I feel bad that I don't have time to do more to help him at this time of year, but there's an army of folks willing to take him for treatments in Victoria, do their own errands, and have their own ferry fare covered in the process. Anyway, let's go there on Friday. I've already booked the day off to focus on the nursery, so I'll just take an hour's break and we can take a walk to the light station. Harvey said we'd actually be doing him a favour by checking on it. He'll be gone, but there's a key hidden."

Tessa stops talking as she slows down in the middle of a curve and turns left into a narrow lane, then begins to pick her way around deep potholes. Kot is intrigued by the total absence of anything that might indicate that this rutted driveway leads to anything beyond a run-down shed.

A second-growth forest borders both sides of the lane, opening on the left some distance along to a sizeable wetland. Spiky vegetation is adorned by red-winged blackbirds sending spring *chicker-eeee-a's* to the sky. The route then curves through a fairyland of old-growth fir and cedar trunks, rising from an open understory that is hillocked with ferns. There are two hundred shades of sun-shot green: deep emerald mosses, grey-green lichen, fresh leaves unfurling from green-black shadows, boulders that have been undisturbed for centuries, now glazed with spring growth. Kot almost looks for hobbits.

The forest gives way to the tameness of cross-fenced meadows, and sunlight shoots through the windshield again. Ahead, Kot can see the roofline of the manor above a high cedar hedge. Tessa drives under a stone archway into a freshly graveled courtyard. To the left, a pedestrian passageway has been cut into the hedge, and on the right is a series of attached garages. A classic wrought iron weathervane adorns the centre of the slate roofs.

Even after the rough driveway, Kot regrets that they're not wearing long gowns, broad hats, and demure expressions. Eager for a good look at it all, she jumps down. They leave Medley in the truck, and Tessa suggests that Kot should begin her assessment of the "blank slate" while she goes to find Hunter.

Kot walks through the hedge opening and stops in amazement. The house design apparently originated in the north of England, or Scotland, and yet it is somehow perfect here as well: a manor house, just as Tessa had described, and not in the least pretentious. The exterior facing is a warm reddish-brown brick that Tessa said the original owner had barged over from the Sidney Island brickworks just before they closed.

The roof has two chimneys and matches the garages, its tiles decreasing artistically in size from trough to peak, making the house seem larger. The windows are tall, with generous cement casings. The two largest, in the upper story, are topped by graceful cement arches. Apparently, the trim was originally custom mixed for Glenhurst at a busy quarry on the shores of Saanich Inlet, now the famously transformed Butchart Gardens.

The symmetry of the main part of the house, with bay windows on either side of its central entrance, is broken by a single-storey glassed verandah on one side and a two-storey wing on the other. Simple cement columns direct a visitor to the pedimented front door that is painted a glossy black.

Kot goes around to the front and walks some distance away. She is not disappointed by that view either. The design is strong, dignified, and timeless and will certainly deserve the same qualities in its landscaping. The building is awash in morning light. It would be bright inside all day, then receive the glow from any sunset bathing the vast meadows to the southwest. As taught, Kot will need to take views from inside the house into consideration.

Outlines of previous gardens remain, long reclaimed by tall grass and weeds. In this area, at least, this is not Tessa's "blank slate," but a huge renovation project. Good thing that Hunter is apparently calling in the big machines.

Over near the paddocks is a low building, built in the same style as the garages, that probably contained the stables. Someone had really thought things through, and Kot is now curious about Glenhurst's history. This is a special place. In spite of everything, she has already been swept into its spell and is feeling a familiar obligation.

She tosses around design possibilities as she takes photos and video snippets on Tessa's old tablet. Tessa was clear that there is no hope of acquiring suitable landscape design software, so Kot will need to use old school methods, matching her images with some measurements for the first round, and eyeballing elevations. At least the grounds were mostly levelled, many years ago.

Tessa encounters Hunter and Roller as they emerge from the elevator, towels slung around their sweaty necks. While they rode, Roller had expressed his amazement that Hunter was allowing Tessa to bring a stranger there, given his determination to keep the property secure from the paparazzi, their technology, and from Hunter's angry exes. He pointed out that he is only one handicapped security guy, while the numbers in those categories are legion. Hunter was about to reply when the door opened.

Tessa laughs at how they look. "Hi there. Should I have called to remind you that we were coming?"

Hunter smiles. "Hey, Tess girl. No, I didn't forget. But sorry, I lost track of time and probably stink."

Roller greets Tessa and wheels down the hall to his suite while Hunter leads her to the kitchen. "He's going to join us in a minute. I want him up to speed with this work, in case I have to leave before everything is done, God forbid. Um, I don't know if you are aware of my latest romantic disaster?"

Tessa looks sideways at him and nods, a little embarrassed at the change in subject.

"Okay. Well, dear Ashley already has my agent's knickers in knots today, and therefore, my balls in a noose as well. Sorry. When I'm upset, I talk like that. Apparently, she's handling her sorrow about me ending things with a full-on smear campaign. A *Variety* article came out this morning that portrays me as a mix of Henry the Eighth, Attilla the Hun, and a wasted addict."

Tessa tries to lighten Hunter's mood. "Yikes. Do you want me to leak that you not only eat quiche, but tofu? The down side might be having to say goodbye to future macho roles."

"That's a kind offer, but maybe hold off for now. Do you want some coffee or something? Where's your new hire?"

"She's outside having a look around. Just water for us both, please. I'll do it. Do you have a lemon?"

Hunter answers, "Sure. There's some in the fridge and a pitcher up there. I'll go get my drawing from my office. Be right back."

Tessa can see Kot smiling about something outside before she wanders further away, looking thoughtful.

Tessa catches Hunter before he leaves the kitchen. "Hunter, while we're on our own…"

Hunter stops in the doorway and looks at her curiously.

"I told you on the phone that Kot has far more design qualifications and experience than I do. But I wish I'd had a chance to work with her for more than one day before coming here. I'm not seriously worried, but I just want to say two things."

Hunter nods. "Okay, shoot."

"First, if you don't like Kot's design ideas, don't worry at all about telling me that you'd prefer to hire someone else. I'd be far madder at you if you didn't do that, okay? And second, if we do move forward, I intend to monitor things closely for clear communications. I want you to let me know right away if you're uncomfortable with anything at all."

"Okay, no problem."

"Good, and just one more thing. Obviously hiring us will be cheaper than going off-island, but it's still going to be a major financial commitment, and I don't want you to be shocked by a quote. You already know that it's super expensive to bring in materials to Atticus, and that a lot of patience is required when some people here like to work on 'island time.'"

"Yeah, I've already learned that the hard way. I'm always amazed that the first guy here ever got it built in the first place. But times were different. The workmen probably came over and camped here until it was finished. Anyway, let's just see what you and Kot come up with. I've been lying awake too much planning things, so it would be great to finally get started." He grins at her. "You may have heard that patience isn't my forté. But no worries. I hear you."

That sounds to Tessa like a partial commitment already. Hunter goes to get his drawing, and after setting up a tray, she watches Kot through the casement windows. Whoever that woman really is and whatever trauma she has experienced, in this setting she looks happy and relaxed.

Hunter returns with a large roll of papers under his arm. When they go outside, Tessa realizes what had been making Kot smile. She was looking at the massive and apparently new Spanish-style furniture positioned incongruously on the weeds and rubble of what used to be a patio, so hopelessly out of place with the classical building style.

Hunter squints into the sun at Kot. His eyebrows rise, and then the trademark grin makes an appearance. Tessa follows his gaze and snorts. About forty metres away, Kot is bent over her tape measure on the ground, her shapely bottom pointed in their direction. Tessa calls to get her attention, and watches Hunter out of the corner of her eye as Kot moves across the yard with her usual grace and energy. He is obviously enjoying the scenery, and as she gets near, Kot's own smile is broad. Her beautiful eyes also seem to be assessing Hunter calmly. Tessa suspects that he's probably wishing he had taken the time to shower.

"Hunter, this is Kot Malone. Kot, Hunter Nott. Apparently, Hunter felt the need to pump weights in preparation for our meeting."

A lot of guys Kot knows don't even pump their own gas, and Hunter at least looks like his typically disheveled adventure hero character. She catches a whiff as they shake hands.

Hunter says, "Great name, Kot Malone. Right out of an old Western."

Kot keeps her gaze level with his flirtatious eyes and shakes her head. "Thanks. But I'd have to work in the saloon or something. I never met a horse I couldn't fall off."

Tessa moves between them and rolls out Hunter's drawing on the table, determined to get down to business. Kot likes that Hunter isn't next to her. She wants to stay relaxed and concentrate on her job.

Kot leans forward to focus on the drawings, and Tessa notes that she is showing none of the silliness of most women—or almost equally, men—on first meeting Hunter. Who knows, maybe Kot is a lesbian. That could be helpful, in Tessa's opinion. Or… what was that intriguing thing Kot had said about having experience with celebrities?

Roller quietly approaches from the house. He is also still in his workout gear, but a ball cap and opaque sunglasses now hide his scrutinizing eyes. All too familiar with the ways that harmless-looking people can find to access a celebrity's home or hotel, he rarely relaxes in his Glenhurst security role, especially when Hunter is there. There are thousands of people with insanely powerful equipment and great patience, attempting to get celebrity photos by any means. Even an angry picture of a star can be worth a lot. But others have more sinister motives, and the truth is that Hunter has included Roller in this meeting for security reasons only. Hunter would never expect him to supervise landscaping work; they both know exactly how that might turn out.

Madonna has escaped from the house and runs through the hedge opening to the parking area to start barking at Medley. Hunter suggests that Kot lets him out of the truck, and the dogs happily race and wrestle around the weedy yard while Kot and Tessa make mental notes about the need for dog management, should they get this job.

The "gardening assistant" doesn't meet Roller's expectations, and also doesn't present like any member of the paparazzi he's ever encountered. She says little and seems relaxed, for one thing, and has nothing in her hands at the moment. She greets him politely, then turns back to Hunter's drawing and his eager monologue about it. Roller watches her from behind his dark glasses. Little mouth twitches and slight tilts of her head probably indicate her own opinions about what Hunter is laying out. If she is faking those tiny betrayals of real emotion, then she is a lot better than most imposters.

It's clear to Kot why Roller had been Hunter's stunt double. His skin is naturally darker, but Hunter has a serious tan. The biggest difference is that Roller now wears his hair long, and tied back. And he can no longer stand. Given Roller's surveillance of her, Kot attempts to conceal her reactions to what Hunter is presenting. His level of watchfulness strikes Kot as inappropriate, unless his role is to protect Hunter from being attacked by an unarmed woman half his size who doesn't appear to be armed with even a phone camera.

Some of Hunter's ideas might be workable, and he has certainly put love and longing into his sketches. But most of it is wildly off the mark, an unworkable hodgepodge of garden features from Morocco, California, the south of France, the Pacific Northwest, England, and Japan. Kot made some of the same mistakes herself, before learning that successful garden designs stand the test of time by respecting the particulars of their surroundings, culture, soil, and exposure. She already has her own design ideas for this place, but it will undoubtedly require tact and persuasion to help Tessa's potential big client to let go of his. She is aware of the man's physical magnetism, but has never been drawn to many celebrities she's met, with their needy egos and expectations. Ben's overly high self-esteem is sometimes even too much for Kot. However, in her books, he is simply an impossible act for any man to follow.

Hunter finishes explaining his drawings and looks up at Tessa, who rewards him.

"Wow, nice, Hunter. I don't see why we can't make at least most of this work." Feeling Kot flinch beside her, she hurries to add, "But I must defer to the pro here. What do you think, Kot?"

Hunter turns to Kot with a look of surprising vulnerability on his face. His hand are anxiously clenching and unclenching.

Kot gives him what she hopes is a supportive smile. "I agree that this is an amazing amount of work, and I hope you stay this excited as it comes together. You've included things you've seen on your travels, and I suspect they were places you enjoyed. Not everyone notices the details that you have, or thought about what makes them feel happy."

Hunter seems pleased, so Kot continues, speaking slowly to match his laconic speaking pace, and pretending that she is thoughtfully considering his work.

"The trick is going to be to identify which components will actually work in our climate and in this particular setting, and then letting go of the elements that aren't viable. The Glenhurst buildings have a distinct character, and ideally, the gardens and landscaping elements surrounding them will enhance their classic charm, rather than distract from it. I think the more that we can find ways to incorporate the overall feeling that you want with compatible garden architecture and plantings, things that will actually survive and thrive on this property, the faster it will grow, and the happier you'll be in the long term. It would sure be fun to find ways to bring it all together."

Hunter barks the abrupt and humourless laugh that often precedes his famous growl in the movies. But right now, it's real.

Hunter turns to Tessa. "What the hell? Basically, she's saying my designs are a piece of shit."

Tessa hurries to interject, but Hunter holds out his hand, clearly trying to control his anger. "It's okay. But I think she needs to convince me she has some pretty attractive alternatives."

His rude use of the third person makes Kot wonder if passive aggression is Hunter's typical reaction to strong women, or a sign of some other negative character trait that Tessa neglected to mention. She tries to engage his eyes, but Hunter stays focused on the romping dogs. Happy to feel more detached than usual, Kot calmly suggests that they begin by getting a wider perspective of the grounds.

She leads the way out to the fence bordering the nearest meadow. Hunter straggles behind, like a petulant child. When he catches up, Kot takes a step away so that she can appear to be addressing all of them, rather than engaged in a battle with Hunter. Repetition of a central message is often necessary, and she tries not to sound condescending or pedantic.

"Hunter, besides its location and privacy, of course, one reason you may have wanted this place is the quality of the architecture." She grins, disarmingly, as she gestures to them. "Well, okay—the gigantic cement planters shaped like baskets with big bows may be a little over the top. But even they were carefully planned to match the window casings. And look how well they've done their job through almost a hundred years of every kind of bad weather and even a few minor earthquakes. So the materials were chosen well. And I absolutely agree with you. Whatever we create here must obviously meet your needs and preferences: the patios, a pool, a rose garden, and so on. That's crucial. But wouldn't it be perfect if we can do that in a way that follows the lead of the architecture?"

Hunter is silently staring straight ahead just a little too long for Tessa's comfort. She jumps in.

"So, Kot, just to be clear, you're not suggesting that Hunter needs to give up any of the functions that he wants, right?"

"Absolutely not." Kot speaks directly to Hunter's stony profile. "My suggestions are based on experience, and meant to lead to beauty and comfort, and, in the end, to an even greater sense of home."

Hunter is stubbornly determined to hide the fact that he is already letting go of some of his cherished ideas. However, still smarting from the barbs of Ashley, he doesn't feel like being dominated, and Tessa's obvious distress is the only reason that he finally nods at Kot and curtly suggests that she carry on.

"Of course. Okay, obviously this may change somewhat, but I think that the landscaping near the house out front here could be fairly formal, to match the building's style and era. Maybe just a couple of dogwood trees and some shrubs. The entry path could be lined with boxwood to echo the European theme, but it would need to be kept trimmed and tidy. Another path could go to your pergola.

But you know, the big kitchen garden—the veggies and herbs and fruit trees, your pool and patios, the rose garden, all of your private, lounging-around areas—those would definitely work best on the other side of the house. Your perennial gardens could be curved sweeps on either side. Most of that seems to get full sun, and we can create shade where needed, including your greenhouse, somewhere that isn't too hot in summer. I'd just need to study the site more and think about it. Obviously the more garden beds, the more weeding and tending is needed, in the early years especially, so that's something for you to consider as we go along."

Kot is deliberately using language that assumes they will work things out. She leads them around to the back of the house. She knows that she should stop soon, but ideas are still spilling out. She has also remembered that every excited amateur needs a little validation.

"The pool and patio area could have planters to contain portable pots for those exotic plants that you want. Then they wouldn't be too hard to move inside or into your greenhouse in the winter, when they might otherwise die. No more cement baskets and bows wanted, I assume?"

Hunter shakes his head and graces her with a small smile.

"The existing ones could be overflowing with annuals, as I'm sure they were originally. So the next step would be comprehensive mapping of all of the areas, not just the measurements, but sun exposure, elevations, and soil types. Then you'd need to approve every detail before anything is finalized. I hear you're planning to be here for a few months, Hunter. That's perfect, because you could supervise everything in person."

Kot catches herself getting dangerously close to sucking up to the client. "So. Enough of my blabbing. Could you be frank with your thoughts please? If we proceed, we'll need to have close communication at every stage."

Kot couldn't possibly have overheard Tessa's conversation with Hunter on that subject, and Tessa is vastly relieved to see the massive improvement in Hunter's mood. Later on, he will confide that it was at that point that he mentally waved adieu to his fantasy of a grotto and the Tunisian arches.

He finally turns to Kot and looks her in the eyes.

"Okay, Kot Malone, I guess that's why you should be doing this work instead of me. But don't expect me to sit in a hard iron chair around a 1920s pool, just because it matches the house, okay? Not happening."

Kot grins and, in spite of himself, Hunter is charmed again. He counters the sensation, by asserting client privilege.

"So, you two, how long before you can show me a general design? I want to finalize things and get going."

Looking to Tessa, Kot asks, "Do we have enough time to get started a bit today? That would certainly speed things up."

Tessa checks the time. "Yes, let's get at it. It's a busy week and my nursery stock will be arriving soon. I'm running out of rationale not to get the garden centre open. But Hunter, in the short term, I'll try to cover off most of the client work alone, and let Kot focus on this design. What do you think your timeframe will be, Kot?"

Kot steps away to think, then says, "I'll aim to have a general design draft ready in a week, or whenever you're free after that, Hunter. Would that work?"

She knows that Hunter has no idea what an impossible thing she has just offered, but appreciates the warmth of his hand as they shake on it. For Tessa's sake, she is relieved to be through the minefield of Hunter's follies, spires, and California dreaming.

Roller is scrolling on his phone, distracted. A triumph. Hunter's phone starts to ring in his pocket. He'd actually forgotten about it, and even about Ashley. He sighs and walks away to talk to his agent. Roller returns to his suite, and Kot and Tessa get to work.

While Kot gets started with Tessa's camera, Tessa takes advantage of being alone with Hunter alone again. "So, how do you feel about working with Kot? And there's no right answer here, Hunter."

"Well, I'll wait for the drawings, but she sure seems to know what she's doing." He grins. "And she certainly doesn't mind contradicting me. I admit that I'm not generally drawn to people who do that, but it's something I've learned to value. At least she understands how special this place is, and what she has in mind will probably be considerably above the generic stuff. So don't worry, I'll push back whenever it's important that I get my little way. Honestly? My main issue now is getting things moving. I wish I'd been able to get here two months ago. I don't want to lose the commitment I got from the machinery guys, so the sooner Kot can deliver something, the better."

"Okay, great. I have to admit that I was impressed, too, thank God. And I'm sorry for my part in your delay. I was frustrated about having no time to do this project properly, and then I met Kot. Hey, I need to check out something else with you, and it's also about Kot. Rob invited me to our next potluck at the café, and I know that you and Roller will be there."

"Sure. Rob ran the guest list by me and I agreed for you to be on it. I think I'm expected to bring the usual truck-full of wine, and Roller's been looking at recipes. Should be fun."

Tessa swats him. "I'm pretty sure I was on that list before you, my friend. Anyway, he asked me if Kot might like to come too, but I obviously want to make sure that's okay with you before I talk to her."

"Thanks. It's fine with me, as long as you trust her discretion. And I'm also assuming that if she is your employee, she will be under the contract confidentiality agreement we talked about, right?"

Tessa agrees without hesitation, and Hunter continues, "By the way, could you come up with some idea of what the design work will cost in total, with estimates for each stage?"

Tessa's to-do list just grew by at least another full day. She will also need to figure out Kot's contract work and pay, separate from her other hours. However, since Tessa has no doubt that the total estimate for Hunter's work will exceed her usual income for three years, she will go without food and sleep to get it done.

"Absolutely. And one more thing. If she could, I get the feeling that Kot would like the entire island to sign her own non-disclosure agreement about her presence on Atticus. Apparently, she's escaped from a bad relationship, but she never talks about her previous life at all. She's definitely afraid of something, or someone. It isn't quite time yet for me to get nosy, but give me another week, okay? And I'm absolutely positive that she has been a victim, not the opposite, so don't worry. Anyway, off we go, and we'll both see you on Saturday evening if I can persuade Kot to take the time off."

Hunter responds quickly. "Well, please make sure she knows it's okay to take an extra day to work on the design, if it means that she can be at the dinner." Tessa notes Hunter's sudden shift in priorities with alarm. He pretends to attend to something over by the garages as the women get ready to leave. He turns in time to catch Kot's smile and breezy wave through the open window, and dutifully identifies his emotion as hope. Hope that they forgot something, and will come back.

How perfect it would be to just shrink-wrap his life on Atticus and hide permanently from the unpleasantness of his working world, although this is perhaps not the ideal time to broach the subject with his agent and producers. Madonna nuzzles his hand, and he strokes her soft head. Maybe she is also missing her new friend.

Hunter is suddenly anticipating Sunday evening's gathering in a novel and enjoyable light. His therapist would suggest that, as usual, he is looking for comfort and validation through a new sexual experience. Hunter heads inside for a shower, thinking that his shrink might be shocked by how much he would simply like to talk more with Kot, get to know her better.

~ SEVENTEEN ~

The Whale
Chatham Islands, Victoria

Through many surface cycles of light and dark, the humpback has been weakened by relentless cramps, her life force dangerously drained.

Back in the Warm Home depths, she had mated with the singing male who was courting her. It had felt right and good, and in time she felt the flutterings of a growing fifth descendant in her belly. She'd lingered with others in the group to protect dolphin companions who were being attacked by the black and white killers. Sharp-cornered barnacles on the humpbacks' pectoral fins made excellent knuckledusters, and inflicted sufficient damage on the transient orcas to drive them away to other prey. The dolphins were exuberant in their appreciation, and the humpbacks departed on their long migration to the Cold Home waters.

It was soon after her clan entered colder currents to the northeast that a malaise had taken hold. She had a night of acute pain before an expulsion stained the water behind her. A sister stayed to comfort her for hours near the surface, but with the arrival of the light, the whale knew that she was no longer carrying new life.

Still sick, she now has no choice but to take many naps. Like one of the wise old ones, she often lolls on the surface, dreaming of the sweetness of her calves. Months ago, one of the vicious surface machines had carved a series of bloody cuts on her flank as she slept, and she'd needed the group's protection until the wounds stopped leaking blood. But the sickness that she has now is unlike anything in the whale's experience.

Her clan had been careful during the long migration from Hawaiian waters, eating no krill in the areas that the ancestors had taught were dangerous. Perhaps she'd ingested some new toxin. There were rumours of such things in the songs of strangers, but until this journey her group had never questioned the safety of its traditional route. One older auntie had quickly lost strength from the illness. She sang weak instructions to the others to carry on without her, and eventually, they sorrowfully did so.

There was a group of grey whales just a hundred kilometres miles away, well within earshot, and for a time they all travelled together. However, like some of the humpbacks, the greys sang as they took a different route, up the long and splintered coast of the very big island that she has finally reached.

Her own destiny now lies east, through the passage with high mountains on one side and rounded hills on the other, and then north to linger in summer Cold Home waters before instinct dictates the next long migration.

The humpback is fifty feet to the tip of her flukes, and before this illness, was in the prime of her thirty-two tons of life. But now she is thin, and not even tempted by the Northern Pacific buffet around her. Her companions remain healthy, and eager to push on to the feeding waters further to the north. She has told them that she is feeling better, and will catch up. And now she is alone.

Between resting periods, she labours through tides and currents to reach the point where the waters of the strait mix with others from a sound to the south. There is none of the usual excitement of this return, and no choice but to swim slowly when she can, and to rest frequently.

She rolls a half-closed eye toward the rocky shore in the spring sun, and looks around. Some of the seals on offshore rocks witness her resonant WHOMPUSSSH *and heart-shaped spray. Then the whale sinks again, resting just below the surface to await the push of the tide.*

Through waking dreams she hears the increasingly distant songs of her clan, as they separate into smaller groups to forage around the green islands.

~ EIGHTEEN ~

Kot stands back to let Tessa open the light station's driveway gate. The predicted rain is beating an erratic percussion on the big-leaf maples above them, and on the hoods of their rain jackets.

Her inclination this morning was to skip this outing in favour of putting in uninterrupted work on the Glenhurst design work. In order to have the draft ready for Hunter as promised, she will need to work on it throughout the coming weekend as well. Tessa is no doubt also anxious to get at assembling her indoor and outdoor display racks, not to mention mastering the challenges of her new inventory and payment software.

However, as they head out into the soft sea air, Kot realizes that she, at least, badly needs this break. The tower on the bluff is a beacon for her imagination. The light stations that she has visited around the world seem to share a mysterious old soul. Building styles and materials vary greatly, especially in BC. Some lighthouses are attached to the residences, some raised on metal supports, some are short and squat, and others resemble the classic tall design, narrowing as they rise. This Atticus Island one reminds Kot of the graceful Fisgard Lighthouse, west of Victoria.

No matter their physical attributes, they are all linked by rugged locations and interesting histories. The lives of the keepers were ones of hardship and routine interrupted by drama, and sometimes life-threatening danger. This light station is relatively accessible in the twenty-first century, but things would have been different at the time of its installation: no ferries, mostly seasonal human presence, and from fall to spring, at least, a job fit for a hermit.

At the top of the rising driveway, Kot experiences the familiar sense of passing into a different dimension. She wouldn't be surprised to see a phantom, rain-slickered keeper waiting in the mists ahead. The residence isn't large, just one level, with probably two bedrooms. That doesn't mean that it wasn't full of a gaggle of kids at some point. The white clapboard siding is exactly what she'd expected. A dilapidated fence encloses the orchard and vegetable garden, once carefully tended to supply the station's fresh produce and canning needs. However, the current caretaker's inability to maintain the garden or prune the trees is sadly obvious. According to Tessa, Harvey's supplies come entirely from the island's grocery store, via caring friends who also bring cooked gifts.

They wander over to the bluff. The rotting wooden staircase descending to the beach would have led to the lifeboat, but now the strong arms of a sharp-edged salal forest partially block access. Following station decommission, a liability-averse federal bureaucrat had probably ordered the locked gate at the bottom and the "No Trespassing" signs to be installed.

Harvey clearly isn't home. Tessa finds the lighthouse key on its rusting ring inside the basement door and offers it to Kot. It feels weighty with importance. From the back of the house, a grass path takes them on a gentle slope to the tower rising above them.

At first, the lighthouse door sticks to the jamb, swollen from damp and lack of use. When Kot pushes it hard, a gust of wind sweeps in and scatters the dry husks of leaves on the circular ground floor.

Tessa's phone echoes shrilly off the bare walls. She pulls it out and looks at the number. "Oh, this is my plant delivery guy. Hello. Hello? Sorry, can you hold on please? I'm going outside to get a better signal." She gestures to Kot to carry on, and pushes the door shut behind her.

The ground level is bare, apart from a low bench and an empty plastic bin. A lingering odour suggests that fuel was stored on this level in the working decades of the lighthouse. A tiny area has a half-wall that encloses an ancient toilet and a rust-stained sink. Kot notices two rolls of toilet paper. Strangely, they don't look old, but cobwebs fill every corner and she isn't tempted to investigate the darkness behind the winding wooden staircase.

There is no telling how long Tessa's call will take and there might not be another chance to come here, so Kot slowly climbs the stairs. Each is worn lower in the middle from the footfalls of almost two centuries. Solid walls partition small rooms on both the second and third floors but she keeps climbing to the top, hoping for a look at the light. There is a faint and incongruous smell of peanut butter. A remnant from years ago, or maybe the byproduct of a chemical process? When she looks back, the lower staircase is already lost in murky curves and shadows.

Near the top, a locked door with a thick windowpane leads to a circular walkway, just below the level of the red-painted lantern. The two railings are thin, and it makes Kot dizzy to even think about being out there in a strong wind. The old abandoned light at the top is dirty, but she stands as close to it as the lightkeepers would have, in whatever state of illness, grief, or exhaustion they must have experienced at times.

She can see Tessa far below, gesticulating as she talks. Kot aches to be sharing this experience with Ben. He had at least pretended to share her attraction to lighthouses. But underneath her habitual yearning, her cherished fantasy of Ben ever changing his mind about them is slowly fading.

Descending the tower again is like being inside a whorled seashell. The windowless space on the third floor is empty, but a tall window in the staircase below it gives a partial view of the bluff and the ocean.

The sun is breaking through, and Kot has a vision of hot and windless summer days, when the station keepers and their families could enjoy some of the location's benefits instead of just bearing their responsibilities.

She'll just complete the tour by poking her head around the entry partition of the second level room, and then she and Tessa can get back to work.

In her second week of living in the lighthouse, Camas had spotted a middle-aged man crossing the lawn below, from the direction of the beach staircase. She'd watched in horror as he continued up the path to the lighthouse, and heard him trying to open the locked door. Camas had stayed at her window until long after he'd given up and disappeared back down to the beach.

There is no telling how many more people might also trespass, especially once the park and campground are officially open. Perhaps someone might even be persistent enough to locate Camas's secret access. Even with her efforts to keep it hidden, it was probably more obvious now that she'd been using it daily. Why wasn't the man living in the house doing a better job of keeping people away? He wasn't even home that much.

Whatever, during the two weeks since that episode, it's been a relief to not feel so threatened again. Until today.

Camas is eating a peanut butter and jelly sandwich and reading a comic book when she hears voices outside and is frozen by the sight of two women already approaching the lighthouse, and then the terrifying sound of a key turning in the lock. There is no vehicle outside, so they must have come on foot, quietly. And now there is no way that she will be able to get outside without being seen. A phone rings below, and one of the women answers it. The outer door closes again, and Camas can hear the same woman talking outside.

For a moment, all is quiet. If the second woman also went outside, there may be a chance to escape behind the staircase and down the hidden cliff path. But now there are soft footsteps coming up the stairs. Camas holds her breath until they continue past her room. Through the crack of the open door she catches a glimpse of a slim woman's back and a chin-length bob of auburn hair. When the footsteps fade toward the top, Camas darts to the staircase window. She's devastated to see that the woman on her phone is pacing the bluff at the rear of the lighthouse as she talks. From there, she would be able to see both Camas's secret exit and the yard below.

Camas is paralyzed with indecision, and the footsteps are descending again. She slips back into her room and crouches behind the door with a blanket over her head in a child's hope of camouflage. She prays that the woman will just continue down to join her friend outside.

Kot pokes her head inside the room and sees part of a sandwich on the floor: proof that she didn't imagine the smell of peanut butter. The sight of an ancient bed with stained and rumpled blankets, a water container, some bins, books, puzzles, and dirty clothing on the floor brings the knowledge that she is an intruder in someone's space even before she hears the sound of fast and shallow breathing behind her. There is also no ignoring the body odour.

Poised to flee if necessary, Kot looks around the edge of the partition. A thin blanket is draped over someone crouched on the floor, trembling. A short person. When she warily lifts a corner, she isn't surprised to see a child, probably a girl, brown eyes wide and wild like a terrified animal. Kot backs away a bit. Partly from the smell, but also to appear less threatening.

"Hello there. I'm Kot. My friend and I got permission to look around the lighthouse, and I'm really sorry if we scared you. We must have. But we're not going to hurt you. Looks like you're staying here for a bit, hey?"

The girl nods once and keeps the blanket held up as far as her nose. Kot finds it hard to estimate the child's age, but guesses that she isn't yet a teenager, and also that she has some First Nations heritage. How long has this poor waif been living here? Is she completely alone? And if so, why? The girl's fear triggers Kot's again, a hard and familiar churning in her stomach, a racing of the blood.

Still, she decides to try again. She speaks softly, not expecting eye contact, but also standing so that the girl can't easily bolt away.

"You're hiding, aren't you? I know what that's like. I was hiding myself not long ago. I had to escape from something very scary." She sees surprise on the girl's face. "I'm pretty sure you want me to keep your secret for now. Are you all alone?" She gets another tiny nod. "Okay. But listen. It really isn't safe for you to keep living here. If I found you, someone else might, too—people who might not understand how you feel, or maybe even someone who could hurt you. Hey, I bet you could really use some good food." Not to mention a long, hot shower with a lot of soap.

Kot sees hesitation, and waits as calmly as she can. If Tessa returns, it might trigger more panic in the girl. It feels better to deal with this alone and as quickly as possible.

When a reply comes, the girl's voice sounds thin and strange from disuse, but she speaks urgently. "I do have food. I know what to eat. I get it from the forest and the water. My mother taught me. And there are other places I find stuff. I don't take much." Her face could only be described as beseeching. "I'm fine. I'm doing great here by myself. Please don't tell anybody I'm here. I escaped from a boat. Just leave me alone. Please!"

The last word sounds desperate, and she drops the blanket to bring her dirty hands together, like a beggar.

"But this must be such a hard life. So cold. And you have to be lonely." The matted dark head of hair shakes quickly in denial. "Well, no matter how careful you are, sooner or later someone else is bound to find you here, and that idea scares me. Plus, without any heating, this really won't be workable when winter comes again."

Kot can see that discussing a distant future is useless with someone that age, and changes tack. "How long have you been here?"

The firm little chin rises defiantly. Someone has certainly taught this girl a few life skills, maybe augmenting an inherently strong character. Another glance around the room confirms that there is no question of this girl's courage and resourcefulness. No child Kot has even known would have been able to figure out survival like this, and pitifully few adults would either.

"I'm not sure. A few weeks, I guess. And I don't care about any of that. Don't worry. I'm doing great. I really am. Please."

Kot is aware that whatever choice she makes is going to profoundly affect this brave child. However, she is totally unsure about what that very fast choice should be. This is absolutely no way for a child to live, and besides, whatever made her run away needs to be discovered, and dealt with. Officially reported, probably. And then Kot catches herself: the big, black pot criticizing a small but apparently capable kettle. Finally, she smiles with as much persuasion as possible.

"Okay, look. I give you my word that, for now, I won't tell anyone you're here. I promise. I need to go, but I'll be back to check on you very soon, just to make sure you're doing okay. Maybe bring you some yummy things to eat. Okay? Do we have a deal?"

Kot hopes that, in the meantime, she might be able to do some research and figure out who this girl is. She also correctly predicts that she may regret her decision, especially during the coming night. But at least she now knows where the lighthouse key is hidden, and roughly which days the caretaker is usually gone.

Camas follows Kot's gaze to her meagre but suddenly precious belongings, and nods with more confidence this time.

"My name is Camas." After saying her name, her gaze flits away again, as if alarmed that she revealed that information.

"Hi, Camas. I used to be Kathleen. But like I said, I'm mostly Kot now. For what it's worth, I also arrived on Atticus as a refugee from the sea."

Kot wonders at her own honesty with even a child. She reaches out to gently touch Camas's cheek, gives her a smile, and hurries outside to intercept Tessa.

Tessa looks anxious as she comes around from the bluff. "He says that the truck with my first gazillion plants is now going to arrive in about three hours, instead of in two days. If he doesn't come over on this afternoon's boat it won't be for another week. Can you spare an hour when we get home to help me get ready? I'm sorry I had to abandon you like that. Did you have a good look around?"

Kot avoids eye contact during her answer, and at the top of the driveway she stops and pretends to tie her boot while Tessa carries on. She looks back at the lighthouse, and catches a glimpse of a small face in the second-floor window. If Camas takes that risk too often, she will definitely be discovered. Kot wonders what the hell she is supposed to do with this situation. As if the chaos of her own life isn't enough.

On their way back to the garden centre, Tessa tells her, "Old Harvey in the house back there told me that he found a strange puddle in front of his wood stove earlier this month. And he's got the idea in his head that someone is stealing things. I hope he isn't losing it mentally now as well, poor guy."

Kot murmurs something sympathetic, and changes the subject to work matters.

~ NINETEEN ~

She'd worked until close to midnight, but Kot's alarm wakes her early. She throws on gardening clothes and carries a mug of coffee downstairs to the garden centre.

After the driver had unloaded close to a thousand plants yesterday afternoon, Tessa looked like she was in shock. So Kot had offered to place as many of them as she could on her own this morning, letting Tessa meet her Saturday client commitments.

Besides the creativity required for the Glenhurst project, this physical work might contribute some useful mental distraction for Kot. She wants to help Tessa make her garden nursery a welcoming place in which people can take pleasure—before, of course, purchasing components of the scenery to take home.

The yard surface is fine gravel, so Kot begins in the covered area and defines two meandering paths by lining and backing them with pots of shade-loving shrubs and perennials. The paths meet out in the sunshine, and then diverge once again to wind through the large yard. Although the work is hard on her back, it feels like the fun of childhood play, using a wagon, no one supervising her, and making a small world of her own in the warming sun and rain-soaked scents of early morning.

Kot masses rhodos and azaleas at different heights, some already in exuberant bloom. The vegetable and herb starters go on wheeled racks that she has assembled close to the store, and inside the rustic entrance gate she creates a cheerful welcome of Japanese maples, ferns, young wisteria, bamboo, and splashes of massed polyanthus.

When they are delivered in the coming days, she plans to tuck the benches, bird baths, sun dials, and small-scale statuary that Tessa has ordered into inviting nooks, surrounded by complementary shrubs, like an established garden that just happens to be entirely for sale.

By eleven, Kot's back is screaming, and she goes upstairs for a hot shower and some clean clothes. Last night, Tessa had mentioned as they drove that, after his appointment yesterday, the caretaker at the light station was kept in hospital for tests, so Kot seizes the opportunity to check in on Camas. She fills two tote bags with the supplies she has gathered, and pulls a hat low over her face for the walk. When she can hear no vehicles coming from either direction, she hurries through the driveway gate and up the bending lane, only slowing when she is out of sight of the road.

Kot still has no clue what to do about Camas without risking the tenuous safety they have both found. Camas said that her mother had taught her about foraging, so there was obviously at least one loving parent in her life, and maybe not that long ago. She is most likely an orphan, or at least feels like one. And if so, why shouldn't she, like Kot, be allowed to hide in what must feel like relative safety, on her own terms, until some better alternative is found. Obviously, finding that alternative is urgent. Through any number of scenarios, Camas will certainly be discovered, and inevitably turned over to the police. Then she would face an uncertain future, probably very much at odds with her nature. Such a resourceful girl might well run away again, probably resulting in a much worse outcome.

Kot's internet search of missing children in BC and news stories about kidnappings turned up no one who could be Camas. All that Kot can think of doing is to keep a close eye on the girl and to take food and supplies while she tries to learn more and build trust. Anything to avoid making Camas run away. However, since everything in the grocery bags she is carrying was purchased with Kot's own meagre earnings, that may not be feasible for long. Nor will coping with her conscience.

Inside the tower, Kot calls out quietly. Other than a faint echo, the only answer is damp silence. When she reaches the second floor, it's obvious that

Camas isn't there, but also that she has made changes. In the past twenty-four hours, she has fashioned a bookcase out of flat pieces of driftwood. Her bins and possessions are now neatly stowed, with nothing on the floor, and the ragged bedding is straightened and tidy.

Kot picks up a framed photo from the upper shelf: a big-eyed toddler, a pretty native woman, and a white man who probably barely got an arm around them before the timer clicked. All three are laughing. There is a lot of love inside that frame, and Kot's eyes fill with tears. She has a strong and sudden urge to get out of there, but puts the grocery bags on the bed and takes a minute to write a note, telling Camas that the room looks nice, that she's kept her secret, and that she will be back in a few days. "*Hoping to talk more.*" She also describes where she lives, and provides the number of the garden centre phone that she carries, although where Camas would find a phone to safely use, Kot can't imagine. She carefully puts back the key, and half-runs down the driveway.

Camas is like a fairy tale character, alone in a tower. There has to be a seriously good reason for that, and in spite of the law and societal dictates, the idea of betraying her feels seriously wrong. Still, Kot knows that she must soon tell Tessa or someone who can publicly take charge. Until that imminent day when a good course of action is clear, Kot fully intends to stay below the radar.

Tessa comes up to Kot's place to visit when she finishes work, raving about what Kot got done in the nursery this morning. She is obviously also looking forward to taking Kot out for dinner. Kot says nothing, but she has lost all interest in the dinner party. She craves rest, her fears of exposure are real, and the Glenhurst deadline looms large. However, if she backs out of this evening's invitation, more than one person's feelings might be hurt and more attention might be drawn to her than if she toughs it out. And strangely, there now seems to be more pressure from Tessa for her to attend the dinner than to meet the work deadline.

When Tessa is gone, Kot groans. Her body needs a long soak in the hot tub on her townhouse deck at home, but a shower might be better than nothing. She is about to step into the steaming spray when her cell on the bathroom counter rings. "Unavailable Number." So it isn't Tessa. Does Kot's promise to answer that business phone extend to a Saturday evening? It's probably a wrong number, but she curses and turns off the tap.

"Petal Pushers Nursery. May I help you?"

"Kot?"

Kot doesn't answer, and holds her breath. The line is full of static. "Who is this?"

The static fades somewhat. "Kot, it's me. Mich. Are you able to talk?"

By the time Kot finally steps into the shower, she's excited and on edge. Her life is about to change again. Mich is planning to come to Atticus tomorrow and stay with Kot for a couple of weeks. As necessary, she will take the commuter floatplane to Vancouver for work, and has also offered to help with the nursery: "All I'm doing is worrying about you anyway. So provided, of course, that you have the decent Wi-Fi that you claim in that remote outpost, here I come. And, Kottie… full confession. This trip is also selfish. I'm trying to drop a clinging TV anchorman. No pun intended. He's awesomely easy on the eyes, but you only have to talk to him for thirty seconds and looks don't count anymore. He also has the attention span of a mosquito, so here's hoping that if I vanish and leave no teleprompter, it will do the trick."

Kot knows that there is probably no anchorman, and that the entire reason for the visit is Mich's concern about her. But she'll take it. The prospect of having Mich here, actually living with her, is simply wonderful. Mich will be careful, and surely the risks are very small by now.

The old bathroom fan offers more noise than function, and in the fogged mirror Kot sees a softened, misty version of her face. Perhaps this first social outing on Atticus Island merits a bit more attention to her appearance than is her norm these days. She has about fifteen minutes before Tessa will pick her up, time enough. Her tools are minimal, but she can blow dry her hair and primp a bit. It would be nice to feel more feminine again. Not fragile, but just a soupçon of girly. "A stitch above slobby," as Mich would say.

Kot opens drawers and gets to work. Some recent second-hand finds should suffice for clothing: buttery soft leather ankle boots hug her tired feet over flattering charcoal leggings, and a once-expensive angora cape will provide warmth over a forest green top. It's almost like being Kathleen Cafferty again, and that feels damned good.

Kot gets Medley settled for the evening, and takes an umbrella outside. The weather has turned wet again and she sinks gratefully into the warmth of Tessa's heated sports car seats, a nice change from the truck. She is struck immediately by her companion's relaxed and happy mood, and the chat with Mich has also elevated her own attitude about this evening to one of pleasant anticipation of great food and possibly interesting company. Still, she intends to firmly limit her wine intake and maintain her all-important barriers. The reward for vigilant behaviour will arrive tomorrow: the ability to talk freely with her one and only best friend.

On the short drive, Kot describes Mich to Tessa and mentions her offer to help with the nursery. She says that her friend is looking for a break from city life, which is maybe her biggest lie yet. Tessa had already agreed to Kot having a guest at some point, and has her own reasons to readily agree to Kot's request.

Kot has passed the Chase Bay Café many times, but has never gone inside before. Tonight, candlelight twinkles through the lead-paned windows into the rain, reminding her of an old London public house in the time of Dickens. Tessa parks in the rear lot, and Kot recognizes Hunter's SUV and Roller's customized van. The truck is likely Robert Baschel's.

Tessa says, "Hey, the gang's almost all here."

Entering the front door of the café through a wave of fragrant warmth is like walking into a grandmother's hug. The perfect distance from a crackling fire, two rectangular tables have been pulled together and covered with crisp white linen. Low candelabra make the crystal glasses sparkle, and all kinds of candles glow from the mantel and windowsills.

Hunter and Roller are back near the kitchen. Hunter is leaning on a counter next to a man wearing a chef's apron who looks to be in his early fifties. That must be Rob.

Kot hangs back as Tessa greets them both affectionately and pushes open the kitchen's swinging doors to assemble her appetizer dish. Halfway in, she remembers introductions, and calls over her shoulder, "Oh, sorry! Kot, this is Rob. Rob, meet Kot Malone."

Rob's smile is warm as he holds out his hand, but then he stares at her so intently that Kot's fight or flight instinct kicks in. She wonders if the vigilant

Roller notices her instinctive calculation of the distance to the door. Beside him, Hunter's grin at Kot is goofier than usual, reminiscent of his dog.

Rob looks away as Tessa returns, then tells them that Toni Campo has been delayed by off-island clients: "In her words, she'll 'throw them on the ferry' and be here soon."

Rob joins Tessa in the kitchen and Roller steps away to take a phone call, leaving Kot alone with Hunter. He has lined up wine pairings for the evening, and pours Kot a dry pinot grigio before refilling his own glass and toasting her, his mouth humorous but his bedroom eyes at full power. Coolly, Kot returns his gaze and clinks his glass.

She is aware of Hunter's reputed knowledge of wine, as well as his generosity, although she doesn't plan to take much advantage of either this evening. Still, she's familiar with some of the labels he's selected for the evening, and their impressive price tags. Way out of her league. Presumably, Glenhurst now has a valuable wine cellar.

Kot is mildly curious to see how long it takes before he steers the conversation to self-focused celebrity stories. She also prepares her defences for some kind of inquisition about what brought her to Atticus, but after the toast he just smiles speculatively at her and looks around the café.

Then he hits her with: "So. No pressure, I'm just wondering…"

Kot tries to look calm and quickly prepares to lie. But after a pause, and perhaps a quick reconsideration, Hunter ends his sentence with: "…how the design work is coming along."

Relieved, Kot enthusiastically uses the opportunity to get more clarity on a few things, allowing her to finish the initial draft with more assurance. Hunter is interested and animated, and Kot finds it easy to keep the conversation focused on him and his property.

Hunter suddenly seems to be done with business and moves closer to her, so Kot proactively begins to interview him about his own connections with Atticus, and the process of buying Glenhurst. As long as the subject isn't herself, Kot is finding it a pleasure to chat normally to an interesting man of any occupation. However, she also hasn't forgotten Hunter's petulance after she didn't gush like a sycophant about his landscaping ideas.

In the kitchen, Rob and Tessa work in companionable silence. Tessa has brought prepared nests of puff pastry and is filling them with chunks of rich French brie, pieces of fresh fig, her spicy homemade apple chutney, and sprigs of thyme. When the baking sheets go into the oven, the flavours will be melded by the melting rich cheese. Rob already has a Peruvian chicken dish in another oven, and a fragrant vegetarian curry for Toni. His soft and puffy pita discs have just gone in, and he only needs to chop garnishes to add at the last minute.

When Tessa turns from the oven she is a little startled to see Rob staring at her thoughtfully, with a knife in his hand.

"Is something wrong, Rob?"

He shakes his head, but his expression shows concern.

"I hope not. I'm just wondering what you know about Kot. What's her last name?"

"Oh. Malone. She says." Tessa pauses. "As a person, and as someone to work with, I think she's pretty solid. In fact, fantastic in many ways."

"Okay, and I can understand why Hunter commented on her looks before you arrived. I also gather from him that she knows how to defend herself verbally. But what has she told you about her history? Do you know what brought her here?"

"To be honest, next to nothing. Steve was too shy to pry—and I've just got the same story that he did: that she's trying to make a new life after an abusive relationship. Apparently, she and her dog arrived at the marina in a kayak. Steve said that she was acting cool but looked like she'd been camping, and accepted his offer of work like it was a life raft. It's pretty clear that she's run away from *something*. You don't just leave your life, grab your dog, and take off with nothing without a damned good reason. And you should see her when we're out in public, even on little Atticus—hiding her face with sunglasses and a ball cap. But her eyes are always looking around. She is gradually less jumpy, and I'm just waiting for the right moment to ask more. We haven't had much down time together. Maybe I need to get her drunk. She's an expert at steering conversations to be all about other people, and of course most folks are happy to talk about themselves."

Rob nods thoughtfully, and Tessa continues, "An old friend of hers is coming to visit from Vancouver tomorrow though, and I'm hopeful I'll hear more from her about our mystery woman. Kot certainly knows what she's doing with gardening and design work, but I'm sure that she was working in some completely different field before she came here. She let it slip that she is familiar with celebrities." Her head nods at Kot and Hunter, laughing about something together over by the windows. "So you have to wonder."

Then Tessa remembers Rob's police history, his undercover work, and wonders what he might know about Kot but hasn't told her. She finally fully realizes for the first time how stupid she may have been, and must certainly appear, to have hired a stranger without knowing more about her and getting references, never mind now depending so heavily on her. Oh, the perils of desperation. She takes a deep breath.

"Why, Rob? Do you think I should be concerned about her? Oh, man."

"I don't know yet. I trust your judgement, and Steve's too. And for what it's worth, my own first instincts match yours." He looks down, then back at her. "But here's the concern. When I did my usual trip to town this past week, Rachel worked here alone, right through lunch. Mondays are slow, and she'd locked up and gone home by the time I got back. But the next morning she told me about a strange guy who came in. He ordered one black coffee after another and just hung around. He was watching the door and people going by on the road, and just before the lunch crowd arrived, he was the only customer. Rachel almost crashed into him as she went out to clear tables. He was on his way into this kitchen. He would have known she was by herself, so it scared her, obviously. He seemed jittery, and she was prepared for a robbery, or to fight him off. But he just pulled a photo out of his pocket, a headshot of a woman, and asked Rachel if she'd seen her. Rachel told him she hadn't, which was true, and then suggested that he order something else or settle his bill. He said he wanted another coffee, and thank God Rachel has such a cool head and didn't try to evict him on her own. She just got him to sit down again, and asked him questions while she worked. He said that the photo was of his older sister. She's disappeared, and the family is worried about her and thinks she's probably on one of the Gulf Islands. It sounded lame to Rachel, but she just got him his coffee and people started coming in for lunch."

Tessa watches her appetizers bake through the glass door of the wall oven, almost willing Rob not to continue. But he does.

"Before he finally left, he wanted to know when the owner would be here, so he could show me the photo. Rachel said that she was vague about that with him. Then the guy said he'd probably head over to Mayne, then return to Atticus and look for me. He gave her a business card."

Rob retrieves it from the drawer under the till, and shows it to Tessa: *Derrick Bond, Private Enquiries*.

"At least he didn't pick James as his fake first name—but so much for the missing sister story. He must have thought Rachel looked impressed, because he got the bright idea to start hitting on her. She probably just said anything to get rid of him and I don't care one way or the other, but she said that she told him he'd be better off hitting on someone who plays for the other team. He called her a 'fucking dyke,' but at least he left.

Rob silently chops a bunch of parsley, slides it deftly to the side of the board, and reaches for the cilantro.

Finally, Tessa turns to look at him. "So what are you thinking, Rob?"

"To be honest, I didn't give it much thought at the time. Just one of those strange encounters we get here, and Rachel said that she only told me about it in case the loser actually did come back, looking for me."

Rob puts down his knife, and faces her. Tessa already knows what's coming.

"And yesterday, he showed up again. Definitely an addict, probably on a combo of things. He skipped the sob story and just showed me the photo. It was a head shot of an attractive blonde woman that I'd never seen before. And yes, it was definitely your Kot Malone. When she came in with you this evening, I couldn't remember at first why I recognized her face, but then I knew. Maybe nothing at all on the guy's card is true, but I think it's likely that someone else hired him to find her. I'm sorry, but I don't want you involved in anything inadvertently, and you need to know the truth. If you want me to talk to Kot, with or without you, I will. Whatever's going on, she should at least be warned."

"Absolutely. Yes, let's talk to her together. I suppose it was good that you could honestly say that you hadn't seen her, at that time. But no matter how hard she tries to hide it, Kot's face will gradually become familiar to more people here." Tessa shakes her head in self-disgust. "Shit, shit, shit. I obviously need to grow up, and not take such a leap of faith about someone I know nothing about. Thanks for telling me, Rob. Do you think he'll be back again?"

"I don't know. Kot is probably a victim, or innocent, at least. If I were still in my old profession, I'd want the goods on the guy looking for her, which is hard when we don't even know his real name or have a photo of him. There's nothing online about an investigator named Derrick Bond. Whoever he is, I don't want him hanging around here, and will let him know that if I see him again. Anyway, let's just enjoy this evening. I'll be done here in a minute. Cheer up."

Rob gives Tessa a hug and peers into the oven at her tray. "Those look done, and they smell fantastic!"

Toni Campo's arrival sends a chilly blast from the door all the way to the kitchen, and Rob and Tessa go out to greet her. Kot is introduced to Toni, who launches into an entertaining description of the anonymous, off-island buyers she has just dropped at the ferry. The laughter flows easily as Hunter refreshes their glasses with a light pinot noir.

Kot is consciously aware of feeling like she has been welcomed into a close- knit community, a caring tribe. There are nothing but good vibes in this café, and Hunter is just one of the gang. She helps Tessa serve her appys on little plates, and for a few minutes the group stands in a rough circle to enjoy them.

Hunter says, "Okay, time for some island gossip. I've been feeling deprived. What have you got, Rob?"

"It just so happens that I can deliver something, sir." Rob turns to Kot, the only newcomer. "You may have already figured out that actual events here can be even stranger than the stories that people make up, and it's sometimes hard to tell the difference. Still, this one isn't even second hand, so … The Tyler boys aren't quite as famous as our friend here," a nod to Hunter, "but they've become sort of island legends. They're opening up something they're calling 'Magic Island Tours.' I don't know whether that refers to the island, or what they will offer their clients, or the substances that inspired their plan, but they asked me the other day if I thought people might believe that you don't need to wear a seat belt if you're riding in the middle of a back seat on Atticus, as long as there's someone sitting on either side. Their truck only has two belts in the back, and they would like to fit in one more person."

Tessa says, "That truck is a wreck. But anyway, I thought both of the Tyler boys had their driving licences suspended for too many DUI's."

"Yes, that is, indeed, a bit of a problem. The punch line to this particular story is that they have someone else in mind. Their dad knows the most about island history, and obviously, he's the only one in the family who's still legal behind the wheel."

The others groan and cover their eyes in dismay. Kot sips her wine, and waits to understand.

Tessa tells her, "Old Man Tyler has never been the most stable guy, but since his wife passed, he's developed a sad habit of trying to drive off cliffs. Luckily, they all have sturdy guardrails, but that front truck fender isn't looking too good anymore. He might not be the perfect choice for a tour driver. Sorry. Island humour."

Rob and Toni bring in the casseroles, pita puffs, Toni's salad of fresh arugula, pecans, and goat cheese, and Roller's arepas de queso. Hunter heads for the chair beside Kot, but is outmaneuvered by Tessa and has to settle for the one opposite.

Tessa smiles innocently across the table. Her determination to prevent Hunter from having close proximity to Kot all evening is stronger still after hearing Rob's news in the kitchen. At least until the Glenhurst plan is finalized, Tessa would like to stay several steps ahead of any flirtations there.

Kot pours sparkling water, the only contribution she was allowed to bring, and catches Hunter watching her. These guys, who think they can have whatever woman they want, just like the creepy Tweeter-in-Chief south of the border. She can nevertheless feel one of her troublesome blushes coming on. She's also noticed that their charming host is pretty much transfixed by Toni at the other end of the table, with no evidence that his feelings are reciprocated. Poor Rob. He seems like a really good guy.

Trying to ignore Hunter, Kot gets Toni talking about her work, and pretending interest in the real estate market on Atticus. The café's small conversations evolve into group ones, like streams meeting a river. Kot is asked about her gardening interests, but to her relief, nothing more personal. She wonders if Tessa warned them. As their voices rise above the rain battering the roof and windows, she relaxes again in the warmth of the café and company.

As dinner plates are cleared, Hunter seizes the opportunity to move to Tessa's vacated chair, and leans toward Kot like an interviewer holding a microphone. Without hesitation he says, "Thank you for being with us tonight, Ms. Malone. May I say, you're looking beautiful, in a manner that might be best described as understated elegance. I know our audience would like to hear what my garden designer has being doing with her life to date. And exactly where, in fact, she has been doing it."

Kot has completely sabotaged herself by dismally failing to stick to only one glass of wine. So here it is, and worse still, the person asking is the famous guy with the puppy dog eyes and tousled hair. That naturally lopsided smile. Her potential employer.

Still, to Hunter Nott or anyone, Kot intends to provide the truth, and nothing but the truth. Just not the whole truth. She summons her own acting strengths, and the accent of a flirtatious southern belle.

"Why, clearly, Mr. Nott, ah've spent my entiah life gettin' ready to do a gawden design on Atticus Island. Y'all know that."

Hunter rolls his eyes and continues to hold the imaginary mic, clearly awaiting a serious answer. Meanwhile, Kot sobers up a bit and remembers her lines.

"Okay, well, I grew up in a pretty village in Eastern Ontario. It's been ruined with McMansions and strip malls since, but there are still a few of the stone buildings from the 1800s. Some unspoiled nature, that kind of thing. It was a safe place to be a child, and I know now how privileged I was. All the neighbourhood kids wandered the countryside with our friends and dogs, damming ditches and things, and in winter, everyone tobogganed at the golf course. Then when we were teenagers, we knocked tennis balls around on the courts beside the village green and necked in cars. I went to Queens, got married young, did some travelling, got divorced, and then moved west. What about you? I should tell you that I don't follow tabloids or much online stuff, so you'll need to start from scratch."

Hunter is delighted that he doesn't have to fight preconceived negative impressions. "Born in Nanaimo, but West Vancouver from the age of three. I also have one brother, two years older than me. He's a nurse, and pretty much the real life hero of the family. We came to the family cottage on Atticus for every summer holiday, and some Christmases. While we were here, my brother and I were also lucky to live free-range. We probably got into almost as much trouble as we wanted to. That old cottage got torn down after my parents had to sell it, but I've never stopped missing that life, or this island. So… it's definitely a dream come true to own Glenhurst."

Kot smiles and nods with interest, making it clear that she is waiting to hear more. Hunter notes the novelty of being with a woman who is really listening to what he's saying, instead of preoccupied with herself or half-gone on pharmaceuticals.

She asks, "How long did you stay in Vancouver after high school?"

"About four years. I was three years into a fine arts degree at Simon Fraser when I dropped out to study acting. I never got the degree."

"That's so sad. Just think of how successful you might have been if you'd stuck with it."

Charmed, Hunter laughs. "Or not, more likely. Then, also like you, I had a starter marriage. We met at the acting school, and then both tried to start careers in LA. Sarah wanted to make it as a model, but she suffered from chronic depression, and it was hard for her to stick with it. In fact, it got in the way of a lot of things. She dropped out of one course of treatment after another. My own career wasn't exactly thriving, and we started to hang out in what I call 'striver circles.' Pretty typical, in Hollywood fringe society. Booze and drugs were everywhere. It was just a phase for me, but Sarah soon headed straight down a black diamond run."

"That must have been a terrible time. Did you guys have any kids?"

"Nah. I made sure of that." He stops, and Kot leaves him the silence. "And in the end, Sarah had a fatal overdose. I found her." Hunter's face reflects real and painful memories.

"How awful. I'm truly sorry."

Kot finds herself genuinely sad for Hunter and has to stop herself reaching for his hand. She is also reluctantly shifting an attitude or two.

"Thanks. It's my therapist's strongly held opinion that I'm still dealing with it, and, of course, with mother issues. The fact is, my mom was—still is—a funny, brave lady who never smothered or rejected my brother or me, just respected us. So I'm not buying that particular therapeutic formula. My personal theory is that most things that are wrong in my life are my own fault, and it's up to me to fix them."

Kot wonders if Hunter is specifically referring to his relationships with women, or if there are other serious issues as well. In any case, his honesty is endearing. If that's really what it is. So hard to tell, with an actor. Her cynical side is trying to fight its way back to the top, but is losing to the cabernet that he poured for her. It really is superb.

She says, "I guess a lot of issues start in childhood, which means digging deeper than we can even remember. Voice of experience, here."

In a corner of his vision, Hunter spots Tessa sending anxious looks their way from the kitchen door. She will probably intervene soon, and while Hunter would like to keep talking to Kot all night, he really just wants to know a little more. He doesn't intend to push her to a point where she won't want to spend time with him, but she seems okay to keep going. And Kot realizes that this getting-acquainted game now requires her to share more personal information, to match his. All right, she is prepared with her own strategy and limits.

"Yes, well, while my ex and I were working abroad and having risky adventures, things were okay. But once we were back home again, there was a big vacuum. It was like each of us had grown in a different direction while we were away, and didn't know how to mesh our gears anymore. Not unusual. And the belief that if we just had a child, we'd find a common road we could both follow—well, that's pretty common, too. I did finally get pregnant, but it was ectopic and I almost died. I was numb for a long time after that, and eventually I knew he was seeing someone else. By then, I was honestly ready to let go anyway."

Kot says no more about her husband, who had evolved from being her biggest fan to someone who never missed an opportunity to belittle her in public. Mich had never hidden her dislike for him, but had reluctantly supported Kot through those years, and on through Kot's struggles to accept a childless future and to eventually let the sun go down on the marriage.

Another gulp of wine, and Kot lurches through the barriers that she had so firmly set. "I lived with someone else for a while later, but a few years ago, I virtually married my career. I've been working in a not-for-profit conservation org, and mostly seven days a week, literally trying to save the world. That's meant dealing with rich and famous donor partners and board members." She gives him a wry look that makes Hunter chuckle. "Please don't share this with anyone yet, but I got pretty burnt out, and was also in what may have been an unhealthy relationship with a donor. So I took off with Medley for a serious sabbatical to look for perspective. In fact, I think I may need a whole new universe of perspectives."

"You and me both. Another thing we have in common. And are you finding any yet?"

Kot doesn't answer as Tessa moves into the seat across the table and brightly asks, "So have you two sorted out all of the plan details by now? Are we still going to meet on Wednesday morning?"

Kot gives her a reassuring smile, glad that Tessa unknowingly drew a big black line under the previous conversation. "Hunter has clarified a few things I was wondering about."

"Ditto." Hunter is grinning at her. He has learned some key information about Kot, although he senses strategic omissions and adjustments. But that's just the smart thing to do, and he did the same.

Kot tells Tessa, "And yes, I'll get some more done tomorrow before my friend Mich arrives, and by Wednesday, I think we'll be far enough along to make a meeting worthwhile."

Hunter smiles broadly at that news, but is now anxious about the gender and context of this Mich person.

"Great. I'll try to be fresh as a daisy this time." Inspiration strikes. "Kot, bring your friend along if you want, if you're sure that he or she will pass the Roller test." To his disappointment, Kot just nods her thanks.

Tessa looks happy, and changes the subject. "Have you had any SARS call-outs since you arrived, Hunter?"

At Kot's puzzled look, Tessa explains, "He volunteers in search and rescue work, flying his own helicopter, and he covers the fuel costs, too." Back to Hunter, "But you use an alias, right?"

"Yeah, and so far no one's breached my privacy. No, there hasn't been a call yet, and I hope that lasts. It depends how many volunteers are available for each particular area. Right now, I just want to stay right here. Selfish, but that's me."

Tessa says, "Wasn't there a dramatic one last year? A boat wreck?"

"Oh, right. That was last November, after I'd just arrived at my Vancouver place. A fishing boat had radioed a mayday call off the Sunshine Coast, but it went down quickly. My bird can't actually rescue anyone, but I had a powerful searchlight retrofitted, the kind that you can move from inside, and

I just happened to spot a life raft. It was quite a distance from where the team had projected the boat was when it went down, so it was just luck. The two people in it were rescued, but the next day the body of the skipper was washed up on a beach further along the coast."

Kot says the obvious, but is sincere. She's also switched to water. "Still, it must be very rewarding work. Bravo."

"Thanks. But most of the time it's a wild goose chase, or someone else finds them. You're correct that it's the urgency and sense of purpose that I like. There's a lot of tedium involved on film sets, waiting to play make-believe."

Maybe it's the mention of film sets, but Kot unexpectedly finds herself wondering if Hunter is romantically involved with someone. Just because he has been flirting with her doesn't rule that out, by any means. Their shared confidences didn't get that far.

At the other end of the table, Rob tears himself away from Toni and returns with dessert plates. They talk as a group again, and Kot listens contentedly. She catches Rob looking at her thoughtfully, but he just smiles and raises his coffee cup to her.

It's close to midnight when Tessa drops her off. That gathering turned out to a lot more fun than she'd expected, more than she can remember having in a long time. Medley explodes outside and they go back down the stairs for his bedtime ramble. The rain has ended, but a few heavy clouds still float across the night sky. Kot remains a little tipsy. She's out of practice with alcohol, but that might change once Mich rolls in, later tomorrow. Her pending arrival seems unreal, and also makes Kot nervous. Meanwhile, she faces another early morning of design work while Tessa does a run to Victoria to pick up more nursery stock.

Medley searches for the perfect spot to do his thing while Kot wanders in the small field, listening to the night and reviewing her conversation with Hunter. Flirting is likely just a habit for a guy like him: separate a pretty filly from the herd and waste no time before mating with her. And besides the fact that she's still in love with Ben, even a short fling with a famous person like Hunter would involve terrifying risks of publicity. And really, does she still need practice in inappropriate entanglements?

The distant call of a barred owl in the neighbouring park brings memories that are still raw. Maybe the resourceful Mich might help her to find a way back home, on all levels. If she can't get there soon, she may not even have a job to return to. She suddenly wonders if home can be defined as simply the place where your stuff happens to be. And stuff can always be moved.

Medley bounds back to join her. Along with Mich, he is her only link between her old life and this one. She stops on the upstairs porch for a moment before going inside. The lighthouse on the point is silhouetted in the moonlight. Alone inside is the bravest person Kot has ever met. She realizes with guilt that, throughout the entire evening, she didn't give one thought to Camas. But now she prays for warmth and comfort for the kindred young soul in the dark tower. By thc time her head hits the pillow, Kot has decided to confide in Mich about Camas.

Maybe her guard has been lowered by wine and fatigue, but something unexpectedly awakens in her body for the first time in weeks. Something triggered by a memory of burning brown eyes and a crooked smile. Kot's eyes open wide again with the knowledge that her currently high libido has nothing to do with Benson Northcott.

~ TWENTY ~

Rob only notices that Tessa's truck is parked further back on the car deck when the *Chinook* is approaching the dock in Chase Bay. Sleepy-eyed, Tessa rolls down her window when he taps on it.

"Sorry, but after last night, the need for a nap was bigger than I was."

"Tell me about it. I slept on the ferry going over this morning. But that potluck was fun, and everything went really fast today."

"Same for me. Every wholesaler had my pick-ups ready to go."

"And it's quite a bonus to get this ferry home, isn't it? I told Rachel I'd be on the evening one, but she'll be finished at the café by the time I get back anyway, so I'll unload on my own."

"How about if we help each other? Kot's taken her friend from Vancouver for an island tour this afternoon, so she won't be around. It's looking like it could rain again, and we'll be able to get things transferred and under cover faster at both places if we do it together."

Rob nods. "Sure. Let's do your stuff first. When do you think you'll be able to open the nursery?"

"Maybe by next weekend. I have enough inventory now. Kot's friend Mich is apparently knowledgeable about all things software, and she's offered her help, so things are coming together. Which doesn't mean I'm not still spazzing out."

Rob laughs in sympathy. "It will all get easier, but running a business is always an adventure. That reminds me—I meant what I said about talking to Kot with you. Let's do it within the next couple of days."

Their tires splash through puddles and up the hill to the nursery. Once everything from Tessa's truck is under shelter, she follows Rob back down to the café. Its "Closed" sign is visible as they approach, but Rob is surprised to see Rachel's scooter still in the back parking lot, along with Toni Campo's Mercedes. Some problem must have kept Rachel at work, but the bright side is that Toni is probably helping and he will get to see her.

An empty semi-trailer thunders and rattles into the ferry terminal, making communication impossible. Rob opens the back of his truck and then hurries up the back stairs of the café while Tessa climbs into the canopied truck bed to prepare for unloading. The driver of the noisy truck applies the brakes and shuts it down as Rob unlocks the kitchen door. At first, what he sees in the dimly lit room makes no sense. But after a few seconds, Rob flees back to his truck and starts the motor.

Tessa yells a warning that she is in the open back and he kills the engine again. He rests his forehead on the steering wheel. What an idiot he has been. It has never occurred to him that Toni's lack of a partner, or at least a series of boyfriends, was due to anything but her busy life and demanding standards. Why the hell has she kept her preferences a secret? Confused questions arise. Rob realizes that even though he ran away from the two women like a terrified child, he would probably now be seen as a threat, especially for young Rachel, his employee. His first impulse is to throw a few things from his apartment into a suitcase and disappear for a time.

Rob's eyes are screwed shut, and his jaw is set. He doesn't raise his head as Tessa climbs in beside him and places a firm hand on his arm. "Hey, buddy. What's going on? Come on. You're scaring me." If Tessa's hunch is correct about what Rob encountered inside, she can imagine the carnage of his heart.

After a minute, Rob removes his hands from the steering wheel and slowly shakes his head in disbelief. But he still doesn't open his eyes.

"Oh Rob. Were the two of them…?"

"I'm so fucking stupid. Am I the only one who didn't know?"

His breathing is ragged. Tessa waits before answering, choosing her words with care.

"Well, I didn't. I don't really know Rachel, and Toni has never confided in that way with me. It's none of my business, but I've wondered. I've also hazarded a guess now and then about your feelings for Toni, Rob, and in that regard, I'm probably not the only one. Still, I doubt that anyone other than you and me and those two in there know for sure that they're an item. I'm so sorry, my friend."

"My God, have I been that obvious? That's even worse. That probably means Toni would have noticed it, too. Maybe even Rachel." He winces in fresh embarrassment.

"Look, young man, you are a very long way from being the first to find yourself in this situation, and I'm also pretty sure that one day you and I will laugh about this." Rob finally opens his wet eyes and looks at Tessa like she's crazy. "Okay, too soon to say that. Anyway, I promise you my complete discretion." She's quiet for a minute. "Rob, may I make a suggestion? I think you'll be glad if you can do it."

Rob gives a small nod.

"Do you think you could make yourself go right back in there, and let them know that you'll keep this confidential? I'm certain that would be a huge relief for both of them at this point, but I also think it might be the best way for you to regain some feeling of control. After all, it's your kitchen, your business, and you can claim the higher ground of an employer. It also can't hurt to act like a friend, if you possibly can. I'm willing to go with you."

Rob stares at the dashboard miserably and doesn't answer. But then he puts his hand on Tessa's as a gesture that he'll do it alone, gets out, and trudges back up the stairs to the kitchen. He seems calm when he returns and thanks Tessa for suggesting that he do that, but says that that he would prefer to leave the unloading until later. Tessa gives him a long hard hug and leaves. Tessa leaves. Rob tries not to run as he heads around the building to the private stairs to his apartment. He locks the door for perhaps the first time ever, and stands back from the window to watch the women leave a few minutes later.

Just before the weekend, Rachel told him that she'd started online property management courses, and Rob had seen the writing on the wall that it might not be long before he'd have to look for yet another assistant. Now he realizes that Rachel and Toni may not just be lovers, but may also be planning to work together. Well, bully for them.

As Toni's car disappears over the crest of the hill, Rob's brain kicks into a review of the past year through a new lens. After Marie left him in such a brutal and cowardly way, he'd felt like a faded blur of a man, lacking shape or substance, a walking question mark without the defining entity of their long marriage. His own reflection seemed to mock him in the mirror. He stopped shaving and avoided mirrors, and when he next checked in, his appearance better matched the tsunami within. Gradually, he'd begun to learn solitude, and soon to wonder if he was missing Marie, specifically, or just having someone else around. In time, he'd started to shave again, and also to parse the advantages of living alone. The complete lack of disagreements, negotiations, and compromises held unexpected sweetness. More recently, whenever he has pictured himself living with Toni, strife wasn't a concern. She works hard, and seems to value equality and justice. Oh, Toni.

He collapses onto the couch with one arm over his face in renewed self-disdain. Once a chump, always a chump.

A disembodied announcement from a ferry carries over the bay. Rob suddenly sits up, punches the arm of the couch, and gives a loud whoop of self-mockery. Yes, he may be male, pale, and getting stale, but life does, indeed, go on. Ignoring the cases of wine down in the truck, he makes a Maori warrior face at his reflection in the window, reheats some leftover pizza, and washes it down with a can of Coke. Heartburn may keep his heartache company later on, but at least he'll still be on the wagon.

Just before dark, he heads back down to the parking lot—his parking lot—to unload his supplies. Soon enough, he'll be facing a completely new kind of early morning with Rachel. He'd like to feel organized, if nothing else.

TWENTY-ONE

Kot is having difficulty standing still as she hides behind a huge pot of bamboo inside the nursery gate, waiting for Mich to arrive. She finished the Glenhurst design just an hour ago, allowing Tessa time to review it before they go to see Hunter.

The distant *thump-thump* of vehicles crossing the ferry ramp drifts up the hill. Most of them turn right, but a small parade splits off to the north, and in the middle of that, a sporty little Audi doggedly tailgates a lumbering camper van until the crossroads, then peels into the garden centre parking lot.

By prearrangement, Mich waits in her car until the remaining vehicles have passed, then drives around to a hidden area at the back, where Kot has gone to welcome her. The two old friends run to each other and embrace while Medley whines with excitement and whines around Mich's legs.

During the lunch that Kot has ready, Mich reports on her efforts to get there secretly, and gets praise for taking such pains. Kot wants Mich to be able to find her way around Atticus independently, so they get into the Audi for an island tour.

Kot immediately enquires about the TV anchorman suitor. Mich tucks her angled swing of glossy hair behind an ear and shows no signs of lying. "Oh he's an okay guy, but basically quite smitten with himself and probably just looking for arm candy. He's likes instant gratification, so I'm happy to provide some character development there. And I'm by no means that desperate. I'm fine enough on my own, at this point." She smiles over at Kot. "I await a true nobleman, as you know. One who can also support himself, at a minimum. Oh, and worship me beyond all reason, of course. But I'm here to talk about your dysfunctional existence, not mine. This is obviously a beautiful place, but you had such a full life, and you must be missing so much, aren't you?"

A work text arrives on the car display, and Mich jabs at the *Ignore* button. Kot directs her to pull into an ocean outlook, where Mich immediately ignores the view and turns to Kot.

"I don't think I've ever been with you, even for just this long, without your phone buzzing a few times as well. Are you feeling isolated? And at night here, it must be, well, pitch black, and it's so quiet that I'm definitely going to need earplugs. How long before you go nuts?"

"That's what's so strange, Mich. I love it. I've also realized that it's also just who I am. I'm actually thriving on being away from the city, never mind trying to fundraise millions. It's a quirky place, but I do feel safer here for now, and that's important."

"Well, I sure get that part. But how are you managing financially? I assume you can't access your accounts."

"Yeah, that certainly sucks. I have to assume paychecks are continuing to go in and mortgage payments roll out. I haven't had to pay rent here yet, and Tessa's giving me cash for now. She'll probably want me on payroll when she has her software set up—which, by the way, she would deeply appreciate your help with. Tomorrow morning, if possible."

"Sure, that timing would work. And I'm happy to mess that up for her, if you'd like to continue getting cash."

Mich finally turns to look at the view, and the tour resumes. They pass the River Run Pub, with big dented doors and a shortage of windows that keeps its interior dark on even the brightest day. The usual suspects' vehicles are parked outside. Further on is a small shopping centre with grocery and hardware stores, a pharmacy, book store, and liquor outlet. There is a short lineup outside the pot store. Then, around more bends and over more hills, they pass a second-hand shop, library, school, and medical clinic. Opposite the clinic is a field full of oxeye daisies just starting to bloom, a herd of alpaca, and several miniature goats. Every so often Mich slows down and peers at the roadside stands selling early microgreens, flowers, and everything from homemade candles to local jams.

She says, "All very cute. But seriously, you must at least be lonely."

"To be honest, I'm missing very few people. That said, I try not to think about how concerned some folks must be, Ben included, from what you've told me. It's probably good that my parents aren't around anymore to worry themselves crazy. My brother must have noticed my lack of communication by now, but I can't risk being in touch with him when anyone looking for me might be also monitoring him. And, it's hard to concede, but my work team may have already figured out how to carry on without me." Kot pauses. "My big concern right now is that you haven't put yourself at risk by coming here."

"Well, remember that it was my choice to come. And my big concern is that I might be bringing danger to you again. So, touché."

Kot squeezes Mich's hand. "I'm so grateful you're here. And you know, after all that stress, and frankly, terror, I have to admit that I've gained a different perspective since I landed here. Maybe we all get so wrapped up in the day-to-day lives that we've drifted into that we lose perspective. Maybe we don't even realize we've trapped ourselves." She's quiet for a moment. "I mean, I've always tried to see a light at the end of any tunnel. But for the first time, I'm wondering whether tunnels and lights can sometimes be confused."

"Whoa. Too much for my simple mind. But it sounds like you might be looking at making changes when you back."

"Yeah, and it's also possible that I'm subconsciously just finding ways to accommodate the present reality. That would make sense. Anyway, I certainly did miss you and the freedom to talk whenever we want. It's been very lonely at times. And Ben—but I was already missing him before. As far as material things go: probably my lovely big bed and bathtub the most. And my laptop and electronics all set up how I like them, or, basically, having them at all. My books and music. Mostly, the ease of having exactly what I like around me, or easily accessible. But in the end, it's all pretty superficial. That said, could I please use your laptop later on to research a few things?"

Mich agrees, with a laugh. Kot doesn't want to upset her, so hesitates before ploughing on. "I got an unexpected rush of gratitude the other day, about my career and home and all that. But Mich, it almost felt like all of it was already in the past."

"Yikes. I hope not. For one thing, I'm sorry, but I doubt that things are going that well without you at work. Jack must have designated someone to take the temporary lead, but of course I haven't made any calls to find out. Maybe it's me who needs to do some adjusting, but this sure isn't what I expected to hear from you."

"I know. Maybe losing all control can also bring freedom. I'll get back to you on that. The fact is, the longer I'm here, the less I'm thinking about that work and those people, and the more I'm focusing on daily life and the people here. Also, after I've been physically working hard all day, I'm too tired to think at all, and I'm sleeping reasonably well. Short of medication, exhaustion seems to be the best treatment for brain worms in the wee hours."

After a couple of hours, they have driven all of the main roads, and Mich claims to know enough to get where she needs to go without complete dependence on the island's unreliable GPS. So they find a sandy beach and relax between Mich's pinging phone messages. When they return to Kot's place later there are boxes and display racks stacked high under the shelter of the store entrance. Tessa must have arrived home on an earlier ferry than expected, and Kot finds a note from her: a reminder that she will need help from them both tomorrow morning, and also suggesting that Kot compensate herself for her recent long workdays by taking another afternoon off after that.

When the dinner dishes are done Kot and Mich get cosy with glasses of pinot noir from the case that Michy brought and in the luxurious notion of having time together in the days to come. Mich wants to hear more about Hunter Nott.

"He's actually quite a nice guy, and his life hasn't always been easy. Tessa and I are going back to Glenhurst on Wednesday, but she told me today that she won't be able to stay with me there for more than a few minutes. She needs to do a big planting job at the marina, so she'll just make sure that Hunter's okay with the plan so far and then leave me to it. She told me to make sure that Hunter behaves himself." Kot rolls her eyes broadly.

"Oh, my jelly knees. Mich winks. "I brought 'the dress,' and if you don't want him what's the harm in me having a go? But the sad reality is that I have to spend Wednesday morning in Vancouver, to puncture a seriously ridiculous idea that one of my clients has come up with. Hey, you know what? You lure Hunter here later on, and I'll put on the dress and have special brownies ready. I'll settle for him fully clothed at first, until the brownies kick in. You can make yourself scarce."

"Sounds like a plan, Mich. But, well, to quote Red Green: 'Be careful what you straddle.'"

In spite of her flippancy, Kot experiences an irrational stab of jealousy at the thought of her beautiful, worldly friend and Hunter together. She puts a lid on the vision, and goes to retrieve the wine bottle. They sit in comfortable silence on the couch, facing each other like bookends, watching the propane flames.

"It's so good to have a fire, especially under what my gran called 'trying circumstances.'" Mich sounds sleepy.

Kot looks at Mich. "I know you're tired tonight, and there's no rush, but I'm hoping that while you're here you can help me figure out what level of threat I might be facing if I go home."

"Well, much as I'd love to, I'm not sure I can. As you said before, it's more than possible that there was some criminal infiltration of the Witness Protection Program, or at least a bad RCMP leak, and that you could be targeted again. And there simply can't be a next time."

Kot sighs. "Yes, there's no denying that. It's what I thought you'd say, so I guess I'll just carry on here and trust that I'll get some kind of signal one day. At least I've already made some friends, and met others who might be worth getting to know better."

"*Ooooh*—saucy. Seriously, though, I'm greatly relieved to see you're doing okay, but I have no brilliant insights to offer yet. However, I must say, most sincerely, that it will be a great day when you can ditch the Echoes of Autumn, or Auburn, or whatever it is. It's a pretty colour, but just not you. So we'd better get some of those insights ASAP."

Kot laughs. She knows Mich is ready for bed and she's also tired after her work marathons, but doesn't want this great relief of an evening to end. She swirls her wine.

"Even with no understanding of what happened—and again, I don't want to sound woo-woo—but this spring has probably been the most aware time of my life."

Mich grins, wryly. "Well, that makes sense, just in terms of feeling like you have to keep your eyes wide open at all times, just to stay alive."

"Yes, but beyond that. For instance, even before the moon appeared out there, I knew what phase it was in. It's close to the same as my last night in the safe house, just before the explosion."

Mich winces, but doesn't interrupt.

Kot goes on. "I find myself noticing things like that, that's all. Like the tides, you know? I had to take the forces of nature very seriously on that crazy kayak trip to get here. But even before that, when I was suddenly shoved into the safe house, I realized that I wanted a better life balance from then on, more time in nature, feeling like myself. Sorry to go on about that, but it's ironic, hey?"

"Christ, maybe I need some life-threatening event to reassess my own life. But I'd really rather not. Lately, I've been remembering my mother telling me

that life is the equivalent of trying to dust in the dark. We cling to our illusions of control…" She emphasizes the last word and looks meaningfully at Kot, "…but mostly we're just bumbling around in the dark and trying not to break anything."

Kot nods. "Or anyone, probably. I love your mother."

Mich gets up, and stretches. "Well, my dear, besides keeping an eye on you and wrangling my work, I want to help you and Tessa. So let's take the wonder dog outside, and then I'll crash so I might be of some use in the morning."

They watch Medley again prolong his outing to the max, and Mich says, "That long ferry trip I did today won't be workable for commuting, so I've already booked return flights for Wednesday and Friday. I told Jenn that I'm trying to get an aunt moved into a care home in Nanaimo and that it's quite complicated. She'll go with that when people ask. And God bless remote technology."

"I hope that works out. Obviously, I have no commuting experience from here. Mich, I really don't know how I would have gotten through the worst of the hell without being able to talk to you. And I hope you can shake off anchor man in this process. I have to admit, at first, I thought you were making him up."

"Oh ye of little faith. But he'll probably melt away in no time, like the wicked witch. No, my big concern about coming here was leaving Rodeo alone. He's just not trustworthy."

"Yikes. I forgot about him." Rodeo is Mich's pet goldfish, named for good reason.

"My neighbour is feeding him, but he's become even more eccentric. I got him a really big bowl, but he still keeps trying to jump out of it. He usually lands on the rim now, and then it's touch and go which way he flops. I duct taped some layers around the edge, so he can bounce back into the water off them, like a trampoline. It doesn't add to my décor, and I think Rodeo just sees it as a new challenge. Oh, and he's also started to chew on pebbles, and it's so loud that I can hear it across the room. Seriously unnerving. I caught his eye the other day while he was doing it, and I swear he leered at me. Sometimes I wonder who he really is."

Mich was also the last person to make Kot laugh like this, back in what feels like another lifetime. She locks the door and falls asleep immediately, her curtains drawn against the light of the moon.

By lunchtime the next day they have helped to get the garden centre considerably closer to opening, and Mich offers to make her work calls from her car while she takes Kot to get groceries. When Mich has a break, Kot suggests a walk, but she waits until they are almost at the light station driveway to tell Mich about Camas, and what is in the daypack she's carrying.

Mich is predictably aghast. "Kot! Your own safety isn't a sure thing. How can you also protect this girl? If something bad happens to her, you'll never forgive yourself."

Kot tries to explain, but Michy's set expression isn't promising. She's right, of course, and the knot in Kot's stomach grows as they climb the driveway. She can't continue to assist a minor to live unprotected and alone. She's also sure that Camas will be justifiably angry that she's brought Mich today. However, doing so is part of a larger strategy, and she's prepared to tell Camas not to push it with her.

Kot calls out as they enter the quiet tower. Camas was out at dawn for water and to forage for food, and Kot's voice wakes her. She leaps to the stairwell, her face panicked when she catches sight of Mich. Both women are smiling, but Camas flies back into her room. Kot isn't in the mood to persuade, but stands just outside and puts in the effort.

"Camas, please don't be scared. This is my best friend, Mich, and she's visiting me. Nobody official, I promise. We've brought you some food and things. We'll just have a quick visit and then go away, okay?"

Kot fully expects Camas to ask her to just leave the groceries on the stairs, but there is only silence.

Mich rallies, and keep her voice softer than usual. "Hi Camas. My name is Suzanne Michaluk, but like Kot said, everyone calls me Mich. I'm pretty sure Kot packed a bag of oatmeal chocolate chip cookies for you. They're my favourite, too. And I saw some chips as well."

Kot is grateful that Mich chose gentleness in spite of her opinions, and knows that Camas is torn between the familiar conditions of fear and hunger. It takes time, but eventually her big hazel eyes peek around the partition.

Mich tries to approximate a maternal smile. "Hi there. I've promised Kot, and I also promise you, that I won't tell anyone else we came today."

Kot hopes that Mich means that, since she's heard no such promise. Camas takes a look down the stairs behind them, and then steps back to allow them into her room. She hurries straight to the window and looks around outside. Kot guesses her thinking.

"We walked here, Camas. And we made sure no one saw us. Don't worry. The man who lives in the house down there is in hospital. Did you know that?"

Camas shakes her head. "He usually just stays in the house. There haven't been any lights on, though." Her lonely curiosity is trumping her fear. "Does he own this property?"

"No, he's the caretaker. The light station is owned by the federal government, like the national park over there, but they're run by different branches of the government. There's no public access allowed to this property these days, but the park is open to everyone. The caretaker's first name is Harvey, but I don't know his last name. His health isn't good right now."

Camas nods as she processes the information. "A man tried to get in here a few days ago. But he went away."

"Oh, Camas, that must have been really scary. I've been careful to lock the door when I leave. By the way, how do you get in and out?"

"I have a secret way." And that is clearly all that they will hear on that subject.

"Okay, well, how are you doing?"

"Fine. I ate everything you left. It was good." Then she remembers. "Thank you."

"You're welcome. I don't know what your favourite foods are, but you need to eat lots of healthy things, especially while you're living like this." Kot starts to unload her pack. "So, I got you cheese and nuts and milk and I hard-boiled some eggs. And here are a couple of freezer bags for your cooler, and some fresh fruit and veggies. And as long as you promise to eat the nutritious things, here are the cookies and chips."

They sit on a blanket on the hard stone floor to unpack the food, and Camas picks up and examines every item that Kot has brought. After a couple of minutes, Mich shifts the conversation toward the invitation that she and Kot had agreed on as they climbed the driveway.

"Hey Camas, I noticed you don't cook here. That's smart."

"Yeah. Smoke and smell."

Succinct child, thinks Mich. "You know, if I were you, I'd be craving a cooked meal like crazy. Aren't you?"

Camas is emboldened now. "Yeah. But I'd way rather eat cold food here than have cooked food in some foster home or jail or somewhere."

Kot says, "Well, what if Mich and I cooked you a meal at my place, and you could bring the leftovers back here? We'd love to do that for you, as a present. No traps, I promise. Just food and a shower."

Camas stiffens, and eventually replies with what sounds to Kot like polite evasion. "I don't know where you live. And you couldn't invite anyone else, so that wouldn't be any fun for you."

Kot replies, "Well, we don't want to invite anyone else, so it isn't a problem. And there's a way we can help you get there and back again without anyone knowing."

Camas goes to the window again. She doesn't want to be rude, and the idea of a hot meal is hugely tantalizing, but maybe having groceries delivered like this is enough. The cost and work for Kot doesn't enter her mind. She watches the clouds building over the ocean in banks of variegated grey and charcoal. The trees and shrubs on the bluff bend and bow in gusts of wind.

She turns to Kot and Mich. "How would you do that? It's light out in the evenings now."

Kot's heart is tugged by the girl's determination to think things through and make her own decisions, but they need to find out more about her right away, not prolong things. Kot would also like to give her at least one secure evening, and maybe include a movie on Mich's laptop. When the food and hot water have done their work, they will push Camas for more information, and then figure out a way forward that will protect her, and not trigger her fears and another dangerous escape.

"Okay, here's what we're thinking."

Kot explains their plan: Mich will drive to the bottom of the light station driveway at a certain time, and Camas would be hiding nearby. Mich would get out to watch and listen, and as soon as she was sure that no one was around she would call Camas to scramble into the car and lie on the back seat. At the nursery, they would cover her with a blanket and carry her up to Kot's apartment, like a sack of potatoes. Kot offers Camas her secondhand watch so that she can be at the rendezvous spot on time.

Finally, Kot pulls out her ace. "Mich has a convertible sports car."

Camas's face lights up.

"And we could drop you off at the end of the driveway again after dark. That's the only part I don't like, because you would have to find your way back to the lighthouse in the dark." Kot knows perfectly well that Camas would have no problem with that. It just sounded like the responsible thing to say. "What do you think?"

Camas looks fearfully back and forth between them, searching for a hidden threat, then nods. "Okay. I'll try. But if there is anyone around, I'm going to sneak back here and not come."

"Fair enough. How about on Thursday?" Kot realizes that days of the week may not be part of the girl's current life. "That's the day after tomorrow. I've found out that Harvey might be coming home from hospital the day after that, and it might be easier for you before then."

Camas just nods slowly, obviously still uncertain. Mich says, "I'll pick you up at five, and if there's any risk, I'll just keep driving, then come back a few minutes later. Okay?" She decides to keep up the momentum. "What would you like for supper? Do you like hamburgers? Or pizza? Spaghetti?"

Camas blurts, "Hamburgers, please." And it's settled.

Camas watches them go down the path and takes note of where Kot puts the key. Then she arranges her new groceries, like Gollum with his gold.

Kot and Mich hurry down the driveway in silence, but once they reach the road Mich doesn't hold back.

"Holy Hannah! Did you say she's eleven? I don't know an adult—besides you, maybe—who could do what she's doing. Incredible. But she obviously can't stay there in the long term. Of course she'll be discovered, for one thing, but you can't get away with sneaking food to her for long, either. Far too many risks. Strange that you're both in sort of the same situation. But at least you have power and a shower. Whew – what a stench, hey? Poor kid. Anyway, I accept that our mission on Thursday is to find out more about her history and who or what she's still afraid of. Maybe I'll loosen her up with a little booze on her burger."

The skies suddenly open again, and they run back to Kot's in the rain, whooping like kids.

~ TWENTY-TWO ~

The *Novicta* docked early this morning, but so far nothing unusual has been reported. Soliniski decides to set a new precedent and leave on time for a change. Maybe perform a token pilgrimage to the gym that she joined at the start of the New Year. She is putting on her coat when Dance knocks once, and her feeble resolution is given permission to bite the dust.

"It's time to move, boss."

"Okay. Because…?"

"Because our mole seems to have made the right call. That stern gantry operator he's suspicious of? He unloaded dozens of containers belonging to a bunch of different companies today, but just in the past hour three of them got special treatment. We don't know how he selected three particular Northcott containers from dozens of others on the ship, but he placed them separately in a row along the rail line. Then they were among the first to be sent for a stage one security scan, right at the end of their working day."

Solinski is actually taking notes. Dance keeps going. "The whole system is computerized, of course. So if there's contraband in any of those containers, someone inside the terminal operations must be involved. Someone supposedly beyond suspicion. And enough profit has to be involved to make the risks worthwhile. However they're doing it, the goal is likely to keep the containers from being flagged, and then get them out of the terminal, lickety-split.

There are three transport rigs waiting in the wings, and apparently what usually happens is that each of them will carry one of the special containers."

"Let me guess. Bellows."

"Bingo."

Bellows Bros. Trucking is owned by middle-aged siblings, both of them full patch Hell's Angels. They've been nailed for procedural transgressions in the past, but so far have escaped doing time. Still, the common belief is that the only reason that their twenty fingers are still intact is because they are solidly stuck into much larger pies.

Solinski said, "Good. But this may be just a decoy, so we need a drone to remain over the terminal. Is the unloading going to continue during this evening?"

"No. The stern crane guy is about halfway through unloading his section, and he's due to quit for the day. He usually does that on time. The trucks may separate if they move, but our best guess is that they will all end up together again, in the Bellows' yard."

"Agreed. I'll requisition two additional night drones to be on standby. As long as their operators haven't buggered off, they should be operational in minutes. I also want the terminal under manned surveillance twenty-four seven from here. Obviously, everything could be legit. But since our guy's seen this happen before, the shit does seem to be piling up and I'll let Batra know. Get us set up to monitor, please."

"Already happening. See you in there."

"Oh, wait—one more thing. I assume that it's because we're focused on the docks area and one of his ships, but the sup also asked me for any updates on the Ben Northcott shooting."

"Right. Well, you know how hard it is to suck info from that silo… but I did learn something from that guy who got transferred in from the Witness Protection Program last week. He invited himself to my table yesterday, in Starbucks." Dance rolls his eyes. "I took the opportunity to probe a bit, but he said that as far as he knew, things have stalled. All that was found was a melted cell phone with no recoverable data. No human or dog remains at the site. It's hard to imagine how, but the witness must have escaped the explosion. A weedy guy was apparently watching the area for a few days but he never got out of his truck. Said he was a birder or something. Didn't really fit, but who knows? There's only random checks on the place now. Presumably, the witness is either dead or still out there somewhere on her own. She hasn't broken any laws, so I'm thinking: good for her. It's likely there's an internal leak in the WPP. All pretty disgraceful, if you ask me."

Dance returns to the surveillance monitor. Before joining him, Solinski scans his bulleted report and forwards it to Superintendent Batra with a request for approval of her tentative plans. She has grown increasingly suspicious that there is also a leak on her own squad. There are too many disgruntled personnel within the force. She has ordered that no one other than herself, Dance, and a trusted techie are to be allowed in the surveillance room, and that no information will be shared outside of it. The implications of her orders are obvious, and she has no doubt that some team members are pissed off. No matter. She is also being careful lately to only use her personal mobile, and to keep it on her.

By the time she joins Dance in front of the monitor, it looks like the suspect rigs have received the necessary security releases and are already on the road. As predicted, the drone follows them to the Bellows' yard, where they are parked beside each other, nose-in, at the rear. The drivers then leave in personal vehicles, and eventually the automatic gate swings shut. Just two company pickups remain inside, both known to belong to the owners. The place is quiet for another half hour.

Solinski calls in a further requisition for standby vehicle trackers. Those rigs might sit in the yard for days, but it's unlikely. She orders pizza to eat in her office, but is only on the second greasy slice when her desk phone rings.

Dance says, "Things to see, Ma'am, tout de suite."

She returns to the surveillance room. The area is quiet now, so the drone has been positioned higher up and focused for a wide view. Two men, presumably the Bellows brothers, are dragging an enormous tarpaulin over the back of the container nearest the rear fence. Then they repeat their efforts on the one next to it. The entry gate opens again, and two unmarked six-ton trucks with unusually high chassis roll into the yard and head for the rear. The gate again swings smoothly shut and relocks.

What follows appears to be well rehearsed. Each truck in turn is reversed against the back of a tarped container. The truck beds are conveniently the same height as the rigs. Then the men manhandle the tarps to create a visual seal between the container opening and the rear of each truck before vanishing beneath the one closest to the yard's rear fence. A transfer of the container contents to the high-chassis trucks has obviously begun.

Dance conjures the voice of David Attenborough: "The exotic mating ritual of the urban six-ton, captured on film for the very first time."

In time, the men start on the second container. Solinski has already ordered activation of the tracking vehicles. The transfers will take time, but those trucks won't be hanging around when it's done.

The third Northcott container has been ignored, and when the transfers are complete and the gate closes behind the departed trucks, the two owners are left to fold the massive tarps.

Dance comments, "What makes me think they may have done this before? Gotta be a reason nobody's interested in that third one."

Infrared drone footage shows the first truck gather speed on the main road. A Chevy beater pulls out of a Tim Hortons and the driver positions himself two vehicles behind. He looks like a teenager in a backwards baseball cap, his head bobbing with the hip-hop blasting from an open window. The drone driver has to take it cross-country at times to keep up.

The second truck takes a different route, followed by an attractive older woman in a Lexus SUV. A heavily tattooed man in a dirty green van waits on a side street in the dusk near the Bellows' yard, but rig number three is apparently going nowhere.

The drone that remained over the yard follows the Bellows brothers' pickups until they park on the main drag. When they get out, the camera is zoomed to catch one of them tilting his head back with laughter and slapping his brother on the back as they enter a restaurant.

"Bon appetit, turds," says Dance.

Solinski makes a note to delve into his recent penchant for the French language, and ensures that there is still surveillance of the Bellows' yard. She would love the brothers to be bycatch in this operation, but bigger fish are more important. It's also still possible that this entire procedure is a smokescreen for something else that has yet to go down in that yard, and she intends to cover that contingency.

By nine, the entry gate of a crowded container holding yard near the Port Mann Bridge is opened remotely, and the second truck is driven in and parked, watched over by a high-flying drone. When a squad with a search warrant arrives in the wee hours, its members have to wake the driver.

But the first truck is still rolling, south now, deep into rural Langley. It turns into a gated property and the young guy tailgating it roars past it on the verge, spraying gravel and still blasting hip-hop.

The assigned drone catches up and its camera catches the truck approaching the rear of an enormous fake-Tudor house. Out beyond the pool and hedges, patchy hayfields may justify agricultural taxes. A dark-coloured sedan sits near the back door. The truck backs in close to the wide doors of a barn and the driver only looks back once as he heads into the house.

Solinski updates her boss, and Batra orders a combined law enforcement tactical operation. There would be any number of volunteers on Solinski's team willing to take part in the raid, but she doesn't delegate anyone from her own squad except Dance. She's getting fed up with having to consider a traitor in their midst. Also, if this operation goes tits up, she knows that it might be quite some time before she enjoys such a smooth deployment of requested resources again. They have two field targets, one of them on hold for now, a third suspect vehicle still sitting in a trucking yard, and any number of others still to be unloaded from the *Novicta.* In an ideal world, how many other freighters should they be monitoring?

Two hours later, the combined forces team is almost invisible in night gear as they creep and silently curse around blackberry tangles in the drainage ditch on the Langley property's perimeter. One team member restrains a leashed dog. The takeout cheeseburger in Dance's stomach is not playing well with his level of adrenaline, but he is honoured to be part of the action tonight.

They scramble over the fence and around the side of the barn. On Solinski's order, the security camera above the doors is disabled, and the clock in Dance's head begins a short countdown to when they can expect a reaction from someone inside the house.

A search warrant is slapped onto the truck, and in seconds a powerful bolt cutter has taken care of the lock on the back. Several flashlight beams jerk around the interior.

The truck is piled high with plastic-wrapped beanbag furniture, some of them child-sized and upholstered with cartoonish fabric. A sniffer dog is lifted onto the high truck bed. Her tail a blur, she returns repeatedly to two of the items. After a reward, her handler takes her further inside.

The clock in her head matches Dance's, and Solinski gives a signal. Everyone except the marksmen tucked behind the front bumpers is out of sight when three black figures leave the house and move in a line towards them, panning arcs with powerful headlamps. Dance catches a reflection off a weapon that looks like a semi-automatic. Solinski waits for them to close in more, then gives another signal. Three leg shots from her marksmen, and it's all over.

She orders ambulances and an armed sweep of the house and property. Then she and Dance don gloves and join the dog and her handler in the now brightly-lit truck. The dog is happily back at work after all the commotion. Solinski is curious to have a careful look around before forensics arrive.

No matter how big a haul this raid yields, investigations might only lead to untraceable people and boarded-up locales. Still, a few deserving folks might eventually find themselves on the wrong side of bars.

~ TWENTY-THREE ~

The back of Tessa's truck is loaded with plants for the marina when she drops Kot at Glenhurst. She anxiously tells Kot to call her as soon as possible with news of Hunter's reaction to the design. Left standing in the early sunshine, Kot takes a minute in the courtyard to settle herself and look around.

The structural brick of the house is rare on the coast, not only because the abundance of native timber would had made wood the more obvious choice, but because, even a hundred years ago, using brick in an earthquake zone would have been considered, to put it politely, unwise. And yet, Hunter said the buildings had passed an engineering inspection with flying colours before he bought the estate. And here Glenhurst stubbornly stands.

The soft green of a nearby honeysuckle vine will soon be broken by colourful little trumpets of nectar, and over a strong trellis a gnarled old wisteria casts a sweet mauve fragrance. The drone of bees provides an orchestral hum behind the snippets of song from newly arrived birds. A magical, secret place, on a beautiful day.

Kot has her design pages in a tube tucked under her arm. She goes around to the back and Hunter opens one of the kitchen's French doors just as she's about to knock. He must have been waiting for her and maybe even watching her. They sit at the kitchen counter and review the drawings over coffee. Hunter has good questions and his happy excitement is obvious. Kot is stunned by his level of confidence in her when he announces that he has already booked the big machinery to start work in two days. He asks Kot to be there to help supervise.

They wander to the bluff and its view of the ocean and neighbouring islands, and Kot has relaxed completely by the time they return. Roller comes out to say hello, but when the talk returns to elevations and design features, he leaves them alone at an outside table, with wild daisies all around and the air like liquid butter. An eagle lands in the top of a fir and watches them, reminding Kot of the one that sat above the beach on the morning that she and Medley had been forced to hurry away from Elegy Island. This feels reassuringly far from that time.

"Hunter?"

"Yes, Kot?" His tone is teasing.

"Could I see a little more of your house? I have to admit, I'm fascinated by it, but I also want to check out some views from the inside before it's too late to change the design."

"Of course. I'd planned to offer you a tour. I told Tessa I'd give you a ride home, and I hope you'll stay as long as you can. Roller's heading to town soon."

Kot wonders what relevance that has. Hunter slowly leads her through the entire house, explaining the original design, the various changes over the years, and his own alterations and plans. Kot is impressed by his historical knowledge, but more by his surprising self-effacement in giving all credit to other people. Still, his comfort in talking about the details of his home indicate to her that his own taste and choices have played a major role.

The rooms are bright, spacious, and free of impersonal or pretentious clutter. Expanses of polished wood flooring are topped with high quality woolen area rugs. Those alone must have cost a fortune. In some rooms the softly coloured walls have natural fir or cream wainscoting, in keeping with the period of the house. Accent furnishings are muted but not boring, and the furniture is high quality and comfortable. In fact, the whole place is simply beautiful. Hunter explains that a few of the bathrooms have yet to be updated because of his desire for peace and quiet while he is there, and his wish to focus on the exterior. "Besides, how many state-of-the-art toilets do two guys really need, surrounded by so much nature to pee in when it calls?"

In his office are a few personal mementoes of Hunter's travels, but no photographs on his desk nor any other evidence that any love interest has played a role in this particular house. Still, he must own other places. Kot wonders if any of his former girlfriends have been here.

She is completely charmed by the house. And, still surprisingly, by the man. Once they have agreed on a couple of design changes Kot feels like they are now on the same team - also a far cry from a week ago.

When she tells Hunter that she has promised to work with Tessa this afternoon he doesn't argue, just nods and gets his keys. His Land Rover handles the driveway far better than Mich's poor little car, and in comfortable silence it feels like a romantic spell has been cast. If Hunter were to reach over and take her hand, she wouldn't resist. Kot sternly reminds herself of the many kinds of hot soup a woman could find herself swimming in by getting involved with Hunter Nott. At least Ben is the devil she knows. She still finds herself happy when Hunter suggests taking a longer route so that he can show her a couple of his favourite spots on the island.

When they pull in, Mich swans down the stairs from Kot's apartment for an introduction to Hunter. After they wave him goodbye, she hardly waits a second.

"Unbefuckinlievable. He is even *better* in person."

She takes Kot by the shoulders and looks into her eyes. "You are spending hours alone with one of the single most desirable men in the universe—and let me go back and emphasize that word: single. Single is good. But instead of laying a solid foundation for quality time without all of those pesky clothes, all you can do is think about the married man who did his slimy best to dump you. You still are, aren't you? I really don't know what to say."

She stands back a bit and raises her chin. "And in case you didn't notice, I put on come-hither makeup and pushed my pheromones to the max, and I got not one spark out of the guy. But his eyes, when he said goodbye to you… whoa, baby!"

"Humph. Didn't notice." Kot waits a couple of beats, then quietly asks, "Okay, to back up again, what do you think is making me unable to accept that maybe Ben really did want to permanently end our relationship?"

Mich shakes her head. "Oh, that one's simple. Stubbornness and determination serve you extremely well in your career, but maybe not so much in personal matters. And I'm talking way back, ever since I've known you."

"Oh. That old hold and fold thing of mine again." Kot grins. "And okay, if you want the truth: Hunter Nott does turn me on, or at least off and on. He's a far nicer person than I expected, and I'm surprised by how comfortable I feel with him. But perhaps you can understand that I also don't trust those feelings. That's surely natural at this point, right? Anyway, I need to eat something and get to work, but I'll tell you all about Hunter's amazing house later on."

~ TWENTY-FOUR ~

The predictable circus began as ambulances arrived and neighbours called the TV news and posted on social media. The forensics team discovered a small splash of yellow paint on the same corner of each container taken to the Bellows' yard, and the bean bag pieces selected by the sniffer dog all have a inconspicuous green dot added to their label and drugs inside. Already, ten kilograms of methamphetamine and nineteen kilos of cocaine have been seized, along with an undetermined amount of carfentanil. Estimates of market value are in the millions, from that one container's contents alone.

The second container, on the truck left in the container holding yard below the Port Mann bridge, contained exclusively heroin, and a lot of it. The third one, still in the Bellows' yard, also contained beanbag furniture. It was clean of drugs but possibly part of a larger decoy operation.

In the painful glare of mid-morning, Dance is driving a ghost car toward the dockyards, Solinski texting beside him. She puts the phone down. "Okay. We monitored the call that the *Novicta* captain made to Ben Northcott this morning, and it sounded like neither of them knows anything beyond the fact that a search is taking place. Obviously, one or both might be hiding things from the other, but whatever, that dock will stay closed until every container on the *Novicta* has been examined. Considering that things were already backed up, our upcoming host is probably not in the best of moods."

"Damn. I was hoping for cookies."

So far, reporters have been unable to attach many specifics to the Langley truck heist, but that will likely change sometime today. Solinski is anxious to have their upcoming chat with Ben Northcott before that happens, and knows that he has recently arrived in his office.

"It's possible that the captain, crew, and Northcott don't know about the smuggling, and it's just mafia dock crew involved. Or it could go right up to the Northcott corporate Board level, and in that case, Ben would also have to be involved. Of course, it could also all be part of a bigger and messier web."

They ride in silence until Dance says, "You know, the plea bargaining around all this could drag out past our lifetimes. And if it is part of that big web, some players will probably get offed, or do it themselves before the whole jar of maggots gets emptied. Best scenario is that a record number of new identities may be required."

The suspects had all lawyered up fast, and the Bellows brothers had opened their act with wide-eyed amazement. Once they were faced with the filmed evidence, the stonewalling began. Still, there was no mistaking their fear.

They swing into the rear lot of the Northcott Shipping building, also the scene of the attack on Ben Northcott several weeks ago. Presumably, folks are still working on that file somewhere in the system, but probably no longer actively looking for the missing witness. Solinski is increasingly sure that there is a link to these current events. Coincidences are highly overrated, except, of course, when that's all they are. In her view, it's always safer to assume the opposite.

They flash their identity cards and receive security lanyards. The elevator doors haven't even closed when they see the receptionist pick up her phone. The windows in the outer sanctum of Northcott's office face the same direction as Solinski's, but there, all similarities end. His PA, Isobel, looks like a model. Solinski estimates that it would have required a good hour and a far steadier hand than hers to get Isobel's face ready this morning. Their ID cards elicit a twitch of her too-perfect nose, suggestive of a stench. She carefully looks at each badge and then their faces. Her glance at Northcott's office door and slow pace of speech suggest stalling. She's clearly not had time to warn him after the call from downstairs.

"Inspector Solinski, Sergeant Dance. Unfortunately, Mr. Northcott's schedule is completely full today, and our board chair is arriving at any moment for an important meeting. Why don't I set up a time later in the day?" Her gleaming smile disappears the second that she swivels to consult her computer monitor.

Dance squares his shoulders and crooks his arms widely as Solinski slips behind him. He drawls, "Aw, thanks, Isobel. Sure is an awesome day out there. Yeah, we know the boss is a busy guy, but hey, no worries. You can just send the chair on in too, when he or she arrives. We'd love to talk to them as well."

Solinski opens the door to Northcott's office, and Isobel yells "Hey!" Ben looks up in annoyance but stays seated. Isobel hot on their heels, Solinski introduces herself and Dance, and Ben is forced to limp from his desk to offer a hand and gesture to seats. Solinski leaves her hand in her pocket and discreetly starts *recording* the conversation on her cell. While it can't be used in court, she prefers watching people to taking notes.

None of the online photos capture Ben Northcott adequately. And his mixed-race colouring also just happens to be Solinski's favourite look for the male of her species. A family photo on a nearby credenza shows his strong hands resting on the shoulders of two teenagers. The human whippet in the middle with expensive hair and a five-thousand-dollar dress must be Lauren, the socialite wife.

With Ben's thanks that she won't be needed, Isobel reluctantly retreats, but they notice him glance occasionally at his desk phone lights. Perhaps his PA has a history of eavesdropping.

Ben loosely folds his hands and dons a relaxed but puzzled expression. "Were you offered coffee? Tea? Nothing, you're sure? I must apologize, but I don't have much time." He winks conspiratorially. "We have a board meeting very soon, and that always means a lot of advance headaches for me. Perhaps Isobel mentioned that I have an important meeting that is due to start in five minutes?"

Ben adjusts his position and winces a little, to remind them of his condition. Neither of the cops speak, and his baritone resumes. Melodic, calm. "Well then, let us proceed with all speed. I've been hoping for more information about investigations since I was attacked. Do you come bearing news? I'm also concerned about the NatureSave employee who witnessed the event, but I've been unable to find out how she is."

Solinski is impressed. As they'd planned, Dance takes the lead, in his deliberately laconic manner. "Wish we could help you there, Mr. Northcott, but we're not in the loop on that. Good to see you're recovering. We're actually here on a different matter. Or maybe it isn't. Who knows? We're hoping you'll help us figure that out."

"I would be happy to, but unless you're here with news about my attackers or the poor witness, I confess to be at a bit of a loss." Ben leans back in his chair with a bemused smile, as if about to hear something completely unrelated to him. "Unless, of course, there is something Captain Yin neglected to mention when he called me a short time ago. I understand that the *Novicta* is undergoing a routine search."

Impatient with the games, Solinski cuts to the chase. "Yes, the ship has been seized for a detailed search of all of its containers, including those that have already cleared inspection and left the dockyard. Mr. Northcott, a substantial amount of illegal goods has already been found within the cargo carried by the *Novicta*."

Ben keeps his eyes steady on hers. "Inspector Solinski, as you are probably aware, I was interviewed some months ago on a similar subject. I'll now repeat what I said then: if illegal goods are getting in, the responsibility has to rest on the policies that have allowed the hiring of known gang members to work on the docks. We have done a thorough review, and found no reason for concern within our company procedures and staffing. We are proud of our ethics, and have an enviable track record. Our company will now take a big financial hit with these delays, and no doubt, with our business relationships as well. So, if criminals have planted smuggled goods within our fleet we will pursue the full measure of the law toward compensation."

The guy is nothing if not fluent. Solinski replies, "Okay, got it. So are we to understand that you would testify in court that you are unaware of any smuggling of illegal goods within the activities of your shipping line? If you do have some knowledge, it will be far better to disclose that now, rather than have it proven later that you withheld that information. Are you clear on that?"

"Of course, but I'm sincerely appalled. If criminals have found a way to take advantage of our company, it cannot happen again. I and my staff are at your disposal, and I'm confident that I also speak for our entire board of directors."

Apart from classic indications of lying—the raising of his brows as he spoke, and his forefinger twice touching his nose—Ben's performance has been flawless, and Solinski doubts that reviewing her recording later will be fruitful. She wonders how many deserving Northcott relatives lost his or her bid for company leadership—and the enormous salary attached—because of Ben's charisma and easy ability to prevaricate.

He asks, "In the meantime, may I count on your complete discretion as investigations proceed?"

Solinski answers, "Probably not. You know how it goes. But thanks for your cooperation."

"Perhaps I should be present during the search? Unfortunately, the timing of all this couldn't be more inconvenient."

Dance answers this time. "Aw, thanks, Mr. Northcott, but that whole dock is now a crime scene, and the fewer people around, the better. I guess what's most helpful to us right now is your assurance that all this is news to you. Good to hear."

Ben gets up, to indicate an end to the meeting, but then turns to face Solinski. "I need to at least be kept informed, as your investigations proceed."

Solinski smiles back. "Thank you for your time, Mr. Northcott."

She is already out of the door when Dance does what she calls his Detective Columbo move. One hand on the door handle, he has turned back to Ben as if with a last-minute thought.

"Oh man, before we go, we should tell you the good news. We've taken a few people off the *Novicta* in for questioning, and a coupla dock workers also seem to really want to be helpful. Just wanted you to know that we're making some progress. Cheers."

As they exit the elevator a tall, silver-haired man in a Gucci suit gets in, every inch an alpha male corporate board chair.

Back in the car, Dance asks, "Wanna bet Ben chooses not to share all that good news with his chair just yet?"

Solinski grunts, holding her cigarette outside the window. "He's so damned smooth. The odds are high that someone in his company is involved.

But if it's Northcott, he must be in deep, and he'd have too much to lose to cave one millimetre at this point."

Dance replies, "Yeah, verbally, he would have been pretty convincing if he hadn't blown it in one big way. When you said that 'illegal goods' were found, he forgot to ask the right questions, like what kind, how much, where—all that. Instead, he went right into the rehearsed shock and indignation thing."

Solinski nods. "My instincts say he's in it up to his molten brown eyeballs. But sadly, my instincts have never convicted anyone."

She decides that it's time to confide in Dance about another hunch that she's developed, and by the time they get back to continue with interviews, they have built the framework of another plan.

Ben returns to his desk and stares into space. He hadn't expected the cops yet. He does another quick online scan of Vancouver news outlets. Nothing connects the seized drugs to more than the trucks in which they were found. No mention of shipping containers. This supports his intention not to bring up the subject with his board chair. If it arises, he will brush off the ship search as routine.

The painkillers he took this morning are still helping, but the leg is taking too long to heal. Lately, Ben has been doing a couple of lines of cocaine at work just to get through his daily high-wire performances and the current level of stress. But he needs to be very careful. Think clearly, and not act in haste. So many moving pieces.

First things first: he will do whatever is necessary to keep this next meeting short.

~ TWENTY-FIVE ~

Derrick's boss has finally requested to meet in person. Derrick finds him sitting at a dirty concrete table outside a McDonald's on the highway. CallMeWayne is wearing the promised red and black ball cap, and is more courteous than previously.

Apparently, Derrick's crazy goose chase around the Southern Gulf Islands has finally been narrowed to only Atticus Island. "Wayne" doesn't share how the information about the woman's suspected location was obtained, and Derrick's curiosity vanishes when Wayne pushes an "interim payment" bag with his foot, literally under the table. He says that they will meet again after Derrick provides positive identification of the target. Wayne's car is barely out of the lot before Derrick is spreading out the cash and drugs on his bench seat.

On the way back to Atticus he figures out the suspected coordinates of his quarry, and plans to start stakeouts and continue until he has good photos. He decides to take a first look today before hitting the pub. He has already made the acquaintance of a regular there, and the high-quality goods that are kept in his vehicle.

Even allowing for some margin of GPS error, the only possible buildings that could contain his quarry are either just out of sight down a waterfront driveway or in what looks like an apartment on top of what is signed as a future garden centre. There is a small Audi half-hidden around the back of that building. Derrick parks the truck out of sight and finds a surveillance spot.

Ferry trips make him sleepy, and the pub is calling, but he doesn't have to wait long before a posh Land Rover pulls into the garden centre's parking lot. Derrick picks up his binos. The guy who gets out looks a lot like Hunter Nott, the movie star. What a laugh. A small dog and then a woman come running down the stairs from the upper apartment. Derrick glasses her closely. Much as he would like her to be his target, she is not. Still, she's easy on the eyes, so he keeps the binoculars on her as she approaches the vehicle. Someone else has emerged from the passenger seat. Derrick doesn't need to pull out the wrinkled photo in his jacket pocket. The woman's hair is a different colour, which only makes sense if she is in hiding, but the face and figure match.

Derrick focuses his telephoto and takes a shot for himself of two shapely bottoms bending over the dog. The Nott look-alike leaves, and Derrick keeps snapping until the women finish talking and head upstairs together. Back in his truck, he sends Wayne a few relevant photos and heads for the pub, feeling like the star he is.

He gets an early call from his boss the next day. Derrick has been deemed a hero and is now invited to upgrade his accommodations from his tiny suite with a nosy landlady to one of the private cabins at Gubbins Bay Marina. In fact, Wayne pretty much insists on the move and tells Derrick to let him know as soon as he has booked himself in. Sweet. Derrick packs his bag and is on his way.

The marina parking lot is almost empty. He takes the path behind a tall hedge that soon borders a row of cottages that are stepped down toward the waterfront, then veers left to the docks. Wayne told him that he deserved to rent the cottage closest to the water, and it looks like a nice place to hang out for whatever time he has to remain on this godforsaken rock. Derrick can hear another slot drop into place as he nears the jackpot.

He adopts a slow swagger across the lawn up to the marina office. It's like a fucking park, with some flowers already in bloom all over the place. As he enters, a woman with short blonde hair greets him. Derrick graces Nora with his most engaging smile.

"I want to rent that cottage closest to the water. I could do you cash in advance for a week, to start. I'll be doing some construction work on the island."

Nora knows that her initial assessments of people are either spot on, partly correct, or way off the mark. In other words, pretty useless. Steve is far better at reading people, but although this guy is rough and kind of wired, he's probably harmless. A casual construction dude, likely to eat in the pub and not be around much. The bottom line is looking uncomfortably low and he's offered cash in advance, so Nora asks for his name and says that she'll check to see if that cabin is available. Nora already knows that it is, but uses the opportunity to Google the name he provided. Nothing at all pops up, but at least there is no negative trail.

The guy has begun to peel off large-denomination bills, like in some old movie. She decides to limit their commitment to a week, their sinking bottom line or not. "Okay, looks like the one you want, the Heron Cabin, is free for the next week. I can start you off there, but after that it's booked pretty solid. We provide fresh linens every second day, and can clean the unit for you if you like. That's another twenty dollars on top of the daily price."

"Hell no. I'll just be crashing there at night. And I don't need fresh sheets and stuff." To fend off the usual nosiness, he adds, "A friend of mine is building a place down the south end, and I'm helping him with some framing. He's just living in a little trailer, so he can't put me up."

Nora used to be able to keep track of who was building what on the island, but there are so many new people moving here now. She hands him the guest rules and the key and watches him shamble back to the parking lot. He pulls a couple of gym bags out of an old truck with the same BC plate numbers he'd used to register, and disappears down the path to his private waterfront cottage while several stubborn red flags still flap in Nora's head. The phone rings, and she is soon distracted by the booking hassles of a Ranger Tug gathering.

Lying on his bed with a view of bobbing boats, Derrick sends Wayne an update. He is chuffed to get an immediate reply that includes what sounds like sincere congratulations and the good news that Derrick won't be expected to run back over to meet Wayne, because Wayne will be coming to Atticus on tomorrow's early ferry. And he'll be bringing more cash and goodies.

TWENTY-SIX

The Whale
Near Sidney Island

She can feel the end approaching, and is glad that her clan is around her again. The meat-eaters won't risk an attack. Her pain is less, but she is overwhelmed by the heavy malaise. She is sometimes able to swim with favourable tides and currents, but moving is exhausting and mostly she sleeps at the surface.

She recognizes the noise and vibrations of the large machines that move between the islands. Sometimes they slow down not far away, and the creatures on them make more noise. On their last migration, her sister's son was killed by one of the machines, and there are stories of others being badly cut up in these waters.

Two other females forage nearby. Occasionally one comes close and rubs against her in support. A daughter sometimes sleeps against her flank. She hears the songs. They are already grieving for her, but before long the others will need to continue north without her.

Waking merges with dreaming. She breathes and moves when she can. And still, she is drawn toward a familiar hill in the distance.

~ TWENTY-SEVEN ~

Mich looks at Medley in her rearview mirror and laughs. His front paws are braced on the door frame, his black nose raised, ears blown back, and tongue flying sideways in a goofy grin.

"That lad needs aviator goggles, Kot."

Kot smiles but keeps her eyes ahead. She doesn't want her speeding friend to miss the turn into Glenhurst's narrow laneway. Once on it, Mich must immediately slow to a crawl and Medley begins an annoying whine.

Kot explains, "He's only been to Glenhurst once, but for a dog who frequently gets lost on foot, he has an amazing memory for car trips. He knows exactly what dog lives at the end of this pile of potholes. *Quiet, Medley*! He might also need to do a dump."

"He went first thing this morning, but perhaps one good turd deserves another."

Kot snorts and stretches her arm back to hold Medley's collar for a minute. "Medley! *Shhhh*!"

He briefly contains himself, and Kot asks Mich, "Did I tell you what Hunter named his dog?"

"No, let me guess. Indi? Chopper? Is it a boy or girl?'

"Female." After a few seconds, Kot asks, "Give up? Madonna."

"Perfect. My devotion grows ever deeper. But seriously, if he's as into you as I think he is, couldn't you just drop the chastity act for the short term?

When you go back to your life, and Hunter jets away to la-la land, it could all just fade away. No fuss, no muss, just memories to cherish for a lifetime. Or not. But at least there would be some excellent stories for me."

"Oh yeah. No mess, no drama, that's me in a bun."

Mich is trying to navigate her expensive car through the pothole canyons.

"This is completely unbelievable. Can't the poor guy afford to maintain his own driveway?"

"Not a priority, I guess. Both he and Roller have four by fours. Hunter also probably wants as few people as possible to ever get to the end of this lane. You can't really blame him for that." She has to hang onto the door grip in the lurching car. "Can we talk about Camas? It was like having a wild fawn come for dinner last night, wasn't it?"

"Yeah, but one that can really pack in the food. She doesn't weigh much, and Lord knows where she stowed two hamburgers, a thousand fries, and everything else she ate. Like you said afterwards, I hope she didn't make herself sick. Maybe we should check."

The car almost bounces into a fence, and Mich shakes her head angrily but stays on subject. "I just don't know what to say. All normal ethics and the law would hold you—and me now, as well—at fault for not reporting a minor 'living at large.' Makes it sound like she's a criminal, but it seems likely that there was someone else playing that role in her life. Her ability to keep secrets is like a spy five times her age."

"I know. It was even more difficult to get her to talk than I'd imagined. But at least now we know that she had loving parents—besides that happy photo she has, you could see that on her face when she talked about them—and that her mom's death was relatively recent. She's clearly devastated at losing her mother, and I didn't pick up anything but sadness about her dad, either. Anyway, she's an orphan who once had a better life, and if she prefers living in a cold lighthouse and eating wild plants, she must be scared shitless of whatever situation she escaped. Foster system, do you think? A stepfather, maybe..."

"Both good possibilities." Mich inches into an unavoidable hole that is full of water, unsure of its depth. "Bloody hell, Hunter Nott. No way I'm driving my baby here again. He'll have to come and get me. And it looks like I'm only going to be able to stay a minute. I didn't allow time for this ridiculous goat track." They reach a slightly better stretch, and Mich dares to speed up a bit. "All I can say about Camas is that you need to set a pretty short time limit for the current situation, given our legal exposure, as well as for her safety. I would suggest that we visit her one more time with food, and if she won't open up, we give her an ultimatum."

Kot knows that Mich is right on most levels. Maybe just not on one very important one. "I'm just afraid that if we spook her, she might bolt again. Then our moral dilemma would be even greater. Right now, we can at least check to make sure she's safe, and help her stay that way. But if I go home—what then?"

"*When*, not *if*. But it's obvious that she likes you, so that's a start. She was watching you in that way girls have when they have a crush on someone."

"Huh. You know, I've felt a strong connection with Camas right from our first meeting and I think she trusts you now, too. Of course, the other reason I've been extremely reluctant to bust Camas is because I don't want to draw attention to myself. I don't even have any ID these days."

"I know. So yes, Tessa will have to take over. And for that to happen, you're probably going to have to trust Tessa with your own story. With the truth."

They are winding through the sunny meadows now, and a tiled gable peak appears above the tree line ahead. Madonna welcomes them, and the two dogs wrestle happily again. Roller's van is gone from the courtyard, but Hunter appears to be home, as promised. As they come into the sun at the back of the house, even at 8 a.m. it already feels like summer.

Mich checks the time. "Oh shit, I have to go. I can't miss this flight."

Kot puts a hand on her arm. "I know, but it's less than five minutes once you're back on the road. Just say hi before you go. I'll show you around here another time." They can see Hunter coming to meet them.

Mich mutters, "Look out Medley. That grin is even cuter than yours."

She congratulates Hunter on all things Glenhurst, and hurries away. Back in the potholes, she has a memory of Kot as a teenager, confiding that she didn't understand the celebrity worship that seemed to engulf their friends. She said that she was always aware of the insecure child within everyone. How grounded she can be, thinks Mich. Still, why hadn't Kot picked up more clues about Ben's lack of commitment? Perhaps love really is that blind. Or, possibly, Ben is just that opaque. Mich pulls onto the road and accelerates with relief. Still, she is already looking forward to getting back to this island on a late afternoon plane, to some wine, dinner, and girl talk.

When the contractor's crew start up the machines in the back, talk becomes difficult. Hunter jerks his head toward the crumbling patio outside the front door. They go through the house and sink into old canvas chairs against the wall. Kot closes her eyes to bask in the sun.

"Mmmm. Feels like that was a long winter. Although probably not for you, hey? Where did you spend it?"

"We were mostly filming on the South Island of New Zealand. It was really beautiful, but I'm not so sure that the quality of the production will live up to the scenery."

Kot chuckles, but asks no more. Hunter appreciates that, since he doesn't feel like providing either the filming or the leading lady details. The folly that was Ashley. They can hear the equipment breaking ground, and he seems to shift gears.

"You have no idea how happy I am to see that starting. But do you think we can ignore the work relationship thing, and just hang out? I really enjoy your company."

Kot smiles. "Probably, boss. As long as you don't get all petulant on me again."

"Ha! No promises there. So. I remember you saying that you don't read the tabloids."

"Nope. Not even at the hairdresser. Is petulance part of your shtick?"

"I have no idea. But anyone who knows me knows that I'm more prone to sulking. I probably just played with my design ideas too long on my own, and I got overly bonded to them. What about you? Hissy fits? No, I don't think that fits. Maybe the silent treatment?"

"Hmmm. For some years, I think I specialized in passive aggressiveness. Now I'm probably more likely to withdraw. Sometimes I also railroad, but only when the mood strikes."

The contractor has found them with a question, so they return to the work area. Even with no known history of First Nations settlement there, Hunter is nervous, for good reason, of disturbing important remains or artefacts, and is relieved that only a minor decision is required. But there is no opportunity for personal conversation until the crew takes their lunch break under a tree.

Hunter and Kot throw together a light lunch and eat at the kitchen table with the French doors open and sun streaming in. Until recently, the man across from Kot was just a famous face and voice, someone whom she'd enjoyed as an actor. Now, she is probably the one doing more of the acting. But she's enjoying the day, so why complicate it with analysis?

Hunter has lined up more questions about her, and she responds openly, describing her former job, its challenges and excitement. She omits names such as Benson Northcott, and any information that might hint at compromises in personal integrity. Hunter seems genuinely interested in her work, and asks insightful questions.

She replies, "Well, not-for-profit work tends to attract idealistic people, and idealism can be sane or screwy. There's also a syndrome that I call competitive martyrdom—sort of like: 'I'm working harder and giving up more than anyone else.' It's silly, and also kind of sweet. Otherwise, egos do need to be firmly parked. What most new folks don't realize is that, in a large organization, for every action there is an equal and onerous requirement for multiple reports, and not everyone can handle the bureaucracy. I was fortunate to find a team who all knew more than I did. Still, to be honest, I now know that burnout can easily overtake people, especially those without families to enforce better work-life balance. I think that idealists can also break their own hearts sometimes."

Hunter shakes his head, intrigued by the shameless integrity of such a foreign world. "I'm impressed as hell. Makes me seriously wonder if my career has been a complete waste of time."

That makes Kot laugh, and Hunter realizes that hearing that could easily become his new daily goal. He waits for the warning voice of his therapist in his head, but nothing comes.

He says, "My cousin works for a health NGO, and from what he's told me, the fundraising part is pretty hairy at times. He said that once commitments are made, if the expected funding doesn't arrive they're completely up shit creek and the stress is unbelievable."

"Right, and that's a reputational thing too, walking the tightrope of donor expectations, but also trying to do what is ethically right. It can certainly keep you awake at night." Kot hates her duplicity in not mentioning that managing various donor relationships can be even worse.

"Believe it or not, it's the same for most film producers. Just possibly less critical to the planet."

Kot is enjoying Hunter's sincere interest, but realizes, again too late, that talking about her career satisfaction would make anyone question why she isn't still enjoying her work there. She is about to reverse the flow and question Hunter in the same way, but her fears are confirmed.

"Okay, Kot Malone. I have to ask the obvious. Why leave a job like that?"

Kot goes to stand in the open doors, her back to him. The workmen are returning to their machines and the contractor is bent over a copy of Kot's already dirty plan. She and Hunter should probably go outside and have a look at things.

She doesn't want to lie to Hunter, but ever since she walked into the store at Gubbins Bay Marina she has relied on half-truths, at best. This time, with this man, it now feels like a tipping point. Hunter has stayed seated, and when Kot turns back to him, her hair is haloed by sunlight and her face in shadows.

"Actually, I didn't choose to leave. And I wasn't let go. I guess you could say I was spirited away."

Hunter seems almost annoyed by her obtuseness. He opens his mouth to say something, but Kot holds out the flat of her hand to stop him, and carries on. "Hunter, absolutely no one in my life except Mich knows what happened. And if I tell you and she finds out, she would probably save others the trouble and kill me herself. The sad truth is that I don't always make the right call."

Hunter stands up. "Hey listen, you don't owe me or anyone your history. I'm sorry if it feels like I'm pushing you. But that said, now I'm really worried."

That was a caring statement, and Kot tries to think of the right words herself. There's surely no added threat to her or to Hunter by telling him the truth. However, there is also that thing about loose lips and sinking ships. She takes a deep breath, and a serious risk.

"Several weeks ago, I witnessed a crime against someone I know well—as in, extremely well. Or at least, for a couple of years, I thought I did. And to be honest, I haven't even figured out the context of what I saw. But apparently, it was enough that I was put into a witness protection program."

Hunter's eyes open wide with shock. "Whaaa?! Oh Kot—" He moves toward her, but again she stops him.

"Let me finish, okay? I was able to collect Medley, but then came a very weird eight days, alone with him on a secluded and thoroughly fenced property outside Victoria. I had very few of my own things, and nothing but questions and a whole lot of frustration. A program support guy brought me supplies every two or three days, but that was it. It was infuriating, and lonely."

Kot looks into Hunter's concerned eyes. "But then the safe house blew up."

"What the fuck! How…?" Hunter is appalled, but then has to wonder if he has found the best-disguised crazy woman yet. The genuine pain on Kot's face argues against that. So is she still in imminent danger, and if so, from whom? And what did she witness?

She doesn't say anything more, so he continues, "I mean, how did you survive that? Is there any chance it was an accident?"

"It happened about a month ago. Since then, I've tried to figure things out. There is no explanation, other than that a bomb was planted with every intention of killing me. With the same information, Michy agrees. So, obviously there was a leak in the protection program itself, at a minimum. My strong instinct afterwards was not to let anyone know I'd survived or where I was—even the police. There was no one to trust, and that hasn't changed. Tessa doesn't even know. Michy is the only one, and she's taken a risk by coming here. A small one, I hope. Since we live in different cities, few people know how close we are."

Hunter moves quickly and hugs her, and this time Kot doesn't resist. It feels incredibly good to be held. He stands back, but takes her hands. "Please tell me everything. I absolutely swear that I won't tell a soul."

So they sit again, and Kot shuts down her doubts and tells Hunter her story. She finishes with, "I guess now I'm waiting for some sign that whoever did it has lost interest in me, or maybe that enough time has gone by. And you know, so far, so good. Atticus feels like a world apart, especially here at Glenhurst. And I've changed my name and my hair."

This is all a lot for Hunter to digest, although not the hair part. He also noticed Kot's blonde roots, but in the context of the modern world, didn't think it merited much attention. What hits him with a wallop is that Kot has probably been in constant fear, and yet managed to act—and act must be the word—ridiculously *normal.* Even humorous. He doubts that he would find such inner resources. Hunter has tried to rescue women before, but this feels different. This just feels right. Kot doesn't need rescuing, and all he wants to do is add his strength to hers.

The genie of her secrets out of the bottle, Kot is numb. Hunter could, quite reasonably, decide that it would be wise to distance from someone who might still be a death target. And Tessa could as well, when she deserves only gratitude and consideration. For the first time since her early days on Atticus, Kot feels a wash of self-pity. Her eyes sting with tears, and she turns to the windows again. Then strong arms enfold her, and she turns to sob on Hunter's chest, lost at last to honesty and openness.

When Kot wipes her eyes, she doesn't try to make light of things, for a change. She also has a clear memory of being held by another man, and even though the protective element wasn't there with Ben, the memory serves as a reminder that this is just a moment in time, illusory. Not something to depend on, moving forward. She also can't allow Hunter to enter the circle of risks that still shadow her life. He is obviously familiar with security issues, but as far as she knows, his actual life has never been seriously threatened.

Then Hunter's hand is cradling the back of her head and when his mouth finds hers, her intoxicated mind shuts down. As the kiss deepens Hunter swings Kot away from the windows and presses her against the kitchen island. If anyone outside makes an appearance, he is prepared to fire him on the spot.

Later, he will let his mind play with how things might have progressed, but a deafening wail suddenly blasts from a device on the nearby counter. Kot breaks away in panic and Hunter curses as he turns it down before picking up a receiver and listening. Kot moves away to compose herself, but Hunter returns to hold her again and look into her face.

His voice is tender. "Kot, that was the search and rescue alarm. You have no idea how much every cell in my body wants to stay here, but they need me to get over to the mainland while there's still plenty of daylight. I'm going to have to grab my gear and go." He nods toward his helicopter, sitting far across the front meadow out in front. "The extra piss-off is that I won't be able to drive you home. I'll see if Marcos can give you a lift."

Kot knows that what she needs right now isn't to make small talk with the contractor, a relative stranger, but some time alone to think. And that might best be done while on the move.

"Hunter, it's okay." She knows that her eyes probably reflect the same warmth and desire she sees in his. She nods at the nearby dogs, now keeping a close eye on their humans. "Medley and I will just have a nice long walk home. That's what I feel like. I'll tell Marcos what's going on, so go. Fly away and be a real-life hero. You know you are, right?" In wonder, she reaches up to brush the now-beloved lock of hair from his brow. "Could you let me know when you're safely back? Do you have my phone number, the garden centre cell?"

"Yeah, I entered that in my contacts right after I met you, of course." He kisses her hard again, and finally lets go with a groan. "Could I maybe see you again tomorrow? I'm sure there will be business things to discuss." That lopsided grin. "Okay. I better go. Can you please give Madonna a scoop of food from that bin and fill up her water when you leave? Thanks."

Hunter looks at her with longing, then shakes his head and grabs a jacket and a bag of gear from the back entry closet. He jogs across the field, away from her. Gone.

Kot watches until the helicopter is out of sight. The house feels empty without Hunter, but she wanders through it again, taking in details that she'd missed before and lingering a bit in Hunter's bedroom. Then she cleans up the few dishes and replenishes Madonna's food and water. Marcos, the contractor, waves his understanding when she yells that she's going to walk home.

No matter how inappropriate, it's definitely fun to feel sixteen again. Everything smells as good as she feels as Medley follows her under the fragrant arch and across the courtyard. She stays on the verge of the lane to avoid most of the potholes and Medley lags behind, entranced by a scent, then runs past her to find more.

Hunter's ability to shift from passion to duty makes her like him even more. Kot remembers her mother's advice during her teenage years: *Kottie, in the end, respect is even more important than love.* She decides to do some overdue research on Hunter Nott, and also resolves to only believe some of what she reads.

Bees are working the wild blue lupines along the lane, and the stretch of wetland still echoes with competing red-winged blackbirds. Kot makes a mental note to advise Hunter and Roller to get rid of the invasive plants taking hold along the driveway before they smother the native ones. The thought of tackling the job together brings a big smile. A cool breeze arrives and she gets her jacket out of her daypack. She'd found it at the second hand store soon after moving into the marina cottage, before even knowing how appropriate the cheerful daisy on its back was going to be for gardening work.

Walking isn't much slower than trying to steer a car safely along Hunter's lane. As they approach the main road, Kot puts Medley on his leash. Since he lost her after the explosion, he never objects. A truck is parked on the other side of the road with its hood open. A man leans over the engine, tinkering with something. Kot keeps walking, thinking idly that he'd been lucky to break down in a place with no ditch, and beside a patch of open ground.

The man glances up, and then stands to look at her. Kot acknowledges him but doesn't stop walking. "Sorry, I'd offer to help, but my dog probably knows more about car mechanics than I do."

"That's okay. I might have it figured out." Kot recognizes a London accent.

He turns back to the motor, but then suddenly calls after her. "As a matter of fact, could you can spare a minute? I could really use an extra pair of hands just to hold this wrench steady. Would you mind?"

His accent sets him apart, but otherwise the guy seems like a lot of others Kot has encountered around Atticus: scruffy, maybe a little down on his luck or his motivation level, but probably nice enough. His tribe appears to be balanced by the well-to-do folks emerging in luxury vehicles from waterfront driveways.

She has been happy on this lovely day, and Kot wants to pay it forward. She heads across the road. "Okay, I might manage that much, but no promises." Once she gets close Kot senses that the man is wired on something and decides to severely limit this encounter.

She stands on the far side of the truck with Medley's leash anchored under her foot, and holds the wrench steady on the indicated bolt while the guy roots around in his tool kit. Medley's patient eyes follow a swallowtail butterfly as it approaches them, then darts away again across the road. The toolbox rattling ends and all is quiet, apart from the bees. The old motor smells of oil and grease.

Kot feels an impulse to drop the wrench and flee. Medley suddenly jerks away, yanking his leash from under Kot's foot. A searing pain strikes her back, and everything goes black.

Rough arms catch her as she falls, then drag her awkwardly onto the truck's rear seat. The man checks that there are still no cars coming, and goes around to the other side to haul Kot in further by her armpits. He pulls a syringe from his pocket and injects its contents into Kot's dangling arm, then slams the rear doors.

Medley had followed his instinct to run away, and now he watches from the darkness of the woods, shivering. Something is wrong with Kot. The man grabs the metal box, bangs down the front of the truck, and disappears inside, where he put Kot. The motor starts, and the truck rolls down the road. Medley chases it through the woods beside the road, but it starts to go too fast and soon disappears from sight. It is taking Kot in the wrong direction from Medley's food and bed, and the place where they are living these days. He knows that he and Kot had been walking in the right direction to get to those things.

He looks around for Mich or Tessa. This may be a strange human game, but no one seems to be around. He returns to the spot where he can still smell Kot a bit. Bewildered by losing her again, he lies down and waits for the truck to bring her back.

~ TWENTY-EIGHT ~

Wayne was holding a gym bag in each gloved hand when he met Derrick at a park trailhead yesterday morning. Derrick followed him along the main trail and onto a tiny deer track that provided scratchy access deep into the forest. Wayne finally reached a small open area and dropped the bags, then began to quietly instruct Derrick in the use of the equipment that was in one of them. To Derrick, this implied a promotion of sorts, but he was annoyed by Wayne's reversion to his former condescending tone, and by his repeated demands that Derrick pay closer attention. Derrick kept his mouth shut, solely on his assumption that the second bag contained another payment instalment.

Wayne laid out exactly what Derrick was supposed to do with the new equipment, and began to test him. Finally satisfied, he narrowed his small eyes. "If you screw this up, I would *not* want to be you, boyo."

Then he repacked the tools and told Derrick to keep to himself from that moment until the end of the "mission." Mission success would apparently be measured by the safe handover of the woman that they'd been tracking, at some as yet unspecified destination. Wayne's last order was that Derrick should wait ten minutes before following him back to the road. He gave Derrick the keys to the truck that he'd driven over to Atticus that morning, and took Derrick's keys in trade. Derrick's truck had become known to a few pub cronies on the island, so Derrick could see the sense in that.

He managed to wait five minutes after Wayne left, and took the opportunity to check out the mystery bag. Inside were some beers, a pile of limp, defrosted pizzas, a few energy bars, and not nearly enough cash to pay for the next instalment of drugs from his pub dealer. He counted it twice, hoping he'd missed something. Wayne was probably trying to create maximum incentive, the bastard.

During the McDonald's meeting, Wayne had confided that this was the biggest mission that his "team" had been given yet. His precise word had been *unprecedented.* And Derrick was to understand that its swift completion was a key prerequisite for full payment. A serious capacity for both menace and generosity had been implied. Wayne had also mentioned that Derrick might be considered for a management role, should he complete this job swiftly and well. At least, that's what Derrick assumed was meant by "a bit higher on the ladder, if you get my drift." If this turned out to be his last grunt job, it would be bloody brilliant. He's a proven star and it's time to move on up. Later yesterday, he'd decided that he might as well finish the job for the promised massive payout.

This morning, Derrick risked parking the loaner truck in deep shadows down the road and used his binoculars to enhance his partial view of the garden centre. He'd figured out that the high percentage of meth in the mix he'd been given was probably meant to keep him on high alert, uninterested in food, and hooked for more. Whatever—it was quite pleasant, sitting there buzzing in the morning sun, and it wasn't long before the two women and the dog emerged. The target was in jeans again. The other one wore expensive clothes and carried an attaché case. She slid behind the wheel of the Audi and lowered its top while the target took the dog around to the passenger side.

Derrick followed at a distance. The Audi turned left into a rough lane and he pulled into forest shadows to wait. It wasn't long before the car blasted out of the driveway again and raced away in the opposite direction. Derrick's target was still down that driveway, but he didn't dare investigate. He pulled onto the wide grassy verge across the road and on an angle from the driveway, still pointed north toward Gubbins Bay. Between trees, he had a long view of the first stretch of the private lane and sufficient notice if someone was coming out.

A joint helped to balance him a bit as Derrick pondered possibilities. Two plans gradually emerged: one to be used in this location, and another if he had to wait until the target was back at the garden centre. It would likely be the latter, but just in case, he collected his tool kit from the back seat. Another little hit of meth delivered a fine sense of invincibility and several hours drifted by with no hardship whatsoever. The only interruption was one of the island's old witches walking by and peering into his window to make sure that he was alive.

It was a surprise when his target appeared on foot in the early afternoon, still some distance down the lane. The dog was intermittently in view, but otherwise Derrick was sure she was alone. He waited until she was behind a long clump of evergreens, then grabbed a wrench and jumped out to open the hood of his truck and turn on the charm.

In the end, he couldn't have imagined a more brilliant outcome. His only—and admittedly addled—mistake was forgetting to factor in the dog. He had nothing against dogs in general, but should have taken it as well, and then painlessly disposed of it. At least the mutt couldn't talk, and Derrick was sure that no one else had witnessed the critical fifty seconds it had taken him to persuade the woman to cross the road, and then get her unconscious body into his back seat. Derrick temporarily forgave the island its boring remoteness in exchange for its low traffic and lack of surveillance cameras.

The mild Taser had worked to get the woman into the truck, and then the injection ensured that she would stay out for longer. Derrick was also chuffed about his competence with the new equipment. He'd nailed both the Taser and injecting someone else for the first time, and had even remembered to pull over at a viewpoint on the way to the marina and wait for the coast road to be clear before hurling her cell phone into the waves.

He has parked close to the tall hedge beside the marina parking lot, and his luck continues. The only people around are down at the docks. He grabs a large wheeled cart from among the group stored nearby for the use of boaters. The worst scenario would be another vehicle coming into the lot during the transfer, but he's temporarily parked the truck at an angle that doesn't allow much of a view and he intends to be quick.

Derrick positions the cart behind the rear passenger door of the truck. He takes a fast look in both directions before awkwardly hauling the woman's limp body out of the truck and into the barrow. He folds her arms so that they don't hang out, and by the time he's piled a crumpled tarp and Wayne's equipment bag on top, there is no way to identify what lies beneath. He tips the unconscious woman onto the floor of his waterfront cottage and dumps the bag beside her. Then he closes the cottage door, neatly returns the barrow, and moves his truck into a designated parking spot.

Back inside with the door bolted, Derrick gets his captive into an old recliner. He grabs ropes from the bag and clumsily binds her legs, arms, and torso to the chair. He is euphoric with his accomplishments and remembers to take photos and send them to Wayne, using a new site, as instructed. He will await his next orders, allowing time to indulge in a well-deserved bonus for his efforts.

The meth is certainly taking its toll on his coordination, but a new excitement has delivered pleasure to his groin. The woman's long eyelashes rest peacefully on her tanned cheeks and the way that her face is flung back reminds him of an old favourite on his porn sites. Derrick doesn't intend to cause harm and doubts that anyone but the target herself might object to what he has in mind. And possibly, even while unconscious, she wants him to enjoy her. Derrick is sure there are women like that, even if he hasn't actually met one who will admit it. Anyway, back in the earlier search phase, Wayne had described this mission as "getting justice for a bro who's been wronged." So this broad is probably not exactly all sweet and innocent.

Derrick is unsure of the purpose of a blindfold, since she has already seen him, but Wayne was firm about the need for it, so his shaky fingers finally knot a cotton rag behind her head. He pulls the drapes shut. Even the way that their stupid hanging bobbles bounce around is sexy. Then he gropes happily and adjusts her clothing to improve his view. The boobs don't come close to the silicone whoppers of his online addiction, but are very nice and right where they belong.

A wash of reddish-brown hair hangs like a curtain over one side of her face, now bringing to mind a provocative film star from the 1930s. Her mouth is slightly open, and a thin rivulet of drool drips from one side. He can't remove her jacket or jeans, but in a haze of bliss he gets to work on himself. But then the drool reminds him that he was supposed to gag her, too. With his pants around his knees, he grabs another rag from the bag and almost falls. She starts to wake up, choking a bit on the tight gag.

The woman's animal whimpering is unnerving, and brings an unwelcome memory of his childhood dog after being hit by a car. Still, this is his first sexual experience since he started using ice, and in his opinion the results are nothing short of inspirational. More than enough to provide some visual memories for future solitary efforts. He takes a few photos as well.

But now the bitch is weakly struggling against the bindings and his phone is buzzing. Watching her writhe, he gives Wayne an update and listens to a series of orders. He hangs up and gets the syringe labeled "2" from the equipment bag. With relief, Derrick injects her with its contents.

A few minutes later, he hits the road alone and lights a plain old cigarette. He isn't tired, hungry, or worried about a single thing. He has a tiny bit of meth left to get him through this trip. After weeks of tedium, he is bloody close to being king of the world.

TWENTY-NINE

Kot's instincts are all that she has right now. The most basic one, survival, requires a complete focus on holding down the vomit. Otherwise, she will choke and die from the gag in her mouth. She suppresses her panic and gradually manages to work the fabric forward with her tongue. She remembers to take deep breaths and the nausea eases a bit, making rational thought possible.

There is no sound of movement or breathing, but she still isn't sure that she is alone. She has no idea how long she was knocked out before waking to find herself bound, blindfolded, and gagged. She has a confused memory of waking once before.

Her upper body is bare and cold, and her bra is pulled down uncomfortably. Her lower body is still clothed, but her breasts feel bruised, and she suspects that she has been abused. She suppresses a strong urge to moan. She needs to stay quiet in case the creep with the truck, or whoever has control of her now, is still within earshot and finds out that she's conscious.

For her to feel this sick, he must have screwed up the dosage of whatever drug he'd used. He might be on drugs himself, but whether that presents only danger or might be used to her advantage, Kot doesn't know.

It takes conscious effort not to hyperventilate, and she can't see or move much. But she can still hear, and try to think. There is still no sound in the cottage, and she grows sure that she is alone.

While her captor hasn't raped or killed her yet, that may be just a matter of time. If he's holding her in hopes of ransom, Kot can't fathom who would be expected to pay. She's positive that she has never met that man before, and is furious with herself for being sucked into his request for help. He must have a role in the continuing attempt to kill her. Excuses of how well things seemed to be going, the friendliness of Atticus, or her own level of romantic intoxication just don't cut it.

Kot can twist her head and neck enough to create friction on the edges of the blindfold and move it until she is able to make out some features of the room. She goes back to work on the clumsy gag until she can spit it out.

The room's dim light is filtered through curtains to her right—curtains that seem vaguely familiar. The air smells musty, like in an old place that has been shut up. She is tied to something that reclines. It reminds her of a dentist's chair, except that it's upholstered. In any case, it isn't possible to move it, especially with her body tied to it. Still, it too seems familiar.

Solely by the fact that she didn't wet her pants while she was unconscious, Kot assumes that it's still the same day that she was abducted. There is no sign of Medley, and she fears for him even more than after the explosion. What might her kidnapper have done to him? Her breath catches in a sob, but tears and panic are more than useless; they're dangerous.

Shrinking her shoulders and arms toward her body to provide slack in the rope yields some progress, but the effort weakens Kot and brings back the nausea. She takes deep breaths through her nose and long exhalations through her mouth, trying to build strength on all levels. Then she rests, and listens.

Beyond the wind in the trees, there is nothing identifiable. After a while, the wind begins to gust, bringing the jangle of sailboat rigging. The next sound confirms her suspicions: the unique squeak at the end of the rasping heron's call could only belong to Herman. She must be in one of the marina cottages, probably unused since last season. She focuses, and also catches the sweet song of circling purple martins around the nest boxes on the docks.

Kot twists her head and raises her shoulder enough to nudge the blindfold askew, then shakes her head until it falls off. The resulting sickness is worth it. The darkening room is a mirror image of the little sitting area in her former marina cottage, and from the light coming in and the closeness of the dock noise, Kot guesses it is the lowest one in the row.

Encouraged by at least being somewhere familiar, Kot is now desperate to attract attention. She yells as loud as she can, but the weakness of her voice is maddening. She stops to work on the ropes again.

Obviously, someone was still searching for her while she was beginning to enjoy her naïve little existence on Atticus. Maybe even while she and Mich had been sitting and discussing it all so cozily. If she can find a way to escape this situation, she will need to forget Atticus and Hunter, Tessa, and even Camas—and disappear again. But after two supposedly safe places have been discovered, where will she find another?

She stifles another sob. That line of thought can't be a priority right now. It's also remotely possible that there is no connection between the events, and that this loser has abducted her for some other purpose. He might be an addict, and that might mean poor impulse control. Even worse, if he's on crystal meth, he could be dangerous and violent.

So many women have been taken, tortured, and abused for a long time before being killed. But at a marina, on Atticus Island? The same unanswered questions remain, the same crushing impotence.

Kot hears Steve's voice faintly in the distance, calling to someone. She makes as much noise as possible, but then catches the distinctive slam of the screen door of their house. How could Steve and Nora have rented a unit to this guy? Does it mean that they are involved in her kidnapping? That seems completely incongruous. Maybe they don't even know that he is using this cottage. Maybe he broke in.

Kot is still groggy from whatever drug he inflicted on her after what must have been a Taser hit. Now, after her apparent failure to attract attention, there is no escape strategy that doesn't require being able to move.

After another half-hour's work, Kot has managed to get one shoulder under the upper bindings and to almost free one arm. But she is also exhausted by another long attempt to attract attention, and so hoarse that trying any more is pointless. If anyone heard her, nothing has been done.

It is quiet outside and so dark in the cabin that she might as well still be blindfolded.

Then a key turns in the lock. He is back.

THIRTY

Since she swung her feet to the floor at dawn Tessa has made satisfying progress on her endless to-do list. And, happily, Kot should be more available to help now that Hunter has approved her designs and work has begun. From here on, Tessa hopes that she and Kot can just check in on Glenhurst as necessary, at least until planting begins. That is, if her new employee is still around after their big chat.

For some reason, Kot hasn't called with the report that Tessa requested, and Tessa is more than curious to see what progress has been made there on this—literally—ground-breaking day. She turns into Glenhurst's lane on her way back to the nursery. Maybe she can also save Hunter the trouble of driving Kot home. He might be mad at her for that, but too bad.

Tessa is now very close to being ready to open her business to the public, and she plans to surprise Kot and Rob with some celebratory bubbly in a few hours. Mich, too, if she's around. Some toasts may also serve to lighten the mood after she and Rob have had that talk with Kot about the man looking for her. While navigating Glenhurst's lane, Tessa's mind drifts back to the early call from Rob this morning. He hadn't wasted time.

"Tessa, unless something has changed, we need to meet with Kot together today. I was taking a load of garbage to the depot yesterday evening and I passed the same sketchy guy who was hanging around the café. He was driving a different truck, but it was definitely the so-called Derrick Bond. How about I swing by the garden centre after you're both finished today?"

Alarmed, Tessa had suggested that they meet around 5 p.m. and said she would make sure they both were there."

"Okay, great. See you then. And what's with the Audi convertible parked behind your store? Is that Kot's?"

Tessa replied, distractedly. "No. It belongs to her friend, Mich. Suzanne Michaluk. She has a PR firm in Vancouver and is staying with Kot for a bit. She's also volunteering for me a bit. She dropped Kot at Glenhurst this morning, and then I think she was aiming for the morning float plane to Vancouver harbour and coming back later this aft." Tessa paused. "Okay. This is getting a little too weird, Rob. Whatever's going on, Kot needs to know that someone has been asking around for her, and may even have located her. The guy may stop at stalking, but neither of us would forgive ourselves if something happened that we could have prevented. Anyway, better late than never. See you around 5."

Tessa had been lost in thought for a minute after the call. Rob's police background was a comfort, as well as the fact that there is someone living with Kot at the moment. They seem pretty tight, and Mich strikes her as fiercely protective. Reassured by having a plan to deal with the issue this very day, Tessa had then buried herself in more immediate tasks.

She now decides to include Mich in the conversation with Kot, if possible. It's definitely high time for some openness from one or both of them.

At Glenhurst, she is pleased with the day's progress and hopes that Hunter is as well. The pool excavation is complete, and the contours of the rear gardens, greenhouse pad, and pool surround are roughed out. The machines now sit abandoned and almost menacing in the afternoon shadows of the perimeter forest. Hunter's car is there, but everything is quiet. The only sign of life is Madonna, wagging madly inside the kitchen.

The French doors are unlocked and Tessa steps inside to fend off Madonna's joy. A copy of the design is laid out on the kitchen table, and the few things in the dishrack are dry. Once Madonna settles down, Tessa calls Hunter's name, and then Kot's. Her only answer is silence. She is confused, and also a little wary of intruding. Surely Hunter and Kot wouldn't have been so unwise as to go upstairs for some koochy-koochy, but Tessa can't come up with another explanation.

She crosses to the windows overlooking the front of the house. The machines haven't begun work out there, and there is no one around. Then she realizes that something in the scene is missing. Hunter's helicopter is gone. Perhaps he offered Kot a trip. *Clever, Romeo.* That must be it.

"So, Miss Maddy, no flies on your guy, hey? At least they left you well supplied, but it looks like you're not even hungry. Not like you, sweet girl."

The critical thing that is also missing is a text from Kot about her whereabouts. Like the promised call that didn't come, that's not like her either. Tessa sends both Hunter and Kot a questioning text, and scratches Madonna's neck as she waits in the stillness for a reply. But of course, they might not be aware of their phones while up in a chopper, so Tessa heads back to her truck. She hopes that the later conversation with Kot won't need to last long or be too heavy. There is probably a simple explanation for that guy hanging around, and there are things to celebrate with the prosecco she's about to pick up. It will all be fine, as long as Hunter gets her employee back in time. She sends him another text to that effect, just in case.

Windows down, Tessa belts out additional harmony for the Dixie Chicks as she swings onto the main road. At first, the sight of the dog sitting on the other side of the road doesn't make sense. It looks exactly like Kot's Medley. The little fellow recognizes her truck and wags his tail, then runs across the road with his leash trailing behind him. Medley it is. And far too clearly, he is all by himself.

Tessa pulls over and leaps out, waving her arms to stop the car approaching from the other direction. Once she has Medley in the truck, she goes back to have a look at the area where he'd been. Even if Kot has just gone into the woods for a pee, she wouldn't leave Medley alone by the road. She calls Kot loudly several times, but is only answered by a siren in the distance. There is an old wrench on the ground, and Tessa decides to leave it there. She notices some disturbance of the earth nearby and steps away. Her happy notion of toasting with prosecco dies an unnatural death.

At about the same time, Rob pulls into the nursery parking lot and goes to peer over the fence. An impressive amount has been accomplished since his last visit. Everything looks expertly set up and ready for customers. Fatigue and low spirits have made him sleepy, and he sits down on one of the benches outside the gate to wait for Tessa and Kot.

A few minutes later, Tessa's truck barrels into the lot, and a dog jumps out behind her. She seems flustered and hurries toward the stairs, calling to Rob, "Hey. Hang on a sec. I just have to see if Kot's home."

Rob watches her knock, then quickly unlock the unit with her own key. Within a minute she joins him again, without the dog and looking worried.

"Have you seen Kot anywhere? She expected to spend most of today at Hunter's to get the landscaping started, but no one was there when I stopped by except Madonna. Hunter's car was there, but then I noticed his helicopter wasn't, and figured maybe he took Kot up for a joy ride. But when I was leaving, I found Medley—her dog—sitting on the other side of the road from Glenhurst's driveway. There's no way Kot would ever have willingly left Medley loose like that. He would have been safely in the house with Madonna. I called several times, in case she was nearby. Something's wrong."

"No, I haven't seen her or Hunter. I guess the best scenario is that they're together, and Medley took off for some reason. But then, wouldn't Kot have gone after him?" Rob's gut is already a long way from his best-case scenario.

"Shit. We should have met with her before now, or I should have had the talk with her myself. It's just been such a crazy week."

"Yeah, for me too. But let's not beat ourselves up just yet. Roller wasn't around either?"

Tessa shakes her head. "No. I'll call him next. I've left messages for both Kot and Hunter. Can you try as well?"

She disappears into the shop, and Rob heads to his truck for his phone. As he waits for the first call to go through, an attractive woman arrives in a convertible and nods at him before marginally slowing down and driving around to the back of the building. Kot's friend Mich, presumably.

Mich heads towards the stairs, aiming to find Kot and a large glass of wine, but Tessa intercepts her. "Mich! Thank God! We're trying to locate Kot. Have you talked to her?"

Mich's heart turns to ice. "No. I just got back from Vancouver. I've tried to reach her a couple of times this afternoon, but it went to voicemail right away and she hasn't returned my text yet."

The man in the parking lot puts his phone in his pocket and comes over to join them. Nothing remarkable about him, but that's not necessarily a bad thing. Mich likes his face, and the easy, confident way he walks. He fits Kot's description of Robert Baschel.

Rob addresses them both. "Kot was at Glenhurst with Hunter today. You must be Mich, so you'd know that, since I hear you dropped her off. I'm Robert Baschel, by the way."

"Suzanne Michaluk. Doesn't Hunter know? He was there this morning and he planned to give her a ride back here. I doubt very much that he would choose to do anything else." She turns to Tessa. "Was his car there?" Mich is trying to summon a veneer of steely calm, currently all that she can offer this nightmare situation.

Tessa quickly fills her in. Hearing about her finding Medley alone cements Mich's dread. "So, we don't know anything that has happened since I dropped off Kot, early this morning?"

The other two look at the ground and shake their heads.

Mich continues, "Hunter was with her then, and he mentioned that Roller had an appointment in Victoria today. Hunter must have left Kot alone for some reason. Otherwise, they would have left the dogs together at Glenhurst. My guess is that something happened to her, near where you found Medley."

Rob says, "Hunter also hasn't picked up messages. With the helicopter gone, he might have got a search-and-rescue call, and maybe Kot went with him. That doesn't fit the dog being abandoned, though."

Tessa says, "There was a wrench on the ground near where Medley was sitting. I left it there."

Her phone buzzes and the others try to get the drift from just her side of the conversation. When Tessa ends the call her face is white.

"That was Roller. He said that Hunter phoned him just before he took off. It was hard to hear, but he gathered that Hunter did get an urgent call for SARS work on the mainland and he couldn't drive Kot home. For some reason Roller doesn't understand, Hunter passed on Kot's number and asked Roller to check in on Kot this afternoon to make sure she got home okay. But Roller is also only getting her voicemail. After he picked up my message, he called Hunter's contractor. Kot told Marcos she was going to walk home, and he didn't see her after that. Roller should be almost back at Glenhurst by now. He promised to call me again after he's had a look around. He's feeling bad because he would have stayed home and provided security for Kot if he'd known she might need it."

Rob mumbles, "He can get in line."

Mich looks away. Her stomach is roiling. She has no choice now.

"I need to tell you both something that maybe Kot should have shared before now, but we both stupidly thought that there wasn't an urgent need anymore. Kot came to Atticus because of a serious threat to her life."

She gives them a short account. "She's been waiting for signs that it might be safe to go home, and trying to watch for danger here as well. There have still been too many unknowns and no reason to trust the police at this point. She doesn't even know who was after her. I'm probably the only person who knows what's happened to Kot, and where she's living. Although now, I'm wondering if she told Hunter as well. That would account for him asking Roller to check on her."

The others are staring at her in horror, and now Tessa's voice is flat. "So that's what it was. No wonder Kot didn't trust anyone with the information."

Describing herself as a murder target would also certainly not have helped Kot find work on the island. But no doubt Kot believed that only she was targetted. And she was probably right.

Mich says, "Kot was starting to feel safe here, and when I came over I kept checking to make sure that I wasn't being followed. But maybe someone found her another way. And now they have her." Or worse.

The proudly professional Suzanne Michaluk turns away to hide her tears.

Rob pulls out his phone again to call a hockey buddy, who is also the senior RCMP officer for the Southern Gulf Islands. He makes two mental notes: first, to make sure that Suzanne Michaluk's car is examined for tracking devices. The second is that the woman is way out of his league.

Tessa's head has started to pound. She rotates her knotted neck and goes through the gate to the comfort of her nursery plants, all so artfully set up by Kot. Out of the corner of her eye she sees a small, dark head duck behind the back of the building. Strange. But her phone buzzes again and she takes the call inside her store, her heart in her mouth until she finds out that the caller is just an excited future customer. Astounding, how quickly priorities can change.

~ THIRTY-ONE ~

Camas spent this morning sitting in her secret lookout, watching people on the beach and the occasional boat going by. She has eaten all of the leftovers that Kot sent home with her last night, and now wishes that she'd saved some. But her stomach is happier than she can remember in a very long time, and she slept well. Maybe Kot and Mich will deliver more food soon—glorious things that can just be opened and eaten, not searched for and dug, picked, or stolen.

One white wall of her tower room is glowing in the afternoon sun when she looks up from her puzzle book. She can hear the rumble of a motor approaching the top of the driveway below, and runs to peer around the edge of the window. A small car stops near the house and an older woman gets out to extract a walker from the trunk before helping the old man out of the passenger side. He is apparently home from the hospital, as Kot had predicted that he would be today. He looks weak, but swats the woman's help away and struggles into the house with the walker, leaving her to carry his bag.

The woman leaves and Camas returns to her puzzle book and loses track of time. When she peeks outside again the sun is lower. Just off the porch, the walker is lying on its side beside the splayed figure of the old man. He isn't moving. Something silver, perhaps an upside-down bowl, is on the grass nearby.

Camas's throat is tight with fear. If the man is alive and she pretends that she hasn't seen him, he could die and it would be her fault. If he is already dead, it will be terrible to be the only one who knows that his body is down there. And the nighttime animals…

Camas unlocks the heavy tower door and takes a fast look around the property below. Then, for the first time since she arrived, she follows the main path down from the lighthouse to the residence. The scene she is approaching is creepy, and she can barely control her panic. If the old man's eyes are open, she knows she'll run. She is relieved to find that he is unconscious, and his rattled breathing means he's still alive. Cat kibble is spilled in an arc on the ground around an aluminum bowl, but there is no sign of the cat that he was probably trying to lure.

Camas gives the man and walker a wide berth and hurries through the open door of the house. At least she knows her way around. She grabs the old-fashioned portable phone just inside the kitchen and dials 911. The woman who answers asks Camas questions, and says that help is on its way. When Camas is asked for her name and relationship to the patient, she thinks fast. She doesn't want to use "Raven" again, and chooses a beloved movie character: "Ilsa." She adds, "I'm a neighbour."

She is asked to take the phone outside and to keep talking to the dispatcher until the emergency crew arrives, but Camas hangs up and races back up the hill. She locks the lighthouse door behind her. Looking out of the window in her room again, her stomach is a knot.

Obviously, other people will be arriving very soon. When they find the man on the grass, they'll look for the girl who called for help. Police might start to search, and maybe they will find the lighthouse key quickly. Isn't that the kind of thing that firemen and policemen know how to do?

Camas can't let herself be trapped in the lighthouse again. She needs to hide somewhere else until the coast is clear. Her field of trusted people includes a solid total of one. Maybe Mich, too. But Kot will know what to do.

Camas can already hear a siren, but it's still far away. She puts Grizz, Mama's ring and scarf, and her photo into her pack and grabs her jacket. She takes her secret exit out the back, and hides in the forest a little distance from the driveway to watch what happens as the howling sirens grow louder.

Camas cowers and covers her ears as first a fire truck and then an ambulance rush up the driveway past her. When they are silenced at the top she sneaks away to the only place of warmth and security she has known since Mama died.

Mich's car is parked at the back, and a truck is in the parking lot outside the shop. There are people on the other side of the building, and Camas hears a man's voice. She can't make out words or Kot's voice from that distance, so she creeps past the Audi and along the back of the building to wedge herself behind a bushy shrub at the front corner.

She pokes her head out for just a second, and her losing streak continues. Camas can only hope, irrationally, that the woman didn't actually see her. She hears her footsteps continue into the building and then a voice in there, and peeks again. A man is talking on a cell phone in the parking lot and Mich is out there too. But there is no sign of Kot.

The older woman must have seen her because she suddenly appears around the corner. She'd made no noise and there is nothing that Camas can do in this living nightmare. It's too late.

"Well, hi there. Are you okay? Are you looking for someone?"

She seems motherly, or even grandmotherly. That might be nice, normally, but is probably bad. Such women like to meddle, and try to fix things.

When Camas doesn't answer, the woman says, "My name is Tessa. Don't be scared. No one here is going to hurt you."

Camas's eyes glance at the upper level of the building. "I need to see Kot."

Tessa is puzzled. Obviously, Kot must know who this girl is. "Well, as a matter of fact, we all want to see Kot, but we can't find her. What's your name? And have you seen her today?"

Camas shakes her head, and ignores the request for her name. "Then can I talk to Mich?"

Tessa warily leads the girl to the others. Too many secrets.

When she sees Camas, Mich blinks rapidly, almost angry at this illogical distraction. Then her face softens. Whatever the reason, Camas must be desperate if she has come out of hiding—and she also has her pack. Maybe she knows where Kot is, and the best way to find that out is to not frighten her further.

"Hi, Camas. Are you okay? Did those sirens that went by have anything to do with you?"

The man joins them, but Camas looks only at Mich to deliver her broken account of what happened and how she called for help. She tells them that she hasn't seen Kot, but needs to.

Camas is shivering and doesn't resist Mich's hug. Mich knows that the girl's precarious lighthouse life has come to a close. With a sigh, she explains, to Rob and Tessa's looks of disbelief, where Camas has been living "for a bit." Then she thinks for a minute, weighing the girl's options.

She tells Camas, "You need to hide again. You'll be fine if you just stay out of sight in the forest across the road. Maybe behind that big old tree we talked about when I was driving you here." Mich points to a gnarly, half-dead maple trunk on the other side of the field and road. "Other people will be coming here soon and they might search everywhere, including my car. Promise you won't try to go anywhere else. If you stay hidden, you'll probably be safe. Okay?"

Camas nods and turns to run, but steps in her way and kneels down to the girl's height. "Camas, my name is Rob, and I'm also a friend of Kot's. We're all very worried that something bad might have happened. Is there anything that you can tell us? Do you know if she was afraid of anyone in particular?"

Camas just shakes her head at him, wide-eyed with fear. Kot, in danger. The horribleness of this day just keeps growing.

"When did you last see Kot? Can you remember?"

"When I had supper here, last night."

Rob looks up at Mich, and she nods ruefully.

Rob knows that Camas is not only a minor, but as a cop, recognizes her as a likely victim, extremely vulnerable, and a clear flight risk. He wonders if the rationale behind Kot and Mich's decision not to transfer Camas to authorities yet was really in the girl's best interests, but has to reluctantly agree with the plan to keep her hidden for now. Sorting out her situation comes a distant second to the emergency around Kot. As long as the mysterious girl is safe, no time can be wasted.

Her headache worsening, Tessa heads into the shop for the extra-strength painkillers that she keeps there. When she returns, Camas is gone and a police car is approaching the intersection with its lights flashing.

Rob's police buddy pieces together the story around Kot, and sends a corporal up to search her apartment and everywhere else. Then, based on the information from Mich, he requests contact with the Witness Protection Program. Instead, in only a few minutes, he is surprised to receive a call from a Sergeant Wade Dance, a senior officer with an organized crime squad in Vancouver. Dance tells him to hold everyone present so that he and his superior, Inspector Annette Solinski, can conduct phone interviews. Rob overhears and asks to speak to his old colleague, Annie Solinski. After a brief catch-up, she takes Rob's statement and notes his personal cell number. Then she and Dance begin their interviews with the others.

Once she has told Solinski everything she can, Tessa goes upstairs to collect Medley and his supplies and go home. Her daughter is going away and she will be looking after her grandchildren overnight. Tessa has priorities, no matter the state of her head or what else is going on. Or what her friend Toni thinks of those priorities.

After the police have finished their search and left, Mich spirits Camas up to the apartment and locks the door behind them. The inaction is killing her.

~ THIRTY-TWO ~

Derrick has barely slept during the past two days, and the meth has removed any interest in food. Far more importantly, he is out of every substance that makes life worth living.

He did another trip to a dock near the ferry terminal in Swartz Bay to exchange the borrowed truck for a fast boat and the assurances that his own truck would be returned when the job was done. He also got new orders from Wayne. Both the orders and Derrick's boat trip back to Atticus Island were rough. Wayne's instructions were to go easy on the chemicals until the job is done, and now Derrick is up against both time pressures and Wayne's ignorance about how much Derrick has been supplementing the drugs Wayne has provided with more from his pub source.

His temper flares when he opens the cottage door. The bitch is already free of the blindfold and gag and has almost freed herself from the upper bindings. This evidence of his own incompetence is infuriating. With a curse, Derrick overturns the chair she is in. It brings down a curtain rod as it topples sideways, and the woman's head hits the wall. Derrick leaves her there and rummages in the bag.

He'll need her to be able to see where she's walking, so he doesn't replace the blindfold. He bends over and roughly binds her wrists together, then cuts the ropes restraining her to the chair. She tumbles onto the floor and Derrick stuffs another rag in her mouth, then pulls out the gun that Wayne had supplied. He almost sounds embarrassed when he tells her that it's "only to show who's in charge." Derrick orders his captive to her feet.

Kot is dizzy as she struggles up with bound hands, and her kidnapper offers no assistance. He is sweating and seems to be on the edge of panic. The gun in his hand fills her with dread.

Not bothering to close the cottage door, he keeps the barrel to her ribs and marches her to the docks. With his left arm wrapped tightly around her shoulders, in the darkness he could be a lover, or assisting a tipsy companion.

The few occupied boats at the docks have closed curtains, and the night is quiet. Further up the hill, Steve and Nora's living room lights are still on. There is a brief hoot of laughter from a dock further down the bay.

Kot has no doubt that this man will hurt her again if she tries to attract attention, but her eyes still roam the night for a witness, for hope. Anyone or anything to justify the risk of yelling out with her mouth full of cloth and the pointy end of a gun sticking into her flesh.

Derrick can't clearly remember the procedures he was told to follow, and he hardly cares. He manhandles the woman onto the boat and pushes her to the floor with a muttered threat. Then he drags a plastic tarpaulin over her, and manages to get the cruiser untied and underway. He keeps the running lights off, counting on the moon to provide enough light to complete the prescribed handover of his prisoner.

Once underway with the woman stowed, Derrick feels a little better. He remembers that by ten o'clock he needs to be about two kilometres off the southern end of Saltspring Island, that looming mass ahead to the right. Then he is supposed to wait for a phone call. It's going to take him twenty minutes to get out that far. He'll be late, but it isn't his fucking fault.

Derrick guns the motor, and the sturdy boat pounds over the choppy waves. At first, Kot heeds his threats and is bounced around under the tarp. Even in the dark, she'd identified the boat at first glance: a twenty-five-foot aluminum Eagle Craft, with a single motor that must be at least 150 horsepower. Highly seaworthy.

She works the gag out of her mouth quickly this time and takes big breaths of the ocean air. She's sure that the wasted creep can't be seeing too clearly, and anyway, he can't keep a close eye on her while also driving. She needs to see where they're heading, and awkwardly grips a side strut with her bound hands to get her head free of the tarp. A blast of salt wind hits her face and Kot is suddenly alert and clear-headed.

She is pretty sure that she knows this ocean world better than the novice at the wheel. He is obviously a mess, gesturing and ranting to himself, but Kot can't make out any words. He'd shoved the gun into the left pocket of his jacket before covering her with the tarp. She'd noted that he's right-handed, so he can't be familiar with how to access a weapon quickly.

They are out of Gubbins Bay, and the lights of the last ferry from Vancouver look pretty in the distance. That means that the final one from the other direction has already gone by and is out of sight. The southern end of Saltspring Island looms ahead and to starboard. In the western sky the landing lights of a plane approach Victoria's airport, and the sky further south is lit orange from the city that Kot used to call home.

She drops to the floor again and presses her back against the side for more stability. She is able to use the tarp to hide her from the view of the driver but still catch some ambient light. Time to get to work.

She starts chafing the cheap jute rope of her wrist bindings against the rough edge of a strut, twisting back and forth for more torque. It burns, but the fibres gradually fray and loosen until she is able to slip one hand free and pull off the rest. Kot looks around for something solid to use to strike the driver from behind, and finds nothing but her own inadequate fists.

Up in the bow, Derrick isn't always sure if it's him or someone else driving the boat, and the night sky and sea are confusingly one. Perhaps it's all part of some hellish dream. His job conditions have deteriorated abominably, and the promised rewards keep fading into the distance.

Why couldn't Wayne have eased his pain by supplying more meth when he gave him the boat? It's not like Derrick has screwed up. Even when he'd resorted to begging, Wayne's response had been a cold: "When, and only when, you get the job done, boyo, heaven shall be yours. So 'til then, just stay on your toes."

Derrick wants to kill him.

He isn't feeling much more in control of the boat than of the entire situation, and he lets both Wayne and the universe know what pieces of shit they are. Then his drunken dad starts yelling at him to answer his fucking phone. He shouts obscenities back at his dad. Only on the fifth ring does Derrick remember that he was expected to have reached the location by now, and be ready for a call. He turns off the motor. The boat slows and rolls back and forth in the open strait.

Terrified, Kot peeps over the tarpaulin. The guy has stood up. He's steadying himself on the back of the seat and looking at the sky, a phone to his ear. His words are slurred, but in the quiet she learns his name.

"Yeah, it's Derrick."

Derrick listens for a minute, interrupts once, and then starts jumping around and screaming in agitation. Kot ducks down out of sight.

"What the *fuck*, man! No way. That wasn't part of the deal. Fuck you all to hell. I done everything you wanted, every fucking little thing, and I done it all good, way better'n anyone else would've. But I never agreed to kill nobody. You want that done, you fuckin' do it yourself."

Numb, Kot sneaks another look. Derrick has collapsed into his seat and is staring at his phone, sobbing. He seems beaten. He has clearly been ordered to kill her. One of his feet starts tapping on the boat floor, on and on, an eerie counterpoint to the water gently slapping the hull.

The wind and waves have stilled, and the boat is almost steady. Derrick isn't a large man, but he has that gun, and seems increasing desperate. A minute later, he starts the motor and pushes the throttle to full. The boat leaps forward and Kot, unready, is thrown toward the stern. With the motor roaring behind her, she crawls to get a grip on the side again so that she can watch Derrick.

He is steering with the other hand and has the gun in his other. Kot is desperate to act. But do what? Jump out? There is nothing onboard that floats that she could take into the water with her. Almost by design. And Derrick could easily turn around to shoot her in the water, or run her over. Or both.

Wayne's orders have sucked Derrick deeper into a psychic nightmare. He'd been told, more than once, that he would be handing off the woman to someone, either in another boat or at some landfall, and that when the job was done and he had returned this boat to Wayne, he would get his truck back and be justly rewarded. So either someone lied to Wayne, or Wayne tricked him. Nothing about this final stage of the mission was ever described in detail, but hadn't Wayne said that was roughly how it would go? All that

Derrick remembers is Wayne being more forthcoming—eloquent, even—about the payment details.

Kidnapping was a big stretch for Derrick, but murder would break a moral code that he didn't even know he had. He has just been ordered to shoot the woman behind him in the head and dump her body at sea. Wayne also added a graphic description of Derrick's own fate, should he fail to do so. And this time he actually promised that after Derrick had done the job, he would "rise in the ranks." Before disconnecting, Wayne had barked that there would be no further contact until Derrick texted him that it was done.

Derrick looks behind and sees that the woman is no longer under the tarp and has somehow managed to free her hands and get rid of the gag again. He briefly wonders what she did that would merit a death penalty. Fuck her. No one would hear her out here anyway. She's quiet, but looks scared, hanging tightly onto the gunnel, her body tense, almost like she might jump.

Mostly to motivate himself, Derrick pulls out the gun, but the tears and ragged breathing have returned. His hand on the wheel is shaking and he isn't even confident that he won't accidentally shoot himself. If he didn't need the drugs so badly, he would just drive the boat as far away as the gas could take him and dump the woman ashore. Maybe he will anyway. There is no one to see that he hasn't followed the orders.

Or… mkaybe he can just complete this appalling mission, and then turn it into a bad dream.

THIRTY-THREE

While his helicopter is being refueled, Hunter keeps his eyes down as he orders a cup of coffee and a burger at Vancouver International's south terminal café. He sits at a distant table with his back to the room while he waits. The caffeine will probably mess with sleep, but his eyes and neck are strained and sore from hours of aerial searching. Not to mention his ears.

Just before dark, a fixed-wing team had finally spotted the lost hiker in a gully, and everyone except the rescue crew could go home. At least Hunter won't have to put up with his search partner's endless chatter during this last leg. His thoughts have pleasurably returned to Kot.

He turns on his phone for the first time since saying goodbye to her, with a rush of almost adolescent eagerness. That is followed by letdown, when he sees nothing from her. But he scans the long list of incoming emails and texts from other people with growing concern, and his phone immediately starts to vibrate. Rob is calling again.

Hunter answers right away. "Hey. I just turned on my phone again. What's wrong?"

"Where are you?"

"YVR South. Refueling before I head home."

Rob's brief synopsis of the situation elicits a surprisingly agonized groan from Hunter. He tells Rob about leaving Kot at Glenhurst, omitting the personal elements. Rob suddenly interrupts.

"Sorry, I need to take this call. Let me know as soon as you get back, okay?" He's gone.

A server delivers Hunter's burger in the nearly empty café and breaks into an awestruck smile when he recognizes him. Hunter thanks him and then turns away again so that a phone camera would only capture the back of what could be anyone's head. He takes two big bites of his burger, chugs the remainder of the coffee, and uses the exit door leading straight onto the tarmac. Soon, his rotors are turning again, and adrenaline is coursing through him. Either Kot omitted crucial information from the story she told him, or the danger she faced was more immediate than she knew. As the discipline of flight routines kicks in, Hunter tries to calculate potential machine damage versus the costs to his own sanity if he doesn't skip his craft's required cool-down period when he lands in the Glenhurst meadow.

Forty minutes later, Hunter is running to his house in a soft and surprisingly warm rain. He'll go back to shut down the rotors after he's talked with Rob again. He finds Roller out in the dark to meet him and trying to wear out Madonna with a ball chucker in case they have to leave her again.

~ THIRTY-FOUR ~

Swanson Channel

The ocean is calm now and behind Kot, the boat's wake is sparkling lace in the moonlight. She can see shore lights that may represent safe havens, but they remain so far away that they might as well be constellations in the sky. And if she jumps overboard and survives the experience, the freezing waters will immobilize her before she can swim far.

Still, Kot can think of no other option to escape the likelihood that the addled Derrick will eventually follow his orders. He is certainly agitated, but hasn't looked back at her again. Kot yanks off her runners and clings to the gunwale, desperately searching the water for something she's previously missed, anything at all to swim to, then cling to.

What she sees instead is something dark protruding from the water dead ahead. It looks like a mound of rock. Derrick is using his sleeve to swipe at his tears and doesn't notice that they are on an imminent collision course. Kot's yell is lost in the noise of impact and the squealing motor.

The boat flies into the air, then tilts sideways. Derrick is thrown like a rag doll against its lower side, and Kot sails off the stern. The hull bounces wildly when it lands, tossing Derrick back and forth. He struggles up, bruised and sore, and cuts the motor. When he looks back, the woman isn't in the boat. He sees the rock that they must have hit, as well as something bobbing up and down in the water close to it. It must be her.

Derrick clings to a remaining thin thread of reason. He hasn't actually killed her, as ordered, but surely this surprising turn of events accomplishes the same goal. He begins to understand the glorious simplicity of things from here. With true Tunstall luck, the decision has been taken out of his hands, and no one need be the wiser.

He searches feverishly for the gun on the boat floor and finds it trapped in the folds of the heavy tarp, along with Wayne's bag. Again, preordained. Holding the weapon with both cold hands, he fires a single shot into the water. His imagination follows the sharp trajectory of the bullet into the depths, like in a movie.

The recoil isn't bad, so Derrick impulsively shoots at the water again, in the general direction of the woman. Then he drops the gun into the bag with the rest of Wayne's equipment. A single running shoe is lying in the stern. Derrick drops it overboard and it floats irritatingly, but slowly fills and sinks. His final bit of inspiration is to cut the anchor line from the boat and throw the anchor and fifty feet of rope overboard. All part of the brilliant story he's come up with for Wayne.

He sends Wayne the prescribed text. The job is done. Wayne's response is instant, telling him to drown the phone and head back to the Swartz Bay dock to meet him.

Derrick knows that life will become awesome if he can just get to his truck and the promised payments. All this will be but a blameless accident, a misty nightmare.

The force of impact and icy submersion is a terrible shock, but once Kot surfaces and coughs to clear her airway, it isn't difficult to stay afloat. She tries to move her upper body as little as possible, unsure of how visible she is. She can't see him, but Derrick must still be onboard if he turned off the motor. He is no doubt looking for her.

She'd be an easy target if he turns around to find her. She would need to sink below the surface before he gets close, and just hope not to be hit by the prop. She watches the boat about two hundred metres away and tries to breathe evenly while preparing to dive. The terrifying sound of a gunshot echoes in the dark. Then another one rings out and something that must have been a bullet hits the water not far from her. But the boat still hasn't moved. She can't help holding her breath, waiting. A minute later, the engine roars to life and the boat races away in the direction that it had been going before.

Derrick may not have been up for first-person murder, but is evidently okay to abandon her to a slower but very certain death.

Kot rolls onto her back and bends her knees, trying to conserve energy and protect her core. She does another futile scan of the water. Already, her mind is turning to mush. She forces her eyes open to the starry sky and begins a structured pattern: wriggling first her right foot, then her left, and matching the movements with her fingers in cycles, counting out loud. She starts to simultaneously twist her neck from side to side, anything purposeful to provide a tether for her mind and senses and to keep her extremities going for as long as possible. But having more of a rhythm would be better, and comfort arrives in the form of the lullaby that her mother used to croon tunelessly, especially on the hot and humid summer nights of Kot's early childhood.

Lula lula lula lula bye-bye, do you want the stars to play with?

Kot gasps out the words, but already her toes and fingers are refusing to do what she wants.

Or the moon to run away with…? They'll come if you don't cry.

She senses the end coming easily, but instead of rising into the air like ether, her body is being pushed up from below. She welcomes the hallucination of being lifted above the water by the rippled boulder that they hit and settles on top of it, spread-eagled. Surface barnacles provide traction, and there is a protrusion to hold onto.

Tattered fragments of her mind wonder if the tide has gone out further than usual. Maybe she has already died. She struggles to open her eyes, and sees a sheen on the water around her. The jacket cuff in front of her face looks stained, as if by blood.

There is a shallow expiration and a little spray from a blowhole to her left. The thing under her moves slightly, and Kot's hallucination alters. She is not clinging to a rock, but to the dorsal fin of a whale. The stain on the water seems to be getting larger. The whale must have been cut open by Derrick's boat. Reliving that hit brings a little more lucidity. Kot was once in a friend's pleasure boat that almost hit a humpback whale. It was lolling on the surface, typically oblivious to danger.

The way that this creature is behaving is apparently intentional. Incredibly, it may be trying to help her, even in its own suffering. Humpbacks, dolphins, others: she remembers that they do this. She's seen videos. They rescue, when they choose to.

Of course, this could also be some form of afterlife. Kot wants to tell someone that even after death it's possible to feel cold and desperate.

Clouds cover the moon and stars, and soft rain pitters into the sea around them. At slack tide, the water is like glass now. Sprawled on the massive whale, Kot welcomes the gentle showers that are so much warmer than the ocean, and clings to the rough fin like a toddler to its mother's neck. Even so, she is losing her grip.

Now she can hear a keening ululation drifting through the depths. This whale is not alone. The clicks and wails of cetacean communications ebb and flow, beyond her understanding. There is another gentle *whoosh* of whale breath, but not from the one she's lying on. Kot struggles to open her eyes one last time, and sees that another whale is now lying alongside.

She hears others sending their spray into the night air. Instead of being frightened, she feels like an infant being cared for by the massive mammals and far from alone as she dies.

Lula lula lula lula bye bye.

Hypothermia is making its slow and deadly advance and Kot drifts in and out of consciousness. The girl has joined her on the whale, but at first she has no name.

Camas. That's it.

Kot slides heavily down the whale's flank.

~ THIRTY-FIVE ~

Steve stands in the bathroom doorway while Nora brushes her teeth.

"I heard a weird noise a while ago, just before I came in. Couldn't place it and it didn't last long. Kind of a faint moaning. Like an injured deer maybe, but I don't think so. Sounded more human. The fellow from the big Bayliner on B was heading down from the washroom, and I asked him if he'd heard anything, and he hadn't."

Nora spits, then smirks. "Maybe somebody got lucky."

Steve chuckles. He turns to go down the hall and says, "I saw that weird guy in the bottom cottage this afternoon. He was getting into a different truck than he had before. Anyway, just thought I'd mention it."

Nora is asleep in minutes, and Steve is about to close his book when he hears the rough roar of an outboard motor starting up. It sounds like it's at their dinghy dock. Then the boat leaves the marina, far too quickly.

When he reaches the porch, the dark outline of what looks like an unlit Eagle Craft is heading out into the bay. No boat like that was registered at their docks for the night. Steve slides his feet into shoes.

The bang of the screen door wakes Nora with a start. That sound usually means trouble after bedtime and Steve is gone, so she throws on a robe and joins him on the porch. There are lights on inside the lowest cottage now and something is hanging down at an angle across the window facing them. They can't see the tenant's truck in the lot, and apart from the fading sound of the boat motor, the night is completely still.

Steve trails behind, still watching the docks, as Nora heads down to the cottage. At her cry of alarm, he hurries to join her. The door was left open, and they survey the disarray in horror. The heavy recliner chair has been overturned, and a curtain rod is dangling by one end, spilling the curtains onto the floor. Spread around are syringes, pieces of rope, a face cloth, and a crumpled towel.

They hurry down to talk to a couple who are regular guests in the slip next to the dinghy dock. Their saloon lights are still on and they open the door in pajamas. The woman reports that a boat arrived not that long ago, while they'd been playing cards, and her husband had twitched a curtain and watched a thin guy in a dark jacket and ball cap clumsily tie up and hurry toward the cottages. They'd gone back to their game. It was a close one, and when the boat left again, neither of them had looked out.

Steve calls the police.

THIRTY-SIX

If anyone is going to organize something to eat it obviously won't be Mich or Camas, so Rob is toasting paninis. And sneaking glances at Mich. He made her a mug of tea, but she has abandoned it during the interminable hour that they've been waiting for more information.

Mich set up a movie for Camas on her laptop, but not even that novelty could hold the girl's attention. She's standing at a window, looking out at the dark road. She has overheard everything that the adults have discussed. Still, she hasn't peppered them with questions, or wanted reassurance about Kot—reassurance that no one can provide. Rob is impressed, and is temporarily successful in pushing aside the moral dilemma of her presence.

Mich keeps her phone in her hand, as if a call from Kot might arrive at any moment. But it's Rob's mobile that rings. He shows Mich the caller ID, then listens for some time before asking a couple of questions. He can feel Mich's eyes like laser beams on his back. When the call is over, he turns to face her. Camas also steps away from the window and begins to rock a bit, with her arms wrapped around her thin chest.

Rob tells them, "The local police just had a call from Steve Elliot, at the marina. Apparently, he and Nora rented a cottage to a guy who matches the description that I gave them of that jerk who was looking for Kot."

Mich looks a little hopeful at even this scrap, but Rob has to continue. "I'm sorry, but there's evidence to suggest that he took her to that cottage and held her captive there. And it's possible that he has since taken her away on a boat, not long ago."

Mich's eyes fill. "What are the cops doing about it? Will they intercept the boat? Tell me they're doing *something*!"

"Well, some marinas are being monitored for the arrival of a boat matching Steve's description of it, but it's impossible to watch them all, especially in the dark, and most managers aren't around this late. It could be anywhere in a wide range of geography by now. Steve also said that the boat's running lights weren't turned on, so it would be hard to see from a distance."

Mich's gaze is frozen on Rob as if she can sense more bad news to come. Rob hates that she's right, and that he's the one to keep on delivering it.

"Kot's kidnapping has been taken over by a special squad in Vancouver. In fact, it's headed by a former colleague of mine. Inspector Solinski, she is now. We should probably assume that it's because Kot's kidnapping is a continuation of what began at that safe house. Or before."

Because of the particular squad that has taken over the case, Rob knows that drugs and gangs are somehow involved. Kot might be just an inconvenient scrap in a much bigger picture. Mich is still watching him intently. He tries to find some positive message to end with, and fails. He takes a deep breath.

"I was told that an official search will apparently begin at dawn."

"Dawn?!"

Mich barely makes it to the bathroom before she vomits. Camas still hasn't said a word.

Rob sees no point in sharing what Annette Solinski had actually asked the Atticus police to pass on to him: by dawn, the official search is being viewed not as a rescue, but as a recovery operation. He suspects that Mich is smart enough to know that anyway.

Rob doesn't expect either of them to eat anything, but he serves the paninis with carrots and pickles. Mich looks pale and pinched when she returns to the kitchen. Rob just hopes that she isn't mentally shooting the messenger. She's calm again, and clearly thinking hard. Rob finds himself wanting to support her better, and even protect her, and his respect for the woman goes up another notch when she turns her attention to looking after Camas again.

Whatever—especially with Tessa being unavailable, he can't imagine going home and leaving the two of them alone, and is already expecting to be up all night. He texts Rachel and asks her to do the prep and run the café on her own tomorrow, or else to just put up the closed sign.

Rob is closing in on some acceptance of Rachel and Toni being together, but his brow still furrows when he reads Rachel's reply. Apparently, Toni is happy to volunteer her assistance from four in the morning until closing, after lunch. He shakes his head at the existential ironies of life, and offers his companions more food and tea. Mich declines politely, but Camas sits down with a big bowl of the ice cream that she'd remembered is in Kot's freezer.

Now Hunter is calling, probably back at Glenhurst by now. With Roller listening in on speaker, Rob updates them both. Camas and Mich can hear Hunter's loud curses.

Rob continues, "I know how this is going down officially—there will be actions taken, for sure, but also some frustration and impotence around the 'looking for a needle in a haystack in the dark' thing. I've only discussed this with Mich very briefly, but we don't see how we can all just hang around and wait, do you? My fishing boat is fast, I have GPS, and I know these waters well, even in the dark."

Mich leans close to Rob, anxious to speak to Hunter, and Rob gives her the phone. She says, "The official search will be far too late. If you have the fuel, would you be willing to do another flight tonight, Hunter?"

Mich hadn't discussed that request with him, but Rob had been working up to ask the same question. It strikes him that she is a person you'd want at your back, and not just in a crisis. Lucky Kot. It also says a lot about Kot's character, to have such a friend.

Without waiting for Hunter to reply, Mich continues to outline her case. "Like Rob said, doing nothing is not an option at this point when there's a chance that Kot can still be rescued. We can plan a search pattern—I hear you're an expert, Hunter—and cover as much territory as possible. I can go with Rob in his boat. We'll take searchlights, and stay out all night if we have to. You can cover a wider area from the air, and if we stay in close touch—well, it's the only chance that I can think of. But we obviously need to get going right now."

Hunter sounds like he is already in action. "Absolutely. Roller's saying he'll come up with me, and we have lots of fuel. And when we find whoever has Kot, I'll rip his lungs out."

All music to Mich's ears, although she wonders if it's just the actor, playing a role. She looks at Rob's face, so close to hers.

"Robert, could you call your inspector friend in case there's anything we should know before we leave? It probably wouldn't hurt to tell her what we're doing, too."

Rob nods. He'd planned on doing that, of course. And while he admires Mich's take-charge nature, and Mich in general, he doesn't intend to take orders all night in his own boat. Still, he liked her use of his full name, and that she seems so comfortable sitting close together.

He tells the group, "Okay. We know that the boat was heading out of Gubbins Bay about forty minutes ago. So far, there's no indication what direction it took, but it's likely that the guy would either head to the Sidney area or across the strait to Vancouver. He may have already reached a private dock." Rob speaks into the phone but looks into Mich's eyes. "The other possibility, and one that we have to face, is that Kot is already in the water." Her blue eyes close.

They quickly agree on Hunter's search plan. He and Roller will leave Glenhurst within five minutes, and fly from the mouth of Gubbins Bay out into Georgia Strait, checking private docks along the shorelines for a boat matching the description. The driver can't have travelled further than that if he's headed to Vancouver through Active Pass. If they see anything, they will contact Rob to alert the RCMP. If they spot nothing on that route, they will return to assist Rob and Mich over the wider ocean path toward Sidney and Swartz Bay.

If necessary, they will all come up with a Plan B. But they won't give up.

Hunter prescribes communications protocols, and he and Roller sign off to prepare a thermos of coffee and grab their gear.

Rob tells Mich that he'll be back to pick her up in a few minutes and leaves to get boating equipment and clothes. As he drives, he lets Steve Elliot know that they will soon be enroute to his marina. Annette Solinski's private number is still in his contacts, and Rob calls her next. Unsurprisingly, he has to leave a message.

Mich decides to take Camas across the road to Tessa's, but Camas has disappeared. There is no way that Mich is willing to search for the uncooperative girl in the rain and dark, so she phones Tessa with the requested update, and tells her that Camas is AWOL again. Mich interprets Tessa's silence as disgust at the situation, and no doubt annoyance at having been excluded from the information loop about Camas. Judging by the background noise, Tessa's grandkids are not yet in bed, and when she signs off she sounds exhausted and worried.

Nevertheless, it helped Mich to talk to someone else who knows and cares about Kot, as does making herself eat some of the food that Rob prepared. She suspects that Robert Baschel is frequently underestimated these days, and that he is probably okay with that. Everyone seems to like and respect him, and he's obviously a smart and solid guy. Also, kind of cute. His warm eyes and sincere smile... she briefly wonders why he left his police career, and clings to the hope that she will be able to ask Kot what she knows.

Mich puts on some of Kot's warm gear, and it also helps to make her friend seem closer. She fills two travel mugs with fresh tea, and grabs a couple of folded blankets and some extra warm clothes for Kot. Mich has never been afraid of long odds.

Under the eaves of Kot's porch, the warm showers are drawing the pungent smell of spring earth. Waiting for Rob to return, Mich looks over Tessa's treetops to the dark water, and allows her tears. More devoutly than a recovering Catholic could ever have imagined, she sends a prayer To Whom It May Concern to guide them to Kot. When goosebumps of hope have arrived and she can see Rob's headlights approaching, she straightens her shoulders and runs down the stairs.

THIRTY-SEVEN

Time has lost meaning. It could be fifteen minutes or fifteen hours since she was thrown off the boat, but in Kot's brief periods of drowsy consciousness, she senses that she is lying between two whales, and that others are breaching to breathe farther away. She hears their enchanted songs through the ocean. It's like that dream that she had back in the safe house. Dying is so easy. *The peace that passeth all understanding…*

The humpback struggles with each shallow breath. Only the warm length of her sister's body against her own has helped her cling to life. For a while, the creature lying between them was making thin, wavering sounds, but it is silent now.

Her entire clan has returned to within a kilometre or two and they call now and then. There is no pain.

~ THIRTY-EIGHT ~

One leaning lamp standard provides a small circle of light in the parking lot of the community-owned dock near Swartz Bay. An hour before midnight, a late model Ford F-150 pulls a boat trailer into the lot and backs to the top of the ramp. Soon after, a battered old truck arrives, also with no lights, and is parked under the trees. Its driver hands something to the F-150 guy, then leaves on foot.

The ferry terminal next door is closed, and only night creatures and the man waiting and smoking in the shadows witness Derrick's clumsy landing at the dock a few minutes later. The man crushes the butt of his cigarette under the heel of his boot as he watches.

Derrick expected Wayne to be on the dock to at least grab a rope, but instead he has to scramble out and fumble with the lines alone. He'd been headed on the wrong course for a bit, but it still only took him twenty-five minutes to get here after he'd sent Wayne the text. But they were uncomfortably cold minutes, and now his hands can barely function. Even after he has looped the line around a cleat a couple of times to secure the boat, he has to scramble back on board to retrieve Wayne's bags of equipment.

By the time he's tossed them onto the dock, Derrick can't remember ever feeling so wretched. He crawls out and stays on all fours. There is a loud hiss from the top of the ramp, and he makes out the fuzzy shape of a man that could be Wayne. Finally, he will get paid. He hauls himself to his feet and clings hard to the railing to join Wayne, who is wearing gloves again. Lucky him.

Wayne beckons Derrick into the shadows and his voice mixes with the low rumble of the night cargo ferry offshore. “So it’s done?”

“Oh yeah. Done and dusted. Now pay me.”

“Relax boyo, that’ll be happening any minute now. Your truck keys are right here in my pocket, and see, it’s sitting right over there and there’s quite a bonus on the front seat. We even cleaned it up for you. But tell me, how do we know she’s dead?”

We. What a fucking pretentious way to talk.

“Cuz after I shot her I tied the anchor rope round her waist and balanced her body over the back of the boat. I dropped the anchor over and she went with it. She sank like a fuckin’ stone. Won’t be anything left down there, soon enough.”

Derrick senses that he may be slurring, but is otherwise pleased with his performance. He hates the way Wayne is just staring at him with his piggy little eyes. Finally, he nods.

“Good. Gun in the bag?” Wayne pulls it out to check the cylinder and his head jerks up. “Two! Why?”

“She was trying to fight me, and it took two. There was no one within miles.” Derrick starts to get into it. “Christ, man, I never killed no one before. It wasn’t part of the deal, an’ like I said, I won’t do it again.”

“I give you my word, we won’t be asking you to do it again. And in your truck you’ll find that our grateful employer has been very generous, as promised. The phone?”

Derrick hands him the most recent throwaway. His own phone is tucked somewhere in an inner pocket. But apparently Wayne still isn’t finished with him.

“Go untie the boat again and centre it while I back the trailer down. Once it’s loaded, you’ll get your keys. Go on.” He turns his back on Derrick’s misery, and heads for the Ford. Derrick wants to jump him from behind, but Wayne has the gun now, and there is no choice. Anyway, he’s too weak to attack a turtle.

Trying to position the boat, he slips on the slimy loading ramp and lands hard on his bum, spewing expletives. Eventually, Wayne tows the dripping boat up into the lot, but doesn't get out. As Derrick approaches, Wayne tosses Derrick's keys through the open window. They land on the ground. "Enjoy yourself, lad. You've earned it."

Derrick scrambles into his truck, afraid that he's been tricked again. But sure enough, a new daypack is sitting open on the front seat. It holds a thick stack of small denomination bills and a lot of what Derrick needs more. The truck smells foreign, and the usual discarded wrappers, containers, and butts are gone. It looks like the whole interior has been detailed, and when he turns the key, the motor starts right away. Nice.

Wayne's tail lights have disappeared, and Derrick fumbles in the bag. A new favourite of his is near the top, and he needs a hit before he tries to drive. He manages to swallow two with a slug of water from the plastic bottle thoughtfully left in the cup holder. Then he closes his eyes and waits.

His chemical friends kick in around the same time as the truck heater. As the magic takes hold, Derrick takes a couple more for the road. He is alone in the dark that he loves. The bad dream is over, and he is a bigger superhero than anyone knows. After all, that woman probably made it to shore.

The southbound highway is empty. Derrick rolls down his window and steps on the accelerator. Each moment is more delicious than the one before. Then his truck takes flight and there are no more moments.

The regional coroner's report later states that the accident victim's blood had the highest concentration of carfentanil ever recorded in BC. A few grains would be enough to kill a sumo wrestler, and Derrick had swallowed enough to fell a herd of rhinos.

THIRTY-NINE

Solinski is enjoying a hot bath in the company of three fingers of single malt and the velvet voice of k.d. lang. A Friday night ritual, when possible.

Dance left work earlier than usual today—some kind of anniversary. Nevertheless, when her phone on the tub surround starts to buzz, she assumes it's him, either with or wanting a late-night update. Instead, she's surprised by a blast from the past: Robert Baschel, at this late hour.

After their conversation, she sighs and adds more hot water to the bath. Solinski sympathizes with the friends of the missing witness and their need for action, but their plan to go searching at night is a futile waste of time. Rob was one of the best cops she ever worked with except that he cared too much, and that trait can lead you down a variety of dark backroads of the soul. Rob had almost trampled them all before he quit. That said, he seems to have recovered and to even be thriving in a new life. And Hunter Nott is apparently a close friend of his. Life sure unfolds.

She texts Dance and he calls just as she's crawling into bed. She fills him in on the report from the Atticus marina owner and the search plans of the Atticus gang, and he replies, "I agree. Kathleen Cafferty may be a cat with nine lives, but odds are, she's been beaten by number ten now. Still, it's gotta be agonizing for them to do nothing. Anything to be done tonight? We just got home."

"Wow. Way past your bedtime. No, we're in a holding pattern."

Dance hears a click and then Solinski says, "Sorry, Wade, I'll call you right back after I take this call. Just a couple more things to pass on."

"Sure. Martin's already snoring."

Solinski calls back in a couple of minutes. "That was the Sidney detachment. There was a fatal SVA on the Pat Bay Highway tonight, south of the ferry terminal. Extremely dead inside was one Derrick Tunstall, age twenty-four, clothing wet with saltwater, and an undetermined amount of cash and a whole Disneyland of drugs onboard. There's a good possibility that he's the guy who had Cafferty. Rented a bachelor condo in an iffy building in Victoria. No official employment. I've ordered an autopsy, but I won't be surprised if he was dead before impact."

"Maybe a planned homicide by his supplier?"

"Correct. Also, the truck was supernaturally clean. We'll see if there are any prints or DNA besides his, but we know where the smart money would be on that."

"So he kidnaps Cafferty, does whatever he was told to do—presumably, murder or deliver her somewhere. Then the dumb ass gets killed by his payment. Classic. Pawn kills target. Pawn gets offed."

"Yeah, not likely suicide. Deliberately swallowing something lethal and then doing a high-speed attack on a highway lamp standard might be considered overkill. So to speak."

Dance grins at her beloved black humour. Solinski keeps going.

"He's probably been given a bunch of burners, but there wasn't one in the truck. He had a personal phone on him that survived the crash. He seems to have used it mostly for voice notes about jobs he was doing, which were mostly entrapment stuff and surveillance. But he also tried to take artsy photos."

"Maybe he was planning to write his memoirs."

"Well, you tell me. The photo I'm looking at right now is from just over a month ago. It's an angle shot of a driveway gate on a country road that I'm betting will create some chatter in the world of witness protection."

"Is the date during Cafferty's stay in the safe house?"

"Yup. Not long before the house exploded. And just this afternoon he took some of a woman blindfolded, gagged, and bound to a recliner chair. It all matches the mess in the marina cabin on Atticus. It looks like she's unconscious, and it's undoubtedly Cafferty, with darker hair. Her breasts were exposed."

"Classy guy all round."

"There's a security camera in the marina's parking lot and the local cops are sending everything over, including their photos of the cabin in question. And hey, remember Rob Baschel told us about a seedy character over on Atticus? Some guy who'd showed him a photo of Cafferty? Rob also saw him hanging around close to where she was living. We're asking him to confirm if it was Tunstall, the dead guy."

"Okay, it's possible that Cafferty was handed over to someone else, but it's more likely that her body was dumped at sea."

Solinski says, "Whether or not she's ever found, which I doubt she will be, we now have a thread to pull hard on. I'm guessing that the safe house was bombed because someone believed that she knew too much, or maybe that she'd heard more than she did when Northcott was shot. Or at least more than she told the Vancouver police about… Or maybe she was lying, to protect someone special. Given what's been turning up in the *Novicta* interviews, there's one clear and smooth-talking common denominator."

"Right. No matter which scenario it was."

"Shit. I just got a text that there were two reports of gunshots on the water tonight. Someone on the northwest shore of Atticus heard them at the same time as a woman on Saltspring. I think I'll let Rob know."

"And Northcott?"

"Sorry, but can you get an emergency full squad meeting broadcast out right now for nine tomorrow. It's going to make me wildly unpopular and we won't get everyone, but it can't wait. Best-case scenario, we smoke out our mole. After that, get some beauty sleep and meet me at the coffee shop at 7:30. We'll go talk to Northcott after that. There isn't enough to bring him in yet."

"Okay. The ocean may have coughed up a body by then."

They say good night and Solinski thinks for a minute before making one more call to Rob Baschel. She's pretty sure he'll pick up.

~ FORTY ~

Rob tries to adopt a light tone as he drives Mich to Gubbins Bay Marina. "I was a little surprised by how quickly Hunter agreed to help tonight. After the day he's put in, he must be pretty bagged."

"Obviously you haven't seen him with Kot much. There are enough sparks to burn even his house down. Kot's actually been fending him off. She's had her reasons." Mich's voice catches. "I'm just more of a carpe diem person."

Rob nods thoughtfully and reaches over to give her hand a squeeze. On a phone call with Hunter before he left Los Angeles, Rob had listened to him swear that he was determined to spend his time on Atticus in celibacy and introspection. *Hah.* That sure didn't last long.

Still, it would be very hard on Hunter to finally fall for a jewel and then lose her so quickly. And in such a way.

When they reach the dock Steve has already filled Rob's gas tanks and put searchlights and night vision binoculars in the boat. The rain is unusually warm but it definitely won't help with visibility on the water. Nora gives them extra coats and blankets and tells Rob that they plan to stay up and monitor their radio in case they can help.

Rob sees that Solinski is calling him again, and moves away to talk to her. After, he keeps her news about the gunshots to himself, but notifies Hunter that he needs to abandon their current aerial search route and assist in what is now the more likely one, towards Swartz Bay. He knows that there's no realistic hope of finding something as small as a human out there, even with the powerful lights, and he can't calculate the possible direction and drift of someone in the water—or a body—from an unknown point at an unestablished time. Besides, bodies don't always float, at least not at first. His primary purpose in this crazy expedition is to gain future peace of mind that Mich—all of them—will know that they did everything possible.

He wonders if the Atticus police have found a tracking bug on Mich's car, and if so, what guilt might do to her.

As soon as he gets a text from Roller agreeing to the new plan, Rob starts his motors and prepares to take the bowline from Steve. A small figure comes racing out of the darkness, leaps into the boat, and scuttles to the furthest corner, as though hoping not to be noticed.

Mich hisses angrily, "Argh! Camas! How did you get here? You were supposed to go to Tessa's. You're not even dressed properly."

"I knew you wouldn't let me come so I hid under something in the back of his truck. I promise I won't get in the way, but I have to come with you."

Rob raises his hands in frustration and curses under his breath.

Mich hurls an extra jacket at Camas. "Rob, let's not waste any more time. She'll have to cope."

Rob's thoughts exactly, although he's aware of the added responsibility. Camas must already be frozen after riding in his truck bed. The kid sure has guts. One determined little beast. When life vests have been snapped on, he gestures to Mich to come forward to the other bow seat, and he heads out into the bay.

There is a spotlight attached to the roof for avoiding logs during early fishing starts, but Rob uses only the boat's running lights for now. Kot's kidnapper would undoubtedly have gone far into open water to do whatever he did. The rain has almost stopped and visibility is improved. Cloud cover keeps the temperature up and the ocean surface is smooth. More like a lake. Rob checks his instruments to confirm that it's slack tide. He figures they have only about an hour of this calm water before the tides push again. Hunter's participation will also be limited by fuel consumption.

Now wearing the coat Mich threw at her and wrapped in a blanket, Camas moves forward and hangs onto the back of Mich's seat, staring straight ahead, and Rob concedes that her young eyes might be assets.

Rob assumes that there are only three likely scenarios: one, Kot has already been delivered to some other captor at a dock or soon will be; two, she was transferred to another vessel at sea, which could be anything, and by now, anywhere; and three, her body was dumped overboard.

He settles his phone into its holder on the dash, sets the radio to the same channel Hunter and Steve are monitoring, and programs his nav system to the community dock near the Swartz Bay ferry terminal. It will be locked and deserted by this time of night, and Rob thinks that a quiet dock in that area might be the most likely destination for the kidnapper to land.

The lights of a helicopter appear in the distance, coming from the north. Hunter is flying well below the clouds, with Roller directing the powerful searchlight over the water below.

The radio crackles to life as they leave the wide mouth of the bay, and Hunter's voice hails the boat by name.

"Come in, Hunter."

"We can see you. To confirm: we'll head over to the Swartz Bay area and work backwards from there until we meet. Over."

"Roger. Maybe start by taking a look at the public dock next to the ferry terminal and its parking lot, and let me know what's there. We're using my roof light and two others. Out."

They briefly watch the chopper continue south, and Rob puts the motors into neutral to give his passengers instructions and searchlights to hold.

"Take one side of the boat each. Aim the lights ahead and then slowly swing them back to the rear, back and forth. Keep the beam on the surface and just above it. We'll go slow."

He moves forward at under three knots and it's so calm that he can occasionally use the infrared binoculars. Still, he feels slightly sick. This night is not going to end well, no matter what.

In the helicopter, Roller knows that his pilot is angry and frustrated. He's now aware of why Hunter is so personally engaged in this search, but Roller is sure that there is only more upset to come and would like to get it over with. He keeps his eyes on the water and diligently mans the searchlight, but says little. They are flying a grid pattern at three hundred feet: low enough to see things on the surface, but not so low that the wind from the rotors disturbs the water. Hunter's bird was built for this, and Roller knows that Hunter will maintain his focus in spite of his emotions.

In this season both the small dock near the ferry terminal and its parking lot are empty. After flying the nearby coast, they begin to work their way back over open water. They are only a few kilometres south of Saltspring Island when Roller's voice suddenly sounds urgent in Hunter's headphones.

"Go back. There was definitely something back there."

Hunter does a one-eighty and hovers a short distance back while Roller steers the powerful light across the water. He obeys Roller's directional requests, but has little hope that he saw anything besides logs. And a part of him is afraid to see anything. But he holds the chopper steady and agrees to retrace their route a little further before resuming the grid. Behind them, he can see the searchlights on Rob's boat illuminating a narrower swath of water.

Suddenly Hunter sees what Roller did. There is something reflective gleaming in the beam of light, part of something large and unidentifiable in the water below. Neither man speaks as they try to keep the search light and chopper steady enough to decode what it is. The object or objects match nothing in their experience; they are not rocks, kayaks, logs, a submerged boat, stumps, or any recognizable animal. It consists of two elongated objects that seem to be partially submerged and connected by a much smaller protrusion. The reflection is coming from that. Hunter goes lower.

Roller says, "Did you see that blow? I think those may be two whales, side by side."

"Maybe, yeah. Is that a person lying between them?!" Hunter's voice is incredulous. His heart feels like it will leave his chest. He reduces their altitude slightly, then yells, "That's Kot's jacket! It has a reflective flower on the back."

In one of his scripts, this would be the point where his body double would execute some heroic rescue on his behalf. But if he's right, in this very real crisis and in this helicopter, neither of them has even a remote ability to reach Kot.

They focus on the tableau below and the green light of the night binoculars only increases the weirdness. One whale again sends a spout of water high into the air. A few seconds later, the other one emits a fine spray, although it could have been the aftermath of the first. Even with the noise and downdraft of the helicopter, Kot hasn't moved.

Rob's radio squawks to life again. He listens to Hunter's broken transmission and shakes his head, confused. He asks if Roller could text him, and a minute later his eyes widen.

"They've found something!" He hands the phone to Mich, and she reads aloud: "Whales and maybe Kot. Follow."

This makes no sense. But Camas smiles in the darkness.

The helicopter descends low in front of them. Hunter waggles it slightly in the official signal to follow his lead, then swings up and away. Rob guns the boat in pursuit and Mich and Camas lean over the sides, salt spray stinging their eyes.

Hunter stops and swivels again, as if to block their way, and another text arrives. *When we go up u stop & look ahed.* A few seconds later, the chopper goes straight up and a bright light beams down from it.

Rob puts his motors into neutral. He aims his spotlight towards the same spot as the helicoper's, then uses his binoculars. Before long, he experiences the humility of witnessing the incredible.

"They're right. That's two humpbacks, with a body supported between them." He used the word body deliberately, and notes Mich's fists, clenched on the railing.

Camas is acting like she might jump off. "It's Kot. We have to get her!" Mich whirls and restrains her, none too gently.

Another text from the chopper instructs Rob to continue to shine their lights on the tableau while Hunter takes the chopper a little further away. The radio squawks to life again.

Hunter says, "Two whales and Kot between them, right?"

Rob responds, "Sure looks like it. But it's… unbelievable."

"Okay. Go dead slow. We're going high and wide but will keep the light on them. As soon as you get close enough, turn off the motors and use your paddles. No sudden movements, and no noise. Standing by. Out."

Quietly, Camas says, "It's okay. They won't spook."

As gently as possible, Rob and Mich slowly paddle the boat close to the whales. Camas is right; neither one moves. Apart from the paddles, it's eerily silent. Rob moves to the swim deck and manages to hook his gaff into the neck of Kot's jacket and pull her within reach. Dead bodies are nothing new to him, but this is appalling for Mich and the child to witness.

Mich bravely helps to drag Kot's limp form onto the transom and then the three of them get her into the boat. Rob puts his cheek to Kot's mouth and his fingers search her wrist. He wonders if he is imagining the faint breath on his face, but is astounded to also feel an irregular pulse. He finds no signs of water inhalation or obvious injuries.

Mich also locates a pulse on Kot's neck and whispers through tears, "She's still alive. Hang on, Kottie."

Rob gives them urgent first aid instructions and goes forward to take a radio call from Steve and Nora. They have been monitoring the search in silence and are offering to call 911.

Rob agrees and radios the helicopter hovering anxiously a safe distance away. "She's still alive, but barely. We're heading back to the marina and she'll be medevaced out. That's her best chance. Out."

He is determined to limit radio chat from here because Hunter might waste time arguing, or even want to transport her to hospital himself. Rob knows that Kot urgently needs the professional hands and equipment that will be waiting at the dock and at every stage after that.

Mich and Camas have already removed Kot's sodden clothing and rolled her in blankets. Rob tells Camas to lie close beside her and then covers them with more blankets before he starts the motors and shows Mich the light marking the opening of Gubbins Bay. With desperate glances back at Kot, Mich accelerates across the smooth waters under broken cloud, and Rob returns to kneel beside Kot and begin CPR. Camas buries her face in the blankets, croons to Kot, and prays.

Only Camas noticed one whale take a breath before they both disappeared beneath the surface. But no one could see it swim gently down as its sister sank into the darkness and sorrowful songs filled the Cold Home waters.

~ FORTY-ONE ~

Kot is in hospital an hour later, and Hunter has flown himself to Victoria airport and rented a car, with a promise to update Mich with even the smallest change in Kot's condition. She will book them accommodation near the hospital, and Rob intends to accompany her on the dawn ferry. Camas is finally asleep in Kot's bed, and Rob and Mich are having tea and toast on the couch in front of the fire before they also try for a few hours' sleep. Mich is sitting close to him, and Rob has rarely felt happier and more comfortable with anyone in his life.

Mich takes a gulp of tea. "Mmmm. I need this warmth. Camas can be a pain, but she also has a weird and impressive collection of knowledge, maybe from her mother. When I tucked her in, she told me that there are lots of stories about humpback whales protecting other species, including humans. Mostly from transient orcas… you know, the meat-eating ones, but from other threats as well. She's seen YouTube video clips. She said that's why she thought they wouldn't abandon Kot."

"It was totally surreal. But some animals do it, and certainly dolphins, so why not other smart mammals? Still, I doubt that many people would believe what we saw tonight. Even I don't."

When Rob's phone buzzes, he expects it to be Hunter. But of course Annie Solinski knows that he will also still be awake. He puts her on speaker, no longer worried about what Mich might hear.

"Hey Rob. I thought you'd want to know that we have the identity of Kathleen Cafferty's probable kidnapper. Or more accurately, ex-kidnapper. Derrick Tunstall. After he got to Swartz Bay it seems he had too much of a bad thing, followed by a spectacular single-vehicle crash. All very unhelpful, since we still don't know who hired him, or what happened to Cafferty. Our best guess is that she was dumped in the water around ninety minutes ago, give or take. The search will start in about four hours, but I don't need to tell you how slim the odds are that she'll be found at all, never mind alive. How are you guys making out? I don't hear a boat motor."

"Fine thanks, Annie. Just enjoying a snack. As a matter of fact, I was about to call you."

Mich smiles and snuggles a little closer as Rob methodically reports the night's events. He signs off with, "It would be good to get a uniform stationed outside ICU at Royal Jubilee Hospital tonight. That's why I was calling you."

There is a pause before Solinski asks Rob, with some delicacy, what recreational substances he may have enjoyed this night. When he finally convinces her that he didn't invent one word of it, Solinski tells him to repeat everything, for recording purposes.

FORTY-TWO

Ben Northcott is in the only situation where he feels remotely safe these days: alone in his car in the dark and an anonymous location, doors locked. The rain obscuring the windshield also helps. He drove like a robot and parked on a random residential street, three blocks from traffic. It should be an adequate distance from the bar he's just left, and he is sure that no one has followed him.

He grips the steering wheel hard with both hands and spits a stream of curses. He feels cornered, like a wild beast in a leather-lined cave and without the moral comfort of any kind of martyrdom. He reclines the seat and closes his eyes. The city's sound track is drowned by the pain in his leg and the cacophony in his head. He needs to brush his teeth and gargle with mouthwash, and not only because of those fruity martinis.

Ben had first connected with tonight's date a month ago, at a charity event not long after the one where he'd talked to Kathleen's friend, Suzanne Michaluk. She had only just met the other man, and had introduced them before she hurried away. Clearly instantly infatuated with the glamorous Ben, he had attempted to impress him with the information that he worked in the Witness Protection Program. It was like a gift from the gods.

Ben had leaned his head close. "Do you think we could have dinner soon? I'm feeling stronger every day." Then he hadn't waited long to set up that first date.

After a few drinks and demonstrating artificial fascination with the young man's work life, Ben had confided, "You know, I'm so worried about poor Kathleen Cafferty. If you can give me any kind of reassurance that she's safe somewhere, I'd be deeply grateful."

It wasn't enough, but Ben did get a few details before the evening was over. And, of course, he hadn't let the guy get even close to first base. But it had provided a good basis to set up tonight's rendezvous. His aspiring paramour had shared that he'd been trying for a professional transfer out of the WPP, and not long after their first date, and with only a small nudge by Ben to a senior RCMP squash buddy, the young man won a junior position on an Organized Gang Squad. Who knows, he might even have earned it.

They'd met this evening in a nondescript bar in East Vancouver, far from Ben's usual haunts and probably appealing to the other man for similar reasons. No matter what it took, Ben's goal was to obtain some critical information to inform his next move, a move that could influence—if not determine—the rest of his life. He had rehearsed well.

The other man seemed almost desperate to impress Ben tonight, and had passed on a large—and seriously negative— nugget of information: his new team, led by Inspector Annette Solinski, is indeed experiencing some success with plea bargains to potential suspects in their Port of Vancouver drug smuggling investigation. Sergeant Dance hadn't been lying.

Ben had struggled to maintain a neutral face at the table. The extent to which each of those suspects is aware of his complicity in the smuggling is a monster of an unknown to Ben. The men who now control him have offered repeated assurances that each player within the "high-end imports" operation has only a fragment of information, and purely on the classic need-to-know basis. That has been the way that Ben himself has been treated, and he suspects that the human pawns lower down are deemed to have precisely no need at all.

He called Lauren this afternoon to tell her he'd be working late. Ben also took the precaution of mentioning a fictitious squabble within the company's Montreal division, and the likelihood that he will need to fly there and sort it out. He thought he heard silk sliding in one of Lauren's dismissive shrugs. Sounding bored, she'd murmured, "Ah. The usual male primate dominance issues."

Lauren's indifference is endlessly useful.

Ben has been working on a handover of the management of Northcott Shipping to an unloved stepbrother. His board may be sniffing something a little off these days, and Ben had not been included in their in-camera meeting after the recent big one. Ben anticipates that his request to relinquish the CEO position will soon be approved, and he can then work out a severance package sufficient to leave the family company completely and shift to unrelated ventures. If he no longer has management control, he should surely be under gradually less external pressure. A blissful dream. Meanwhile, the plan is something that Lauren, in turn, doesn't need to know.

At the end of the workday, Ben had waited until Isobel had left and then locked his private bathroom. He removed his jacket and tie, rolled up his shirtsleeves, and after looking in the mirror had undone a couple more buttons. Satisfied, he put on his black leather jacket and left it open, then headed to the nearby pizza joint to eat just enough to keep his stomach from growling during the upcoming ordeal.

By the time that he had settled into an intimate corner of the bar with his date the greasy food had begun an acidic rhumba in Ben's stomach. Still, through the course of those girly martinis, his seductive eyes led the conversational slow dance that he does so well. The other man slid a little closer around the vinyl bench, his voice low while confiding that he was 90 percent sure that Ben is not personally in the crosshairs of the *Novicta* smuggling investigation. Emboldened when the smoldering hunk across the table expressed feigned gratitude for such reassuring news, he'd inched closer still.

The young detective claimed to have the trust of everyone, from Solinski on down, and expressed confidence that if there was any recent information about either the smuggling interception or the missing witness to the attack on Ben, he would almost certainly know about it. From everything he'd heard, although her corpse is still a no-show, the witness remains missing and is increasingly presumed dead. His hand closed over Ben's as he expressed sympathy for the probable loss of a friend. They grimly agreed that gang activity is hopelessly out of control and that there is, tragically, probably nothing unusual in such an outcome.

Ben didn't ask, and his date saw no reason to reduce the admiration in Ben's eyes by admitting that he no longer has any links with the Witness

Protection Program, nor, to be honest, any real involvement in the smuggling investigation. Besides, he knew an innocent man when he met one, especially if he was falling in love with him. Only when he woke in the night with a splitting headache, did the sweaty awareness arrive of having just earned consecutive jail terms if Ben wasn't discreet.

Ben had gently extricated his hand and paid the bill, pleased that the effort expended was matched by information gained. But outside in the darkness his companion claimed a second-date full-tongue kiss and some early groping. Ben shyly withdrew in the sudden glare of turning headlights and managed a fond goodbye without yielding to his urge to punch the guy. He didn't anticipate a need to use him again, but Ben has learned the hard way not to burn bridges.

He has been diligent to avoid paper or electronic evidence, and regularly dumps the cheap phones he is given. He has also been careful—no, meticulous—in compartmentalizing his life, as if in an orderly chest of drawers. Property, wife, kids, and extended family kept in the virtual top drawer and open to the world. Girlfriends, including Kathleen, in the middle one, locked and lined in red satin. The imaginary bottom drawer is nailed shut. It contains his most damning and self-destructive secrets: his drug addiction and gambling debts and the increasingly threatening blackmail. For some time, that lower drawer has been threatening to burst open from the additional subterfuge required to hide all of those secrets.

The same masters who now control him had begun by obtaining a number of distinctly compromising photos of him with Kathleen, taken by a hidden camera back when Ben thought that a messy and expensive marriage breakup would be the ultimate in bad outcomes. Those were the days.

He sees now that the whole enterprise of using him has been expertly designed and carried out by seasoned professionals. As the stakes grew, agreeing to just a few untraceable container additions had seemed a manageable risk. Again, that was then. And after a few months Ben learned that certain containers sometimes held humans as well.

His attempt to draw a firm line around the use of his ships resulted in increasing threats, then being shot in his parking lot, just to underline who actually holds all the power.

Ben still thinks that he might have been able to contain the situation and maybe even come up with a solution, had Kathleen not shown up at that precise moment like a haunting from his past. She'd not only witnessed the shooting but could have heard everything that was said. And, of course, his attackers were understandably unhappy that Kathleen would be able to accurately describe them and what went down, leading to other links.

They soon made it clear to Ben what his choices were: cooperate in the elimination of the witness, or have something unfortunate happen to one or, eventually, both of his children. Even if he can somehow emerge unscathed through the police investigations, Ben has no illusions that the stakes won't continue to grow.

Still—and this does cause him genuine sadness—by showing up when she did, Kathleen had unwittingly written her own death warrant.

Much of his conversation with her when he was sedated in hospital wasn't clear in Ben's memory, but he'd remembered one thing: she was in a safe house on a country road outside of Victoria, behind a gate with a keypad. The first date with his admirer had added the information that it was a fenced acreage west of Elk Lake. That was enough for his mob controllers to take things from there.

Ben had found the bombing of the safe house shocking, in an arm's-length kind of way. However, something inexplicable must have happened, and with no body and no clue about Kathleen, he has lived in a new level of purgatory in the weeks since.

During his chat with Mich at that gala, Ben had confided that he hoped that Kathleen was at least somewhere safe. On one of the Gulf Islands, for instance. The surprised flicker in Mich's eyes had been enough to make it worth attaching a tracking bug to the bottom of her little Audi in the dark when he left. He'd made sure that their conversation included a follow-up from a previous one: a light discussion about their respective level of satisfaction with their current vehicles.

And sure enough, before long Mich did lead them to Kathleen. It was a huge relief to get confirmation last night that the deed had finally been accomplished with no possible links to him. Ben is determined not to think about what it's taken to keep himself and his kids safe. He intends to honour his good memories of Kathleen, and henceforth lead a better life.

He can now hear the urban background noise, the traffic on wet streets, the usual siren and horns, and the repeated chords of a distant train as it transits a series of level crossings. His nerves are hopelessly stretched, but Ben needs to figure out his remaining options. An objective, clear-headed decision must be made.

He is trying to cut down on all meds and chemical assistants, and his notable lack of success is disturbing to him. In the better life ahead, that must also change. He pops a couple of painkillers and waits for his mind to settle.

Finally, one possible course of action rises to the top. He ruthlessly lays bare every aspect of the preparation, execution, and probable aftermath. Then he makes himself face the necessary losses and finds that he isn't afraid of them. Anything will be better than the current, ever-worsening reality. He will need to sort things out with the kids, but that can wait.

There is a lot to be arranged tonight but the chilly calm settling over him brings a strange energy. He'll do what is needed, and then lie down for a while. Ben's car soon merges into the herd of headlights aiming for the Lions Gate Bridge.

FORTY-THREE

Armed with surveillance photos from last night, Solinski didn't have to work hard to convince Superintendent Batra about the probable links between the Northcott attack witness and the current smuggling investigation. While one coincidence can be fragrance-free, there is now a growing stench. Batra also assigned Solinski continued leadership of integrated investigations.

Also, with mysterious gunshots, a helicopter, and searchlights on the inland waters last night, a lot of people are justifiably clamouring for more information beyond a vague "search-and-rescue mission." Until they corner Ben Northcott, Solinski is trying to control the flow of information to the media. It will be a relief when she can actually hold a press conference.

Kathleen Cafferty's condition is no longer critical but she remains unconscious and under police guard in hospital. Dance and Solinski plan to get over there today and talk to her as soon as she is awake. Apparently, some of the Atticus Island people they interviewed before will also be on hand for an encore.

But first, there is something big to accomplish closer to home. The squad members are straggling into the meeting room, and Dance is buzzing. It required a lot of coffee, but he and Solinski are ready to implement the plan that they'd hatched in the café early this morning. They even have a few minutes to spare.

Solinski is at the far end of the meeting room, watching each of her squad get settled. Even on such short notice most are already here, and one person in particular. Besides the understandable grumbling, she is getting curious looks.

Dance starts off by providing an historical summary of the two related cases, then hands over to Solinski. She tells them about a second successful plea bargain that was achieved late yesterday with one of the dock stevedores. She has the attention of everyone in the room as she sketches a schematic diagram of names, places, circles, arrows, time lines, and question marks. A few jaws fall open when she gets to last night's events in the waters off Saltspring Island, and she experiences a presentation high: the synthesis of unprecedented events, leadership, a rapt audience, sleep deprivation, and all that coffee. Dance watches the group, trying not to betray his focus on one member in particular.

When Solinski is finished she waits through the initial wisecracks and incredulity before acknowledging a senior member's arm in the air.

"With this new info, it seems likely that the plea bargain testimony will prove that Ben Northcott is involved. Are we going to start tightening a few screws?"

The question was unscripted, and they couldn't have asked for a more perfect one. Over the rim of his mug, Dance zeros in on someone and catches exactly the micro expressions that he'd hoped to see. Maybe that course he'd taken wasn't a waste of time after all.

Solinski looks at Dance to answer, and he nods emphatically at the group. "Absolutely. In fact, Inspector Solinski and I hope to take tea with Mr. Northcott directly, and enhance our understanding of the nuances of just that."

More than his French affectations, Solinski despairs over Dance's penchant for channeling Inspector Morse. They answer a few more queries and she stands up to assign the next round of grunt work. Then, she and Dance are first out of the room.

Solinski nods to the uniform waiting down the hall and he immediately pretends to be fascinated by his phone. Another cop joins Dance and Solinski in the elevator. Going down.

A junior squad member with an ill-advised moustache lingers behind as the group gabbles their way down the hall, then, unnoticed, turns around and heads in the opposite direction. He passes a preoccupied uniformed man in the hall, scoots into the grimy stairwell, and hurries down two floors. Alone, he leans against the landing wall and selects a number from his personal phone contacts. His face shows disappointment when the call goes to voiçe mail but he rallies to leave a warm and urgent message.

Starting back up and deep in thought, he finds the stairs blocked by the burly cop he'd passed in the hallway upstairs. Another is approaching from below, his hand on his holster. The promising world of Ben Northcott's biggest fan explodes in the experience of being on the wrong side of handcuffing and a reciting of his remaining rights.

On the ground floor, Solinski is waiting for her squad leak and the cops gripping his arms. She looks him up and down with wordless disdain and takes his phone from one of the officers. Back in her office, she grimly finds no surprises on it at all. With last night's surveillance photographs of Northcott and this man in a bar together, and an admittedly poor one of some mouth-to-mouth action in the shadows outside, this evidence of calls and texts is all that is needed to nail the leak. The big bummer is that Northcott may have already picked up the warning message.

She and Dance hurry to a marked car. No need for discretion on this visit. Both Ben's home and office have been watched for the past hour with no sightings of him or his vehicle yet. Since it's a Saturday they head for his home first. Progress is slow on the clogged streets, even with flashers on. Solinski handles calls up and down the hierarchy.

The nav system directs them to a winding driveway lined with blossoming trees. Dance steps onto the cobblestones in front of a carriage house three times the size of his apartment and screws up his nose. "Do little people creep in by night and dust away the blossoms?" He rings the bell. They wait a bit, and he does it again. Eventually, there is the echo of locks being released, and Lauren Northcott appears in the doorway. She is wearing a long silk kimono and kitten-heeled slippers with fluffy pompoms straight from the 1950s. Solinski observes that photos fail to capture the steel in Lauren's eyes.

Dance uses his friendly voice but sticks one foot over the threshold. "Mrs. Northcott? I'm Sergeant Dance and this is Inspector Solinski. Could we have a word with your husband, please?"

Without her contacts, Lauren can only make out the photos on their ID cards, but pretends to examine them anyway. Ben's business is uninteresting apart from its critical support of their lifestyle. However, the presence of police on her doorstep is abhorrent. With overly vigilant neighbours, she needs to send them packing and is already inventing a reason for having summoned these dreary cops. At least they're not in uniform, but why couldn't they have had the courtesy to use an unmarked car?

"Oh dear. I'm afraid not. Ben had to go to Montreal this morning to sort out some company business. Maybe someone else can help you? I would normally suggest that you contact his PA, but of course she's off today. Perhaps on Monday?"

Lauren starts to close the door, but Dance shoves his arm out to keep it open.

Solinski asks, "How long ago did he leave? And what airline is he booked on?"

The fake smile disappears. "I have no idea. I didn't see him this morning. And frankly, I don't expect my husband to report to me about his frequent business trips."

Lauren Northcott could be reading from a teleprompter, as smooth as her husband and chilly as satin. She seems aware that this is as far as they can invade her domain without a warrant. But then she surprises them with a dazzling smile as she releases her hold on the door and adopts a tone of gracious warmth.

"I'm sure that Ben would be very happy to help you to the extent that he can. However, this is making me late for an appointment. Thank you for stopping by, and I wish you a very good day."

With surprising force, Lauren suddenly heaves the heavy oak door shut and Dance's arm takes the brunt. The locks slide noisily into place again.

Dance takes revenge by flipping on the siren as they leave. Solinski orders a priority search for Northcott's flight booking to Montreal and an airport apprehension if he's still on the ground. They have just entered Richmond when the information arrives that, in fact, Ben Northcott will soon be boarding a one-way flight to San Jose, Costa Rica.

Dance mutters, "*Quel surprise.* No extradition treaty there. What do you think, boss? Enough time before we head over to Victoria?" Solinski nods.

They abandon the car with its lights still flashing at the curb of YVR's international terminal, and take the long hallways at a run. They reach the gate just in time to witness two security guards step into the path of a tall man who was about to hand over his boarding pass.

At moments like this, Dance remembers why he loves his job. And he isn't sorry when Solinski tells him that she will head to Victoria alone to do the interviews, while he takes charge of follow-up with Ben Northcott.

FORTY-FOUR

Kot can't lift her eyelids, and struggles to break through the thick fog in her head. She isn't sure who she is, never mind where. There is a low hum of machinery, and a whispered conversation that she can't decode. Something heavy is covering her. It feels good, but her hands and feet are icy. She moves her arm, and something attached to it catches on whatever is on top of her.

There was a boat involved, darkness, freezing water… with a sigh, she surrenders to sleep again until someone starts rubbing her shoulder. A familiar voice says, "Kot. It's me. Are you awake? Open your eyes, okay?"

Kot wants to please this voice and turns her head slightly towards it. Of course. It's Mich. Nice. She drops off again. But firm hands begin to jostle her, and a man speaks close to her ear.

"Kathleen, I'm Colin. I'm a nurse, and you're in intensive care in the hospital. How are you feeling?"

Exhausted. Angry at you. But maybe if she answers, he'll stop bugging her. Kot slurs, "*Feetercold.*" It works, and the jostling stops.

"It's not surprising your feet are cold, and all the rest of you. You've been through a lot, and we're very glad you're back. There are heated blankets on you." He tucks them more tightly around her feet. "We're giving you extra oxygen through a special membrane. Your insides are also getting warmed up through an IV. Pretty soon you'll feel a lot better. But here's the thing, Kathleen. You have to try and stay awake now. Do you understand?"

Understanding and agreeing are different things, and Kot only wants him to go away. She nods, and floats back down to somewhere just below consciousness. The nurse adds something to the IV drip to help Kot surface and stay awake, and quietly tells Mich that her friend's mental clarity and physical condition are likely to improve together.

Mich and Rob had found an armed cop guarding the ICU door when they'd arrived early this morning. Mich had to prove her identity, then wait to be admitted while he phoned someone. She was allowed in, but there'd been no question of anyone else going with her.

Half an hour later the vibration of a call from someone with the Vancouver RCMP makes her nip out of the ICU to take it. It's Solinski calling. She's been informed that Kot is awake, and is coming over to interview her as soon as she can get there, and then needs to talk to Mich, Rob, and Hunter. There is the roar of what sounds like a floatplane motor in the background, and before Mich can ask for any new information Solinski is gone.

Mich returns to her chair close to Kot and takes her hand, relieved to at least be where she needs to be. She lets her eyes close and her thoughts drift where they will. She knows now that Kot told Hunter some of her story while they were alone at Glenhurst yesterday, and it had led to a deeper connection. How could that be just yesterday? However, Robert has made it no secret that he has come to Victoria primarily to support Mich. She falls asleep in the surprising comfort that knowledge brings, and wakes with a start when the privacy curtain is yanked open.

An older nurse efficiently flicks Kot's IV and checks the machines. Then she turns and gives Mich a quick once-over. Her accent is all Caribbean warmth and music.

"Honey, you look all in. This girl's gonna wake up any second, and then they're plannin' to move her up to 4C, so I gotta ask you to leave for a bit. Why don't you get yourself down to the crappeteria? I bet it's been a while since you took care a' yourself, and your friend here don't need you passin' out just as she's gettin' better. It's gonna be about an hour before she's settled upstairs. Go on now."

Mich nods, recognizing an order beneath the veneer of good advice. She certainly feels awful, and some caffeine and splashing around in a washroom sink wouldn't hurt. A text from Rob arrives while she's in the elevator: *How's K? And r u okay? u eaten? Can bring food up.*

What a nice guy. Apparently, they hide in unexpected places. Feeding people is obviously one of his things, but there are lots of other impressive aspects to Robert Baschel. She heads to the cafeteria to pass on Solinski's interview plans. When he sees her coming, Hunter leaps up and demands every detail about Kot.

The guard has been reinstalled outside Kot's new room when Mich finds her again. The heated blankets remain, but Kot is sitting up and her hair has been brushed. A cup of warm broth and some ubiquitous white saltines are on the tray table in front of her. Best of all, Kot seems alert. She gives Mich a wan smile. "Hi."

Mich smiles back. "Look at *you*! Some people will do anything to get a private room. And I have to say, until some arrests start happening, I intend to make sure that you spend the rest of your days in here with Mr. Beefcake on guard outside."

Kot looks confused, and Mich points a finger at the door. "Maybe no one's told you, but there's a big, burly hunk of cop out there, entirely in your honour. He's been following you around. He weighs more than both of us together, and he's packing something nasty. A little late, since he's obviously exactly what you've needed for the past six weeks."

Kot's eyes suddenly fill and she whispers, "So they haven't arrested anyone? I don't think I can take it if I have to disappear again." She stops and swallows hard. "I've started to remember things."

Mich kicks herself for her flippancy. "Oh shit, I'm so sorry. That was incredibly thoughtless. I'm sure we'll have news soon. You're safe now, and like I said, I'll be making sure things stay that way. And now it isn't just me watching out for you, either."

Kot has closed her eyes as tears flow, so Mich changes the subject.

"Hey—guess who was quite the little superhero?" She tells Kot about Tessa finding Medley waiting by the road. "He's staying with Auntie Tessa until you get home. I wish I could have brought him over with me. Medley kisses are such a good way to wake up."

Kot smiles through the tears. "Yeah, I wish you could have brought him, too. I can't believe I didn't think about him, first thing. I can't wait to get my brain back. Can you help me put together what happened? I remember bits and pieces, like being thrown off a boat when it hit something in the water. But I also have a memory of being on top of a whale, and that can't be right. I need to understand how I ended up here."

Mich urges her to keep trying, and with a few prompts, Kot gradually remembers more.

"A cabin. Like the one I lived in at the marina, but a reverse layout. I was tied up and gagged, I don't know for how long. It got dark. The guy was parked just off the main road when I left Hunter's driveway. He had the hood of his truck up, and I remember he asked me to hold a wrench for him. Medley jumped away, and I felt a sharp pain. The jerk must have tasered me. Something made me really sick later, so he also probably injected me with something. When I came to, in the cabin, I was tied up, and gagged and blindfolded. While I was unconscious, he must have pulled some of my clothes off. I think… yeah, it was the same creep who was driving the boat."

Kot rests again and Mich tries to control her anger. A minute passes before Kot turns her head and looks straight at Mich. "Yeah, it was the same guy. I must have woken up briefly. He was circumcised. Maybe that will help with ID?"

Mich's eyes are flint and she looks away. But the point is to keep Kot going forward and back in time, as memories emerge. Kot remains hazy about her time in the ocean, but retains the increasingly clear memory of being on top of a whale.

"It was bleeding. Very weak. I thought we would both die at the same time. But still, it was… completely peaceful." Her eyes close with the memory.

Mich replies softly, "That experience must have gone deep, and will probably never leave you. We were so focused on you, but Camas says she saw the whales sink after you were in the boat. There was a second one, you know. They kept you above water, lying between them."

Kot insists on hearing everything that Mich saw, how Camas was with them, how they came up with the search plans, and about the rescue. Then she tells Mich about her time with Hunter at Glenhurst and her decision to walk home. Soon, they are both pulling tissues from the box on the tray table.

Kot says, "That must have been torture for Camas to have to leave and get help. I'm proud of her. And she was sure that the whales wouldn't leave me? I wonder why. She's quite something, isn't she?"

"For better or worse, she certainly is. Rob and I left early to get over here, and she was still asleep in your bed. She knows that she can go to Tessa's anytime, but I won't be surprised if she's sneaked back to the lighthouse. That old man isn't likely to be back home yet, if he's even still alive. Never mind revealing herself to the others, Camas was pretty scared by police being around. We all protected her pretty well, I think, hard as that must have been for Rob, in particular. I think Tessa is mad, but that will pass. Anyway, Camas's lighthouse life is over, no matter what happens next. And now you and I aren't alone with that dilemma."

Kot silently begins to process that information. Then Mich says, "Oh… I forgot. The Vancouver detective who's in charge of the investigation will be here soon. Inspector Solinski. Rob actually used to work on the same squad as her and calls her Annie. She wants to interview you, and then the rest of us. She'll do Tessa and Roller on the phone. Do you think you'll be able to manage it?"

Kot doesn't answer at first. She dreads the level of disclosure that the interview will inevitably require. She sighs deeply. "I don't suppose I have a choice. She'd better accept that I'm still pretty out of it. It's good that you just took me through it all, but I'm having trouble even hanging onto what you said. Can you stay and help while she's here, please?" She adds, "I didn't know that about Rob. Him being a detective before."

Mich gives Kot's hand a big long squeeze. Kot's eyes open in a quizzical stare and Mich grins, but they are interrupted by a sharp rap at the door, followed by a faint odour of stale tobacco and the appearance of a middle-aged woman with a hint of humour around her mouth.

Inspector Solinski introduces herself and peers at Kot as if seeing the *Mona Lisa* for the first time. Mich is forced to follow Solinski's instructions to go and collect Rob and Hunter, then wait together in the solarium down the hall.

Solinski is clearly in a good mood when she finds the three of them there half an hour later. She interviews each separately in the chapel next door, and then questions them together. She's learned that a group interview can allow for the triggering of forgotten scraps of useful information. She also watches them for signs that might indicate surprise or even alarm at what one of the others says. However, there are no important discrepancies in their stories, and Solinski enjoys the rare and welcome sense of undisputed evidence forming a neat pile. She only regrets looking like road kill while doing her first celebrity interview with Hunter Nott. It's obvious that he is smitten with Kathleen Cafferty, but Solinski remembers reading that his lovers rotate more often than the rotors on his helicopter.

After Solinski is gone, Kot vacantly watches the rays of sun washing the opposite wall of the quiet room. Incredibly, It's fewer than twenty-four hours since Hunter left her in a haze of happy confusion and raced across the meadow to his helicopter. Mich said he's waiting to see her, but Kot isn't ready. It had been a psychic shock to finally divulge the whole truths of her life to a total stranger with a legal duty to record them.

Kot is also aware that she is a completely different person from the one that she'd told Solinski about: the one still trying to recover from being suddenly dumped by Ben Northcott, and waiting in her car for him to emerge from his office. And even from the one who'd walked down Glenhurst's driveway, just yesterday. It's going to take some time to get to know her new self.

But already, great relief is overtaking the chronic stress of secrets. She's still far from feeling any lightness of spirit, but might be headed in the right direction. While telling Solinski her story, it struck Kot for the first time how insignificant the relationship with Ben could have been in the longer term if she had just been able to let it go. She still cares for Ben, but is, at last, no longer in love with him.

Solinski offered no information about who was responsible for the attempts on Kot's life—and Kot did ask. However, she actually said that Kot should expect to feel a lot safer soon, so there must be some progress.

Kot sinks into a deep sleep. When she wakes, the low sun is fully bathing her bed, and not Mich's hand, but a big, warm one is holding hers. Hunter leans over her anxiously and kisses her cheek. A weary version of that crooked grin makes an appearance.

"I'd tell you never to let that happen again, but I'm thinking the chances of that are slim to none anyway."

"Hi there. Was I drooling?"

Rob and Mich go outside with Solinski to wait for her taxi, and Rob asks for any updates she can share. She purses her lips and gestures to him to step aside with her.

"This is in strict confidence for now, Rob, although it will probably hit the news soon. We have a shipping CEO in custody in relation to both this case and another one. I can't say any more."

A sudden lull in the surrounding noise means that her words carry farther than intended. The effect on Suzanne Michaluk is dramatic. She turns white and stares at Solinski, then quietly chokes out, "Ben Northcott?"

Solinski shrugs and gets into her cab, hoping that the woman, a public relations pro, can be discreet. As the taxi pulls away from the curb she watches Rob protectively put his arm around Mich and head to a bench against the wall. Again, too bad he left the squad. But… good for Rob. Her attention returns to her phone. She needs to be ready for a full press conference soon after she lands.

On the advice of his lawyer, Northcott still isn't talking. Dance's voice message said, "We'll let him ponder life in a cell for a bit. You can bet my ass he was deeply involved in both the bombing and the second attempt on Cafferty's life. Probably slid into some deep shit with some inappropriate friends."

No matter Northcott's silence, Solinski suspects that his house of cards will really collapse by later today, when the complicit dockworkers' testimony is entered. Meanwhile, she'll restrict her press comments to revealing more details of the drug heist. She may also state that a link between last night's ocean rescue and any other investigations, as various outlets speculate, is yet to be determined. She will allow, however, that said rescue did indeed involve humpback whales. That should help the media stats, although also increase the demand for further feed.

Meanwhile, Mich is embarrassed to be falling apart in such a public place and in front of Rob. "It's just all way too much."

Rob suggests that she takes some deep breaths and they go back upstairs to the empty private chapel. They settle in one of the pews and he puts his arm around her shoulder. Mich bends over and covers her face with her hands. Rob just waits quietly.

A couple of minutes later Mich sits up. "I can't tell you why I'm upset, because I'd be betraying Kot. But it will probably all come out soon. I've never liked or trusted him but even in in my worst nightmare I didn't think Northcott was capable of this. I sure hope that Solinski didn't tell Kot what she told you. I'd better get back to her."

Rob asks no questions. "I'm sure that Annie wouldn't have said anything to Kot yet. Not until there's more certainty about suspects, and Kot is recovered enough to cope. But Mich, once the facts are established, Kot should be told the truth right away, no matter how upsetting it is. It will be worse still if she hears or reads it somewhere. She'll get stronger every hour now and might even be sent home tomorrow."

Mich nods and finds a tissue to blow her nose, pulling herself together. Rob continues, "Why don't we go up to her room together? I'd like to say hi before I head for the ferry."

Rachel has let him know that she and Toni pulled off a flawless day together, and Rob finds that unaccountably bothersome. As long as Mich is coming back to Atticus soon, he needs to get home.

But Mich still doesn't make a move to leave the chapel. She says, "Kot will also want to thank you, for sure. You know, things sure developed fast with Kot and Hunter."

Rob is pleased to see her tired smile as she adds, "Gardens must provide fertile grounds for all kinds of things." He chuckles. He likes everything about this woman: her intelligence, her humour, the lovely lilt in her voice, and her spirited resilience. And last, but by no means least, the way she looks. He would be grateful to have Mich as a friend, since it's highly unlikely that she would ever want more than that with a guy like him.

Still, she doesn't seem to mind being alone in a chapel with him, and something makes Rob consider taking an unusual risk. He is clasping and unclasping his hands between his knees, and finally looks sideways up at Mich.

"I suppose you'll be heading back home to Vancouver after Kot's recovered?"

"Yeah. Once she's out of danger, I'll need to. My goldfish must be pining. And duty calls."

"Seems a pity."

"At least I know now that Kot has good support, and maybe she'll go home soon. But I'm already dreading having to deal with what I've missed. There's usually at least one major fire to put out every day at work, and someone is always having a hissy fit about nothing. My assistant is trying to handle things but she's not thrilled either. She's trying to figure out how long it can possibly take to get my aunt settled into a nursing home."

Rob smiles, but straightens up in resignation.

Mich seems to read him and puts her hand on his arm. When she turns and to face him his eyes remind her of warm caramel. "The thing is, Robert, your crazy island seems to have sunk its little claws into me. Maybe some kind of fatal attraction."

Rob smiles back. "Huh. We're usually a crashingly boring bunch."

"Oh yeah? Sorry, but that seems like quite a stretch at the moment."

"Well, I'm glad that at least we haven't scared you off completely. Millions would have been, by now."

"To be honest, what really drives me crazy on Atticus is the number of drivers who signal before they follow a bend in the road."

"You're right. That level of courtesy is hard to find."

"I'm sorry if this is prying, but were you really on a drug squad or something? Is that how you know Inspector Solinski?"

"Yup. For eighteen years. Organized crime stuff. She and I worked our way up together. Always a small world, hey, at least in this country. I still miss parts of that job, but definitely not most parts."

"Why did you leave?"

"It's kind of a long story. 'Burnout' would probably be the popular term. And don't go imagining any heroic halos. I had some vices myself. Hopefully all past tense now. Annie always kept a better lid on her stress remedies than I did. But there were other factors."

Mich replies, "I'm sorry, and I'd very much like to hear that story sometime. And someone said that you're separated from your wife? Maybe permanently?"

"Also true. Just not properly finalized." Rob looks away in embarrassment. He feels like an idiot for not having insisted on a divorce by now. What has he been waiting for? At this moment, with Mich's hand somehow now tucked into his, no reason seems good enough.

His emotions are all over his face, and Mich tilts her head with humour. "Say, I hear they've found a fix for that."

Rob laughs. "You're kidding! Really?"

"No, seriously, there's some legal process. You know, if a guy really wanted it…"

Looking into her eyes, Rob would swear that Mich seems to be flirting specifically with him, and not, as Toni does, with the world in general. But then, clearly, what does he know?

He tries to sound confident. "So, let's say, if a particular guy were to investigate that subject, maybe with some vigour, you might be willing to offer personal support now and then?"

"That, my friend, is what they call a strong possibility."

Mich is pretty certain that a downside to this lovely, dented man is probably a sad lack of romantic initiative. She steps out of the pew and opens her arms wide. The strength of Rob's hug, his response to the quick kiss she gives him, and a later phone conversation combine to make Mich consider the immediate future with new curiosity. Kot needs to recover fast and be up for meaningful conversation.

When they are granted access to Kot's room, she and Hunter are watching the TV on the wall. Kot looks stunned, her mouth hanging open and her brow furrowed. The reporter is mid-sentence, and the screen shows footage of spouting humpbacks and a Google Earth screen shot of the Southern Gulf Islands. One spot in Swanson Channel is marked with an X.

"…still no evidence who fired the shots. It also remains unknown who was piloting the helicopter, or manning the boat's searchlights out there. This is certainly not the first time that these gentle giants have offered assistance to other mammals, but as far as we know this is a definite first in the Salish Sea. How the as-yet-unidentified person ended up in the midnight waters southwest of Atticus Island remains a mystery. But stay with us for more on this developing story. Belinda Aylesbury, Global BC."

Mich is angry that publicity-savvy Hunter thought that it was okay for Kot to watch news coverage of the gunshots last night. She grabs the remote, and turns the damned thing off.

A relatively minor story appears the next day in the *Vancouver Sun* about a previously undisclosed attack on shipping magnate Benson Northcott several weeks ago, outside his company's office building near the Port of Vancouver dockyards. Solinski ensured that the release specifically included the information that the only witness to the attack was, unfortunately, unable to overhear what was said nor adequately identify Mr. Northcott's attackers. That much was true, and making it public might give that sole witness a little more security while legal processes unfold.

FORTY-FIVE

Mich was correct. Camas wakes up in Kot's bed mid-morning and only wants to use the bathroom before she sneaks back to the lighthouse. She sees that Mich locked the deadbolt when she left for the first ferry, and Camas is pretty sure that Kot and Mich are the only ones with keys. But what might have happened to Kot while she's been sleeping?

All of the blinds are shut and the fridge is making a comforting hum. Camas crawls back into bed with a bowl of cereal. Her chronic anxiety is sky high after this latest seismic shift in her life, and the unbearable thing is knowing that she can't spend more than a few minutes back at the lighthouse. Just long enough to pack a few more things and escape before it becomes too late. If she tries to keep living there, how long will it be before one of the adults that she met yesterday reports her, and the police or some official arrives to capture her again? No, once again she needs to find a place to hide and then get far away. The certainty of that makes her feel sick, and she puts the bowl down. It's too much and so unfair. She isn't very old, and out of fear has worked so hard to be strong.

Staying in Kot's place for even one day must also have risks. Kot promised to protect her, but is she going to come home soon? Or at all? And will she still feel the same? Camas doesn't know how to find these things out. Maybe she should at least wait for Mich to return with news. She peeks through the blinds on the back window and sees the little Audi is still parked down below. Mich will definitely come back for that.

The fridge motor goes off, and the place is silent. Camas has food if she feels like it again, a nice bathroom, and a luxurious bed. She also has the beginnings of a headache as well as the nausea. With no obvious option, she decides to stay where she is for now, with the door locked and the blinds closed. Maybe she can figure out how to watch something on Kot's laptop. But she's still so very tired.

She wakes about an hour later to the sound of confident footsteps ascending the outside stairs. Camas leaps out of bed and into the bathroom, but the deadbolt is already springing back. The intruder is the older woman who had discovered her behind the bush yesterday, and whose house Camas was supposed to stay in last night. She can't remember the woman's name.

Tessa quickly finds her and reintroduces herself before going around opening most of the blinds. Camas blinks painfully in the sudden light. She wonders whether trying to run away would be futile. She manages to say hello but is furious that this woman has a key to Kot's place.

Tessa loads the dirty dishes from last night into the dishwasher and puts the kettle on. Then she turns to Camas, not unkindly, and suggests that they sit down for a chat. Camas perches on the edge of a chair, half-turned away. Tessa assumes that the expensive robe she's wearing belongs to Mich.

"First of all, I heard this morning that Kot is conscious. She had a close call, but she's through it okay and just needs to keep recovering. She might even be able to come home tomorrow—if this is going to be her home in the future. Which I don't suppose anyone knows yet, including Kot."

She finds Camas's big smile at the news about Kot rather sweet, and wonders how long it's been since it last appeared.

"I'm still not clear on all of the details of last night. So maybe you can fill me in since I hear that you inserted yourself into the scene. But secondly, you need to understand that every adult who has kept your secret—that you have been living alone over there—" Tessa waves her hand toward the tower on the bluff "—has actually broken the law. Out of kindness, but it can't have been an easy decision for any of them, nor one that I necessarily agree with."

Seeing Camas stiffen and glance look at the door, Tessa mentally gives her head a shake and softens her tone.

"Still, it was what they thought was best at the time and so far, no harm has come of it. This is also a kind community, on the whole. People will want to continue looking after you. But before I even think about joining your illegal support club I need to know a lot more about you, and I'd like to hear it from you. I've raised kids, and now I have grandchildren and a lot of experience in what can go well and what can go wrong. I guarantee that nothing you say will shock me. Okay? Why don't you just sit over there on the couch and try not to act like you're going to run away any minute. There's no need, I promise. Now, tell me how old you are, and about your family and where you lived before, and if you can, what happened to you." The kettle whistles. "I'm going to make us some hot chocolate. Okay?"

Camas says thank-you but doesn't drink from the mug when it arrives. She still feels awful. She reports the initial information like an army recruit to a senior officer. Now and then, Tessa interrupts with soft questions, choosing her words with increasing care. Camas then struggles to relate the events of the past year, her mother's death, her lack of extended family, and an almost-twelve-year-old's summary interpretation of her step-father's abuse and neglect.

After the girl has described her escape from Brett's fishing boat, her concussion, and precarious life since then, Tessa understands Kot's instinct to respect her fierce self-reliance. She also learns that Kot had discovered Camas during that visit to the lighthouse when she had gone outside for a phone call. How long ago was that now? Camas tells her about how Kot and Mich brought her groceries and puzzle books, and invited her here for dinner and, in Camas's words, "a whole lot of questions."

After dropping off her grandchildren this morning, Tessa was determined that dealing with Camas would take priority over the rest of the day's demands. Whether she found the girl at Kot's apartment or the lighthouse, or had to initiate an official island search for her, Tessa intended to assume the role of the only responsible adult in the group. She'd planned to find a way to confine Camas for long enough to contact Social Services. Now, she is far less sure. Her new instinct to wait a bit is almost annoying. She also believes that Camas is telling the truth about knowing of no surviving close family.

Of course, they must involve the appropriate legal agencies, but perhaps, once Kot is back, Camas's Atticus friends can first have an open and productive discussion about her. Anyway, there can be no harm in waiting and talking to Rob. He, at least, Tessa knows well and solidly trusts. Meanwhile, she won't let Camas out of her sight.

The child is looking at her fearfully, silent and self-contained. Tessa goes to sit beside her and give the rigid girl a hug.

"Thanks for sharing all that, Camas. I'm deeply sorry. You've been brave and resourceful through some extremely tough times and you deserve a whole lot of help. I actually own this building. Kot is my tenant and also works for me in my gardening business. Until she gets home and we know what her plans are from here, I think it's going to be best if I keep you hidden at my place down by the ocean over there. I assume you've met Medley. I'm looking after him for Kot and she would love to know that you're helping. He's out in my truck right now, and when you get in with me it will make his day. I think he's really worried about Kot too."

Camas has brightened at Tessa's inspired mention of Medley.

"So why don't you pop into the shower and we'll find you some clean clothes, even if they're a little big. I'll take that wet pile home to wash."

"I got wet on the boat. But I had to go with them, and I helped." Then Camas adds, "I feel kind of sick."

"Oh no. A shower might help that too, and then you can lie down on my couch. I'm dying to know why you felt that you had to go on the boat, and all about what happened last night, but I guess it can wait until you feel better. Anyway, scoot in there and use soap and shampoo while I find some of Kot's things for you to wear. I think that we'll do a quick stop at the light station and use the bags in my car to pack up all of your belongings as fast as we can. There's no one there right now, but with so much going on I don't want to be there for more than a few minutes. You know, Camas, you are going to have a far safer and more comfortable time if you just trust that we're going to try and make sure that the future is brighter for you, no matter what. Can you do that?"

Camas never lies. "I don't know."

"Well, one step at a time, so off to the shower."

Tessa is like the neighbour that Camas and Mama had before they moved, and they had both learned the futility of arguing with her. Anyway, a hot shower will feel good, and after that, Camas plans to just keep her pack handy and her running shoes on.

~ FORTY-SIX ~

After only two days of recovery at home with Mich and Camas Kot announces that she's ready to go back to work. Tessa has to reluctantly help to make sure that she doesn't. Kot's survival high wears off at about the same time that Inspector Solinski calls to tell her about the impending charges against Ben Northcott, including his probable role in the attempts on Kot's life.

Kot's shock and denial transition into a level of anger that feels like hatred. Toward Ben, but also toward herself, and it takes therapy and a lot of support from friends to get her to eventually even leave her apartment. Ashamed, her belief in her own judgement is in shatters. She'd allowed herself to become addicted to the familiar pain of loving someone who was unavailable on every level. Someone who had finally detached so far as to help plan her death. More than once. Others assure Kot that she should remain a loving and trusting person and proud of it, that Ben is an extreme aberration and that everything that happened was on him. But Kot thinks differently.

The eventual legal proceedings might possibly create some distance and bring gradual understanding, and for justice to be done, Kot knows that she must give public testimony of deeply private things. But she won't be able to look at Ben, and will need safe hands to support her. She has also accepted that she must submit her formal resignation to NatureSave, before it is requested.

And through it all Hunter has been there, with his caring and his boyish enthusiasm and self-effacing humour. Not to mention the gob-smacking sex. Not many days after she got home a couch cuddle evolved into a level of joyful abandonment that took over her small apartment. And amazingly, on that front, nothing has changed since.

Hunter is trying to be patient, but is open about what he wants: Kot in his life and house, as soon as possible, and on whatever terms she needs. But Kot isn't even close. She feels emotionally ancient. These days, every little decision seems to demand dispassionate and lengthy consideration; co-habitation, especially, would be far too big a step.

It's going to take time to shift from living within a fictional reality to standing in relative peace in its ruins, but for now Kot takes comfort in what she privately labels a "creeping growth in personal integrity." She is summoning gratitude, and trying to heed the recent advice of her dearest friend: "*For Christ's sake, cheer up. Against all odds you're alive. And you're not only still brilliant and beautiful, but have a reasonably presentable guy who is madly in love with you. You have the luxury of choices. Anyway, you owe me.*"

Tessa finally opened her garden centre, right at the height of spring planting season, and the traffic was immediately more than she could manage. Almost every day a young man drifted in on his bicycle to wander around. He never wanted help or bought anything, but appeared to take great interest in every plant and how it was doing. When Tessa discovered that he was a horticulture student he suddenly found himself working there.

Meanwhile, word about Kot's design work at Glenhurst spread quickly on Atticus, second only to the rumour that she seduced poor Hunter Nott. Oh, and how a pod of orcas carried her aloft to an RCMP boat while fifty synchronized dolphins raised their fins to point to the nearest hospital. Legitimate requests for Kot's design work must be distilled from the flood of others before Tessa only them on to Kot.

His lawyer located Marie and Rob has filed for divorce. Mich lives with him part-time these days as they navigate the vistas and potholes of a new relationship. She sometimes helps out in the café on Saturdays, but the allure of Rob's early mornings escapes her. Another big development is reshaping Mich's life. Her professional success and Hunter's contacts have resulted in a long-term contract with a Vancouver production studio that will allow her to work remotely, earn more, and let go of most other work. She and her assistant will soon work remotely and let go of the big office expenses. Still, Mich has no desire to let go of her city apartment. She is trying to persuade Kot to realize what sweetness is evolving from Kot's bad but loving decisions.

However, on the same day that Kot was released from hospital Mich's little Rodeo achieved his personal best, and it was a leap too far. When the neighbour went over to feed him the next morning Rodeo was stiff on the floor, a full two metres from his fish bowl. Mich picked up the neighbour's voicemail message: "…but honey, that's the first time I ever see'd a dead fish wearin' a smile."

Both, in Mich's words, "in f'ing transitions," Kot and Mich are able to see more of each other than they have in years. On the June solstice they take an evening walk to walk down to the park beach where Camas had washed up. Talk turns to the men in their lives and Kot shares her concerns about the pressure she's getting from Hunter.

Mich replies, "Well, at this point I agree with you. He's obviously head over heels, but you're smart to monitor his behaviour once he's back in la-la land and surrounded by women who… well… he's a babe magnet and not exactly known for his relationship stamina." She is quiet for a minute. "Maybe the best anyone can hope for is honesty."

Kot nods, chewing on the juicy end of a grass stem. "Wow. You've certainly changed your tune about Hunter, now that I've followed your advice. Believe me, I'm going to keep things slow and assess his staying power. Mine, too, obviously. The other thing that worries me is his little temper flare-ups. I mean, what if they're erupting from a molten core of permanent pissyness?"

"Yeah, and how can you even tell something like that about a person unless you live with them for some time? I have some concerns about Rob, too."

"About him falling off the wagon?"

"No, not so much that. He's very strong-willed. It's smaller things, but when you put them together, maybe not. Like he insists on calling me Suzanne. Apparently, he considers it more"—she makes air quotes— "feminine. I always thought Suzanne was a weird choice for an Irish woman and a Polish guy to pick as my name, but at his age I should certainly have a veto on the matter. Rob and I also have some significantly different views on what constitutes a healthy daily diet. But I should say that the biggest issue for me so far is the constant virtual presence of The Ex. Marie may be gone physically, but she's still everywhere around here. People love telling me how much they liked her and miss her, and how devastated Robert was when she suddenly left. Blah. Blah. And there's always a sideways look at me, hoping for a reaction." Mich shakes her head in frustration.

"You thinking you'll never measure up? Don't let it get to you. It's likely just the island prejudice about anyone who doesn't live here full time."

"Well, it probably keeps some part-timers wanting to stay that way. People may also be trying to protect poor little Rob from the evil city bitch. Most folks don't know his own checkered back story. Anyway—back to you. I wonder what even constitutes 'normal' when someone has a lifestyle like Hunter's. We've both crawled around enough blocks to know that the real relationship test is when you're living with humdrum routine."

Kot agrees. "Right. And again, you have to live together for some time to get into that, and then try to find a way back to having fun together again. Hunter obviously has more freedom than I do, and I'm not sure he could even handle much humdrum in his life. Anyway, for the foreseeable future, I'm flying solo. I feel shaken to the core, and it's like I'm trying to rebuild from ashes. Who knows who I might end up being? It's possible that Hunter may not be attracted to that person, or me to him. Anyway, right now it feels like the ultimate personal repositioning exercise."

Mich chuckles. "That's good. P.R.E. We should use that. But believe me, you're a long way from ashes."

Kot says, "But it's more than possible that I'll never fully trust a lover again. And if not, why bother?"

"I guess you'll just have to give it time. Passion is a crummy glue if two people start moving fast in different directions."

Kot turns to Mich with a wry smile. "My God, girl, who knew you'd become so wise and maternal? Anyway, never mind Hunter. I need to put my energy into Camas and making a living. Not to mention Medley. Plus, I'm still learning not to look over my shoulder constantly."

Mich puts her arm around Kot. They watch some young otters swimming behind a parent, the birds on the ocean, and the sun dropping into it until Mich complains that it's time to go home because her bum has seized up on the hard log.

So far, Camas's claims of having no family have matched the searches done by Child Protection Services. Kot is still nervous about potentially losing Camas to some long-lost relative—even a loving one. Still, there's little chance that Camas would leave Kot willingly in favour of living with a stranger. The bonds between the two grow stronger all the time, and Kot has won a Temporary Guardianship Order. She hopes to attain permanent guardianship, and Camas will soon be old enough to have her wishes considered in that decision. Meanwhile, the girl is healthy and growing, and excited to attend the island school in the fall. And what a change in her. A quirky, sly sense of humour is steadily emerging. Sometimes, she is downright chatty and laughs out loud. Child abuse and other charges related to his failure to report a runaway and possibly drowned minor are proceeding against her stepfather, and Camas is also having therapy to deal with the stress of testifying about Brett.

Still, these days, neither Kot nor Camas cries much.

One area where Kot has made surprisingly certain progress is where to call home. She woke up one day knowing that she was finished with her Victoria townhouse and wanting to be financially unencumbered. Relieved to be so sure about anything, Kot put it on the market and already has a conditional sale.

Harvey, the caretaker of the light station, had fallen from a major stroke and passed away in hospital within a week of Camas finding him. Now, thanks to strong local references, it seems likely that the new tenant in that house might be Kot Cafferty. The property is conveniently situated to the garden centre and the yard would be paradise for Medley. She has reason to expect a lease offer within the next couple of weeks. Kot recently took a solitary walk up to the lighthouse bluff and looked down at the house. Everything felt right, and now she is sure of one more thing: she badly wants to live there.

She is welcome to continue renting Tessa's suite, and won't say anything to Camas unless a formal tenancy offer arrives. But she thinks that Camas would enjoy turning her first refuge on the island into a proper home together, living beside the park without having to also forage from it and from the ocean to stay alive. They could invite friends over. Laugh. And live in peace.

~ FORTY-SEVEN ~

The sky is already brightening, and unless Kot can shake off that dream, there's not much chance that she'll fall asleep again. At least she doesn't die in this recurring one, although it is just as vivid as the one that she had in the safe house, just before the owl called and everything exploded.

She slips out of bed and gets a pot of coffee going, then wraps the soft couch throw around her nakedness and stands at the window to watch the dawn unfold.

In this dream, she is always sitting sideways, alone in a strangely open seating arrangement inside a square metal-walled service vehicle of some kind. It is humming along, but no one is driving it. She can't see anything because the windows are covered over. Strangely, nothing bad has resulted from this complete lack of control. She is worried about the situation, but so far has done nothing to take charge.

Kot usually wakes up at that point, but this morning the dream carried on and she'd started to rip the paper off the vehicle's windows. Her movements created an imbalance, and when she looked out it was teetering on the edge of a drop-off. Then it slowly tipped backwards and started to fall through the air. Kot braced her legs and clung hard to something, feeling her stomach lurch. Magically, she remained conscious when the car landed in a shrubby ravine. Hunter suddenly appeared and managed to clamber down to the wreck. He was loving but also irritated. He told Kot that she might lose her right eye, and then left to get medical help.

Kot felt stupid, full of regret that her lack of trust had caused the disaster. She tried opening the eye that Hunter thought was so badly injured, and found that she could see just fine. In fact, she wasn't really hurt at all. She urgently wanted to tell Hunter that, but he was gone. Then she woke up.

Smiling, she pours steaming coffee into a mug and snuggles into the chair with a view. Not much analysis is needed for this dream, especially with this new, extended version that includes Hunter's first appearance. Her subconscious obviously still sees a need to bludgeon her over the head, making the reasonable assumption that she may yet… still… be resisting the message. Food for thought. Or maybe, Kot wonders, she should try *not* to think. Just keep her eyes and mind open and trust her angels. Simply enjoy the journey for a change, not force anything or try to manage all outcomes. It's still a foreign concept, and one hell of a learning curve. But already, at moments like this in the grace of a summer morning, a surge of unexpected gratitude hums within her.

The dusk of dawn is transforming into another golden day, and the sky is the colour that Kot's mother used to call robin's egg blue. When the sun crests the horizon it pours onto the bay like melted butter. The region's usual summer drought began early this year. The white lighthouse glows against the parched, wheat-coloured grass on the bluff, and the dark waters of Chase Bay are transformed to sparkling blue. A perfect start to July first: Canada Day.

Kot has the day off, but the island will be busy with everyone's visitors and the usual tourists. If she wants to see any wildlife, she'd better get going before everyone else does. She can see the gables of Tessa's roof through the trees across the road. Camas spent last night there, earning a little money by helping with Tessa's rambunctious twin grandchildren. They both adore Camas and are easier to manage when she's around. Still, Kot is pretty sure that Tessa's invitation to Camas to stay the night was offered solely to allow Kot and Hunter one night of unencumbered romance.

Kot's mouth curves in a smile again when a deep voice calls from the bedroom.

"Come back to bed! I'm freezing!"

"Oh no. So sad. Isn't Medley doing his job?"

She goes to the doorway. Medley keeps his eyes firmly closed and nestles deeper into his nest of bedding. Hunter rolls over drowsily to look at her and growls, "He's a poor substitute."

"You know, it's gorgeous out there, and I'm feeling like an early paddle. Want to come?"

Hunter may choose to catch up on some well-deserved sleep, but Kot knows that she will go anyway. It's time to reclaim what is rightfully hers.

Acknowledgements

My thanks to Rory Dickinson, to my talented designer Jeremy Bohn, and to the others on my team at FriesenPress for so courteously bringing *No Safe House* into the world.

To the brave friends who reviewed earlier drafts: Shawna Barrett, Wendy Bone, Allan Bogutz, Nancy Curtis, Bill Deverell (also for the title suggestion), Charlotte Forish, Jonathan Garnett, David Sheffield, Kathi Springer, and Sarah Stonich, your generosity of time, honesty, and enthusiasm got me past every exit ramp to Quitting. Thank you.

Deep gratitude to Jan Kirkby for editing multiple drafts of this book. Every writer should be blessed with such a kind and eagle-eyed friend.

Fond thanks to author and friend Ann Coombs for a personal introduction which led to helpful tips from professional editor Julia McDowell. And thank you, Julia.

Hugs to my dear partner, Ian Syme, for picking up the slack as needed, and to my loving family and friends for their interest and support. Also, forever cuddles and scratches to sweet Gubby, who stayed beside me until almost the last word and his last breath. Joyful echoes of him live on in Kot's dog, Medley.

Most of all, thanks to you, the reader. I enjoyed writing this book, but without you at the end, it's just a bunch of words.

Jan (Rumball) Garnett
2024

Printed in Canada